Praise for *The Wedding Sisters*

"Filled with unforgettable characters and deep insights, *The Wedding Sisters* is a heartwarming and modern take on love, marriage, and family. Completely compelling and impossible to put down . . . I loved it!"
—Anita Hughes, author of *Rome in Love*

"This story of three sisters who all plan high-profile weddings in the same calendar year is a smart, fun read that will leave you thinking about the nature of love, the spectacle of wedding planning, and what's really important in life. Prepare to be charmed by *The Wedding Sisters*."
—Brenda Janowitz, author of *The Dinner Party*

"*Little Women* meets *High Society* in Brenner's sparkling story of three sisters finding Page Six–worthy love. But while the hunt for the perfect white dress, and the partner to go with it, will draw readers in, it's the exploration of the power of families that makes *The Wedding Sisters* a modern romance that you will fall in love with."
—Karin Tanabe, author of *The Gilded Years*

also by jamie brenner

The Gin Lovers
Ruin Me

The Wedding Sisters

jamie brenner

st. martin's griffin ⚑ new york

THE WEDDING SISTERS. Copyright © 2016 by Jamie Brenner.
All rights reserved. Printed in the United States of America. For information, address St. Martin's Press, 175 Fifth Avenue, New York, N.Y. 10010.

www.stmartins.com

Library of Congress Cataloging-in-Publication Data

Names: Brenner, Jamie, 1971– author.
Title: The wedding sisters / Jamie Brenner.
Description: First Edition. | New York : St. Martin's Griffin, 2016.
Identifiers: LCCN 2015050411 | ISBN 9781250045744 (paperback) |
    ISBN 9781466845367 (e-book)
Subjects: LCSH: Mothers and daughters—Fiction. | Marriage—Fiction. |
    BISAC: FICTION / Contemporary Women. | FICTION / Family Life. |
    FICTION / Romance / Contemporary. | GSAFD: Love stories.
Classification: LCC PS3602.E6458 W43 2016 | DDC 813/.6—dc23
LC record available at http://lccn.loc.gov/2015050411

Our books may be purchased in bulk for promotional, educational, or business use. Please contact your local bookseller or the Macmillan Corporate and Premium Sales Department at 1-800-221-7945, extension 5442, or by e-mail at MacmillanSpecialMarkets@macmillan.com.

First Edition: June 2016

10 9 8 7 6 5 4 3

*My husband taught me a very important thing
about writing—and about life: If you want a great story, put a
wedding in it. This book is dedicated to him.*

acknowledgments

Writing a book—like planning a wedding—takes a lot of time, patience, and the sometimes irrational belief that it will all work out in the end. I want to thank the following people who helped walk me down the aisle: My agent, Adam Chromy, whose early notes helped give this book its heart and soul; Dan Weiss, who heard my idea for *The Wedding Sisters* over lunch and said let's do it; my editor, Vicki Lame, who patiently gave me what I needed for this one: time to figure it out! And my college friend Dana Bash, who in making time to say "hi" one busy workday, gave me an unexpected but invaluable behind-the-scenes look at political journalism. A special thanks to professor and memoirist Dori Katz, who so candidly and generously shared her story with the congregants at Temple Emanu-El and inspired me greatly.

Thanks to my daughters, Bronwen and Georgia, who show me—every day—the remarkable beauty of sisterhood.

Finally, I thank my beloved husband, who makes my dreams come true.

The Wedding Sisters

prologue

The bright sound of giddy laughter pulled Meryl's attention from the book she was reading. She glanced across the room at her husband, Hugh, and they shared a quick smile.

"The mixed blessing of working from home," he said, raising his eyebrows.

"I still can't get used to having this much space," she said. Their Upper East Side apartment, a perk of his new teaching job at a nearby private school, made her feel like a real grown-up—even more so than their three young children did.

Hugh turned back to his work in progress, a biography of Louisa May Alcott. He scribbled something on one of the dozens of handwritten notecards strewn across the dining room table, shaking his sandy blond hair out of his eyes. Meryl loved the old-fashioned way he conducted his research. And she loved that sometimes he chose time at home with her instead of the solitude of the library.

A shriek, followed by a thump, broke through the silence.

Meryl put her book down. "I'll go check on them."

The hallway leading to the girls' bedroom appeared to be post-tornado:

a trail of discarded ballet tutus, Mary Janes in three different sizes, Disney princess nightgowns, sundresses . . . and an unspooled roll of toilet paper running the length of the hallway.

Biting her lip, Meryl quietly pushed open the half-closed door to the bedroom to find her three young daughters giggling and jostling for position in front of the full-length mirror. Eight-year-old Meg stood earnestly in her favorite white dress, a lacy, impractical frock that her grandmother had picked out from a store on Madison Avenue. Six-year-old Amy twirled in a white T-shirt and white tulle ballet skirt, while toddler Jo wore only her Pull-Ups, messy red lipstick, and a tiara with a paper napkin tucked into it.

"Hugh," Meryl called out, "get the camera."

She watched as Meg methodically taped a paper napkin to her sister Amy's hair, and then did the same for her own.

"Your veil looks better than mine!" Amy cried out.

Hugh appeared beside Meryl, camera in one hand, the other gently finding the small of her back. "What's going on?"

She pressed her finger to her lips. "You've got to see this," she whispered.

"Put on your dress," Meg ordered Jo.

"No!"

Meg, one hand on her head holding the napkin in place and the other holding a white sundress, began chasing Jo around the room.

"Noooo!" yelled Jo.

Meryl pushed open the door, and three wide-eyed little faces turned to her.

Meg stopped in her tracks, but Jo continued her circular dash around the bedroom, crying, "No! No! No!"

"We're having a wedding and Jo won't be a bride!" Meg's face was flushed with indignation.

"And Meg won't let me wear her other white dress. And I don't have one!" Amy said.

Jo began to cry.

"Okay, okay, girls, let's settle down. Josephine, darling, come here." Meryl scooped Jo into her arms, kissing her plump cheek, salty with tears.

"Daddy," Meg asked, "can you please walk me down the aisle?"

"Me too!"

"Girls, I would be honored to walk you down the aisle," said Hugh, gallantly offering his arm. Meg reached up for it solemnly. Crisis averted, Meg and Amy made their way into the hall. Meryl carried Jo along.

Meg adjusted her veil, her brow furrowed with concentration. Meryl planted Jo beside Amy as they waited their turns.

Hugh grinned. Then, shaking his head, he walked slowly down the hall while humming "Here Comes the Bride." Meg gazed up at him adoringly.

Meryl knelt down, camera in front of her face, adjusting the lens until Hugh and Meg were clearly in the frame. She felt her chest tighten, overwhelmed with love for her family.

She also felt an intense need to capture the moment—to hold on to the innocent joy forever. Even with a photograph, she knew that she couldn't. This day would pass, the girls would grow up, and she and Hugh would get older. But she told herself that even when other things changed, one thing would not: They would always have each other. She and Hugh and the girls.

Hugh looked at her and, as if reading her thoughts, gave a wink.

Meryl snapped the perfect photo and smiled.

Eight Months Until the Wedding

Eight
Months
Until the
Wedding

one

It was an "all hands on deck" kind of night. At least that's how it felt to Meryl. Unfortunately, judging by everyone else in her family, she would be doing the heavy lifting alone.

It was only noon, but in her nervous excitement, Meryl couldn't wait to set the table with the good dishes. She hated to put too much pressure on this dinner, but she felt an overwhelming sense that everything had to be absolutely perfect. She couldn't help but fuss.

"Remember, honey, it's not about you," Hugh had said on his way out the door earlier that morning, a comment that both rankled her and served as useful caution.

"I'm doing this for Meg," she had responded in a huff.

He had kissed her on the forehead with a knowing smile, squeezing her hand.

They were finally meeting the parents of the man her daughter was going to marry. Meryl had read up on them in the *New York Times* and *Vanity Fair,* even seen them on CNN, but that had only served to make her ill at ease. They're just people, she reminded herself. And we're going to be family.

She dialed her mother's cell phone despite the odds being that she wouldn't answer. At eighty-six, her mother did not embrace technology and she made no apologies for it. Still, Meryl felt more comfortable knowing she had a cell phone, though in that particular moment, it served only to increase her frustration.

"Mother, it's me. I just want to make sure you'll be ready for me to pick you up at three for the dinner tonight? Please. It's important to us."

She hesitated, wondering if she should sign off with "I love you" or "Looking forward to seeing you." But that's not how they spoke to one another, and it would seem odd to tack it on now—desperate. As though Meryl needed her there tonight. Except, she did. Meryl hoped beyond hope that, for just one night, they could seem like a normal family. If not for her own sake, then for her daughter's.

That was the thing about weddings: they forced family members to deal with one another, like it or not.

Meryl drew back the dining room curtains and gazed out at the East River. The view was the best thing about their apartment, her favorite part of her home of the past twenty years. She always found it so calming. Meryl couldn't imagine living anywhere in Manhattan without a view of the water. But then, there had been a time when she couldn't imagine the girls being grown up and gone from the nest. And now it was normal not to see them for weeks at a time. More and more lately, it was as if Meryl needed an excuse to see them—to tear them away from their very busy lives.

She missed them.

Meg, Amy, and Jo. Named for the heroines of their father's favorite Louisa May Alcott novel, the much-cherished book that had set the course for his entire professional career—and their romantic life, if she was being honest.

Carrying the names of literature's most beloved sisters was a lot to live up to, but Meryl felt that her girls did the originals justice. They had equally as distinct personalities—Meg, the easy daughter. Amy, endlessly dissatisfied. And Jo, the rebellious tomboy with the world's biggest heart.

Meryl found it infinitely fascinating to watch them clash with and complement one another as they grew up, in a constant primal dance of love and hate, envy and unconditional love. Meryl was an only child, and she took immense joy in bearing witness to sisterhood. She had often felt lonely as a child, much the way she did now.

If only it wasn't so difficult these days to get them all in one damn place.

She used to be able to rely on Amy to show up regularly. Amy, who still craved Meryl's undivided attention. But even that was coming to an end; a few weeks ago, when Meryl invited Amy and her boyfriend to their standing Sunday night dinner, Amy had begged off, saying she and Andy were staying an extra night in East Hampton. They never rescheduled.

Amy's boyfriend was the son of fashion designer Jeffrey Bruce, and Amy was living what—at least to Meryl—seemed to be a very glamorous life, working for the company and traveling the world for industry events. Yet despite all of it, Meryl knew Amy was still playing catch-up to her older sister, Meg.

Meg, Amy felt, was the favorite, the perfect daughter, the one for whom everything came too easily. At the same time, Amy secretly worshipped her. It was a dynamic Meryl had hoped would change as Amy grew older and more confident—when she created an identity for herself outside of being one of the Becker sisters. But so far, no such luck.

Lately, Meryl felt something close to panic. She knew it was irrational, but she felt motherhood slipping away from her. And what was she if not a mother? Was this how it would be from now on? An occasional phone call. Seeing the girls here and there, a family dinner maybe once a year? Unfortunately, she made the tactical error of expressing her disappointment to Amy one night, at which Amy had scoffed and said, "Oh please, Mom. It's not like you even really cook."

This wounded Meryl deeply in ways she couldn't fully pinpoint. True, she didn't cook—but wasn't it about spending time together?

Her cell phone rang. Meg.

"Hi, Mom! Where are you?"

"Home, sweetheart. Where are you?"

"Just got into the city."

"I thought you couldn't leave D.C. until late this morning?"

A pause. "We didn't. But instead of driving, Stowe's dad brought us in the helicopter."

"Well. That's one way to beat the GW Bridge traffic!" Meryl laughed, trying to make light of it, but the truth was, she was uncomfortable with the prominence and extraordinary wealth of her soon-to-be in-laws.

Meg's fiancé, Stowe Campion, was the scion of a Philadelphia steel dynasty. And his billionaire father, Reed, was a Republican senator in Pennsylvania. Republican!

"Reed has a last-minute work event tonight," Meg added sheepishly. "Tippy wants to meet up with him after dinner. Is it okay if we come a little early?"

"Wait—Reed isn't coming tonight?" These people were unbelievable. A work event was more important than meeting the parents of their future daughter-in-law? They had a wedding to discuss, for God's sake. It was bad enough that the Campions had rebuffed every overture Meryl made during the last year. She understood they were busy. But this? Well, it was what her mother would call "insult to injury." And for once, her mother would be right.

"I'm sorry, Mom! I am. He feels really bad, and we'll definitely see him another time. But for tonight, a little earlier . . . okay?"

"No problem," Meryl said, trying to sound nonchalant. Her time-line was now officially screwed up.

And she still had to pick up her mother—never an easy feat.

"What can we bring?"

"Just yourselves," Meryl said in a singsong voice that sounded foreign even to herself.

Well, at least she would finally meet Tippy.

Before Meryl Googled her, she had imagined Stowe's mother, Tippy, to look like Barbara Bush: no-nonsense, sturdy, all-white hair, and pearls. But while Barbara Bush's whole life was etched on her face, Tippy Campion had the smooth, age-defying complexion of the obscenely rich. A face that, after a certain age, could be achieved only through a regimen of chemical peels and Botox and filler and other things that Meryl probably couldn't imagine. Tippy had buttery blond hair and a lithe frame that was always dressed in Tory Burch (daytime) and St. John (evening). She was beautiful; not a former, faded beauty, but a contender, even now. And her husband, Reed, had movie-star good looks that had translated faithfully to his son. It was no wonder the media was fascinated with them.

Meryl put her phone in her bag and rushed out to East End Avenue to grab a cab across town to her mother's. There wasn't time to wait for the M79 bus. She dialed her mother's landline and was relieved when the home health aide, Oona, answered.

"I'm on my way now, Oona. Can you please have my mother ready? Sorry—it's earlier than I said originally, I know."

Hiring the home health aides had been an extravagance, but also, as Meryl had rationalized to Hugh, a necessity. When her father died ten years ago, she didn't want her mother living alone, even though she seemed relatively healthy and capable. Unfortunately, moving in with them was entirely out of the question, since her mother and Hugh were oil and water. And Rose would never have agreed to move into an assisted living facility, and truthfully, she didn't need one. The home health aide seemed like the perfect compromise. Regrettably, there had been an almost semiannual rotation of nurses. Her mother fired them all. Oona, eight months on the job, seemed to be the most promising, and Meryl had high hopes they could make it to the twelve-month mark.

"She told me to tell you she don't want to go, Mrs. Becker," Oona said. Her Caribbean accent was musical. It managed to make even this rather undesirable news sound pleasant to Meryl's ears.

"What? Why not?"

"She says you know why not."

"I'll be there in fifteen minutes." *Great.*

Her phone vibrated. She was surprised to see her husband's number appear on the screen.

Hugh, a twelfth grade English teacher, was usually unreachable between the hours of 8:30 A.M and 3 P.M. every weekday. Once he disappeared behind the granite walls of Yardley, an Upper East Side private school that was arguably more difficult to get into than Harvard, he was happily in his own little universe.

"Hugh? Aren't you at school?"

"Yes—it's lunch."

Of course it was. She was distracted. "Everything all right?"

"It's Janell," he said. "She is really starting to push back when I try to help. It's like she's afraid to fail, and so she's purposely sabotaging herself."

Janell South was Hugh's most promising student so far that year.

Meryl sighed. She hated to be impatient, but she really didn't have time for one of Hugh's student dramas right now, not today.

Hugh prided himself on being a champion for his students, and she had always loved that about him; after all, she had been one herself once. Usually Meryl liked to hear his stories and act as his trusted sounding board. But she didn't have the mental space for Hugh and the Yardley students today. The Campions were coming for dinner. Finally!

"Hugh, I have to call you back," she said. "Or call me back. Or I'll just see you at home later, honey, and I promise we'll talk all about it. Everyone is coming earlier than I thought, and I still have to get my mother."

Meryl asked the cabdriver to let her off at Seventy-second and Broadway. She'd walk the rest of the way to her mother's West End apartment. Even though she was pressed for time, it was already October, and she couldn't ignore the orange-gold leaves on the ground or the changing light. Fact was, the truly beautiful days were numbered. And she never could resist walking down the block where she had grown up, the spot where her favorite bookstore used to be. Growing up on the Upper West Side—before it was the least bit fashionable or even particularly desirable—Meryl's favorite refuge had been Eeyore's bookstore on Broadway near West Seventy-ninth Street. There, her lifelong love of books had taken root.

The first book she remembered ever so subtly planting facedown by the cash register was *Fifteen* by Beverly Cleary. Meryl had been ten. It was the most romantic book she had ever read, and by the time she was in middle school and walking to the bookstore by herself, she was snatching up Barbara Cartland and Victoria Holt novels by the excited armful.

In college, the bodice rippers were replaced by the classics and, of course, the mandatory *Feminine Mystique* and Mary McCarthy's *The Group*. But by that time, her obsession with romance novels had been supplanted by her first real-life romance—a romance sparked by the worst English class Meryl had ever suffered through.

It had taken Meryl three semesters to get into the coveted American Literature II: 1865 to the Present class with Professor Dunham. Students who loved reading—who lived and breathed it—wanted Dunham. They knew he was the toughest, but he was also charismatic and brilliant. For true lovers of literature, he was the only one to trust as their guide from Whitman to Roth.

Unfortunately, Meryl got more than she'd bargained for. She struggled with Faulkner and stumbled with Thomas Pynchon. The optional "office hours," run by Dunham's TA, became essential to her academic survival.

At first, the soft-spoken TA, Hugh Becker, barely registered with her. He was a means to an end, her lifeline in a class that she had wanted so badly but was now her personal *Titanic*. Becker was tall and thin, blond and blue-eyed—not at all her type. But he had the artistic hands of a pianist or painter, and when he spoke about "The Beast in the Jungle," he was as passionate as Neil Young with a guitar. And she noticed— she wasn't *completely* blind after all—that when he spoke of Henry James's heroine May Bartram, he looked right at her. Every time.

Disappointingly, Meryl got a B+ in Dunham's class. She'd never earned anything less than an A in any English class, ever. She was angry at herself, annoyed with Dunham, and eager to wipe the slate clean with a new semester. She didn't think about American Literature II, Dunham, or his fair-haired boy Hugh Becker again, until she got an invitation in the mail three weeks before spring semester ended. It was the final days of her sophomore year, and Hugh Becker had invited her to a party—his book party.

He had published a book! Nonfiction. *Abby May Alcott: An American Mother.* It was incredibly impressive to Meryl, an almost unthinkable accomplishment. She toyed with writing a book someday—a novel. Or maybe short stories like Susan Sontag. But Hugh Becker had done it— he was a published author.

The party was in a town house just off lower Fifth Avenue. Meryl dragged her roommate along, and they were the youngest people there. With feigned sophistication, they drank white wine and ate cheese and crackers. Meryl felt out of place and slightly bored and decided she would eat just enough that she wouldn't have to buy food for dinner. And then she spotted Hugh Becker across the living room at the same time he saw her, and if there was such a thing in real life as "electricity" between two people, she felt it in that moment—an exhilarating spark.

Hugh Becker was not nearly so uptight as he had seemed in class; he knew his way around the town house (his agent's), and he confidently ushered Meryl into a small bedroom left vacant by the agent's college-aged son. There, he proclaimed his overwhelming attraction to her, his desire for her—confessing that he had barely been able to contain it the entire semester and had never been more relieved for a class to finish. Meryl, astonished, asked, "Why?"

"Well," he said, giving this serious thought, as though answering a question posed in a lecture hall. "You're beautiful. And temperamental. And you're not overly impressed by work it's taken me a lot longer not to be overly impressed by."

He asked if he could kiss her, and she was thrilled by the shocking turn of events. She had never even fantasized about Hugh Becker, and now she found herself wanting nothing more than to feel his hands on her body. She'd had sex with only two men in her life, and as soon as Hugh Becker's mouth pressed down on hers, she knew that very night he would be her third. And, quite possibly, her last.

For the past decade, Meryl's mother had lived alone in a six-story building that had a tiny lobby. Meryl did not know any of the other tenants; her mother had moved into the place the month she became a widow, and never bothered getting to know anyone. Not surprising: While Meryl was growing up, Rose had kept to herself even as the other mothers formed friendships and alliances at school drop-offs and pick-ups and on the PTA boards. But Rose kept a low profile. That's how she put it, "low profile." "I like it that way," she'd said.

Growing up, Meryl had taken these things as a matter of course, not recognizing the behavior as odd. Her mother was different from the mothers of her friends, but that was because Eastern Europeans were different. There was a wariness that ran bone deep.

Her mother had stomach problems. And insomnia. All just a part of her mother, like her blue eyes and ash blond hair and Polish accent.

The elevator was small, with a sliding door that had a round, gated window. Something about it made Meryl feel like any ride could be the one that ended in a free fall to the basement, so she opted for the stairs.

On the third floor, out of breath and vowing to make it to the gym sometime that week (month?), she rang her mother's bell.

"I feel bad you wasted a trip over here, Mrs. Becker," said Oona, opening the door and shaking her head.

"I'm not leaving here without her, Oona. Now, where is she?"

Oona led Meryl to the bedroom and briskly knocked once before opening the door.

Meryl's mother was fully dressed in a white blouse, gray tweed skirt, full makeup, her signature eyeglasses with the oversized round black frames, sturdy shoes, and her nails manicured with clear polish. She was watching *The Bold and the Beautiful*, a show she watched only begrudgingly now that they had recast the leading male character, Ridge Forrester. As a teenager, Meryl had watched soaps like *The Young and the Restless* and *As the World Turns* along with her mother. The common vocabulary of soaps was one of the few things they shared. Her mother had never been one for deep conversation. In her world, everything was black-and-white. There was very little to discuss.

"Hi, Mom. Meg is coming early, so we have to get going."

Her mother shook her head and tsk-tsked. At first Meryl thought it was her irritation at being rushed, but then she realized the disapproval was directed at the television screen.

"Her own sister's husband," her mother muttered.

"Mom, did you hear what I said? We have to get going."

Her mother turned to her. "I'm not going anywhere."

"What? Why not?"

"You know why not."

Not this again. Meryl inhaled deeply and took a brief reprieve from her mother's stubbornness, instead appreciating the rare opportunity to look at Rose's paintings, which hung on every wall. Her mother had only ever displayed her art in the bedroom while Meryl was growing up. It was as if her mother didn't want anyone else to know that she was an artist, even now. At times, Meryl had encouraged her mother to try to sell some of her work. But Rose had huffed and said, "It's just a hobby. Your generation only wants to turn play into work instead of finding an honest profession." Meryl found it sad that her mother couldn't even fully embrace the joy she got from painting. Her mother never seemed to find joy in much of anything—ever. And Meryl never quite understood why.

"You're really going to do this to Meg?"

"I'm not doing anything. This is about the choices you made, Meryl." When her mother was angry, the Polish accent became more pronounced. "What did you think was going to happen when you married a man of poor character? Of course your daughter doesn't know any better."

Meryl sighed. "Mom, it's just dinner. I'm not asking you to walk her down the aisle. It's a family dinner, and I'd like for you to be a part of it. Don't you want to meet her fiancé and his family?"

"I don't need to meet him. I know all about that family. A bunch of anti-Semites."

"They are not anti-Semites, Mom." Just Republicans. Stop it, she told herself.

"I can't sleep at night, you know."

"Because of Meg's engagement?" Meryl asked incredulously.

"The club where they want to have the wedding used to be restricted. I expected more from Meg," said Rose. "But then, why should I expect anything when you've done nothing to make them value who they are and where they come from."

Meryl sighed. Rose's criticism was nothing new, but it was difficult to take from a woman who never spoke about the country where she'd been born, never shared photographs of her childhood, had not raised her particularly Jewish—and yet had been endlessly, blatantly hostile toward her marriage outside the Jewish faith. Her mother acted as though Meryl had turned her back on some rich heritage—as if she'd raised Meryl in some parallel universe.

Meryl had thought her relationship with her mother might mend when Meg was born. Surely there was nothing better for a mother and daughter to bond over than a new baby—a first grandchild! But any hope for a new beginning was dashed when, upon hearing Meryl and Hugh's choice of name for their baby, her mother refused to speak to them or to see the baby for the first month of her life. And then, the only thing she said to Meryl was that she had "dishonored" her grand-parents by failing to name the baby after one of them so that "their soul can rest in peace." To be honest, the Jewish tradition of naming the baby after a deceased family member had never even occurred to Meryl. She had been so charmed by Hugh's idea of naming the baby after a char-acter in *Little Women*. Back then, she had found all Hugh's quirks and obsessions romantic and endearing.

Her mother turned back to the television, tight-lipped, her hands clutching the remote as if it were the controls of a plane losing altitude.

Meryl thought of the food hastily shoved into the refrigerator at home, the flowers that needed to be bought, and the unfortunate possibility of Meg, Stowe, and Tippy somehow arriving at the apartment before her.

"Look, Mom, I really would like for you to be there."

It was an understatement. She was surprised by how very much she wanted her mother by her side for dinner that night. Yes, she had three grown daughters of her own. Still, she sometimes yearned for her mother. But she had learned long ago to accept Rose's limitations. As she used to tell Meg, Jo, and Amy: "You get what you get, and you don't get upset."

Meryl took another deep breath, trying not to get too emotional. "And I know the girls want you to be there. It would mean a lot to us. But obviously I can't force you out of this apartment and into a cab. So I'm going to ask you one more time: Will you please just get your shoes and coat and let me take you to my place for a nice family dinner?"

Her mother turned, her blue eyes as bright and angry as the day Meryl had announced her engagement to Hugh. An anger that had forced them to elope; an anger that had not softened in three decades. And Meryl already knew her answer.

"No."

It was Meryl's own fault, really. It always had been. In the earliest, fragile days of her relationship with Hugh, she'd shared a secret with her mother that should never have been shared.

And she'd been paying the price ever since.

two

"I'm nervous," said Meg Becker in a stressed, quiet voice. Sitting on the edge of the king-sized bed in the hotel room overlooking Columbus Circle, she felt strange staying at a hotel in the city where she'd grown up.

Meg moved uneasily toward the window, pausing as her reflection overcame the view. Her blond hair skimming her shoulders, her slim frame hugged by a cashmere V-neck sweater and black pencil skirt. Elegant, symmetrical features had always greeted her—wide blue eyes, sharp cheekbones, sensual but refined lips. But today, her outer composure belied her feelings. Inside, she was a scattered jigsaw puzzle.

"What are you worried about?" Stowe, her fiancé—fiancé! She still wasn't used to the word—glanced up at her from his laptop.

"Your mother. My mother. My *grandmother*," she said, sitting down on the bed again heavily.

"You're never nervous," Stowe said as he slid closer to her, taking her hand. Kissing her neck, he sent a shiver of delight through her body. "And there's no reason to start now, sweetheart."

"Untrue! I was nervous the day we met," she said, smiling. Think about the beginning, she told herself. Focus on being in love. Forget about dinner!

"That's right. You were. But then, you were going on live television for the first time." He gave her a wry smile in return. "So I think we can let that one slide."

She first saw him in the green room at the show *Real Time with Bill Maher*. Meg, a senior editor at Poliglot, a political Web site, had gained notoriety with an article on Elizabeth Warren calling out ABA lobbyists on the Senate floor and had been invited on the show as a panelist. The other two panelists were in the room, a loud, liberal actor with a new movie out and a chip on his shoulder, and Reed Campion, a rising star in Republican politics and a Pennsylvania senator. Campion and the actor chatted each other up while Meg was left to anxiously check her e-mails and mentally replay her talking points. She was the first person from Poliglot invited on such a high-profile show, and her bosses had warned her not to fuck it up—in pretty much those exact terms.

And that's when Stowe, a member of Campion's entourage, approached her. If she hadn't been so nervous about the show, she would have been cowed by his staggering good looks. But as it was, she was just relieved to have someone keeping her mind occupied before it was time to go on live television.

It wasn't until the show was over, until after he had already asked her out for a drink, that she learned he was the senator's son.

They were both strangers to L.A., and this, at least, put them on equal footing. Unsure of where to go, they took a recommendation from someone on Bill Maher's staff and ended up at the Standard Hotel on Sunset.

They sat out by the pool, under the stars. Meg's first thought was that her sister Jo would fit right in, with her long hair and peasant blouses, her denim shorts and ever-present flip-flops. But Meg, with her ponytail and pearls and Chanel ballerina flats, was a fish out of water. Fortunately, Stowe—with his close shave and short dark hair, his fair skin that seemed like it had never seen a day at the beach, and his jacket and tie—was equally out of place. If anything, their contrast to the strange exotic birds of L.A. that surrounded them just made them seem all the more perfect for each other.

With the show behind her and her confidence back, Meg was finally able to notice that Stowe Campion was *GQ*-cover-model gorgeous. And smart. And ambitious.

And how hyperaware she was of his thigh next to hers.

"How did you manage to take time off to come out here?" she asked, smiling playfully. "Don't they keep you guys chained to your desk until you're in your fifties, at least?" At thirty, he was the youngest partner at the D.C. law firm Colby, Quills, McGinty, and Dean.

"The gods of timing were on my side," he said, leaning closer to her. "We're taking depositions out here on Monday. I was able to swing an extra day or two."

"Timing is everything in life. So they say." Meg swallowed hard. She had never wanted a guy more. Her desire unnerved her. She had been so focused on work the past year and half that she'd barely even dated.

Finally, when it was nearing one in the morning, she reluctantly stood to leave. She could have sat there talking to him all night, but the control freak in her needed to be the one to punctuate the evening.

"So." They locked eyes, and her stomach fluttered.

She was staying at a hotel on Santa Monica, and he was staying at a family friend's house in Beverly Hills—with his father. Clearly, if they were going to take their little party elsewhere, it would have to be to her place. But she couldn't bring herself to invite him. Meg Becker did not make the first move. Ever. Plus, if she was going to sleep with someone on the first date, it would at least have to be an actual date.

And yet she regretted her unflinching stance when, two weeks later, she still had not heard from him—despite the fact that he'd tapped her number into his phone before walking her to her car.

Back in D.C., Meg suddenly became overly interested in the work of the senator from Pennsylvania. She sat in on a few less-than-newsworthy votes on the Senate floor, justifying it to herself—and to her boss, Kevin—that he was an up-and-comer, a politician worth watching closely.

But she never managed to see Stowe, try as she might—though Meg would never, ever, admit to *trying* to run into him.

And then she got annoyed. Why hadn't he called? Just like that, her interest in Reed Campion's senate voting activity disappeared entirely. But one afternoon, while she was running up the steps to the carriage entrance of the Capitol to record a quick interview with the senator from South Carolina, Stowe was walking out.

He noticed her first. "Meg Becker," he called happily.

Before she turned, she knew on some subconscious level, some animalistic part of her soul that was already half in love with him, that it was Stowe.

She pretended not to remember his name.

Stowe held out his phone, displaying her name and number in his contacts, and gave an apologetic smile. "I was premature in saying they don't keep me chained to my desk," he said. "But I've escaped for the day. Is there any chance in hell that you're free for dinner tonight?"

And that, as they say, was that. Deep down, in her heart of hearts, Meg knew she was done—off the market. One year later, he put a ring on her finger. And it was official.

And now, they were mere hours away from their parents meeting for the first time. Well, his mother and her parents anyway. As soon as people got wind of Reed's calendar putting him in New York that weekend, his office started getting calls. Meg understood; after a year with Stowe, she knew that Reed—traveling constantly from their home in Haverford, Pennsylvania, to his office in the capital, Harrisburg, to D.C. for meetings and votes on the Senate floor—was difficult to pin down, family occasion or not. But her mother would never understand. She would consider this yet another example of the Campions "not making an effort."

About six months into her relationship, Meg let it slip that the Campions were in New York for the weekend. Big mistake; Meryl thought for sure they would reach out and suggest coffee or a drink with the parents of their son's girlfriend. They didn't. Eventually, Meryl decided to just suck it up and do the reaching out herself. Phone tag ensued, and the end result was that the two mothers never actually spoke until the day after the engagement, when Tippy called Meryl to say she was "so delighted" for "the kids" and that they would be in New York soon to take them to dinner.

But Meryl didn't want to be "taken" to dinner. She wanted to host dinner at the apartment, so they could all get to know one another. "After all," she'd said to Meg, "We're going to be family."

Meg didn't have the heart to tell her mother they would never really be family—not in the way her mother envisioned. The Campions were a closed circle, and they had their own way of doing things. More was not merrier. The Campions were more like a club than a family, and they were certainly not looking for new members.

Patricia "Tippy" Gaffney Campion was a Main Line blue blood who had been born, bred, and educated in the rarefied air of the Philadelphia suburbs—the Baldwin Academy and then Bryn Mawr. She'd raised her three boys in a sprawling stone home in the woods of Villanova. They summered at "the shore" and at the country club, Philadelphia Racquet and Hunt. Meg, having grown up in Manhattan and attended one of its more exclusive private schools (albeit on a free ride since her father was on staff), was no stranger to elitism. But she had never encountered anything quite like the sheer myopia of Tippy Campion. Nothing, absolutely nothing, outside her sphere of interest and influence mattered.

Meg was already dreading the land mine that would be Thanksgiving and Christmas every year, when she would be forced to alternate between being with her parents and Stowe's. There was a chance the Campions would invite her parents to family events, but she knew that Meryl liked "having the girls at home." Meg liked it too.

And what about Amy and Jo? They wouldn't want to travel to Philly to have holidays at the Campion house.

She rose again to look out the window. This was just part of merging your life with another person's. These things would work themselves out. *I just have to get through tonight.*

"My mother is going to talk to your mom about the wedding planner," said Stowe, coming up behind her, his arms circling her waist.

Meg turned, and mistaking the expression of surprise on her face for happiness, he kissed her.

"Stowe, I told you my parents aren't wedding-planner-type people," Meg said. "Mom won't want a stranger getting involved and second-guessing her. My mother wants to just run with this—she's so excited about it. It would break her heart not to do it herself. And frankly, I'd rather just plan it with my mom."

"Hon, of course you'll be planning it with your mom. The wedding planner will just help with some of the logistics that would bog you guys down, like dealing with all the vendors. She'll make sure everything is efficient, easy."

Meg pulled away from him, crossing her arms in front of her chest and frowning. This was a vote of no confidence from Tippy. Not for her mother, but for her. The wedding-planner issue was a reminder of the one thing Meg didn't want to think about this weekend: her certainty that Tippy did not approve of her.

Meg Becker was never disliked. Meg was the one people aspired to be around, to be like, and to be liked by. She was occasionally intimidating, but just until you got to know her; she was a girl's girl—a loyal friend, a straight shooter at work, the voice of reason among her squabbling sisters. She never stole someone else's boyfriend, took credit for work that wasn't hers, or upstaged someone when it was their turn to speak. She was polite and well-informed, opinionated but not judgmental. She dressed stylishly but not flashily. She was ambitious but not cutthroat. She was beautiful, yes—but in an understated way. Jo was less classically beautiful, but when she walked into a room, every head turned. Meg could fly under the radar if need be.

But with Tippy . . .

"Stowe, I don't want to worry about efficiency. Planning our wedding isn't something I want to just check off my list like an article I have to write. In some ways, I've been looking forward to this my whole life." Meg smiled, thinking of all those times she and her sisters had played "wedding" as little girls.

Stowe took her hands in his, drawing her closer. "That's not what I meant, Meg. It's just there's a lot to do, we're all busy—including your mom—and we are lucky to have a pro at our disposal. Why not use her?"

She didn't want a pro. And yet, she found it difficult to say no. It was a new and undesirable side of herself that had somehow appeared to coincide with her relationship with Stowe: people pleaser. And this people-pleasing was undeniably specific to one person in particular: Tippy Campion.

Meryl unwrapped the triangular brick of Jarlsberg from its cellophane wrapper and removed the lid from the plastic container of mixed, pitted olives. No, she "didn't even really cook." But the table was set with beautiful dishes, the crystal candlesticks she and Hugh had brought back from a trip to Ireland, and Meg's favorite tablecloth, the green and red bird toile print that Meryl had bought on Madison at a cute little shop that had long since been replaced by a Gucci or Alice + Olivia or someplace else she'd never set foot in. In the oven, Meryl was reheating bruschetta, and the house smelled like she'd been cooking all day. So there.

Hugh walked in, heavily dropping his books and messenger bag on the entrance table.

"Hugh, put that stuff in your office, please. They'll be here soon. Oh, and my mother isn't coming after all," Meryl told him.

Hugh shrugged as if to say, *What's new?*

He seemed quiet, distracted. Usually, when he was stressed out, it was because he was grading subpar exams, failures that he took personally. But it was only October—too early for end-of-the-semester nerves. Maybe he'd hit yet another "wall" in writing his book. But it was doubtful after all this time that he was letting his ever-stalled project get to him. So it must be Meg's engagement.

She had to admit there was something both thrilling and unnerving about Meg marrying into such extreme wealth—that money would never be an issue for her. It was something Meryl could barely imagine. And Amy seemed headed on the same track with Andy. Only her youngest daughter, Jo, seemed to be living a normal existence for a twenty-something, working at a Brooklyn coffee shop and dating an equally cash-strapped law student.

Meryl tried to imagine the early years of her marriage, only without worrying about money. While Meryl and Hugh had never been impoverished, there had been many months in the early days when they lived on cereal and missed payments on the electric bill. Not that they cared; they were just happy to be together. But since the Yardley job, they managed to live extremely well within their means. The girls had attended Yardley for free. Meg earned an academic scholarship to Georgetown, and Jo had gotten a partial scholarship to NYU. They paid full tuition only for Amy's four years at Syracuse. They had been renting the same summer house for two weeks in August on Fire Island since Meg was a toddler—and the fee somehow barely went up. And, of course, the one thing that made their life in Manhattan infinitely more livable than those of a lot of their friends: the beautiful, three-bedroom, prewar apartment with a view of the river that Yardley provided them for a fraction of the market value.

They had been lucky. But their daughters were about to become even luckier. So it surprised her when Hugh said that he liked both Stowe and Andy, "despite the money."

"Despite the money?" Meryl said. "Doesn't every parent dream of their kid marrying rich?"

"No," Hugh said, frowning at her. "They dream of their children being happy."

"Yes, well, you have to admit, money helps in that regard."

But in saying that, she felt like she was betraying some core value they had once shared—a pact they had made to live a life in the pursuit of art and culture. Certainly Hugh, a high school English teacher, and Meryl, with a career in book publishing, were not motivated by making a fortune. A fact that made the extravagant wealth of their daughters' partners all the more curious.

And though she hated to admit it, her life with Hugh suddenly seemed provincial, as if they'd raised their girls on a farm. At least, she was afraid that's how it seemed to the Campions.

Maybe Hugh sensed that attitude as well, because he certainly didn't seem to share her excitement about the engagement.

"Can you at least pretend to be looking forward to dinner tonight? Between you and my mother, I feel like I'm in this thing alone."

"I'm sorry. I'm preoccupied."

She wanted to tell him to snap out of it, but he looked so defeated. So she put her hand his arm and softly asked, "What's going on?"

"It's just work stuff," he said, shaking her off.

Then she remembered: the call earlier in the day when she'd been running to her mother's. Janell South.

Janell South was a senior who had come to Yardley two years earlier, a scholarship student. There weren't many of them at Yardley, but
the ones who made it there and lasted tended to be exceptional. She
had grown up in the Bronx, shuttled between foster homes, before
recently settling with her adult half sister in Harlem. According to
Hugh, she was a talented writer who shared his passion for the American classics.

"What's the problem?"

"Janell handed in a plagiarized paper," Hugh said.

"Oh, Hugh—are you absolutely certain?"

"I recognized entire passages from McKnight's book on Hawthorne."

"I'm sorry! I know this is a huge disappointment. Will they let her
finish out the semester?"

Yardley had a zero-tolerance policy toward cheating, a hard-and-fast
rule that was enacted in the wake of massive cheating scandals at
Stuveysant High School and Horace Mann. Hugh sat on the advisory
board that had passed the measure.

"I'm sure they wouldn't."

"You mean, won't."

"No, I mean if I had reported it, they would expel her immediately."

Meryl's eyes grew wide. Just last year, Hugh had overseen the dismissal of Todd Boswick, a junior who cheated on the Regents Exam.

"You didn't report her? Hugh, you can't be serious. You can't just
take it upon yourself to make exceptions to the rules. That's why
you and the board voted for zero tolerance—to take the guessing and
favoritism out of it."

"This is different."

Todd Boswick, son of a hedge fund billionaire, was barely passing
his classes. He skipped class, routinely got busted for having his cell
phone or other contraband, and he talked back to teachers. Todd was a
kid who thought the rules didn't apply to him. And sadly, in the grand
scheme of things, they didn't. Because of his father's wealth and stat-
ure, he was already ensconced at a neighboring private school.

But there would be no such safety net for Janell South.

"Hugh, I understand why you feel that way and that you feel bad.

But it's not your job to cover for her. You have to report this or you're as much at fault as she is."

"Well, it's too late for that. I told her I was giving her a warning."

Meryl looked at him in shock. "Hugh! You helped put that code of ethics in place, and now you're just ignoring it?"

"Don't Monday-morning-quarterback me, Meryl," he responded angrily. "I was agonizing over this all day, and you couldn't be bothered to talk for five minutes. And I couldn't just wait to deal with it. So I did what I thought was right."

It was then that Meryl realized this was about more than just Janell South. Hugh was pissed. He was pissed that their daughter was marrying into a family that expected a lavish wedding. He was pissed that Meryl was on board with that idea even if it meant straining them financially. And yes, he was pissed that a rule put in place to keep spoiled rich kids in line had bitten his pet student—a poor student—in the ass.

"Fine. You did what you thought was right. In that case, don't hide in here, 'agonizing over it' when we have a family dinner tonight. Please, just forget about this for now. Enjoy tonight." She looked at him imploringly. "For Meg."

After a moment, he sighed, his shoulders relaxing. "You're right."

"We have a wedding to plan." She smiled, hoping to make the school stuff recede, to bring him into a joyful moment.

"Make sure to keep the spending under control, okay? Within reason."

"I will."

"Promise?"

"I promise."

He kissed her, and as if on cue, the doorbell rang.

"That's them!" she said, her voice shrill, her heart leaping.

"Meryl, relax. It's just dinner."

three

Josephine "Jo" Becker never thought twice about what to wear, but tonight it was somewhat of a problem. Her usual jeans, high tops, and T-shirts were out: the Campions were coming to dinner. Or, rather, THE CAMPIONS. She had come to think of them in all caps.

She made herself a soy latte, ignoring her waiting customers. Café Grumpy was wall-to-wall Brooklynites. Contrary to its ironic name, the café was warm and pleasant, with earth-toned exposed-brick walls, tin ceilings, and bright orange accents, simple wooden furniture, and eclectic design details everywhere—the occasional freestanding bookshelf, a potted plant, round wall clocks. Today, the entire staff happened to be moving in slow motion because last night one of the baristas had her burlesque debut nearby at the Bell House. Jo made it home a little after three in the morning—she was considered an early defector, lame, a "pussy." She would have made it an all-nighter if her girlfriend hadn't declined to join the Café Grumpy crew in their night of debauchery. But Caroline was in law school and always studying; nights out were temporarily on hold. Jo did not—*would not*—complain, even if every single minute apart left her feeling raw-nerved and aching, still, three years after they got together.

Jo's heart sped up erratically just thinking of her. *God, I love her.*

She pulled her phone out and texted Caroline. *Clocking out soon—will u be ready to go? My mother will stroke out if we're late for this one.*

There had been a time when Jo would have dreaded dinner with her uptight mother, her cranky grandmother, her two bickering older sisters, and her dad checked out thinking about his book or his students or whatever else occupied that man's mind—he never seemed to be quite there. The bad vibes used to stress her out. But not anymore. With Caroline by her side, even her crazy family was something she could take in stride. That's what the kind of head-over-heels love they had did to a person.

Jo could still barely believe her luck; she'd fallen in love with her best friend—and somehow, in the most unexpected and gloriously dizzying turn of events, that friend loved her back.

Caroline. Smart, funny, beautiful—in a way Jo never thought could exist—Caroline.

For half of college, Jo suffered in agonizing silence. Jo knew as soon as she met her that Caroline Winter was straight as straight could be. She was from Vermont. She dressed in L.L. Bean and J.Crew, and when frustrated she said, "Shoot!"

They had been assigned as roommates freshman year of NYU. Jo had been just a little bit awed by Caroline from day one. She was like a different species, with her translucent milk-white skin and deep red hair the color of autumn leaves. She'd never taken the subway and she'd never eaten Indian food.

Jo became her tour guide to New York City. As the youngest of three sisters, she was rarely the one to introduce someone to something. She was always the last to know, to experience, to discover. It was intoxicating to be the more experienced one, the person in the know. And experiencing her hometown through the eyes of someone new made her appreciate it in a completely different way. She'd always prided herself on being a freethinker and very different from her older sisters, but sometimes it was hard to really know where their influence stopped and her true likes and dislikes began. She was the first to admit that a lot of the time she found her own interests simply by rejecting Meg's and Amy's. But in the budding of her friendship with Caroline, Jo's passions and personality seemed to crystallize for the first time. In getting to know Caroline, she discovered herself. And one of the things she discovered was that she was in love for the first time.

Jo swallowed this love, keeping it a tiny ice-hard secret deep in her heart. She and Caroline were inseparable, meeting after classes, grabbing dinner at Dojo or John's Pizza, and pulling all-nighters studying.

It was heaven. Until November, and Christmas break was on the horizon. The thought of being separated for two entire weeks was unbearable to Jo, though she couldn't admit it to Caroline. The fact that she couldn't eat and couldn't sleep was crazy, she knew. She flubbed at least one exam over her preemptive heartache. One thing was clear, she needed some distance from Caroline.

Jo started sneaking off to study by herself, finding other friends to meet for dinner, waking up early on weekends to go running and avoid their usual routine.

"I never see you anymore!" Caroline said good-heartedly one afternoon.

"Well, you're going home in ten days, so we might as well get used to it," Jo said, trying to sound nonchalant and failing miserably.

"Yeah. Unless you come with me."

What to say about that first trip to Vermont? Chastely sharing that queen-sized bed in Caroline's childhood bedroom was the most erotic experience of her life. That first morning she woke up before Caroline, and in the sunlight shining brightly through the gauzy pink curtains, reflecting off the snow on the ground, she was able to stare unabashedly at her friend's porcelain skin, the curve of her cheekbone, the cleft above her full upper lip. Every morning in that house was Christmas morning.

And then, second semester, just weeks after New Year's, disaster struck. His name was Derek Ebernoff.

Caroline met him in psych class, partners assigned to do a group project on Skinner. Jo was disturbed to notice that Caroline found every excuse possible to talk about him. The nights spent working on the Skinner project became later and later. And then one night when Caroline didn't return to the dorm room, Jo burned with the fury of a spurned wife. But unlike a wife, she had no grounds to complain.

Caroline and Derek became a couple.

Jo started drinking. She smoked a lot of weed. Anything to keep the images out of her mind: Derek Ebernoff kissing Caroline's lips. His hands on her small breasts, his fingers between her legs, cracking Caroline's patrician reserve in ways that Jo could only fantasize about. Derek, hearing what Caroline's moan sounded like. He would see her cheeks flush in ecstasy. Derek, holding her naked and trembling body in his arms, that long russet hair falling against his chest.

It was, in a word, hell.

Jo tried to muster some romantic interest in other people. There was no shortage of attention, male and female. Jo, with her long brown hair fading to a burnt umber color midway down her back, her high cheekbones and almond-shaped brown eyes, her effortless boho chic style of a young Sienna Miller, and most attractive of all, her indifference. But her few hookups during that time left her cold.

She made a new friend, a cute blond guy named Toby—Tobias Hedegaard-Kruse. They met in line at the Genius Bar in the SoHo Apple store, and when they bumped into each other again on the way out, they discovered they were both NYU students. There was something different about Toby—he had a quiet confidence, a deeply contented way about him that disarmed her. Months later she learned that at least part of this reserve stemmed from the fact that he was Danish royalty. But by that time, Toby had become her new BFF. It was as platonic as her friendship with Caroline—minus the searing, desperate attraction. At least, not on her part. She began to suspect that Toby had feelings for her, but she tried to ignore that terribly inconvenient realization.

And then, just when she was starting to emerge from the depths of her heartsickness, when she had accepted the loss of Caroline to Derek Ebernoff, it happened.

"It's over," Caroline sobbed.

For forty-eight hours, they didn't leave their dorm room as Jo ministered to her like a parent with a bedridden child. When the fever broke, she had her best friend back. Jo introduced Caroline to Toby, but they didn't really work as a threesome. When Jo and Caroline were together, their closeness sucked all the oxygen from the room. And then summer came. Toby went to Europe, Jo stayed in New York, and Caroline returned to Vermont.

Jo was back in agony. She lasted not even a week before buying a plane ticket to Vermont. There was a heat wave in Bennington. Late at night, Jo and Caroline lay on top of the patchwork quilt, wearing tank tops and their underwear, as the window units wheezed out a paltry amount of cool air. What had they been talking about that first night? Jo couldn't remember now. But she did remember—would always, until her deathbed, remember—how Caroline had leaned forward and brushed her lips against Jo's. A lit match to kindling.

"What are you doing?" Jo had asked, barely daring to speak, to breathe.

"I know how you feel about me," she'd said, her voice surprisingly steady and even.

"Oh."

"And I love you too."

Three years later, it felt as fresh and new and exciting and unbelievable as that first night they'd made love. It was everything Jo could ever ask for, and so there was no reason to think about next steps, about the future—if it weren't for Meg's engagement. As soon as Meg and Stowe announced their intention to spend the rest of their lives together—and to make that vow in front of all their family and friends—Jo couldn't help but think about doing the same.

She didn't envision diamond rings and white gowns and walking down an aisle on her father's arm. But . . . *something.* Because she wanted to spend the rest of her life with Caroline. And maybe it was time she made that official.

Jo looked up from the espresso machine. She felt Toby's presence before she saw him. This, she suspected, was because mostly everyone in the café had turned to look at him. Aside from his height and his blond good looks and his vague familiarity (Toby had briefly dated an actress from an HBO drama and became a temporary *Us Weekly* staple), something about him simply screamed I Don't Belong in Brooklyn.

"I was just nowhere near your neighborhood," he said, leaning over the counter with an impish grin. It was a quote from *Singles,* one of their favorite movies, which Jo had unearthed during her obsessive retro grunge phase junior year.

"I hate to tell you, this is so hardly worth your while—I have to bolt in, like, five minutes."

"Big plans?"

"Dinner. Command appearance. Meeting the in-laws."

"Great. I'm starving."

"Are you serious?"

"Not really. As much as I'd love to meet a real live Republican in New York City."

"I think we'll be steering the dinner conversation as far away from politics as possible."

"Can Meg get through a dinner without talking about politics?" Toby raised an eyebrow.

"Something tells me she is learning—fast."

"Right. So let's grab a drink after. I know your ball and chain is working too much to go out, and you're becoming an old lady."

"For your information, I didn't get home until three this morning. And there's not enough caffeine in this whole place to power me through another night out."

She glanced at the clock. Her shift was officially over. Reaching behind her waist, she untied her orange apron and hung it on a low hook.

"Meet me out front," she told him while she headed to the basement to clock out.

The day was brisk, the daylight low and fading fast, leaving no doubt that the colder temperatures were there to stay. Jo hated this time of year. She was a child of summer—flip-flops, tank tops, sun-kissed skin, sand in her hair. She had considered going to Berkeley for college but knew she would miss New York too much—cold winters and all. And thank God she hadn't. She would never have met Caroline.

Toby walked her the two blocks home to North Henry Street, pausing to look up at the five-story redbrick building with a shingled awning over the entrance door. "This place looks like such a shithole," he said.

"Cranky much?"

"I just miss you. I knew things would be different out of school, but . . . they're really different."

"You just need to stay busy. You need a job, Tobe."

"Jobs are for money, and I have plenty of money."

"Jobs aren't just for money."

"Oh? Are you getting some deep-seated satisfaction from serving the country's favorite legal drug topped with foamed milk?"

"Ah, fuck off, Tobe."

He looked at her then with a thinly veiled longing she recognized. It had been painful when she experienced it with Caroline, and it was difficult to see that same unrequited passion reflected back at her. She reached up and hugged him tightly.

"Have fun tonight. I'll catch you later in the week."

Jo climbed the stairs, her exhaustion lifting.

She wiggled her key in the stiff lock, then pushed open the heavy door.

"Hey, babe," she called out, dropping her keys in the bowl on the flea market table in the entrance foyer. "Caroline?"

Jo shrugged off her coat—a long suede treasure lined in faux fur that she had found at Vice Versa Vintage ("Vintage garb for man, woman, and beast")—and headed to the alcove in the back, where Caroline had set up her office. The desk was empty.

"I'm in the bedroom."

Jo smiled, tossing her coat and bag on a chair. She pushed open the bedroom door. Caroline was on the bed, the end of a pen in her mouth, her books spread out. She was in a V-neck white T-shirt and yoga pants, her long red hair up in a messy knot. Her complexion was paler than usual, bordering on wan. Her mascara—brown, not black—had migrated to smudges beneath her lower lashes. And her mouth—oh, her mouth.

She wasn't dressed for dinner.

"Hey, we gotta get going." Jo climbed onto the bed, moving her laptop out of the way, and pulled the pen from her lips so she could kiss her. She tasted like cinnamon raisin toast.

"Uh-huh," Caroline said. Her voice sounded husky, like she hadn't spoken all day. Either that, or like she'd been crying.

"Everything okay?" Jo said.

"No," Caroline said, hugging her knees to her chest.

"What is it?"

"I can't go to dinner."

"Why not?"

"I . . . I've met someone," she said.

Jo didn't fully process what Caroline was saying. She'd met someone and . . . what? The words could have meant anything. But the expression on her face could mean only one thing.

"You met someone? Who? Where?" But even as Jo asked it, she knew. The study group. The study group that took up more of Caroline's time than was even remotely reasonable, even for law students.

"Jo, please don't make this harder for me than it already is."

Jo sat on the edge of the bed and whispered disbelievingly, "You cheated on me?"

Caroline nodded.

Jo bit her lip, willing herself not to cry and trying not to lash out at her. "Okay. I'm . . . I'm glad you told me." She wasn't. "I'll get over it with time. I will. I just need to know it won't happen again."

"Jo." Caroline's face softened, her expression pained. And that's when Jo knew, but she refused to know.

"Jo, I'm in love with him. I'm moving out."

The fashion headquarters of Jeffrey Bruce International were in the heart of the Meatpacking District—the trendiest neighborhood in all of Manhattan, and one of the farthest from Amy Becker's parents' apartment on the Upper East Side. She was going to have to leave work early for the command appearance to meet Meg's future in-laws. Amy didn't know how she was going to stomach the next nine months of everything revolving around Meg. Well, really, everything *always* revolved around

Meg. But now, with her engagement, it was official. And justifiable. And more intolerable than ever.

Amy knew she should be happy for her sister. And on some level, she was. Truly. But for God's sake, she'd been dating Stowe Campion for only a year! Amy had been with Andy for five years, and *they* weren't even engaged! Why was everything always so easy for Meg?

A knock on the glass door. She looked up to find Andy.

"Hey," he said, smiling. "What time do we have to get going?" Andy had curly dark hair and big puppy-dog brown eyes. The first time she saw him, in a friend's dorm room, pregaming with shots of tequila before a night out, she'd thought, That guy's cute. "Cute" summed up Andy. At age twenty-five, he still had something boyish and collegiate about him. Maybe because she'd met him while they were still teenagers, he would always seem like one to her.

"Ugh—I don't know. Soon."

"Did you tell Stella? We're going to miss the four-thirty marketing meeting."

No, she hadn't told her boss, Stella. Stella Chung terrified her. She had a fashion-industry résumé a mile long, and she was only thirty—having started as an assistant to Anna Wintour, then on to a couple of years at Vera Wang before becoming the marketing director at Jeffrey Bruce. Oh, and she'd pretty much made it clear that she hated Amy. "Hate" was maybe a strong word, but Stella was obviously resentful at having Amy dumped on her desk. Every time Stella called her name, practically spitting it out, it was like she was muttering "nepotism" under her breath. Amy didn't want special treatment at the office. Of course, if it weren't for special treatment, she wouldn't have this job. But she tried not to think about that. On a day-to-day basis, she worked hard to earn her keep like everyone else. If anything, she worked extra hard to prove her worth. She wanted people to forget that she was Andy Bruce's girlfriend.

Which made it seriously uncomfortable to have to knock on Stella's door and tell her, "I just wanted to remind you that I have to miss the meeting at four thirty."

Stella looked up from her stainless steel desk, which was spotless except for a razor-thin laptop. Her black hair framed her face in a bob so sleek, it looked like a helmet. "Did you tell Jeffrey that you were going to the shoot next week?"

"Um, no. I think maybe Andy did?"

"I would appreciate it if you didn't make presumptions. I don't need you at the shoot—I need you here at the office. Understood?"

"Yes. Absolutely. Understood."

Amy tried to hide her disappointment. She loved going to photo shoots for the print ad campaigns. Jeffrey had taken her along with him once or twice when he visited the sets. The glamour of it was dizzying.

When they were growing up, her sister Meg had always been the glamorous one. The infuriating thing was that Meg was so stylish yet had zero interest in fashion. Like everything else, style was effortless for her. And, like everything else, Amy had to work at it—hard. Even now, a junior executive at Jeffrey Bruce, likely marrying into the family of one of the biggest American designers of the past thirty years, having hung out with the top stylists in fashion, Rachel Zoe to name one, and having worked on fashion shoots with Cara Delevingne and Kendall Jenner and Gigi Hadid, Amy was still awed by Meg. The more she met fabulous people, the more she knew that Meg was the chicest of them all. Apparently, Andy's father agreed with her, having said (jokingly?) on more than one occasion, "We should get your sister into one of our ads." The comment had left her with a pit in her stomach that never quite seemed to fully disappear.

Her only consolation was the certainty that Meg would *never*. Meg was serious. Meg was a journalist. She was into Politics with a capital *P*. She might look like Grace Kelly, but she talked like Andrea Mitchell.

"Oh, and I hear congratulations are in order," said Stella, looking at her pointedly. "I hear your sister is marrying into the Campion family. She's like the new Jackie Kennedy. Which would make you—What was her sister's name? Oh, who can remember. At any rate—have a lovely dinner."

four

It was time.

Meryl opened the front door with a flutter in her chest and a bright smile on her face. "Hi, everyone!"

"Hi, Mom." Meg leaned in to hug her, and Meryl happily breathed in her eldest daughter's Chanel Allure.

And then, because she couldn't hesitate any longer, Meryl turned to the woman by her daughter's side. Tippy Campion.

"So nice to finally meet you!" Meryl said warmly.

"Tippy Campion," the woman replied, extending her hand.

Meryl was startled. She had been going in for the cheek kiss. Instead, she took Tippy's lead. Then she greeted Stowe with a kiss and ushered them inside.

Stowe handed Meryl a bottle of red wine. She caught a glimpse of the label and did a double take: Screaming Eagle. Arguably the most coveted cabernet in the country—available only by mailing list or at auction.

"Stowe—you shouldn't have," she admonished him, trying to hide her shock.

Tippy handed her a box from Ladurée SoHo. "I couldn't resist stopping by. It's just my favorite bakery outside of Paris," she said.

Meryl thanked them and steered everyone to the living room, where the cheese, crackers, a sliced baguette, and five varieties of pitted olives were set out.

"Is Gran here yet?" Meg asked.

Meryl tried to keep her expression neutral. "Gran was feeling tired, sweetheart. Another night. I'm sorry."

"Is she all right?"

"Fine. Just tired," Meryl repeated.

"And Dad?" said Meg.

Where *was* Hugh? "Excuse me for one minute." Meryl took the wine, making her way to the back of the apartment. Hugh's office door was closed. She knocked once, impatiently, before turning the brass knob. "Hugh, they're here. What are you doing?"

He looked up from his computer. "I was trying to get an hour in on the book."

The book.

He had not published anything since *Abby May Alcott: An American Mother*—a book that was heralded by reviewers as "definitive" and "groundbreaking." At the time, he had told his agent that his plan was to publish books about Louisa May, and then follow these with a collection about the entire family dynamic. But this proved overly ambitious, and somewhere along the line, he pared it down to just the Louisa May biography.

That was twenty-five years ago. The book was still a work in progress. His agent had retired.

"Now?" Meryl asked, exasperated.

"Okay, okay—I'm coming."

Back in the living room, Meryl found everyone still standing. Awkwardly.

"Please—everyone. Sit."

Meg introduced Tippy to Hugh, who ignored all social cues and kissed Tippy on her cheek.

"I apologize that my husband couldn't make it," said Tippy. "One of his fund-raisers got wind that he was in town, and it's the only time they overlapped."

"We understand. Another time," Meryl said automatically. Except she didn't. At all.

"Where do you stay when you're in New York?" Hugh asked.

"The Vesper Club."

The front door opened.

"Amy! Hi, honey!" Meryl rushed to hug Amy as if she hadn't seen her in months and extended a hug to Amy's boyfriend, Andy.

He handed her a bottle of prosecco, Meryl's favorite.

"You didn't have to bring anything," Meryl told him with a smile, as she did every week. Andy had been coming to family dinners since their sophomore year at Syracuse. And his parents, Eileen and Jeffrey, had come once or twice. She hated to compare, but it was a stark contrast to the Campions. And Jeffrey could easily have found the same excuses if he'd wanted to. Jeffrey Bruce was just as high profile as Reed Campion—more so, really. But for some reason, Meryl had never felt uncomfortable around the Bruces. Maybe it's because she knew that even though Jeffrey Bruce had a fashion empire, he had at one time been just an Upper West Side kid like herself. There was something familiar about them—relatable.

"Thanks so much for making it here early," Meryl said to Andy.

"No problem! I'm starving. Early dinner is always good with me." He grinned.

"We barely could finish out the workday," Amy said. "What was the big rush?"

Amy had been in a foul mood for weeks. Since Meg's engagement, to be precise.

Meryl supposed that was normal—jealousy between sisters. The day Meg announced her engagement, Amy snorted, "Well, that was quick."

"They've been together a year, hon," Meryl had said, then immediately realized her mistake. By then, Amy and Andy had been together five years, and no ring had yet been forthcoming.

"Everyone's in the living room. Go say hello while I go open the wine."

In the kitchen, she leaned against the counter, thankful for the minute to catch her breath. While she had been disappointed that Reed couldn't make it tonight, now she was thinking it might be for the best. Hosting the senator would have been far more pressure.

"Can I give you a hand?" Tippy appeared in the doorway, startling her.

Meryl was about to say she was already finished and would be right out, but realized she hadn't even retrieved the wine opener yet. "Oh, I've got it! Please, relax. I'll be right out to join you."

"Actually, I'm happy for the moment alone. Before we all sit down to dinner."

"Oh?" Meryl tried to seem nonchalant, maybe even pleased for the chance to chat, but she felt self-conscious as she uncorked the prosecco.

"The kids have us on quite a timeline, don't they? Nine months! Who can get something major accomplished in just nine months?"

Well, Mother Nature, thought Meryl.

"Meg and Stowe seem to know what they want. So that helps."

Tippy seemed not to have heard her. "It's going to be a large affair," Tippy continued, "and I just want you to know that we are happy to pay for everything. We don't want the kids to feel they have to cut corners. It's a once-in-a-lifetime event, after all. At least that's what we all hope, isn't it?" Tippy laughed lightly.

Meryl didn't know whether to feel appreciative or insulted. Was this just a gesture acknowledging that the Campions clearly had the money, so not to offer would be rude? Or did they really think that Meryl and Hugh couldn't provide an adequate wedding? The distinction between the two was vital, and as she stood there wrestling with it, she found herself speechless.

"Having the wedding at the club makes it so easy," Tippy said. "Just a few phone calls, and we can take care of everything—"

Meryl finally snapped to attention. "No—you don't have to take care of everything—anything, actually." Then, realizing how it sounded, she soft-pedaled. "Thank you, though. For the offer. But Hugh and I are happy to throw the wedding. Parents of the bride—part of the deal, right?" She laughed awkwardly.

"Well, at the very least, you absolutely must take advantage of our event planner, Leigh. I insist. She is a genius, and does all our affairs—I don't make a move without her."

"Oh, I don't think—"

"And it's not just campaign events and fund-raisers. She did the Prescott wedding last spring. You must have seen that in *Town and Country*. Breathtaking."

"Tippy, I appreciate the . . . thought. Really. But I'm looking forward to this being a project for Meg and me. And of course—your input is always welcome. But aside from that, I don't think we need another person in the mix."

Tippy looked at her as though she were about to speak to a delightful but very young child. "Meryl, I completely understand the sentimental aspect of the event. And there will be plenty for you and Meg to do together! But if we're going to really pull this off by the spring, we need someone on the ground full-time. And I'm sure you have other things to do."

Meryl didn't want to admit that, no, she had little else to do. That her freelance work had all but dried up recently. In the age of blogging and "virtual" book tours, a time when most major newspapers had done away with their book review section, the need for a freelance book publicist was not what it had once been. Even just ten years ago, small authors were going on multicity book tours. When she started at HarperCollins in 1984, the publicity department at the publisher had taken two entire floors at the office on East Fifty-third Street. From what she was hearing from the few of her peers who had managed to hold on to full-time employment, the ranks had thinned considerably. This made her feel a little better about the premature end to her corporate career.

"Meryl, trust me. Having the wedding planner will keep things on track," Tippy said. "And then you and Meg can just enjoy the fun parts. Plus, Leigh works with all the vendors so frequently, she gets deals on everything. It's win–win."

The kitchen door opened, and both women turned to find Meg. Meryl's stomach seized up and she wondered how long she'd been at the door, how much she'd heard.

"Sorry to interrupt—but, Mom, Jo just texted me. She's not coming."

Jo spent nearly a full day's tips taking a cab from Greenpoint to the Upper West Side of Manhattan, and cried the entire way.

When she called Toby, he had answered on the first ring.

"Where are you?" Jo sobbed.

"At my flat. What's wrong?"

"I'll tell you when I get there."

Now she wished she were still in her bed at the apartment. Caroline was gone, but she could curl up in a ball and just wait for the pain to kill her, because surely this much agony could only result in death. There was no recovering from it.

"I love you," Caroline had said. "You know I do. And because I love you so much, what happened between us happened. But I'm not *in* love with you."

" 'What happened between us happened'? What the hell does that mean?"

"It means that I don't think I'm gay."

Gay, straight—what the fuck difference did it make? They were in love. They were. They had passion. They had best friendship. They had everything.

"So what are you saying? You're 'in love' with this guy?"

"Yes."

Yes. The single word, a bullet.

Caroline was moving out. "But I don't want to lose you as my best friend. I would die if I lost that," she said.

She would die? *She* was the one who would die?

The cab left her off at Eighty-first and Central Park West in front of the Beresford, a magnificent, storied Italian Renaissance building.

After three hours of anguish, her eyes were swollen, her nose red, and she was still dressed in the clothes she'd worn to her eight-hour shift at the coffee shop. She was embarrassed to present herself to the doorman, a white-haired Irishman in a green and gold uniform.

After the doorman confirmed her status as an approved visitor with a quick call up to Toby, she made her way to the gated, prewar Otis elevator, complete with a white-gloved operator.

"Good evening, miss," he said when they reached the twentieth floor. He slid open the gate, and Jo hastily made the quick left turn to Toby's apartment, one of two on the entire floor.

Toby was waiting in the doorway. "Lovers' quarrel?" he said.

Jo burst into tears.

"Oh, for fuck's sake, come inside so I can pour you a drink."

Jo was not entirely comfortable at Toby's apartment. She always half expected his parents, the count and countess, to descend from the spiral staircase in the center of the duplex (never happened).

She folded herself into a ball on the couch, underneath an enormous oil painting of the royal arms of Denmark, the coat of arms of Prince Henrik, Denmark's prince consort and Tobias's uncle.

The furniture was antique and heavy and distinctly European, with ornate rugs and lots of dark wood and heavy curtains. The place was, for lack of a better word, palatial. Tonight, for the first time, it felt welcoming and safe. The Beresford was a fortress against the outside world, and Jo, a wounded bird, needed its protection.

Toby poured two vodka and tonics into crystal tumblers and joined her on the couch. True friend that he was, he did not demand to satisfy his own curiosity but instead let her sip her drink and calm her nerves.

When Jo finally spoke, it was only to keep her mind from replaying the image of Caroline's face as she walked out the door. "It's over with Caroline. She ended it." The words didn't sound real. They sounded like lines from a play about someone else's life.

"Damn, Jo. I'm sorry." He retrieved a bottle of Stoli and two shot glasses. "Did you see it coming?"

"No. Not at all. I was completely blindsided."

"Was this a fight?"

"No. It wasn't a 'heat of the moment' thing. She'd clearly—" Her voice broke. "—she'd clearly thought it out. Planned to tell me. Was tormented by it."

"I hate to ask you this—I don't want to upset you more, but . . ."

"Yeah. There's someone else. A guy." With this, a sob came loose, hard and abrupt, a branch suddenly falling from a tree with a sickening crack.

"Fuck," Toby said, pouring two generous shots. "There's only one thing to do at a time like this. And lucky for you—though you mock my lack of gainful employment—I have nowhere to go tomorrow and am therefore available to get completely, irrevocably annihilated with you." He handed her a shot, then raised his own for a toast.

She ignored him and downed the drink, welcoming the burn. "I just don't know what to do," she said, lost.

"There's nothing to do," said Toby wistfully. "If there's one thing I've learned, it's that you can't make someone want you."

"How could she do this to me? We love each other."

"Don't beat yourself up, Jo," Toby said, pouring another round. "The best thing to do tonight is not think too much."

Jo drank, and she drank some more. "I started in the friend zone, and I'm ending in the friend zone," Jo said just as it became difficult to speak clearly.

"I hate the friend zone," Toby said.

"What do you know about it? You sleep with every woman you meet."

"Except the only one who matters," he said softly.

Even through the haze of alcohol, there was no missing the intensity in his blue eyes. His eyes were filled with longing, the longing she had recognized when they first started hanging out but had become inured to over the years. Now, raw with her own grief, she couldn't ignore the pain that was just under the surface of his gaze.

"No, no, no, Lord Tobias Hedegaard-Kruse. Don't do that. Don't make me feel bad. You are rich, you are gorgeous, and you get laid more than any guy I know. I will not feel bad for you!" She poured them both another shot. The room tilted, and the heaviness of her heart lifted. The small shred of rational thinking she had left told her that she would be sorry in the morning, but for now it was sweet relief.

"Sex is nothing," he said, now slurring too.

"Sex is nothing? Can I quote you on that—when we're not hammered, I mean."

"Let me finish," he said, taking another shot. "Sex is nothing compared to love."

"What do you know about it?" she countered.

"I know I'm in love with you."

I'm in love with you. Even through the thick sludge of alcohol slowing her brain synapses to a fuzzy mess, she couldn't avoid the irony. The love of her life had told her just hours ago that she loved her but was not in love with her, and now her best buddy was telling her that he was in love with her.

"Oh God, Toby."

"Yeah," he said. "Tell me about it."

five

"I'll help you clear," Meg said, the first one to offer when it was obvious the dinner party was hurtling toward its conclusion. All that was left was dessert.

All in all, Meryl felt it had been successful. The conversation, while lively, had steered clear of politics. Hugh entertained Tippy with a long-winded but charmingly eccentric story of his trip to Germantown, Pennsylvania, to visit the birthplace of Louisa May Alcott. The building was apparently not far from the Campions' house in Haverford, and Tippy realized that, come to think of it, that was where she'd bought one of their pianos. There was a plaque outside.

"And wasn't Louisa May Alcott's father a teacher, too?" Tippy asked.

"Yes!" Hugh said, delighted.

"I guess I do remember a few things from school!" said Tippy, equally delighted.

Stowe and Andy found they shared an interest in the NHL, and debated the Rangers versus the Philadelphia Flyers. The only one who didn't get into the spirit of things was Amy, who resisted contributing to the conversation no matter how often Meryl or Andy tried to engage her. Luckily a copious intake of wine had kept Meryl calm and smiling. They'd gone through three bottles at least. Still, she made a mental note to talk to Amy about this tomorrow. She couldn't act out for the next eight months until the wedding. She would have to get over it.

"Oh, before I forget," said Tippy. "And this is something Reed and I had planned to share with you together, but goodness knows when he'll be available!" She laughed before continuing, "But I can't possibly wait any longer: We'd like to throw an engagement party."

Meryl looked at her, stupefied. The bride's parents were supposed to throw the engagement party, at least according to the small stack of books on modern wedding etiquette she'd bought. She wanted to do everything just right for Meg and had already marked key passages.

Meg and Stowe, beaming at each other, were the first to speak.

"Mom, that's really generous. Thanks," Stowe said.

"That would be amazing," said Meg.

Amazing? Meryl looked at her daughter incredulously. Meg wasn't typically prone to hyperbole.

"Sounds terrific," said Hugh, refilling Tippy's glass.

Meryl shot him a glance, but he didn't notice.

What could she say? Thanks, but that's not necessary? The truth was, she hadn't thought about throwing an engagement party. It wasn't essential, and it was a huge added expense. But if the Campions wanted to contribute in that way, fine. All it did was solidify her feeling that she absolutely didn't want any more input from them—financial or otherwise.

The only one who looked as unhappy as she felt was Amy. And as irritated as she was with her, she couldn't help but feel a twinge at her middle child's being so unhappy.

"I think it's time for dessert," Meryl said, picking up her plate and Hugh's. Meg stood and collected her own and Stowe's.

"Let me help," Tippy said, making a polite, halfhearted attempt to rise from her seat.

"No, please—relax. We'll be done in no time," Meryl said, and waved her away.

She couldn't help but glance at Amy, who made no move to help clear the dishes.

Andy did not fail to notice, however. "Why don't we take a quick walk before dessert?" he said to her.

Amy shrugged.

"It's so lovely that you live right on the water like this," said Tippy. "If I didn't have to meet up with my husband, I'd suggest we all take a stroll."

Andy, not wanting to wait for Tippy to reconsider her stance on the matter, hustled a reluctant Amy out the door.

Hugh, left with an audience of three, opened another bottle of wine.

"I haven't seen your father drink this much in a long time," Meryl commented in the kitchen.

"At least everyone is enjoying themselves," Meg said.

"Did you know about this engagement party?" Meryl said.

"No—total surprise. But really nice of her, don't you think?"

"*Very* nice."

Meg pulled on one rubber glove, and Meryl's eyes unwillingly fell to the two-carat, flawless solitaire diamond on her daughter's left hand. It was a beautiful ring. When she'd commented to her youngest daughter that the ring belonged in a Tiffany's ad, Jo said it belonged right where it was: on Meg's finger. Meryl was duly chastened. Time to get on board the Campion train. It seemed it was going to be quite a ride.

"What was Tippy talking to you about in here before dinner?" Meg asked.

She didn't turn around, and Meryl was relieved that she didn't have to face Meg. She didn't want to tell her that Tippy offered to pay for the entire wedding. She knew Meg would be equally mortified, but at the same time, it was a lie of omission and Meg would see it on her face.

"She suggested we use her wedding planner," Meryl said.

"And what do you think about that?" Meg asked nonchalantly. Too nonchalantly. This was clearly not news to her.

"I told her thanks but no thanks," Meryl said. "What did you think I'd say?"

Meg turned around, an exasperated edge to her voice. "Mom, don't."

"Don't what?"

"Be offended."

"I'm not offended. Why didn't you talk to me about this if you knew she wanted it?"

"Stowe only just mentioned it to me today. You know, it really will save money in the end because she gets such great deals from the vendors."

"Yes, so she said. It's not so much the expense, Meg. Your father and I are more than capable of throwing your wedding. I don't need the Campions trying to make it into one of their events. Not to mention, I don't need them overly involved with the cost and the budget and other things that frankly aren't their business." This came out harsher than Meryl intended, and Meg had registered her resentment.

"I think she's just trying to help. In her own way," Meg responded stiffly.

Meryl's face softened. "Honey, I don't doubt it. But I told her—nicely—that I am really looking forward to planning my daughter's wedding—your wedding, with you—and I don't need help from a stranger."

"How did she seem to take it?"

Meryl looked closely at her daughter. "Are you worried about offending her? Meg, it's your wedding."

"I know, I know. And I'm not worried—I just don't want to freeze her out of the process, you know. She should be a part of it too."

"Don't worry, Meg. The Campions aren't the only ones who know how to be political."

"Oh my God, you *are* pissed. Mom, please don't be."

"I just wish you'd told me instead of letting me get ambushed in my own kitchen." She wondered if Meg also knew about the far more unsettling offer to pay for the entire wedding.

"I would hardly call it an ambush. Forget it—she offered, you said no. It's fine. Let's just move on."

"Gladly. Do you have time to come back for the afternoon sometime in the next few weeks to do your bridal registry?"

She nodded. "I'll try. Anyway, we should get dessert out there. Tippy has to go meet Reed."

"Right!"

The box from Ladurée was on the corner of the counter. Meryl opened it. "Macarons?" she said.

"Yes. The bakery flies them in daily from Monaco."

"You're joking."

"No. At least, that's what Tippy told me."

"If it's true, that's outrageous!"

Meryl took the chocolate cake down from the top of the refrigerator, where she'd left it to stand to reach room temperature. "I hope Amy doesn't miss dessert," she said quietly.

"What's her problem tonight?"

Meryl sighed. "Meg, she's always been competitive. And she's been with Andy for years now, and you meet Stowe and boom—engaged. It's just hard on her. You'd feel the same way if you were her."

"Okay, first of all, we dated for a year before he proposed—that's not exactly 'boom, engaged.' Secondly, Stowe and I are the type of people who know what we want and go after it. It's not my fault Andy is dragging his feet. He's a nice guy, but he really seems to just coast on his father, you know what I mean?"

"Honey, it's not her fault either."

"I know, Mom. I'm just saying, if she's annoyed with anyone, it should be with Andy, not me. And there's no use in her taking it out on me for the next eight months. She should be happy for me. And if she gets engaged someday, I'll be happy for her."

They carried the dessert into the dining room. Meryl had hoped that by some chance Amy would be there, but was not surprised to find she wasn't.

"These macarons look delicious," Meryl said, placing down the tray. Really, she had to lighten up about Tippy. She had made an appearance at dinner, seemed to be having a good time, even, and Meryl had made it clear they didn't need any help with paying for the wedding, thank-you-very-much—everyone could move on and just enjoy the planning.

"They fly them in from Monaco every day," Tippy said.

"Really?" said Meryl. She and Meg shared a conspiratorial smile, and for the first time all night, she felt close to her daughter. She would never admit to having a favorite, but there had always been something about her relationship with Meg—a shared language, an effortless connection. Even when Meg was a teenager, when everyone warned Meryl not to take it personally if she pulled away, their closeness hadn't diminished. With Amy, there were always her moods, her sense of entitlement, her competitiveness. And Jo, a sweet girl, was certainly the most good-natured out of them all, but Meryl always had a hard time understanding her.

"Should we wait for Amy?" asked Hugh.

"I think we should just start without them. Stowe's dad is expecting Tippy to join him soon," said Meg.

"No, it's okay," said Stowe. "We don't have to rush."

"Darling, she's right. I have to get going," said Tippy.

Tippy left with effusive praise for the dinner and apologies for Reed's absence. When she leaned in to give Meryl an air kiss, she said quietly, "Please think about our conversation."

Meryl didn't know if Tippy meant the part about them paying for the wedding, or the part about the wedding planner, but she nodded politely.

"I'm glad you two can stay awhile longer," Meryl said to Meg and Stowe. She had expected they might leave with Tippy, but the pair didn't seem to be in a rush.

Her hand was still on the door when it pushed open again. She jumped back, startled.

"We're back!" Amy called.

"We just saw your mother in the hall," said Andy. "I'm sorry we took so long. Didn't mean to miss dessert."

Was it her imagination, or was Amy beaming?

Instinctively Meryl looked down at her daughter's hand and saw a splinter of light coming from the enormous cushion-cut diamond ring on her finger.

"Amy . . ." Meryl trailed off, eyes wide.

"We're getting married!"

"Oh, sweetheart, congratulations. Come here—you too, Andy." Meryl opened her arms, hugging her daughter and future son-in-law. Over Amy's shoulder, she glanced at Hugh, who had visibly paled—

a "deer caught in the headlights" look on his face. Another wedding to pay for.

"Hon, why don't you uncork a bottle of champagne," Meryl said to spur him out of his paralysis.

"Congrats, you two." Meg said. "What *interesting* timing."

Meryl shot her a look: Not now. Yes, Amy always seemed to be chasing after Meg, playing catch-up if not one-up. But this was different.

Hugh appeared with the champagne, quickly pouring six glasses. He and Meg both gulped it down before Meryl could make her toast. She glared at the both of them.

"To my two beautiful daughters, their wonderful husbands-to-be . . . and to a year of weddings."

"To a year of weddings!" everyone cheered.

Everyone but Hugh.

six

Amy gazed adoringly at the ring on her finger.

Three hours into her engagement, and she felt married already. They'd lived together for two years in a dream apartment in TriBeCa, they worked together, and now with Jeffrey and Eileen telling her, "Call us Mom and Dad!" the wedding seemed like just a formality. But what a great formality it would be! Her cheeks hurt from grinning so much.

It all felt exactly right, exactly as it should be. The duration of her relationship with Andy was unheard of among their friends.

They'd had only one "break"—junior year, when Amy went abroad to Spain and Andy went to Italy. It had been painful—the break had been Andy's idea. But it was probably the thing that helped them go the distance. They both realized they weren't missing out on anything, except time together.

"Ame, come look at these mock-ups for the new ads," Andy called from the bedroom.

She moved reluctantly from the couch, not wanting to think about work just then. It was the night of their engagement. She wanted to revel in that.

Sometimes it was hard to find time for romance. It was so easy to fall into being best friends, and coworkers, and family, in a way. It was important to take time away from all that to be a couple.

Amy padded into the bedroom, closing the curtains on the oversized windows overlooking Greenwich Street.

"What do you think?" he asked.

She climbed onto the king-sized bed and glanced at the images on his laptop screen. "It's very . . . rustic."

"Yeah. I know. Dad loves it. You're going to the shoot, right?"

"Stella said she didn't need me."

"It's not about whether or not Stella needs you. If you want to go, go. You're into the shoots, right?"

"Yes, but—"

"So it's a done deal. Dad will tell her."

"I don't think we should, you know, go over her head on this one."

Andy squinted at his MacBook, scrolling through images of catalog models wearing various combinations of the latest higher end of Jeffrey Bruce menswear—the top-of-the-line pieces that sold only in places like Barneys and the Jeffrey Bruce flagship stores. The looks would be finalized before the print shoot next week, when the "real" models—agency models who costs thousands of dollars an hour—would wear the clothes for ads that would run in *GQ, Vogue, Esquire.* Everywhere, basically.

"Do you think your dad was upset I didn't ask him before proposing to you?"

Amy shook her head. "My dad isn't like that—that whole 'standing on ceremony' thing."

"So can we go ahead and tell my parents we'll have the wedding at Stonehill?"

Stonehill was the Bruces' hundred-acre East Hampton estate, which rivaled something out of one of her father's beloved novels set among the British aristocracy.

"Yeah. Sure."

"And, Ame, I didn't talk about this with my dad or anything. And I don't want to tell you what to do, but—"

"Of course I want to wear a Jeffrey Bruce dress," she reassured him; she had decided that long ago. Andy was visibly relieved. "Did you doubt that?"

"Well, I know you love Monique Lhuillier."

Actually, it was Meg who was obsessed with Monique Lhuillier. It had been her sister's first and only Pinterest board. Wearing a Monique Lhuillier dress was the only context in which Meg had ever discussed getting married. And, following Meg's lead, Amy had quickly found herself enamored with the gowns by the superstar designer.

"I love you," she said, leaning forward and kissing him.

"Love you too," he said, giving her a peck and immediately turning back to his computer.

She sighed inwardly. When was the last time they'd had sex? She was pretty sure it had been at Stonehill, over a long weekend. Labor Day? But no—that would make it six weeks! And yet . . . possible.

A few months ago, Amy had almost asked one of her friends how often she and her boyfriend had sex. But she was too embarrassed to go through with it. More recently, walking to the subway with Jo after a dinner a few Sunday nights ago, she had almost asked her. But judging from the way she still mooned over Caroline, it was obvious they probably still banged every day.

The thing was, she and Andy had been together longer than any couple she knew. Longer than some marriages lasted. It was normal to hit a sexual plateau—wasn't it?

Unfortunately, it was definitely *not* normal how, during these lulls, her thoughts always drifted back to her one and only one-night stand.

How was it that a guy who hadn't known her at all had known so absolutely how to touch her?

It had happened that summer in Spain. She would never cheat on Andy, and—given their "break" status at the time of this insane, unforgettable sex—had never cheated on him. Technically speaking.

Afterwards, she probably wouldn't even have thought about Chris at all—that was his name, Chris. It wasn't Juan or Pablo or any of the foreign-to-the-tongue kind of names he would have if they had met in a Woody Allen film. He wasn't even Spanish. Chris was an exchange student from Skidmore. He was as Midwestern as they came, with sandy blond hair and blue eyes. He was a lacrosse player.

When he had fingered her, she hit the moon.

Lying side by side in the twin bed she slept in at her host family's house—a family that went out for dinner at ten at night and usually returned after she was already asleep—she'd already had an orgasm by the time he moved on top of her.

Amy shook her head, scattering the unwelcome thoughts.

Her eyes fell to the ring on her finger—her gorgeous, cushion-cut, three-carat Tiffany engagement ring. A ring that was bigger than Meg's. But then, Meg didn't want a big ring. Meg was nothing if not understated. But Amy did want a big ring, damn it.

And, at that moment, she wanted to be fucked. By her fiancé.

She pulled the laptop from his hands.

"Hey, babe," he said when she kissed him on the mouth.

"Hey." She pulled off her T-shirt. Andy, finally getting with the program, kissed her more ardently. He took off his boxers, and she was gratified to see he was already hard. She closed her eyes, her lips curling into a smile, and when he slipped his fingers between her legs, she willed herself to feel excited.

She didn't.

Andy was lost in the woods down there. Even when she showed him—touch me here, touch me like that—he went about it in such a literal and rote way, she couldn't help but think she was better off masturbating.

Then he moved on top of her and it felt . . . good. It always did. After a few minutes of practiced, rhythmic motion, she finally felt a climax within reach. Amy always tried to prolong that sensation of building pleasure, trying to time it so that she and Andy could come together. She rarely could, because Andy tended to go on and on. By the time he climaxed, her own orgasm had come and gone and she felt as detached from his orgasm as a casual bystander.

Her phone chirped. Who was calling at this hour?

"I should probably get it," she groaned when she saw her mom's face pop up on the screen.

"Hey—everything all right?" she asked, trying not to sound breathless and finding it pathetically easy.

"Hi, honey. I just wanted to say congratulations again. Your father and I are just so thrilled. And I can't wait to start planning with you. But," Meryl paused, "I also wanted to give you a heads-up. Jo and Caroline broke up. She's devastated."

"Oh no! Is that why she didn't show up tonight?"

"Apparently. I'm hearing this all secondhand from Meg."

Amy frowned. Of course Jo called Meg first. Jo had always idolized her eldest sister, and Meg—despite her impatience with Amy—always had time for the beautiful baby of the family.

"I'll call her in the morning. I promise," Amy said. "Love you."

She hung up and set her phone to Do Not Disturb except for Jo's mobile number. Just in case.

"Jo and Caroline broke up," she said to Andy.

He nodded sympathetically. "That sucks."

"She's devastated," Amy said.

He pulled her close. "We're very lucky to have each other."

"I know," she said, pulling on her T-shirt and rolling away from him.

Jo woke, dry-mouthed and overheated, under a heavy down comforter. Groggily she pushed herself up and reached for the water glass on her bedside table. It took her a few seconds to remember where she was and why, and then it all came rushing back to her. She moaned, quickly blinking away the tears that threatened to start falling again.

She glanced at the other side of the bed. Toby wasn't there. She groped around in the dark for her handbag and retrieved her phone.

Finally, in a darkness broken only by the glow of her phone, she dialed Caroline's number. It went straight to voice mail. She imagined Caroline's phone in its purple plastic case, sitting on some strange nightstand in some strange guy's apartment.

"I can't go through this alone," she whispered, her voice cracking. "I can't do this without you. What am I supposed to do, Caroline?" Starting to cry, she hung up.

She quickly gulped down her water and stepped shakily out of bed.

Tears blurring everything, she stumbled over her shoes as she wandered into the living room. Toby was asleep on one of the couches. She crouched in front of him, willing him to wake up.

When he didn't, she touched his arm. "Tobe?" she said.

He stirred. "What's wrong?"

"I don't want to be alone," she said, voice wavering.

He sat up, running his hand through his mop of blond hair. "Aw, Jo. It's going to be okay."

"Will you keep me company?" she asked.

"Yeah, all right. God, my head hurts."

He followed her into the bedroom.

Jo crawled back under the covers on her side, and Toby fell under heavily on his side. She lay flat on her back, staring into the darkness of the ceiling. "I just left her a message," Jo said.

"Not a good move," Toby sighed. "Though, I blame myself."

"What? What are you talking about?"

"Friends don't let friends drunk dial."

"I'm sober."

"Then there's no excuse."

She groaned, turning her back to him.

"I'm trying to bring some levity to the situation," he said.

Her crying grew louder.

"Oh, Jo—come here."

She didn't move, her body shaking with sobs.

Toby rolled closer, draping an arm over her, spooning her, pulling her in tight. "I know you're hating life right now. But it's going to be okay, Jo. Look, how many people end up with the person they dated in college? It doesn't happen—not in New York, at least." He kissed the back of her head. "Try to get some sleep."

He moved away, and she turned, grabbing his arm. "No, don't. Stay like this, like you were," she said, her voice hoarse.

"Okay," he said, pulling her close again, mumbling into her hair. "Whatever you need."

What she needed . . . what she so desperately needed right now was to feel wanted. She had lost the woman she loved. Was it her fault?

"Tell me again—what you said earlier," Jo whispered.

"I said a lot of things earlier."

"How you feel about me."

He sighed. "Jo . . . why?"

"Because. I need to hear it."

"I'm in love with you. Okay? Does that make you feel better?"

"It does. I know it doesn't make sense, but it does."

But barely. Every part of her hurt, as if her broken heart had infected everything. The pain was unstoppable. She reached for her phone again.

Toby wrested it from her hand, holding it behind his back. "Jo, don't. Go back to sleep. Okay? You'll feel better in the morning."

The phone glowed, and she moved on top of him, reaching for it. "Give it back," she begged. She grabbed his wrist, shaking his hand like a maraca.

He laughed. "You are your own worst enemy right now, do you know that?"

She was so frustrated, she wanted to scream. She did scream. "Fuck!"

He put the phone down and held her by the shoulders. "It's okay. *You'll* be okay," he said.

His face was inches from hers. She felt his caring, his love, his safety. And she wanted more of it. *Fuck it.* She kissed him hungrily. His mouth opened to her, and her body flooded with endorphins. It was better than the alcohol.

"Jo . . . wait . . . ," he said, pulling back, sitting up.

She kissed him again, pulling off her T-shirt. She knew she had great breasts, perfect breasts.

He touched them longingly and gave a pained sigh. "You're killing me, Becker," he said.

"Don't talk." She straddled him. He was hard. How long had it been since she'd had a guy inside her? Not since freshman year, spring break. A party, someone she knew from Yardley. She was drunk, she was missing Caroline, who was with Derek Ebernoff at that point. It was an utterly forgettable encounter.

She tugged off her underwear. Toby flipped her over, so she was on her back. He touched her between her legs. His hands felt big—different. He went down on her, and his stubble was an odd sensation. But he knew what he was doing, and the pleasure was such a staggering contrast to the tension and pain she was in, she gasped.

"Yes," she said.

He moved on top of her. "Are you drunk?" he asked.

"No. Are you?"

"I don't know."

He moved inside her, and it felt good and so alien that she could hardly think to miss the softness of Caroline's flesh. This was something else entirely. No thoughts, no tears, no pain . . . just a satisfying hum deep in that gnawing, greedy part of herself.

He cried out when he came, and afterwards he held her close, his lips pressed to her damp forehead.

"Toby?"

"Yeah?"

"You're a good friend," she said.

Maybe she should be satisfied with that. Maybe friendship was more important than love. You couldn't trust love. Love hurt.

seven

"Two weddings," said Hugh.

Meryl climbed into bed next to him, feeling giddy as a schoolgirl.

"I know! Oh, Hugh, we're so blessed. Both our girls marrying wonderful men. They are going to have incredible lives. They'll have everything they ever wanted."

"Two weddings," Hugh repeated.

"We'll manage. Come on—don't worry about that tonight. Aren't you happy?"

Hugh put down the student papers he had been reading on the nightstand and turned to her. "Of course I'm happy. But Meryl, we now have *two* weddings to pay for. Two *expensive* weddings. Why does Amy have to get married so soon? If she had a yearlong engagement, we could at least catch our breath."

Amy wanted to get married in May—the month before Meg's wedding. Meryl did see that as a problem—but not for the same reasons as Hugh. It was a new level of one-upmanship.

"I'll try to talk to her about it."

Relieved, Hugh turned off his bedside light. He kissed Meryl on the cheek and rolled over.

"Don't you think it's odd," Meryl said slowly, "that Stowe's father couldn't make it tonight? I mean, we're going to be family. Do you think they think Meg isn't good enough? That we're not good enough?"

"No, I think they're just busy people. And I think you need to manage your expectations for what our relationship is going to be with them."

Meryl sighed. Hugh could note every social more and protocol of the characters in a Henry James or Louisa May Alcott novel, but apparently couldn't recognize the breach of one in his own life. "And the Campions are not the ones who should be throwing the engagement party. That's a prerogative of the bride's parents."

"Says who?"

"Emily Post!" Meryl said, reaching for her own bedside light, feeling around in the dark for the dangling metal chain to turn it on. She waved the book at Hugh.

"What is that? I can't see without my glasses," he said.

Emily Post's Wedding Etiquette.

"Oh, for God's sake, Meryl. What do you need that for?"

"To do things right. Remember what a mess it was when we were going to get married? My parents not talking to us? Your parents balking at the idea of helping us throw a wedding? Eloping at the last minute? I don't want that to happen to our daughters, Hugh. We're going to give Meg and Amy perfect weddings."

"I'm a little surprised that with all their billions, the Campions haven't offered to pay for Meg's wedding."

"Actually," said Meryl, "they did."

Hugh smiled. "Well, why didn't you say so? That's great news."

"No! It's not. Hugh, if they pay for it, they call all the shots. Tippy wants to put a wedding planner in charge, have it at their country club— basically treat this like just another event to get done on their checklist. But this is special to me. To us—me and Meg. I don't want anyone taking that away from us. This experience is priceless, Hugh."

Silence settled between them.

"Meryl, you have to be realistic. The way Meg and Stowe are talking—the way his parents are thinking—this wedding is going to be beyond our means. And now Amy's engaged—"

"We'll find a way."

"I don't agree with you, Meryl. Not one bit. If the Campions want to contribute to the wedding, let them. We have to be practical."

"Oh, *now* we have to be practical? You're never practical! You live in a world of ideas, the life of the mind, the idea of a book that has consumed half your attention for our entire life but you've never finished. And when I try to encourage you to get the damn thing written, you tell me that I'm missing the point—that it's the journey toward the end that matters, not the finished book. So don't tell me now that I have to be practical."

Hugh sighed. "Fine. But maybe now's the time to start thinking about working again full-time."

As if she hadn't been looking.

"Believe me, I have some calls out."

Silence.

"Meryl, just be sure you're doing this for the girls."

"Who else would I be doing it for?"

"Like you said, we didn't have a wedding—"

"Don't be ridiculous, Hugh. This isn't for me. I know it's not about me." She paused. "But yes, in a way, it's for all of us. For our family."

Meryl couldn't sleep. The conversation had settled into an uncomfortable place in her gut, along with too much food and wine.

Hugh's insinuation that these weddings were somehow more for her than for Meg and Amy—well, it stuck in her craw. She had no regrets about their own wedding: it had been bare bones, but it was completely romantic. Just the two of them. She wouldn't necessarily have changed the way they got married. But she probably would have changed a few of the decisions she made leading up to it.

She tossed and turned, finally giving up on sleep around eleven. She turned her phone back on and checked a weather app for the temperature outside. At fifty degrees, it was warmer now than it had been earlier in the night. Tomorrow would be beautiful.

She wished it were morning already, so she didn't have to struggle to quiet her mind. She figured she had two choices: she could have another glass of wine or two, or she could go for a walk. The wine was the simpler way to go; the walk, the healthier one.

Meryl, thinking of the imminent dress shopping, opted for the exercise. She pulled on a pair of yoga pants and her sneakers.

The apartment door opened silently but closed with a loud click. She waited a beat.

In the daytime, she didn't like to go outside without at least mascara and a touch of color on her cheeks. She often thought about Nora Ephron's line that your just-woke-up face of your twenties is your all-day face of your forties. And at fifty-four, well . . . she felt bad about a lot more than her neck.

But under the cover of night, in the crisp air of early fall and walking on the East River promenade, she felt free and she felt young.

She loved this walk. It was the path she'd followed pushing the girls in their strollers. The place she'd come to read during the rare moments she could steal for herself. The bench she sat on the night her father had died, crying, looking at the winking lights of the bridge. She loved that seagulls flocked to the waterside, and she loved that sometimes she smelled salt in the air. In the summer, if she closed her eyes, she could imagine she was a little girl again, back at the Jersey Shore, when her only worries were washing the sand off her feet before walking into her grandparents' beachside condo and if the line at Sack O' Subs would be too long. This was a shore before casinos, when there was nothing to do but take long strolls on the boardwalk and see a movie at the Ventnor theater. It wasn't just that her life had been simpler, it was that Life with a capital L had been simpler.

The East River did not bring her back to the shore that night. The air was dry, the only birds a few lone pigeons resting on the backs of benches and pecking along the ground.

Ahead of her, a couple walked linked arm in arm. She felt a pang, thinking of Hugh back in the apartment, with no idea that she was out.

She should have woken him up, said, Let's take a walk together and revel in this night of good news—a turning point in their lives. But he didn't share her unfettered joy. He was thinking practically, and she was being romantic. It was a disconcerting role reversal; she wished they had talked longer, had ended up in a better place. Maybe she would wake him when she got home. Maybe they could even have sex. She smiled to herself; that was certainly one way to celebrate the engagements.

Meryl passed the northernmost part of Carl Schurz Park and followed the curve around the back of Gracie Mansion. The Federal-style house, painted pale yellow with green shutters, was the official home of the mayor of New York City—except during Michael Bloomberg's twelve-year tenure, when he opted to live in his East Seventy-ninth Street town house instead.

Meryl was suddenly parched. Too much wine. She would loop around to York Avenue and stop by the 7-Eleven to get a bottle of water.

Jazz music filled the air as she got closer to Gracie Mansion. The backyard, obscured by tall fences, was lively with the sound of a party. She was in luck; Meryl ordinarily wouldn't cross through the park at night, but she knew that if the mayor was entertaining, the walkway to Eighty-eighth Street would have a heavy police presence. She could cut easily through the park to the convenience store on York.

Sure enough, a police car was parked on the grass behind the Gracie. Meryl felt like an interloper even though she was on public grounds. On East End, drivers in town cars were idling, waiting for party guests. She pulled up the hood on her Yardley fleece, suddenly eager to get back to the safety and privacy of her warm bed.

But first, water. She walked briskly to York and made a left for the 7-Eleven.

The convenience store was as crowded as if it were the middle of the afternoon. She glanced at the hot dogs on the rotating metal trays. No, Meryl. She kept walking to the refrigerated water near the back.

"Meryl Kleinman?"

She turned automatically at the sound of her maiden name. "Scott?"

So this was what happened when you walked out of your apartment in the middle of the night; you ran into someone you hadn't seen in twenty years—while wearing a fleece hoodie and no makeup. A very good-looking someone. A someone who had made an appearance in more than one postmarital fantasy.

Scott Sobel.

What was he doing in her 7-Eleven?

"Hey!" He leaned in for the awkward greeting hug. "This is crazy! Do you live around here?"

He was dressed in an impeccable suit, clearly coming from or on his way to an event. She was wandering around in yoga pants and tennis shoes. It was safe to assume she lived in the neighborhood.

"Yes—right on Eighty-fourth. What are you doing here?"

"A party at Gracie Mansion. A colleague of mine is making a documentary about it."

"Oh . . . wow. For TV?" Scott was a prolific producer of reality television, most of which chronicled the lives of the newly rich and the more newly famous. She'd watched his first show out of sheer curiosity because it had his name on it, and became shamefully addicted.

A woman with long honey blond hair and luxurious houndstooth coat approached them, holding two coffees. She handed one to Scott.

"Camille, this is Meryl Kleinman, Meryl, Camille McGuiness."

"It's Becker now, actually. Meryl Becker." She shook the woman's hand, painfully aware that she had left her wedding ring on her nightstand.

"Meryl was just asking if your doc is for TV."

"We're hoping to get theater distribution," Camille said. "At least in New York and L.A." She had a clipped British accent. Meryl guessed she was in her midthirties. When Meryl had been in her midthirties, she had been doing what? Pretty much what she was doing now: freelance PR, married to Hugh, raising the girls.

"So what are you up to these days?"

"I work in book publishing. Freelance publicity."

"Of course! I should have known. Camille, this girl always had her face in a book. It could be the most perfect beach day, and all the other kids would be running to the ocean or playing horseshoes or volleyball, and Meryl was having none of it." He grinned playfully.

Meryl was tempted to say that she had just been thinking about those summers at the Jersey Shore—but she worried it would sound sad. Or worse, imply that she thought about him, which she did. But only in the way of any woman remembering one of her first crushes. She had been fifteen. He was a seventeen-year-old lifeguard at the beach—as remote as a movie star. Until one night—a night that burned into her mind as only events from your adolescence can—when she ran into him at her friend's older brother's house party just a few blocks away from her grandparents' condo.

Scott took her for a walk on the boardwalk that night. He kissed her in the darkness, leaning against the metal rail, against the backdrop of the rushing ocean and the thick, humid salt air.

It was the greatest moment of her life up until that point. In some ways, still one of her life's great moments.

The next day at the beach, he acted like he barely knew her name. And the summer came to a quick and anticlimactic end. But Scott knew enough people in the periphery of Meryl's social circle in high school and later in college that over the years she would occasionally run into him at a party. But that hadn't happened in decades.

"Crazy. Weren't we just kids on that beach? Time flies, right?"

She nodded, thinking that he hadn't changed a bit. He was still the sun-kissed beach boy, object of her urgent, youthful desire. A few gray hairs and crow's-feet couldn't compete with that memory.

Camille shifted impatiently. "We should get going," she said.

Scott nodded. "So listen, I'm in New York for a few weeks, getting a show off the ground. We should grab coffee."

He pulled out his phone. Meryl realized he was waiting for her phone number. She recited it, feeling vaguely uncomfortable giving out her number to a man. But he was just an old childhood friend. Well, "friend" might be overstating it. But if friend was overstating it, then it was certainly nothing more than that and therefore harmless.

Meryl arrived back at her apartment more restless than when she'd left a half hour earlier. And she forgot all about waking up Hugh.

eight

"D.C. is finally starting to feel like home," Meg told Stowe.

It was a strange thought to have walking through the white corridors of the Russell Senate Office Building. But she realized, following Stowe to his father's office, that it was true. Of course, she would never admit this to her mother. She knew Meryl still had a fantasy that Meg would somehow end up back in New York, finding a way to parlay her journalism career into a job at *The New York Times* or even CNN's New York office. There had been times when Meg thought along those lines herself. But that was before Stowe.

"My father just said the same thing."

Reed was in D.C. only a few times a month, but today was one of those times. There was a vote on the floor, and so it was a quick stopover in Washington before heading back to Pennsylvania.

Along the edge of the rotunda, a CNN reporter was conducting an interview. Meg felt an itch to get to work, but Stowe wanted her to stop by Reed's office to meet his new communications director, a woman named Hunter Cross.

"Knock knock," Stowe said, opening the door Reed's office.

"Kids, come in," Reed said, standing behind his desk and waving them forward.

Perched in the seat in front of him was a striking woman with shoulder-length auburn hair wearing a chic tweed dress. She stood to greet them, her smile as bright as a beauty pageant contestant's. But her eyes, falling on Meg, were cool and appraising.

"Meet Hunter Cross, my new director of communications," said Reed, beaming.

"Hi, Stowe—good to see you again," Hunter said.

Again? When had Stowe met this woman before?

"This is my fiancée, Meg Becker," Stowe said, either ignoring Meg's quizzical look or missing it entirely.

"Ah, the journalist," said Hunter. The phone in her hand buzzed. She glanced down, frowning. Then she turned to Reed. "Stackhouse has a Web site live. Presidential exploratory."

"What?" Meg said, reaching into her bag to find her own phone. Senator Leland Stackhouse had promised her an exclusive if he was going to announce a bid for the Democratic nomination. Heart pounding, she quickly scrolled through her e-mails. Nothing.

"No tip-off for you?" Stowe said.

Meg looked at him, shaking her head. She loved that he understood her work. Still, they tried not to talk politics too much. While they weren't so diametrically opposite as, say, Mary Matalin and James Carville, they did have their differences. And of course, Reed and Tippy considered her a raging liberal.

"Don't feel bad," said Hunter. "I'm sure his people are working with their contacts inside CNN. It's very hard to break into that circle."

Meg looked at her, incredulous. "I have my own relationship with the senator. I'm sure this was an oversight."

Hunter gave her a smug grin. "Of course it was."

Meg turned to Stowe. "I have to get to the Hill, see if I can catch him before the vote at eleven."

"They're calling the vote early, Meg, so I'm heading over. You can ride with me," Reed said, grabbing his jacket.

"Great."

Meg texted her editor that she was headed to the Capitol building to try to get something for them to post by noon—to make sure their camera guy was on-site. At worst, she'd get a few quotes for an article. Hopefully, she'd get an on-camera interview that they could post on the homepage.

She followed Reed to the basement level and through a redbrick corridor. The senators traveled to and from Russell via an underground rail car. Climbing into the red vinyl seat across from Reed, she checked her phone for updates.

"So what do you make of this Stackhouse business?" Reed asked. "Does he have a shot?"

Meg smiled. "I think you and I both know he doesn't. But he can certainly shake up the debate."

Reed nodded. "Well said."

She liked Reed. She knew a lot of people found him intimidating—his good looks and his wealth set him apart from most politicians. But he reminded her so much of Stowe that she found it easy to be herself around him. Much more so than around Tippy.

"I want to try to get something on camera," she told him. "For Poliglot. I wish he'd given me some notice about this. He'd promised."

"Politicians!" Reed said, shaking his head.

"Exactly."

The car sped through the tunnel, wind whipping her hair around her face and making it difficult to talk. She checked her phone again. A text from Amy, *Omg did you see Page Six?* No, Meg had not seen Page Six. She stopped reading the New York gossip column in college. She wished Amy could say the same, but her younger sister had a never-ending thirst for anything to do with the limelight.

Crazy busy, she texted back. *Call you later.*

The car stopped. Reed helped her out. He was distracted now, also checking his phone. They took the stairs.

"I'll catch you kids for dinner when I'm back in two weeks," he said.

"Yes!" she called after him.

He headed for the Senate floor while she made her way to a small anteroom off to the side.

Leland Stackhouse was waiting for her. "Kevin told me you want to do a quick on-camera," he said. Leland Stackhouse was a fifty-two-year-old three-term senator from Wisconsin. He was white-haired, tall, and lanky. He wore bad ties but had a winning smile and, because of his policy and personality, was normally was one of Meg's favorites. But not today.

"What happened to the heads-up?" she asked pointedly, not about to let him off the hook.

"It's just a Web site, Meg."

She pulled a compact mirror from her bag and reapplied lipstick.

"I'm ready when you are," the cameraman told her.

Meg motioned for the senator to stand closer to her, in front of a United States Senate emblem and a bookshelf. Under bright lights, cameras rolling, she asked,

"How close are you to actually running for president?"

"I've set up an exploratory Web site called DemocratsforProgress .com to see if there is a path for me, a base, outside of Wisconsin. I'll probably know by April."

Meg nodded, then named the other contenders for the nomination. "They speak to the same base that you're going after. So why you?"

"This is what I have to offer: Progress is not just a word, it's a concept that has to be put into action. Who has an alternative to the floundering foreign policy our current president has enacted? We can't pretend that we'll have peaceful coexistence with enemies abroad—or domestically. But neither can we make a move toward isolationism."

Meg heard her phone ring inside her bag. Damn it, she forgot to turn it to vibrate. Senator Stackhouse didn't miss a beat, and while he'd started off with platitudes, after a few minutes, she felt she got a couple of good sound bites, and the video would be worth posting. When they finished, he thanked her, and she said, "I don't want to be surprised again in April. A text next time? Smoke signals? Make me work for it— I don't mind. Just keep me in the loop."

He laughed. "I have to get to the floor."

She nodded, already distracted, checking her phone. The missed call was from Amy. She frowned. What was going on?

• • • •

Jo woke up next to a sleeping Toby, with a dry mouth and her eyes nearly swollen shut from all the crying. The first thing she did was look at her phone. Four new messages—all from her mother and sisters.

Her stomach churned, and she ran to the bathroom to vomit. The bathroom was surprisingly small, considering the scale of the rest of the apartment, but that's the way it was in the old buildings.

She flushed the toilet when she was finished and rested her head on the cold marble floor. It felt good.

"You alive in there?" Toby rapped lightly on the door.

"Unfortunately."

She hauled herself up, pulling so hard on the towel rack, she was afraid it would come down bringing the wall with it. She looked at herself in the mirror and groaned. It was as bad as she expected.

Opening the door, she found Toby wearing only his drawstring pajama pants (plaid, preppy, totally cute) and bare chested. His blond hair was tousled, his cheeks full of their ruddy European color. He was a gorgeous specimen—a gorgeous specimen she got very up close and personal with last night, if her memory served.

Disaster.

How could she have slept with him? Cheated on Caroline! No. Caroline was the one who'd cheated. Fell in love with someone else. And left her. Forever. Tears started to sting the back of her eyes again. God, was she *ever* going to stop crying?

She brushed past Toby, out of the bedroom, blindly headed for coffee like a heat-seeking missile.

Mercifully, Toby did not follow her. She pulled open the cabinets until she found the yellow box of Gevalia coffee pods. What she really needed was a latte, but that would involve venturing into the outside world. She felt brittle, fragile—completely helpless. What was she supposed to do now? Every day of the past three and a half years of her life had revolved around Caroline. Or at very least factored her in heavily. Today was not—could not—be any different. Should she call? Should she just go back to the apartment and wait for her to show up? She had to come by eventually if only to collect her things.

Jo slumped over the black marble countertop. As the caffeine hit her system, she felt a sense of urgency, a certainty that she had to get back to the apartment as soon as possible.

It was all clear to her now: Caroline was just having relationship jitters. Meg's engagement had inspired Jo to want to jump into the relationship deeper, but it had the opposite effect on Caroline. Totally normal! The last few Sunday night dinners had been so wedding-centric. Meg's guest list, Meg's dress, the bridal shower . . . Jo didn't take it too seriously, but maybe it was freaking out Caroline.

She had to talk to her—and now—tell her she understood, forgave her. Really, they were lucky they hadn't had a bump in the road before now. And the guilt over straying must have made Caroline confess. She didn't *really* want to break up—she just wanted absolution.

The fog of misery slowly lifted. Jo looked around for her phone but couldn't find it. Grabbing her mug, she rushed back to the bedroom, sloshing coffee on her shirt.

The shower was running. That was what she needed, but there was no time. Standing by the bed, the sheets still rumpled—Oh God, poor Toby! She was such a jerk.—she dialed Caroline. It went straight to voice mail.

"Hey, babe. It's me. Look, I want you to know that I totally get it. Yes, I lost it a little last night and, I mean, you weren't making the most sense. But I think we just need to talk. I'm coming back to the apartment. If you're home, please just hang out till I get there."

She looked up to find Toby standing in the doorway, his hair wet, a towel around his waist.

"Can you give me a ride back to Brooklyn?"

"Are you sure you're ready?"

"I live there," she snapped.

Toby looked hurt.

"Sorry, Tobe—I know you're trying to help—and you did help last night. I was a total basket case. And you were . . . you were so great. But Caroline and I are going to work this out."

"Okay," he said. "But do you want, I mean, should we talk about what happened last night?"

No, negatory, not in this lifetime. How could she talk about it when it was something that never should have happened—something she would pretend never did?

"I'm okay with just letting it sort of be, you know what I mean?" she said. She kissed him on the cheek and then looked through her handbag to make sure she had her keys.

Meg called Amy when she was just outside the Poliglot office on North Capitol Street. "Is everything okay?" It was starting to rain, and she was eager to get to the video to start transcribing it.

"Did you read Page Six yet?"

"Are you serious? Amy, I was in the middle of an interview when you called."

"Check it now. On your phone. Call me back."

Irritated, Meg hung up and opened her browser to the *New York Post*, scrolling down to the gossip section.

It took a few heartbeats to realize what she was looking at. A photo of her and Stowe—a shot taken last month while leaving the restaurant Filomena with Reed and Tippy—was on Page Six.

Sister Act Too

Turning work into play has been mastered by a pair of Upper East Side sisters: Poliglot editrix **Meg Becker** gets cozy with fiancé **Stowe Campion**, son of billionaire Pennsylvania **Senator Reed Campion**, while little sis **Amy** goes from **Jeffrey Bruce** flak to future Mrs. **Andrew Bruce**. A walk down the aisle has never looked more like a climb up the social ladder.

Meg felt her face flush. She looked around the street, half expecting every passerby to be staring at her.

Her first impulse was to call Stowe, but before she could dial, the phone came alive in her hand and Amy's image filled the screen.

"Crazy, right?" Amy squealed.

"Unfortunately, yes."

"Isn't it hilarious?"

"That's not quite the word I would use."

"You look gorgeous. Of course they didn't even use a photo of *me*."

"Yeah, Amy . . . I don't think you're really getting how absolutely uncool this is for me."

Since the engagement last month, she'd gone out of her way to minimize all mention of her relationship at work. Everyone knew she was dating a Campion. But now that they were engaged, it was different. She had to make it clear to her boss—and the staffers working under her—that it would in no way influence her reporting, or the editorial choices she made for the site. She worked for Poliglot, not for Senator Campion.

But something like this . . .

"Who leaked your engagement?" Meg said.

"I don't know! And who cares. You might as well get used to the attention. What did you think was going to happen when you married into that family?"

"Amy, I have to get to work."

"Okay, one more thing—have you heard from Jo? Her phone's going straight to voice mail."

"No. Listen, I'll talk to you later."

Meg hung up and walked back into the office building. Her only consolation was that no one in D.C. read Page Six.

The Poliglot office occupied the sixth floor of the building. She'd first walked in the doors as a college junior looking for an internship, and she'd been working for them ever since. Eight years later, she still felt a high flashing her ID card at the security desk, knowing she belonged.

Closing the door to her office, she couldn't resist looking at the offending Page Six post one more time.

A knock made her jump. She shoved her phone into her bag like it was contraband.

Her boss, Kevin, opened the door. "Got a minute?"

"Yep." She slid behind her desk, logging on to her computer.

Inside, he closed the door. Meg felt the weight of the trillion things she had to get done before the two o'clock editorial meeting, including getting the Stackhouse story live ASAP.

"How'd things go with Stackhouse?"

"Fine. Got some good stuff. I have to look at the video. Definitely enough to post."

"Did you call him out on not giving you notice?"

"Of course! He laughed it off. Said it's just a Web site."

"Asshole."

"It could be worse. He'll never get the nomination, so it's not exactly like we lost the scoop of the century."

"I know. But I feel like this is a warning shot. Things are going to be moving quickly from here on out. And I don't want to be playing catch-up every damn day."

"You think I do? Trust me—I'm more frustrated than you are."

"I know, I know. So that's why I was hoping you'd have a sense about where things are with Reed."

"Reed? What about him?"

"I heard he's off to the Middle East next week," Kevin said.

"That's right."

"What do you know about it?"

"I know it was organized by the State Department and the Senate Banking Committee."

Kevin nodded. "Everyone thinks he's going to run."

"What? Says who?"

"You're really going to play this game with me?"

"Kevin," she said slowly, her mind racing. "I am not playing anything. This is the first I'm hearing about this, and if Reed were thinking about running, I don't think that would be the case."

Kevin nodded, considering this. "Meg, you're a very important part of the team here."

"Thank you, Kevin."

"And your part in this team is changing."

"What?"

"I see you in a much larger role."

Meg's heart began pounding. She'd imagined this conversation countless times in her head over the past year or so. She had steadily worked her way up the masthead to senior Congressional editor. But she had her eyes on the prize, namely the White House beat.

"Obviously I'm thrilled to hear that," she said. "What do you have in mind?"

"Senior editor, White House," he said. "I figure I can take it to the powers that be after the new year."

She nodded coolly, as if this were absolutely to be expected.

"That is, if nothing goes wrong," he added.

Meg nodded again. It took a few seconds for his comment to register. "What? Wrong? What do you mean?"

"Oh, I don't know," Kevin said with an exaggerated casualness.

"I'm confident that nothing will go wrong," she said, narrowing her eyes. "I've performed solidly for five years." She ticked off a list of half a dozen stories she broke about the current administration, and added a few about the Middle East that she didn't break but augmented notably. Her media presence on behalf of the Web site—Bill Maher, CNN, the Sunday morning shows—was unspoken but obvious. She didn't like being put in the situation of making the case for her promotion like this—impromptu, pre-caffeinated, with her mind barely bouncing back from the Page Six debacle.

Kevin held up his hands. "Meg, you're preaching to the choir," he said. "That's why it would be such a disappointment for another outlet to break the news of Senator Campion officially running for the Republican nomination for president of the United States."

Meg froze. Was she hearing him correctly? Her promotion depended on breaking the news of a campaign that didn't even exist?

"First of all, Reed Campion is not running for president. Secondly, even if he were, it's unethical for me to leak information—it's bad for me personally, and it's bad for all of us professionally."

"Meg, I'm not asking you to leak anything. And I'm not even asking you to make us look good by breaking the news first. I'm just asking that you save us the embarrassment of *not* breaking the news first, since it's all over the papers that our editor is practically a member of the Campion family." He dropped a copy of Page Six on her desk and tapped the paragraph with her name in bold newsprint. "Do you get what I'm saying?"

Meg nodded slowly once more—anything to get him to leave her office so she could call Stowe.

He smiled at her on his way out the door. "Big things ahead, Becker. Big things."

He left the newspaper behind.

nine

Meryl woke up with every intention of drumming up more freelance work.

But then there were the voice mails.

First, from Jo.

"Mom, sorry I missed dinner last night. Caroline and I are having a . . . I don't know. A rough night. But I'm on my way over there now to work things out. Fingers crossed. Sorry again. Love you."

And then Amy.

"Hi, Mom! We didn't get a chance to go into detail about Andy and my thoughts about the location of the wedding. I didn't want to hog the floor, so the speak, but I *do* want to nail that down. Give me a call later. Oh—and Jeffrey is designing a dress for me! Love you!"

Meryl made coffee and pondered the facts: (a) Amy was going to get married in a one-of-a-kind Jeffrey Bruce gown—a dress that cost more than a year of their rent; (b) Jo was having relationship troubles just as her sisters were happily getting married. Jo was the least competitive of the girls, but still, it wasn't exactly ideal timing. She hoped Jo was right, that they'd work it out. Meryl really liked Caroline—as did Hugh.

While neither of them had been surprised when Jo came home with a girlfriend, they were surprised that the girlfriend was Caroline.

"She just doesn't seem that way," Hugh had said.

"What way?"

"Gay."

"And Jo does?" said Meryl.

"Nothing Jo does would surprise me," he'd said. And Meryl had to agree. Jo had always done things her own way, in her own time. Meg had been the easy baby, the obedient toddler—not even the twos were that terrible—and an ambitious and studious teenager, and Amy had been the colicky baby, the tantrum-prone child, and the lazy teenager. But Jo had been an odd hybrid. She did everything late—talking, walking, reading. The more Meryl tried to push her into something, the more she resisted. But she when she finally did it, she embraced it and ran with it. It just had to happen on her timetable. By middle school, Jo had become fascinated by astrology. Meryl's Aquarius child had found the explanation for her sensitive and rebellious soul, and Jo seemed to take comfort in the belief that there were forces in the universe that would buffet her and guide her along her path in life. She started looking for "signs," and to this day tended to make unexpected decisions based on things that Meryl and Hugh considered less than firm ground but knew nonetheless that it was useless to fight her on. "Jo is going to do what Jo is going to do," they would tell one another.

The third voice mail was from the superintendent of her mother's building.

"Mrs. Becker, Tom Curello here from the Clarion. Please give me a call as soon as possible."

Meryl jotted down the number. Had her mother forgotten to pay the rent again? Things like that were happening more and more lately. "Part of aging," her mom's physician had said. Basically, everything undesirable fell under that category. Lately, Meryl wished she had a sibling. Watching your parents age—and in the case of her father, dying—is terrifying and lonely. Of course, her mother had always been a challenging person. Not just overly opinionated, but also enigmatic in a way that Meryl could never quite explain. She had memories of her mother shutting herself in a dark room for entire days. Those days were fewer and fewer as Meryl got older, and now it seemed she'd almost imagined them. But if she'd had a sibling, she could discuss these things with someone who really understood.

At least she'd done that right. No matter what life threw their way, her girls would always have each other.

"Mr. Curello? This is Meryl Becker returning your call."

"You need to get over to the building immediately, Mrs. Becker. We have a situation."

From the passenger seat of Toby's car, Jo stared at the entrance to her apartment building, the lump in her throat growing. Her home looked different than it had the last time she saw it in daylight, and she knew it was because she was seeing it through different eyes. This time yesterday, her life had been whole. Now it had a giant crack running through it.

"Thanks. For everything," Jo said, kissing Toby on the cheek.

"Maybe I should walk you in," he said.

"Tobe, I'm a big girl."

"I know. But these things are rough."

"How do you know? You've never had a serious relationship. At least not in the five years I've known you."

"That's because the woman I'm seriously interested in happens to be in love with another woman. Isn't irony great?"

Regret flooded through her. In her blindly selfish quest, groping in the dark (literally) to stanch the bleeding of her heart, she had done some damage to Toby's.

She opened her car door, filled with sudden urgency.

"I'll text you later," she called out, rushing to the front door without so much as a glance behind her.

She took the stairs two at a time, and by the time she got her key in the lock, she was out of breath. "Caroline?" she called out as she pushed the door open.

A strange man jumped up from the couch.

A strange, gorgeous man. Tall with dark hair and blazing green eyes and a hipster beard (moderate length, as far as those things went), he looked like a young David Gandy.

"Jo," he said.

"Who the fuck are you, and why are you in my apartment?"

She already knew the answer to both questions, but that did not make it okay. And she wanted to hear him say it.

"I'm Drew Finley. Caroline's . . . friend."

"Where's Caroline?"

"She's not here. She thought it would be easier if I picked up her things."

Jo felt like she might vomit. "Get out," she said.

Drew Finley was clearly not used to being unwelcome. Drew Finley had probably never been rejected in his entire life. And surely, Drew Finley had never come home to find the person who was trying to steal away the love of his life standing in his living room.

"I'm really sorry," he said. And he did look apologetic. He looked like he would hug her if she'd let him. In some perverse way, she wanted him to. What was so great about being in the arms of Drew Finley? What the fuck, Caroline?

"Well, I'm sorry for *you*. Because Caroline is clearly just having a first-year post-college crisis. Maybe it's the stress of law school. I don't know, and I don't care. The point is, this is going to pass. We are in love, and we have a history, and a future—and you don't factor into any of that."

Jo marched to the front door and opened it, making a sweeping gesture with her arm. *Get the fuck out.*

"I've asked her to marry me," said Drew. "And she's said yes."

Meryl's mother was still screaming when she walked into the apartment.

It was a sound she would never forget, as if, God forbid, her mother were being stabbed to death. And apparently, her mother had been going at it for forty-five straight minutes.

Oona was in the hallway, talking to the superintendent and her mother's neighbor from across the hall. Meryl pushed her way past them, into the bedroom, where her mother stared straight ahead, wide eyed, rocking back and forth as she emitted her endless, bloodcurdling screams.

"Mother! Mother, what is it? What's wrong?"

Her mother looked at her, still screaming, but something in her eyes shifted, a sudden clarity, and she reached out hesitantly to touch her. Meryl moved forward and pulled her mother into a hug, and the screaming stopped. Her mother began rambling in her native Polish, a language she dropped as soon as she arrived in the United States and never bothered to teach her children.

"I'm here, Mom. It's okay," Meryl said. It felt strange to have such physical contact with her mother. Rose Kleinman was decidedly *not* a hugger. And she certainly was not overly affectionate in the past few decades with the daughter who had so bitterly and irrevocably disappointed her.

But the hug seemed to work.

"Meryl," her mother said.

"What's wrong? What's going on?"

Her mother shook her head, looking around the room.

"Mom, wait here a minute, okay? I need to check on something. Will you be okay for a minute?"

"Of course. I'm fine. What time is it? Is it time for my stories?"

Meryl found the remote and turned on CBS for her mother's soap operas.

"Mom, I'll be right back."

Out in the hallway, the neighbor had retreated back into her apartment but Oona and Mr. Curello were still talking.

"What's going on? What happened, Oona?"

"Mrs. Becker, this is the third time this has happened this week. The last time was at two in the morning, when she woke up half the floor and the family living in the apartment below her," said Mr. Curello.

"What? Oona, why didn't you tell me?"

"I thought you knew. I thought you knew that she do this."

"No, I had no idea this was happening."

"Mrs. Becker, this has become a tremendous disturbance to the other tenants in the building. I've gotten word from management that the tenants downstairs have threatened to stop paying rent."

"Oh my God. I'm sorry. I—"

"Management won't be renewing your mother's lease."

Meryl's stomach dropped. She scrambled to think of when the lease expired. Was it this December? Or next? Had they signed a two-year last time?

"I understand," she said quietly, glancing back inside the apartment. "I need to talk to her." Meryl went back to the bedroom and closed the door. "Mom, what's going on?" she asked.

"Nothing," her mother said.

"Did you realize you've been screaming?" She didn't know what was more terrifying—the thought that her mother was doing this on purpose, fully aware, or that she had no recollection of the episodes.

"Maybe it was a bad dream," her mother said.

"You were speaking in Polish."

An expression crossed her mother's face that she'd never seen before, a look of intense vulnerability. Rose didn't like to talk about Poland, the country she'd left when she was just seven years old. Meryl's grandparents had moved to America in 1937, just two years before the Nazi invasion of Poland. Rose admitted that they had always planned to visit, to return someday to see the friends and family they left behind. But their town had been wiped off the map. If Meryl's mother rarely spoke about Poland, her grandparents never did. And oddly, they had somehow gotten rid of even their Polish accents, while Rose's speech was still thick with it.

"That's nonsense," Rose said. "I don't even remember Polish. If this is how you're going to behave, just leave."

Meryl did not mention the lease. She would talk to Hugh first. She wasn't entirely sure it was even legal for the building to take that kind of action, though she suspected it was.

She held it together the entire cab ride back to the Upper East Side. But as soon as she paid the fare and stepped onto the curb at Eighty-fourth and East End, she lost it. Her mother, so fierce, so eternally independent and stoic, was finally showing a crack. And Meryl had no idea what to do about it—didn't even know where to start.

Her phone rang. Amy. Meryl swallowed hard, clearing her throat, hoping her voice sounded normal.

"Did you get my e-mail?" she squealed.

"E-mail? No, hon. I've been with Gran."

"Mom, drop whatever you're doing and check your e-mail. Call me back."

Meryl juggled her bag and her keys and her phone so that she could click onto her Gmail. Amy had sent her a link to the *New York Post*. She clicked it, and a photo of Meg and Stowe filled her screen. Incredulous, Meryl scanned the text. She laughed, covering her mouth, the crisis with her mother momentarily forgotten.

"Oh, honey, look at that," she said as soon as Amy picked up again. "You're officially a boldfaced name."

"So crazy, right? Jeffrey thinks it's great. I mean, the tone of the piece is snarky, but that's just Page Six. And all publicity is good publicity, right? I've got to run to a meeting—don't tell Daddy. I'll call him later."

Meryl felt the day turn around. Whatever was going on with her mother, she would figure it out. There was too much to be happy about to let it get her down.

By the time she walked into her home, she had a smile on her face again. But then she saw Hugh's canvas messenger bag on the dining room table. What was he doing home?

"Hugh?" she called.

She looked at her phone. It was barely noon.

His office door was closed. Heart pounding, she didn't bother to knock, opening it to find him sitting at his desk and staring into space.

"Why aren't you at work?" she asked, alarm in her voice.

A part of her, the irrational but deeply hopeful part, thought maybe he'd somehow sensed that she needed him, that after thirty years, their connection was just that strong. That's what marriage was at its best—you didn't have to tell your partner to look out, that you were falling. They were just there to catch you, the ever-present net.

"There's a problem at school."

"What kind of problem?"

"It's Janell. She plagiarized another paper. In Ethan Pogrebin's class."

"Oh, Hugh, I'm sorry. I know you really had high hopes for her."

"He turned her in. And she said she felt it was unfair because I had given her a warning, so why couldn't he?"

Meryl's stomach dropped. "She told Ethan you gave her a warning," she said slowly.

"No. She told Harrison."

Harrison Winterbourne, the school chancellor.

"Okay, so why are you here instead of at school, dealing with this?"

"I've been suspended. Pending a disciplinary inquiry."

"Suspended! *For what?*"

"Breach of ethics."

"Jesus, Hugh! I told you!" She paused, and took a deep breath. "Okay, okay—I'm sure they just have to go through the motions with this. How long will a disciplinary inquiry take?"

"A few weeks. A month."

She shook her head, hugging herself. "It will be fine. I just wish . . . Hugh, I just wish you had talked to me about all this."

"I *tried* talking to you," he said. "You were too busy worrying about dinner that night."

She looked at him blankly; then she remembered his phone call while she was on her way to her mother's the day of the Campion dinner.

"Let's try to look on the positive side," she said, trying to find one. "If you're home for a few weeks, you get to be more involved in the wedding planning. Maybe this is a blessing in disguise."

"Yes, well, about that: We need to put the spending on hold for now."

"That's not the kind of involvement I was hoping for." She tried to smile.

"The suspension is without pay."

What?

Math was not her strong suit, but she immediately calculated the loss of income for the next four weeks and considered how tight their budget was to begin with. And this was the key time they would be putting down deposits for everything: the dress, the florist, the band. They had savings. But not what they should, thanks to the market bottoming out in 2008.

"Okay, let's think. Let's think." Meryl paced in front of Hugh's desk. "You just need to talk to Harrison. Go in tomorrow, tell him it was a misunderstanding. Beg if you have to. Hugh, this cannot happen."

"It's not that simple, Meryl."

"Of course it is. It might not be easy, but it *is* that simple."

"It wasn't a misunderstanding. I believed—still believe—that Janell deserved one warning. That she should be punished, but not thrown out. The policy we put in place is too dogmatic, and needs revision. I see that now."

She wanted to strangle him. "Hugh," she said, sitting across from him as she took his hand, trying to be calm. "Do you really think that this is the time to draw a line in the sand?"

"I made a mistake with that zero-tolerance policy, Meryl. And now a girl's future is at stake."

"Our future is at stake!"

"Don't be melodramatic."

"Okay—how about your daughters? Did you give them any thought when you took your high-and-mighty stand for educational justice?"

"I don't appreciate your mocking this. They'll be fine. Meg is marrying into one of the most powerful families in this country. So is Amy. I don't think you can put them on par with a parentless girl from the Bronx who is about to lose her one shot at a real education. At college. At a better life."

"Is this your way of pushing back about the weddings? Of making sure I don't 'go overboard'? Of making me go to the Campions with my tail between my legs, taking help from them? Well, I won't. These weddings are going to happen one way or another."

"I have no doubt," he said.

"What's that supposed to mean?"

"I just know how you get when you set your mind to something," he said.

"You know what? I wish you would set your mind to something other than your goddamn students—and the book."

"Our girls got a first-rate education at Yardley, thanks to my position there."

"Yes, and they grew up among the children of the rich and famous, and now they have certain expectations for weddings that you suddenly don't want to meet. What did you think would happen with them going to that school? You expose them to the best of everything, and then tell them not to want it for themselves? Don't act like Stowe Campion or Andy Bruce are coincidental. Once we sent the girls to that school, their paths were set."

"That's not true."

"I think it is. So don't act surprised now, or like none of it has anything to do with you. It has everything to do with you. I would have sent them to PS 290 and East Side Middle and Eleanor Roosevelt High School. But those options weren't good enough for you, because you're an academic snob. So our daughters grew up with the elite, and are now marrying into the elite, and big weddings are a part of that deal. So I would appreciate it if you didn't act like this is all my fault."

The doorbell rang.

Hugh, clearly relieved for the distraction, brushed past her to answer it. She leaned back and found that she was shaking. It was so like Hugh to pull something like this. He was more into the idea of something than what that idea or ideal actually meant. The private school for the girls: great in theory, but it exposed them to things beyond their means. Writing the Alcott book: great in theory, but after two decades, a cloud of unfinished business hanging over him. Maybe even marriage: great in theory, but maybe somehow emotionally messier than he had bargained for. Creating a family did not have the neat dramatic arc of a Louisa May Alcott novel. Not even if you named all your daughters after the characters in one.

"Where's Mom?" The sound of Jo's voice snapped her to attention. Jo, in distress.

Meryl rushed into the living room, suddenly in full mother-bear mode. With all the drama concerning Rose, she'd forgotten to check on Jo.

Jo's long hair was in a messy knot on the top of her head, her face drawn. Without hesitation, she flung herself into Meryl's arms.

"It's over," she cried, her thin body racked with sobs.

It felt strange to hug Jo. She wasn't a hugger, and at five foot eight, she was the tallest of the girls and a full three inches taller than Meryl. But still, her baby. Meryl kissed the top of her head, inhaling her organic, tea tree oil shampoo scent.

"Baby, are you sure?" Meryl asked, not wanting to offer advice until she knew more.

"She's met someone else. A guy!"

Oh, dear goodness. That had to hurt.

"Is there a chance this is just temporary? Something she has to explore before you two get any more serious?"

Jo shook her head, her body trembling. Meryl tightened her arms around her, embarrassed by the reflexive pleasure she felt in being able to comfort her.

"She's going to marry him."

"Oh, Jo—I'm so sorry."

The sobs again. "Looks like everyone's getting married. And I never will."

"Jo, you know that's not true."

"It is," Jo said, her voice heavy with conviction.

Hugh appeared with a bottle of Sam Adams. He uncapped it and handed it Jo, who took it gratefully, disengaging from Meryl long enough to take a deep swig. Meryl tried to catch his eye, but he avoided her, their unfinished conversation hanging heavily between them. But it would have to wait until Jo was calm and ready to go home. The last thing she wanted was news of this work crisis to get back to Meg and Amy before they resolved it. They were good girls, and if they thought for a minute that the weddings would strain Meryl and Hugh, they would refuse help. And Tippy Campion and Eileen Bruce would be planning the weddings that Meryl had spent the past few decades dreaming of. Ever since the girls played dress-up brides, maybe even before that. Maybe as early as the first day she held Meg in her arms.

"Mom," Jo said, tipping back the beer again. "I can't go back to the apartment. Okay if I crash here tonight?"

"Of course, darling. You don't even have to ask. This is your home."

The look on Hugh's face was undeniable relief. A reprieve. Conversation officially on hold.

Jo's phone rang. It was Meg.

"Aren't you going to get that?"

Jo shook her head. "I can't talk to her. I know she wants to help. But she can't possibly understand. Her life is always so perfect. And mine is falling apart."

ten

Meg ignored Stowe's text. Hunter Cross wanted them to "put their heads together" about the Page Six piece? It was really none of her business.

Or was it? Her conversation with Kevin had left her so unsettled, she couldn't think straight. Could it possibly be true? Reed running for president?

She told herself she would discuss it with Stowe at dinner. They had reservations at Il Canale. Stowe had to travel the rest of the week to take depositions in Seattle, so they were treating tonight like it was a weekend. Normally, they didn't talk about work over dinner. Dinner was for reconnecting after a long week. And after dinner, they would fuck.

They didn't "make love." Meg and Stowe fucked. It was one of the surprises—and delights—of Stowe Campion. Despite his patrician good looks, his unflappable composure, his buttoned-up way, all the way, everywhere—in bed, he was animalistic and thrilling. She wished that they could just skip dinner and get to the fucking part of the night. She, too, dealt with the world always buttoned up and on her game. It was exhausting. In Stowe's hands, she could finally relax. And she *really* needed to relax.

Il Canale was nestled on a side street off M, the main strip of George-town. It was unassuming, with such outrageously good, authentic Italian food, it belonged in Queens or Little Italy. Stowe's parents preferred Filippa, an institution. But Meg found it stodgy and overrated, and she and Stowe had been trying to convert them to Il Canale for months.

Stowe was already waiting for her at a table. "Hey, babe," he said, giving her a quick kiss on the cheek. "I'm starving. And I might need to take a call, so I have to leave this on. Sorry."

Early on in their relationship, they'd agreed to silence their phones at dinner after one comical night in which they both took turns leaving to take calls and basically spent an entire meal not speaking to one another.

"Mutually assured distraction," Stowe had said, finally turning off his phone as they ordered dessert. She'd followed his lead, and it was now their unofficial policy.

But tonight she saw it as her opening.

"No problem," she said. "Actually, since work is already on the table, so to speak: I had an interesting conversation with Kevin today," Meg said. "He basically told me he was putting me up for a promotion."

"Meg—that's fantastic. You deserve it, of course. Truthfully, it's overdue. But then, maybe I'm biased." He flashed a smile and kissed her again.

"Yeah, I'm beyond excited."

"Did he say anything more specific?"

"Senior editor, White House." She couldn't help but smile as she said the words. God, she wanted it so badly. Maybe more than she'd ever wanted anything. Except for Stowe.

"Well then, that gives us something to officially celebrate tonight."

"As if we needed more."

He took her hand. "We're fortunate, Meg."

"Yes, we are . . ." She trailed off, wondering if her areas of good fortune were colliding in a very unfortunate way. "Stowe, the thing is, Kevin made it seem like my promotion had a contingency."

When Stowe didn't take the bait, she pressed her nails into her palm and continued. "He basically asked me to find out if your father is going to go after the Republican ticket. And to break the news on the site.

I told him that was ridiculous. I mean, it *is* ridiculous, right? You would have told me if your father was thinking about running for president."

"Well, aside from stating the obvious about how out of line he is—"

"Stowe, he's a news guy. Your dad's a senator and he's hearing buzz. It isn't out of line." She noticed he didn't answer the question.

"Yes, but it's out of line to make a promotion you deserve contingent on a specific story. One that relates to you personally and is therefore a conflict of interest."

"Well, I told him your father has no intention of running for president, so it's a nonissue. Right?"

"Right," Stowe said, studying his menu. Even though he always ordered the Bolognese.

Meg's heart began to race. "But if your father *were* to announce his candidacy, I hope he would consider letting me break the story."

Stowe glanced at her and sighed. "That's not how it works, Meg."

"Uh, yeah—it is. That's exactly how it works. And you know it."

"Okay, but he hasn't decided to run, so it's a moot point."

She pulled the menu away from him. "What do you mean, 'hasn't decided'? Is this a possibility? Is that why he brought in a new communications director?"

"Meg, please calm down. Anything's a possibility. You know how my father is."

"No," she said, "I don't. And if you've been talking to him about this and somehow decided to shut me out, then I guess I don't know you very well, either."

"Meg, you might be all work, all the time—but believe it or not, when I'm with him, he's just my dad. I don't grill him about his plans for the entirety of his political career. And he is surrounded by very savvy people, ninety-nine percent of whom he would talk to about this stuff before he discussed it with me. And if he was dealing with something that was confidential in nature, he would be smart enough not to put you—a member of the press—in a compromising position to know about it."

"So he *is* running."

"Jesus, Meg! Did you hear a word of what I just said? No, he's not running."

"But if he were, you wouldn't tell me."

"Would you want to know something you couldn't write about?"

"Why couldn't I write about it?"

"Meg, I'm not going to go around and around in circles on this."

"What? Is that the most outrageous suggestion in the world? I'm a journalist, and Poliglot is a major news outlet. Why wouldn't your dad want me to break the news?"

"His office has other press relationships. And Poliglot isn't exactly CNN."

"For our generation, it is. Have you looked at CNN's demographics lately?"

"Meg—he's not running. Drop it."

"Fine."

"Why are you pissed at me?"

"I'm not." But she was.

They ordered, finishing their glasses of wine faster than usual.

"By the way," Stowe said, breaking a long silence. "My mother told me to tell you that she can get you a personal fitting with Monique Lhuillier."

"I already have an appointment at the shop with my mother next week."

"No, I mean a fitting with the designer herself."

"Are you serious?"

"Yeah. She did my mother's dress for the Correspondents' Dinner last year."

A pause.

If Stowe was keeping something from her, it would take a lot more than a custom dress fitting to make it okay.

"Thanks, but . . . I just want to go to her showroom with my mom and my sisters. I don't want to do anything crazy," she said uneasily.

Stowe reached for her hand, holding it from across the table and looking into her eyes. She wanted to melt into his gaze, but she was still extremely unsettled by their conversation.

"How did I find the only woman who would pass up the chance to be fitted for a wedding gown by the designer herself? But whatever you want, babe. You might as well indulge in your last year of being anonymous, since this time next year you might be a public figure. With my father running for president and all." He reached across the table and squeezed her hand with a wink.

She smiled, a real smile, and breathed deeply with relief. He wouldn't joke around if he were lying to her.

Would he?

"Very funny." She ordered another glass of wine.

With Jo tucked into her childhood bedroom just halfway down the hall, Meryl was careful to keep her voice low.

"Hugh, I'm not angry about the situation at school. You had good intentions, and things happen. What's upsetting me is that you won't even try to fix it. If you just talk to Harrison and admit your mistake, this will all get resolved. Everyone makes mistakes. If he sees that you're repentant, he won't let this go too far."

"But that's just it, Meryl, I'm not repentant. I don't believe Janell should get expelled."

Meryl knew when Hugh got like this—idealistic, on moral high ground, defensive—there was no reasoning with him. And there was no point in trying. Hugh was beloved at Yardley; hopefully this would all just blow over. They could ride out the four-week loss of income. For now, there was a bigger issue at hand.

"Listen, Hugh, I got a call from the super at my mother's building today. Apparently, she's having these . . . episodes. She screams like she's being murdered, God forbid. I had to rush down there. It was extremely upsetting, to say the least."

"What's going on? Did she tell you anything, or was it more of her usual closed-off MO?"

She didn't blame Hugh for being cynical about her mother, but she wished for once he could put his feelings about her aside. "She didn't even seem to know that she was doing it. It was like she was in a trance or something. I'm telling you, it was really disturbing."

"Did you call her physician?"

"Yes. I'm going to bring her in for testing. But he says it's probably not neurological."

"Then what is it?"

"Psychological."

There had been times when Meryl was a teenager that her mother had fallen into deep depressions, not leaving her room for weeks at a time. Her father always dealt with it, and when the storm passed, her mother acted like nothing had happened. She wasn't a "sharer"—and she clearly wasn't about to start now. Meryl did believe she wasn't aware of the yelling, that something subconscious was going on.

"Do you think it's some kind of early dementia?"

"Good Lord, I hope not."

"Well, we'll just have to cross that bridge when we come to it."

"The thing is, regardless of what's causing it—we're already at the bridge." Meryl took a deep breath. "They're not renewing her lease. She's disturbing the other tenants."

"Can they do that?"

"We can try to fight it, but I don't know—"

"Don't worry, Meryl. We'll find someplace else. You said she never really felt at home there, anyway."

"It's just . . . I don't think she should live alone right now, Hugh."

"She's not alone. She has full-time care."

"But I'm really worried about her."

"See what the doctor says first."

Meryl looked at Hugh. She felt as though she were talking to a stranger. When had a gulf opened between them?

Jo woke up confused, and then remembered why she was at her parents' apartment.

"Fuck," she groaned, realizing, too, that she was late for her shift at the coffee shop. She should call so she wouldn't get fired. But she simply couldn't bring herself to care.

At the breakfast table, her mother, in her eternal inability to "read the room," suggested Jo come with her to help Meg with her bridal registry.

"Do you really think I'm in the mood to do something wedding related when I just lost the love of my life?" she asked, fully aware of how melodramatic she sounded yet still finding it an understatement.

"The timing isn't ideal for any of us," her mother snapped uncharacteristically.

"Um, okay," said Jo, chastened.

Besides, she didn't want to be alone all day. She didn't like to be alone under the best of circumstances, never mind in this state, with her heart dissolving to ash.

She wasn't like her mother, who could always curl up with her favorite book for hours, or Meg, who was the most independent person she knew, or even Amy, who could always run out for a little retail therapy. Jo felt most comfortable around other people, especially when she was hurt or upset. She'd never understood the impulse others had to slink off to a dark corner in solitude. Solitude was not her friend.

And while having two sisters was a cluttered, competitive, loud, annoying existence at times, it also meant rarely having to be alone. With Meg and Amy, she had two built-in best friends.

And today she needed one of those friends. Even if it meant doing something she'd almost rather eat nails than do.

Her phone rang. Toby.

"Where are you? I stopped by the coffee shop, and they said you were a no-show."

"I slept at my mom's last night."

"Things didn't go so well with Caroline?"

"Toby, I really don't want to talk about this right now."

"Well, why don't you come over here?"

The thought of hiding out at Toby's was tempting. But then, there was the unfortunate fact that she'd slept with him.

"Can't—thanks, though," she said. "I'm going to meet Meg at Bloomingdale's to help with her bridal registry."

"Wow, you really are in a bad state."

She snorted, laughing despite herself. "Later, Tobe."

Jo had to give her mother some credit—she didn't ask her that much about Caroline during the ten-minute subway ride to Fifty-ninth Street. Either she was being extraordinarily sensitive, or she really did only want to talk about Meg's wedding.

"So I don't know if this country club thing is Meg's idea or if the Campions are strong-arming her into it," she said, leaning down as she held the metal pole. Jo had a seat at the edge of the subway bench, the metal bar pressing into her side. The car was too hot, the heating system prematurely activated given the warmth of the October day.

"Uh-huh," she said, certain the elderly Asian woman next to her, peering up at Meryl intently, was more interested in this conversation than she was.

"I mean, I'm sure it's a perfectly fine venue, but the wedding is usually in the hometown of the bride's family, not the groom's."

"Whatever, Mom. I think you should just roll with it."

Meryl, squinting up at the map of station stops above Jo's head, ignored her.

"We're next," she announced, as if Jo hadn't been riding the 6 train her entire life.

At Fifty-ninth Street, Jo took comfort in the tide of people sweeping her off the train. Her mother, a few feet ahead, glanced back to make sure Jo was behind her. She could have caught up with her mother, but she was happy to have the temporary buffer.

Lexington was crowded, and her mother walked with brisk purpose. Jo's legs were longer, but she still practically had to trot to keep up with her.

"Are we late?"

"A half hour early, actually," said Meryl. A white-gloved attendant opened the door for them. "I want to get the lay of the land first."

Oh God. She didn't need an extra thirty minutes of looking at china and flatware.

Her mother fumbled for her glasses and scanned the directory. "We're headed to the third floor," Meryl announced, loudly enough that a passerby looked at them.

"I'm going to check out the shoe department. I'll meet up with you at eleven thirty."

"Oh, come to the registry with me. It will be fun!" her mother said.

"Later, Mom."

They parted on the escalator when Meryl got off first.

Alone in Designer Shoes, Jo felt lost. She should have stayed with her mother. Damned if you do, damned if you don't, she thought.

The salespeople appraised her—was she worth their time? Was there a commission to be had in talking to the woman in jeans and Converse sneakers with the lank unwashed hair?

The verdict must have been no, because she moved to the shelf of Chanel boots without interruption. She thought of Amy and Meg, and how if they were the ones walking into this department, they'd be surrounded, swarmed, bees to honey.

Maybe Amy was on to something with her love of shopping. Would trying on a pair of nine-hundred-dollar Chanel combat boots fade the memory of Caroline? Somehow she doubted it—even if she could afford to buy them.

"They would look good on you."

She turned, prepared to tell the salesperson thanks, but that she was just looking. But the woman—dressed in a baby blue cashmere cardigan, a scarf knotted loosely but perfectly around her long neck, and carrying a really cute Marc Jacobs—was not a salesperson.

Their eyes met, and Jo felt something. A ping. A jolt. Impossible. Jo was in love and Jo was heartbroken and any illusion of feeling was just a traumatized mind and heart playing tricks on her. It was like someone who had lost a limb, waking at night with pain in the foot that no longer existed. But she had to admit, this woman was exquisite. She had flawless, creamy skin, shiny dark hair cut into long layers framing her face and falling past her shoulders, and intense, nearly black eyes that were big and almond shaped and slightly exotic looking.

"These would look good on anyone," Jo said. She turned them over to look at the price tag again. "And for nine hundred dollars, they should."

"I couldn't pull those off. I'm stuck with this sort of thing." She held out a ballet flat.

"Don't sell yourself short," Jo heard herself saying, her tone—dare she admit it—flirtatious. "Try them on."

The woman smiled at her, as if accepting an outrageous dare.

A bow-tied salesman appeared. "Can I help you?"

"Yes, actually. I'll try these in a seven." She held Jo's gaze as she said it.

Jo, her heart beating fast, her body responding in a way that she hadn't even felt for Caroline in a long time, felt like she was having some sort of anxiety attack. It's fuck or flight, she told herself.

"Good luck with the shoes," Jo said.

And she got the hell out of there.

On the third floor, her mother was deep in conversation with an older saleswoman. She had dyed red hair and a tweed jacket and black slacks that did nothing to slim her extremely wide hips and ass. The woman wore glasses on a beaded chain around her neck, and nodded at whatever Meryl was saying, her face tight with extreme seriousness as if matters of national security were being discussed.

Meryl spotted her and waved vigorously, as if guiding a plane to landing.

Yeah, Mom, I see you.

"This is my youngest daughter, Josephine," Meryl said as soon as Jo was in shouting distance. She was holding a gilt-edged dinner plate with a giant H design in the middle of it.

"Congratulations on your engagement," the woman said.

"Uh, no. I'm not the one getting married."

"The bride-to-be is my eldest daughter, Meg," said Meryl.

Jo, still rattled by her odd attraction to the stranger in Designer Shoes, just nodded distractedly. She wandered off to look at a glass case filled with Lalique figurines—fish, goddesses, Buddhas. She wondered which ones Meg would pick out. Maybe the ballet dancer on the top shelf. Meg had always liked ballet. She took Jo to see *Swan Lake* when Jo was in ninth grade, and then when the Natalie Portman movie *Black Swan* came out, they went to see it together. Jo was so turned on by the sex scene with Natalie Portman and Mila Kunis, she was too embarrassed to enjoy the rest of the movie, as if her sister could somehow guess what she was thinking in the close darkness of the movie theater.

"Honey, Meg's here!" her mother called excitedly. Jo turned to see her sister, practically glowing with her classic beauty, turning heads in her camel cape, her blond hair pulled back at the nape of her neck, her face pale but her blue eyes shining.

Meg kissed her mother hello but then made her way quickly to Jo, pulling her into a warm, Chanel Allure–scented hug.

"I'm so sorry, kiddo," she said. "It totally sucks."

"Yeah," Jo said, holding her tight, feeling the prick of tears.

"You're going to be okay," she said, a whisper. Then, kissing her on the cheek before pulling back, she put an arm around her and they faced the room together.

"So how much of this crap do you think I need?" she said.

Jo laughed.

"Meg, come over here. This is Helen, and she's going to help us get organized."

"Okay, but we should wait until Leigh gets here."

"Who's Leigh?"

"Leigh Beauford. The wedding planner. Tippy told you about her, right?"

Jo saw her mother's face turn a shade of purple she'd never seen before.

"I told Tippy we didn't want a wedding planner."

"Well, Mom, she didn't get the message, because Leigh came in from Philly this morning just to help out, so let's keep that thought to ourselves, okay?"

"No, it's not okay—"

"Shhh—she's here. Hi, Leigh!"

Jo turned to follow the direction of Meg's greeting, but all she saw was the woman from the shoe department. Jo couldn't help but look down at her feet.

She was wearing the Chanel boots.

Their eyes locked. Had she followed her here? How had she known? Surely, the woman was not going to the bridal registry—

And why was Meg talking to her? Why was Meg waving them over?

"Mom, Jo, this is Leigh Beauford. Our wedding planner."

eleven

Meryl felt like hurling the Hermès dinner plate at the pretty brunette wedding planner.

"I'm sorry—there must have been some miscommunication. We don't need a wedding planner," she said instead.

She didn't dare look at Meg, who was no doubt giving her a death glare. And Leigh Beauford didn't even seem to be listening. She was looking at Jo, whose cheeks were undeniably flushed.

"I've got to go," Jo said. "Meg—good luck. I've got a . . . thing."

Go? Go where? But Meryl couldn't worry about Jo's abrupt departure when Tippy Campion's minion was busy crashing her party.

"Mom, it's fine. No harm in having a third opinion. Let's consider Leigh our tiebreaker," Meg said, smiling graciously at the woman standing before them.

Helen, sniffing out a budding argument in her midst like a narcotics canine at Penn Station, had distanced herself, and was nowhere to be seen.

Why was she so upset? Meryl didn't know if it was Hugh's job fiasco, Tippy's wedding planner, or Meg's refusal to take her side, but she suddenly felt like crying. She knew she was being irrational, so when she felt her phone vibrate, she was grateful for the distraction and the chance to pull herself together.

She fished her phone out of her bag. *Any chance you're free for drinks tonight?*

Meryl looked around the room, as if therein was the answer to who on earth was texting her.

"Mom?" Meg prompted. "Leigh suggested we start with the dinnerware."

"Kate Spade is doing some really modern, fresh things for casual dining," said Leigh.

Who is this? Meryl texted back.

"For the fine china, I'm partial to Wedgwood," said Helen, who had reappeared, somehow sensing the storm had passed.

"Yes, I agree. Shall we start there?" said Leigh.

"Absolutely. As I was telling Meryl, I like to start our brides with the formal ware and build out from there."

It's Scott. I'll be in your neighborhood around seven. Work for you? Pick any place.

Tonight. Was she free? Of course. When was the last time she and Hugh had gone out after dinner? Hugh probably wouldn't even notice she was gone.

Meryl smiled to herself. Where could they go in her neighborhood? Someplace that wasn't too old and stodgy or too loud with a million TV screens airing the hockey game. Jo had mentioned someplace recently— a place she said was "More Brooklyn than Brooklyn." Meryl typed back, *There's a place called Bondurants on 85th.*

See you there.

"Mom, are you coming?"

Meryl looked up. Helen and Leigh were already walking to the next room. Meg took Meryl by the arm. "Are you all right? Everyone's acting crazy. And where did Jo run off to?"

"I don't know," said Meryl. "I'm sorry, honey. I was distracted. Oh, but Meg, this woman Leigh. It's not necessary and I don't think we should encourage her by bringing her along today. I'm not using a wedding planner. We're not celebrities."

"Why is this so threatening to you? It can only help. We have a lot to do in not a lot of time. I'm working like crazy, and you could get a freelance job any day because you know how that is with you. Tippy's in Pennsylvania and I'm in Washington with Stowe. If we can have another person on board to fill in the gaps, I say great."

Meryl didn't know what to say. That Hugh had lost his job and she felt like the entire wedding was slipping through her fingers? That she felt less important than the mega-family Meg was marrying into? That she was afraid Tippy, with her well-preserved beauty and WASPy elegance and contacts all over the place, was going to replace Meryl in Meg's life? That Tippy could hire someone to do Meryl's job made her feel all the more useless? She could barely admit these things to herself.

"Mom. Mom! Your phone's ringing," Meg said impatiently. Good Lord, she was right. Meryl pulled it out again.

"Mrs. Becker?"

She recognized the Queens accent, and her stomach tightened into a knot. Mr. Curello.

"Yes?"

"We need you to come get your mother. Now."

This time, when Meryl arrived to find her mother screaming, the police were waiting for her.

"We can't tell you what to do, Mrs. Becker," an officer said. "But you probably should consider a different living arrangement for your mother sooner than later."

Meryl could barely register what he was saying, not while her mother was screaming like that. She looked around for Oona. "Where's her caretaker?"

"We're talking to the nurse," the officer said.

"Talking to her . . . about what?"

"Just to make sure there's no problem—you know how things can be sometimes. We need to file a report."

"Oh, I don't think Oona is causing this. But for God's sake, I don't know what is!" She pressed her hand to her head.

Her mother was perched at the edge of her bed, staring at the wall with her eyes wide open again.

"Mother," Meryl said quietly, then again, more loudly. Her heart raced at the volume and pitch of the scream. Feeling frantic, she paced for a minute by the bedside. Then, remembering what had worked last time, she threw her arms around her mother and held her tight. Sure enough, the screaming stopped.

Then, as if waking from a dream, her mother shook her head slightly, looking at her askance. "Meryl. Did you call before you stopped by?"

Meryl shook her head, choking back a sob. "No. No, Mom, I didn't call. I'm sorry."

She sat next to her on the bed, searching for the remote to turn off the television. Since when did her mother have the TV on all day? She knew she watched *The Bold and the Beautiful* and *The Young and the Restless,* but it was too early for those shows. "Mom, I want you to come stay with me tonight."

"With you? At your apartment? Don't be ridiculous, Meryl. Why would I do that? Are you okay? Is it the girls?" Her voice lowered. "Did Meg break off that engagement?"

"It's not me. Or the girls. We're fine. It's you I'm worried about."

Before her mother could erupt in protest, one of the police officers came near the bedroom doorway, gesturing for her.

"Why are the police here?" her mother asked.

"Mom, pack some things. We'll talk about it in the cab."

"I'm not going anywhere until you tell me what this is about, Meryl."

They looked up at the sound of Oona storming into the room. She was crying. "I'm sorry, Mrs. Becker, but I can't be doing this no more. I quit!"

Her mother admitted to having "episodes." The nature of these episodes was vague, and her mother was not enthusiastic about clarifying. "I guess you could say it's like a bad dream. But I'm awake."

"What are you dreaming about?"

Her mother shook her head. "Nothing."

But Meryl knew it was something. She would take her to Lenox Hill for a brain scan and whatever else Dr. Friedman wanted to do to rule out a mini stroke or Alzheimer's or any of the myriad things Meryl was petrified of hearing. But deep down, Meryl suspected it wasn't anything a brain scan would find. On some level, a deep, primal gut sense, she knew something was bothering her mother. Had *always* been bothering her mother. And that something was finally catching up with her.

After dinner, when her mother was settled into Meg's old bedroom, Meryl told Hugh, "She needs to be here with us. At least for the foreseeable future."

"Meryl, is that practical?"

"She's my mother."

"I know. And I also know your mother. I can't imagine she'd agree to this. I mean, the woman refuses to so much as come for dinner, and now she's going to live here?"

"She's not happy about it, but she's not really fighting me either. I think she's scared. These episodes . . . she's not even aware of them happening. This is a problem I have to deal with."

He hugged her. "I get that. It's fine. Of course she can live here. Although, with Jo back, it's getting to be quite the full house."

"Jo isn't staying here tonight. She's with Toby." Meryl raked her hands through her hair. "It isn't exactly a cake walk for me, Hugh. My mother drives me crazy from across town, never mind under our roof. I just can't imagine how this is going to go."

"Not to mention we might not have this much space next year."

"What are you talking about?"

"Well, if I lose my job, we won't get to stay in this apartment."

Meryl felt like someone kicked her in the chest. She literally gasped, reaching for her nightstand to steady herself. "The apartment. I hadn't even thought about the apartment."

She was so busy worrying about the weddings, she hadn't thought about the other collateral damage from Hugh's job being in jeopardy.

"How can you say that so casually? And you're not going to lose your job. That's not happening."

Her phone rang. She checked just to make sure it wasn't the girls before she ignored it. It was a 310 area code. Oh my God. Scott.

She'd completely forgotten.

"Hello?"

"Hey—you picked a great spot, but it would be better if you were here, too," Scott said. She heard the noise of the gastropub in the background.

"I am so sorry—family emergency," she said. "I feel terrible. Any other night this week?"

"Tomorrow breakfast? I'm heading back to L.A. tomorrow."

"Yes—that works."

"I'm staying at the W Union Square. What's good around there? City Bakery? Say, nine?"

"Perfect. See you there." She hung up the phone.

Hugh looked at her quizzically. "Who was that?"

"Oh . . . a job lead. A publicist I was supposed to meet for a drink," she lied. Why was she lying about it?

"Great!" he said. "We might need your steady income around here."

She glared at him. "Are you happy about all of this?"

"Of course not. I just don't think it's the catastrophe that you're making it out to be. Most people these days don't have the same job decade after decade. We've been fortunate. And frankly, I'm ready for a change."

"Well, I'm not! This is . . . too much change. Everything is out of control," she suddenly started sobbing.

"Meryl, we'll figure it out."

"*We'll* figure it out? You figure it out! I'm tired of being the one to figure everything out!"

Walking into the bathroom and slamming the door, she indulged in a good hard cry. She cried over leaving Meg with the wedding planner to register. She cried over her mother's behavior.

And she cried over lying to her husband.

twelve

Jo wondered what heartbroken women did in the days before Netflix and HBO Go. The ability to lie in bed for hours on end, binge-watching entire seasons of her favorite shows strung together like an emotional all-you-can-eat buffet, was the only thing getting her through this.

That, and Toby.

They sat propped up side by side in his king-sized bed, surrounded by bowls of popcorn, bags of Doritos, his laptop and phone, her phone and her e-reader, and the remote.

"I could seriously stay here forever," she said, cueing up yet another season of *Girls*.

"We really don't have to leave the apartment. At least, not until we want to," he said.

"If only! I need to find another job."

"No, you don't," he said. "What do you think, I'm going to charge you rent?"

"I still need money, Toby. Unlike you, I don't have someone funneling cash into my Chase account every month."

"I'll get you a debit card to my account," he said.

"Oh my God, stop. Tobe, I love you, but you don't have to take care of me. Honestly, all I need is your company. And maybe a copilot over the next few months as I deal with all this wedding shit. I love my sisters, but God, it's just so not my thing."

She thought of the bridal registry department, the cabinets and tables filled with expensive, delicate, shiny things—some useful, some absurd. She could never imagine owning any of it. If she and Caroline had gotten married, they would have eloped. Scratch that. Her mother would be devastated. Instead they would have done some cool destination wedding—maybe Jamaica. And they would have told people no gifts, and then when they came back to New York, they would have woken up on a lazy Sunday, made love, and then headed to Bed Bath & Beyond to buy a few things that would signify the start of their life as a married couple.

Jo reached for her drink. It was a kamizake, made with fresh lime, triple sec, and Tito's vodka. Toby said it was the one cocktail he knew how to make, and clearly he'd perfected it.

"I don't know," Toby said. "This whole wedding thing sounds like a good gig to me. You basically have people buying you things for a year straight, culminating in a big dinner with all of your friends and family and then a vacation with your favorite person in the world. Hell, I'm jealous."

"Yeah. Me too," she said quietly. "But I can tell you it's not in the cards for me. I am never going to let myself fall in love again. It's just too painful."

"Yeah, good luck with that. It's human nature. You can't fight it."

She thought of the surge of desire she had felt for the wedding planner. It was shocking she could feel something so strong, when she felt so broken, and it dismayed her that she had so little control over her impulses. Jo realized her biggest fear wasn't what she'd told her mother—that she'd never fall in love again. It was that she would.

"I can fight it," she said.

"Well, I can't," said Toby, looking at her with naked longing.

Before she could say anything to neutralize the moment, he leaned forward and kissed her.

Jo knew it was wrong—but he was such a good kisser, and his arms around her made her feel safe and cared for, and so even though she knew she was being weak, she let him tug off her T-shirt, and when she felt his mouth on her breasts, his hardness through his jeans as he pulled her into his arms, she gave in to the animalistic need for skin on skin.

Toby pulled on a condom, and she watched the process with a detached fascination. When he moved back on top of her, she found herself eager for the sensation of being filled by him. The sensation of him entering her, the hardness of his cock, was so different from Caroline, which was exactly what she needed, and undeniably satisfying. There was no question this was just fucking—it was clean and simple, and if he had messy emotions about it, well, frankly that was his problem. He was a grown man and he knew the deal.

At least that's what she told herself as he kissed her neck, moaning her name as his body trembled and she drew him closer. She wouldn't come this time, she could tell. But the closeness felt good.

"My God, Jo," he said, her body tensing, his hips bucking. His eyes were closed tight, his face tense with the orgasm that rocked through him. Jo watched him, touched by the intensity of his experience and struck with a sudden pang of worry. Be careful, she told herself. *Be careful.*

City Bakery was a two-story, cafeteria-style food mecca for the Union Square professional crowd.

Scott texted her that he was already there, at a table on the second floor.

Meryl ordered a coffee—for once not even tempted by the pretzel croissants, and walked up the narrow metal staircase.

She was nervous. Judging from that brief encounter at the 7-Eleven, Scott Sobel made her feel like a starstruck fifteen-year-old girl all over again. What were they even going to talk about after all this time?

He spotted her and rose from a corner table. She smiled and headed toward him, letting him embrace her.

"You made it!" he said.

"Scott, I'm so sorry about last night."

"Oh, I'm just teasing," he said. "Don't even give it a second thought.

I'm just glad we were able to fit this in before I head back to the West Coast."

Meryl shrugged off her coat, draping it on the back of the chair next to her, and sat down facing him across the table.

Scott was the physical opposite of Hugh. As a teenager, he'd been dark and exotic looking—almost Mediterranean. He had thick, shiny dark hair, a little lighter now but still brown, not gray. He had an aquiline nose and a full upper lip, dark eyes with heavy brows and thick lashes—bedroom eyes. When she was younger, she'd heard the expression on one of her mother's shows, and though she didn't know exactly what it meant at the time, when she saw Scott for the first time, she knew instantly what it meant.

"So how the hell have you been, Meryl Kleinman?"

This was crazy. She was still attracted to him. It was absurd—like her brain synapses were stuck back in 1975. She could practically hear the Barry Manilow song "Mandy"—God, how she'd loved that song. It made her so sad and so happy at the same time. It had been magical.

"Becker," she said. "I'm married." *Yes, Meryl—you're married!*

"I know. I remember. It just feels good to say your old name. God, when did I see you last? Before the other night, obviously. That party at Columbia?"

"Probably."

At the time, she'd already been dating Hugh a few weeks. She and Scott had said hello. He had been with an attractive woman—of course. They were still young then. They didn't matter to each other yet. Nostalgia hadn't set in, making them golden to each other.

"You look exactly the same as that night on the boardwalk," he said.

Oh my God. He remembered. "I don't feel the same," she said, blushing.

"Who does?" he said, smiling at her. "Except, I have to say, sitting here with you—it's the closest I've gotten in a long time."

She glanced down at his ring finger. Bare. Of course, a lot of men didn't wear wedding bands these days.

"Are you married?" she asked.

He shook his head. "No. Never got married." He said it almost apologetically.

"You never found the right person?" She paused. "I'm sorry," she added. "It's really none of my business."

He laughed. "This is what friends do after decades—they talk about their lives, right?"

"I guess you're right."

"How long have you been married?"

"Thirty years." It sounded outrageous, even to her.

Scott whistled. "Wow. Meryl, that's impressive."

Was it? There had been times when she thought about leaving. Likely they both had. But the feelings had passed. So the fact that she was still married wasn't necessarily impressive. She wanted to be happily married. Or at least to feel content.

But she didn't. Not lately.

"It's not, really," she said.

"You're so self-deprecating. I love it. Usually I'm surrounded by complete narcissists."

"I guess it takes a certain amount of that to want to be on a reality TV show."

"I'm sure what I do seems pretty crazy to you."

"Not at all! It's interesting. In fact, I watched your first show. The rodeo housewives."

"Really? I'm flattered."

"Well, don't be too flattered. I grew up watching *The Young and the Restless* and *As the World Turns*. Not exactly highbrow entertainment."

"Highbrow, no. But they serve a purpose. We need narratives about love and family to make sense of our lives—just like centuries ago we needed myths to make sense of the natural world."

"I never thought of it that way."

"So what else, Meryl Kleinman Becker?"

"Well, I have three grown daughters."

"I know."

"You do?"

Had he Googled her? Did that mean something? Did he think about her?

He smiled at her, a knowing, intimate smile as if he knew exactly what she was thinking.

It took her breath away.

Amy dreamt about her wedding. Every night since the engagement, her sleep was filled with vivid images of white gowns and six-tiered cakes and flowers—oh, the flowers! Purple was her signature color, and the arrangements of dark eggplant calla lilies, anemone, hydrangeas, purple zinnias, and poppies and roses—she could smell them, feel their velvety petals.

In the morning, she would jot down notes from her dreams, a wedding coming together piece by piece from the place of her deepest fantasies.

So far, she hadn't shared any of her wedding brainstorming with her mother, who had been disappointingly absent since the Friday night dinner. She had barely called Amy even though there were obviously a million things to talk about. Amy tried to fight the knowing feeling that her mother was simply too caught up in Meg's wedding planning to start getting Amy's off the ground. Typical.

Amy shrugged off the vestiges of her fantasy wedding slumber and the rising panic that—as always—she was being eclipsed by the bright and shining star that was Meg. For years, with Andy by her side, it had seemed like she was finally catching up. Meg might have been born with innate style and Grace Kelly good looks, but Amy had the fashion bona fides. By senior year in college, her social calendar included New York Fashion Week, the European shows in February, Art Basel parties in Miami, the CFDA awards. Meg seemed uninterested in it all, but their mother loved hearing all the details—who wore what, the kind of food that was served. For the first time, Amy had felt like the special one.

And then came Meg's new boyfriend, Stowe—and his family, the Campions. Fashion was exciting, fashion was important. But it wasn't political power.

Amy showered and got dressed. Andy was already gone, an early meeting. The apartment was filled with flowers, well wishes and congratulations from friends—Jeffrey Bruce's friends. Marc Jacobs alone sent an arrangement that was lavish enough to be a centerpiece at their wedding.

Over coffee, she opened her laptop. Andy's mother, Eileen, had given her a list of potential wedding planners. "To use or not to use, whatever you want," she had said, and Amy knew she meant it. Eileen had also made it clear that they were happy to pay for whatever "you kids" need, but that she didn't want to "overstep." From what Amy had seen from the preliminary planning of her sister's wedding, her parents did not want anyone else paying for the wedding—any part of their wedding. Her father was very old-fashioned, and her mother was prideful and, let's face it, a bit of a control freak.

Amy had spent fifteen minutes clicking through the Web sites of various wedding planners, when she realized she was in danger of being late. There was no margin for error today—she wasn't going to the office, but instead to Milk Studios on West Fifteenth Street for the menswear shoot.

The studio was hip and glamorous, a glass-enclosed space with panoramic views of the Hudson. But for the past week, she was a little less than focused, just a little less awed by her entrée to the workaday world of Jeffrey Bruce International. Now she wasn't just dating a Bruce. She wasn't just working at Bruce. She was on the cusp of becoming a Bruce.

Amy Becker Bruce. She mentally played with the name constantly, chewing it like the most delicious salted caramel. In meetings, she was tempted to doodle it onto her legal pad, but she didn't dare, in case Stella caught sight of it and became even more wary of her.

Stella had made it clear that she did not need Amy at today's shoot. Amy had been prepared not to go. And then the Page Six story broke.

Amy didn't know who fed the news of her engagement to the city's notorious gossip site, but she suspected it was someone from inside the Bruce camp. Jeffrey certainly seemed happy about it, somehow missing the completely pejorative slant of the piece. (Her sister clearly hadn't.) Amy had long had the feeling that Jeffrey Bruce was probably even better at branding than he was at design; every aspect of their lives reflected the Bruce aesthetic: fresh, clean, sporty, all-American bordering on preppy.

Andy confided in her that his father worried about relevancy.

The advent of social media baffled him. The fact that a thirteen-year-old blogger sitting in the middle of nowhere could somehow matter sent him into a tizzy. Now everyone chased that ephemeral thing that would make them "viral."

Jeffrey loved that Amy and her sister had landed on Page Six. He loved that the photo of Meg included Stowe Campion. Blue-blooded Stowe, who embodied the Jeffrey Bruce lifestyle and aesthetic.

Jeffrey had called Amy into his office that morning, along with Paul Derribond, head of the in-house public relations team, and a petite, blond Southern woman named Camille, who handled the outside PR when Jeffrey Bruce needed reinforcements, like during Fashion Week or for crisis management. Together, they dissected the Page Six piece with an intensity Amy had not seen since her sophomore-year study group had prepped for a midterm exam on Milton's *Paradise Lost*. Jeffrey declared that Amy was now a "brand ambassador." Camille and Paul had clucked approvingly, and the meeting had a high-energy, positive vibe that was both thrilling and baffling.

The next thing she knew, Stella informed her, with obvious bitterness, that she would be going to the menswear shoot after all.

Amy dressed in jeans and a gray cashmere Bruce sweater with high black suede Bruce boots. The boots were impractically high-heeled, but she was running so late, she was taking a cab to the shoot anyway.

The studio buzzed with the self-important energy inherent in fashion, along with Arctic Monkeys playing at an obscenely high decibel, considering it was barely nine in the morning. The stylist, a teeny-tiny waif of a woman who channeled 1960s London, was busy with one of the male models while the other two stood nearby.

Amy grabbed a soy latte from the coffee bar and took a seat next to Stella, who barely glanced at her.

After a few minutes of awkward silence, Amy asked, "Is there anything I can do?"

"No," Stella said, scrolling through the look book on her tablet. Her one terse syllable said everything. *No, there is nothing for you to do because your presence here is completely unnecessary, which is why I told you not to come in the first place.*

Amy pretended to be very busy with her e-mails. When she exhausted that, she looked at the models, three perfect specimens of male beauty. One, African American with bright blue eyes. Another, with tousled sandy brown hair and pouty lips, looked like a male Angelina Jolie. The third had longish dark hair that obscured his face. He was bending down, fixing his twelve-hundred-dollar chocolate brown suede Jeffrey Bruce work boots. When he stood, shaking his hair back, tucking a lock behind his ear, he looked straight at Amy.

And she lost her breath.

He was the most magnificent person she had ever seen, in person, in print, on the screen—in her wildest imagination.

He didn't have that one startling declaration of beauty as the other two did—dramatic ice-blue eyes or lips with an almost cartoonish sensuality. And yet he stood out more than either of them because the perfect composition of his face was once in a lifetime. It was a work of art, nature at its most sublime. Maybe proof of the god she barely thought about.

She could only imagine what his girlfriend looked like. What kind of woman had the self-confidence to be with a guy who was prettier than she was? Andy was definitely cute, but there was never a question that she was the better looking of the two. She remembered reading somewhere that people tended to couple off with partners of the same relative degree of attractiveness. She didn't remember where she'd read it, but now, thinking about the couples she knew, the theory behind the article seemed to prove true.

Meanwhile the stylist, Brandi, and the photographer, Rupert, were carrying on about the clothes.

"This jacket is just . . . no," said Brandi, yanking the blazer off the broad shoulders of Mr. Perfection. "Rupert, give me a minute to pull another option. Unless," she said, looking dutifully at Stella, almost as an afterthought. "You're totally married to this one."

"Let me see what else you have," Stella said, hopping down from the metal stool, handing Amy her thin laptop to hold and muttering, "Make yourself useful."

The photographer busied himself with the other two models whose clothes didn't offend Brandi.

"We're changing you, Marcus," she called from somewhere behind a screen or a wall or something else making her invisible. "Lose that shirt."

Mr. Perfection—apparently named Marcus—began unbuttoning the lavender and gray plaid shirt he wore. Amy averted her eyes, as unnerved as a virginal heroine in one of those turn-of-the-century novels her father loved so much.

Someone's assistant handed Marcus a glass of champagne. Amy found herself yearning for a drink herself, but couldn't. Not on the job. Even if her job today entailed very loud rock music and ridiculously beautiful men. Even if the job was currently making her feel more extraneous and cloddishly unattractive than she'd ever felt in her entire life.

And then, Mr. Perfection ambled over to Amy's spot on the sidelines.

"Guess the jacket's not working," he said with a sheepish grin.

She realized that she was supposed to say something professional. As a rep from Jeffrey Bruce, she was supposed to assure him that they had plenty of other wardrobe items for him to wear, that they would get what they needed for the ad—not to worry.

"Guess not," she said.

"At least, I hope it's just the jacket they have a problem with."

Did this astonishingly gorgeous creature really think something—anything—could be wrong with him?

"I don't think you have to worry," she said, smiling up at him.

"Really?"

"Yeah. Really." She tried hard not to look at his chest.

"You work for them?" he asked.

Her smile grew wider. He had no idea who she was. This guy just saw her as a staffer, maybe even an intern. He had no idea she was practically a Bruce herself.

"Yeah," she said.

"Cool." He smiled at her again, and her knees turned to Jell-O.

"Okay," said Brandi, appearing with a T-shirt and leather jacket. "Crisis averted."

"Wish me luck," he said, winking at Amy.

She watched him saunter back to the other two, under the bright lights, ready for the shoot. She found she was holding her breath. Amy looked down at her engagement ring.

Pull it together, you idiot.

"Did I Google you?" Scott repeated. "Yes—guilty as charged. I did Google you. But that's not how I know about your daughters."

Crap. Had she said that out loud? "So you're a *New York Post* reader."

"In a town full of celebrities, they are writing about your kids." He smiled.

"Yeah. Well, it's been a slow news month."

"It's interesting stuff, Meryl."

"That's one way of putting it. Crazy is another. Stressful, yet another."

"Who is handling everything?"

"The wedding? I'm trying to. There's a wedding planner but—"

"No, I mean your PR."

"Oh. I am."

"You don't want a professional? I'd be happy to put you in touch with a few people."

"I have all the publicity I need. More than I need, actually. My daughters—well, my eldest daughter—is very sensitive about this stuff."

He smiled. "She'd better get used to it. Fast."

They sipped their coffee.

"People love crazy, impossibly true stories. Reality shows are the new soaps."

"That's very true," she said. "The whole 'truth is stranger than fiction' thing."

"Exactly. But it's not always about it being strange or circuslike. I think there's a trend toward wanting to see real people with a hint of fantasy. And viewers want positivity. Take the Kardashians. Yes, there's a lot of drama and extreme wealth and jet-setting and celebrity. But what's the take away from every episode? At the end of the day, they're still a family. No matter what."

Meryl nodded thoughtfully.

"That's why I think your daughters would make a great show."

"Wait—what?"

"Think about it: three sisters, two getting married and embarking on that new phase of life at the same time. Both marrying interesting—and wealthy—men. Both building their own careers. I mean, it's all there, Meryl. It's gold."

Was he serious? She hoped not.

"I don't think so." She laughed nervously.

"Meryl, I wouldn't bring it up if I didn't think it was a real possibility."

"Scott, I'm sure in your business this is a normal thing to think about and talk about. And maybe most people would find this idea . . . flattering. But trust me—my daughters would never go for it. I told you, my oldest got very upset just about that Page Six piece."

"That's because it's someone else taking control of the narrative. This is about you—all of you—owning this story. And making a fortune off it."

Meryl swallowed hard. How much money, exactly, did he mean by "fortune"? But no, she wouldn't ask. Wouldn't even give him an opening.

And then she realized, this coffee wasn't about connecting with an old friend, nostalgic remembrances of a seaside kiss in another lifetime. This guy was all business.

"Scott, I hope this isn't the reason you wanted to get together, because I'm afraid you've wasted your time."

"No! Absolutely not. I just . . . It's the way my mind works. I'm sorry."

"Don't apologize—it's an interesting thought. It's just not for us."

"I get it. Most people don't want to be Kris Jenner. It's just, where some people see an egomaniac, I see a woman who built an empire."

A woman who built an empire. Meryl imagined not just managing the wedding, but building a brand as well. Money would never be a problem again. She wouldn't have to look for a job—she'd create one for herself. *The Wedding Sisters* TV show, books . . . a line of wedding-day cosmetics.

Maybe it was time she became a little more business minded. Maybe then she wouldn't be in the position she was in.

"Honestly, my life isn't all that interesting."

"I think that's going to change," he said with a smile.

Afterwards, everyone went to nearby Hogs & Heifers for drinks. That's what you did after these things. Amy texted Andy, *We're on our way to Hogs. Want to meet us?* He wrote back that he was too slammed. *Do you think I should head back to the office?* she wrote. He replied, *No. Have fun, Brand Ambassador* ☺

Only one in the afternoon, the bar was nearly empty except for two men at the end of the bar, Con Ed workers whose truck was parked out front.

Rupert ordered a round of shots for everyone, including the Con Ed guys. Amy fell into place near the edge of the bar, wedged between Brandi and Stella. She was extremely aware of gorgeous Marcus on the opposite side of Stella.

Rupert was busy telling a story about the early '90s, when Hogs was the only bar in the neighborhood. That was back when the Meatpacking District really was for meatpacking, and Rupert would come out of the bar in the early morning hours and there was literally blood in the streets from the butchers already at work. Meat hung from hooks outside the buildings that now housed shops like Scoop and DVF and Jeffrey Bruce. This was just a few years after Amy was born, a fact that made her feel blessedly young, but also as if she had missed out on something.

The bartender, a woman with inky black hair and tattoos and wearing an off-the-shoulder Metallica T-shirt, tight jeans, and a cowboy hat, poured them another round of tequila. Amy was torn between being uncomfortably buzzed with her boss, and eager for the alcohol to take effect and dull the jumpy feeling she had around Marcus.

At some point, the bartender began doing shots with them, and Stella left to take a phone call.

Marcus edged down a spot at the bar, now elbow to elbow with Amy. "Do you play pool?" he asked.

"No."

"Want to learn?"

"I'm a bad student," she said. It came out much more flirtatiously than she'd intended.

"Oh, come on. I don't believe that."

She hopped down from her barstool and followed him to the pool table. While he set up, she examined all the framed photos of the bar's celebrity clientele. She squinted at one of Brad Pitt and Gwyneth Paltrow. She had very short hair and he wore a somewhat cheesy leather jacket. Had they been a couple?

"Okay, we're good to go," Marcus said, the balls arranged in a perfect triangle at one end of the table. He handed her a cue, and when she took it from him, their knuckles brushed. The contact felt hot and electric. It was like the heat packet Andy's mother had given her once to keep in her gloves to stay warm while skiing—instant 150 degrees against her skin.

The little heat packets had amazed Amy at the time. It wasn't that they were particularly expensive or even difficult to find. It was more that it was yet another example of how there was never a moment of discomfort in the lives of the Bruces. And when she was with them, she was cocooned in the security that came with extreme wealth and celebrity. She had seen this kind of wealth when she went to school at Yardley. But then it had been secondhand. Her father was staff. In the Yardley family, she was the poor relation. But now, she was the real deal.

Marcus put his arms around her to show her how to lean forward, positioning the cue between her thumb and forefinger. Every cell in her body lit up, on high alert. Through the haze of alcohol, she was intensely aware of everything—his smell, woodsy and masculine. The song playing: "Bullet the Blue Sky" by U2. She turned to look at him. A mistake. His intense beauty, the slope of his nose, the arc of his cheekbones, and his blue gray eyes focused on her, gave her the sense that the room was tilting. And the only way to right her equilibrium was to lean against him. His arms tightened around her, and desire shot through her like a drug.

Some animalistic sense of self-preservation caused her to glance up, across the room to where Stella was now watching her.

Amy abruptly pulled away from Marcus, startling him. She mumbled something about needing the bathroom.

The bathroom, a tiny, graffiti-scarred cabinet of a room, offered the refuge she needed to collect herself. There was no mirror, and so she could not confront her guilty reflection.

When she emerged, she headed for the bar. She would talk to Stella, assume her rightful place with the other Jeffrey Bruce executives. But Stella was nowhere to be seen.

"Where's Stella?" she asked Rupert.

"Called back to the office."

"I should get back to the office, too."

"Don't be such a suit. You're too young for that," said Rupert. "Come on, we're going to my place."

Rupert lived in a town house on West Tenth Street, a four-story building with a starkly modern and minimalist interior.

"Please take your shoes off," Rupert told everyone. "These floors cost more than God."

The walls were covered in photographs of all the celebrities Rupert had worked with over the years—ten years at *Rolling Stone,* fourteen at *Vanity Fair.* Kurt Cobain, Kate Moss, Princess Diana. He shot the Jeffrey Bruce ads only as a favor, because Jeffrey had given him his first break. Jeffrey was a genuinely nice guy; people told Amy this again and again, as if they'd stumbled upon a unicorn. For the millionth time, she thought about how lucky she was to be in his orbit, to be a part of his family.

She texted Andy, *I'm at Rupert's house. Leaving soon.*

Ask him to show you the photo of Madonna and my dad.

Okay! Love you.

"Andy said I should ask you to see the photo of his father and Madonna," Amy said. It was the first time all day she had acknowledged or referred in any way to the depth of her personal relationship to the company. She looked to see if the comment registered with Marcus, but he was absorbed in his phone.

"Oh, Jeffrey would kill me. He hates that photo. That was back when he dyed his hair, which no man should ever, ever do."

"Amen," said Brandi.

"You think?" said Amy.

"Um, yeah. Whom would you rather look like at fifty—Johnny Depp or George Clooney?"

"Gotcha."

"Let's get the grand tour out of the way," said Rupert.

There was an elevator, and they filed into it. Rupert took them to the top floor, and the doors opened to a short flight of stairs that led to a rooftop deck.

"Not too shabby, Rupert," said Brandi.

They had a view of the entire West Village and a partial view of the Hudson. Amy knew the sunset must be phenomenal.

"How long have you lived here?" she asked.

"Long enough that I prefer the bar to the view. Shall we, people?"

Everyone followed Rupert back to the stairs, quickly and wordlessly, as if he were the pied piper of the West Village. Everyone but Marcus.

Amy didn't move. She had the sense that the moment was somehow precious, but couldn't quite put her finger on why. Maybe she was reluctant to leave the fresh air. Yes, that was it. Already, it smelled more like winter than fall. Soon it would be too cold to enjoy the outdoors.

Amy tried not to take too much notice of Marcus. She leaned over the brick balustrade, pretending to be absorbed in the scenery. Her heart pounded. She felt the weight of his presence as heavily as if they had planned this together, a secret rendezvous. She wondered if she had somehow missed a subtle cue from him, some inadvertent collusion that had passed between them.

She felt his eyes on her. The urge to look at him was excruciating. The fact that she didn't indicating a willpower she never knew she possessed. And the longer she resisted, the stronger she felt. This was nothing, she told herself. She needed to go back downstairs. But she was frozen.

Marcus was the one who moved first. Months later, when mentally flagellating herself, she would remind herself of this.

As if it made any difference.

At first, she thought he was just walking toward the farthest end of the balustrade to get a better view of the water. That was what her mind reasoned as she stayed rooted in place, even as he moved directly behind her, pressing his body against hers, moving her hair out of the way so he could kiss the base of her neck.

She felt it in her pelvis, in the deepest part of herself.

When she turned to face him, to find his mouth with her mouth, there wasn't a thought in her head. His lips, his teeth, his tongue—she devoured him, every part of her throbbing, and from her throat rose noises she didn't recognize, like the sounds a small animal would make.

He unbuttoned her jeans and slipped his hand between her legs. His touch was like an electric prod.

"Yes," she gasped.

And then his pants were down, and he lifted her, somehow holding her against the balustrade as her legs wrapped around him and he pressed inside her with a soft moan.

"My God," she said.

"Yeah, baby," he growled, his mouth open and wet against her neck, his thrusts hard and even.

The only thing tethering her to the earth, to reality, was the hard brick wall grazing her back.

There was no condom. She was on the pill, but still.

"You can't—we aren't using any—"

"I'll pull out," he said, and somehow in the alternate universe she currently inhabited, this was okay.

She looked at him; his eyes shut tight, his eyelashes long. That perfectly carved nose, like a caricature of male beauty. She threaded her fingers through his shiny, dark hair—and she came so hard, it scared her.

"Fuck," he said, and true to his word, jerked quickly out of her. She felt the liquid heat of his come through her pants, and the logistical problem this created was not immediately clear to her; all she felt was a dizzying excitement.

She would deal with everything else later.

thirteen

Meryl could finally breathe easy.

The battery of tests came back negative. Her mother was healthy.

The CT scan, the X-rays, the brain MRI, and something Dr. Friedman called an MMSE showed no sign of anything wrong.

"I can refer you to a geropsychiatrist. Depression is very common at this stage of life."

Meryl took the name and number, but knew her mother would never agree to see a psychiatrist. This was one of the few arenas in which she resisted embracing American culture: medication and psychiatry. That, and dieting. Though her mother never needed to diet; she was always incredibly, effortlessly slim.

So: no evidence of dementia, Alzhiemer's, stroke, or brain tumor. So what, then?

"Fancy," said Rose outside the Monique Lhuillier bridal boutique on East Seventy-second Street. It was not a compliment.

Meryl shot her a look. "Mother, if you're not going to be positive—"

"Seriously, Meg. I feel like I should have worn a ball gown just to come along today," said Jo.

"You look fine," Meryl said, suddenly wishing she'd taken Meg dress shopping alone.

"Gran, she is the most incredible dress designer," said Meg. "You're going to love everything, I just know it."

"We'll see," said Rose.

Meryl glared at her mother. The least her mother could do was fake it for an hour. She wasn't even sure why Rose had agreed to come along.

Meryl also wished Amy had mustered some enthusiasm and joined them. She had an image of all three sisters together on this occasion, but Amy had insisted she needed to be at work.

Not wanting to take no for an answer, Meryl had tried another tack: "You should at least see what Meg picks out so you know when you're telling Jeffrey what style you want."

"I'm not *telling* Jeffrey anything, Mother. He's an artist. And I'm certainly not letting Meg's dress choice dictate my own."

And that was the end of that.

The door opened and they were greeted by a woman in a charcoal gray pantsuit. She had dark hair and olive skin and she could have been twenty-five or forty-five—Meryl could not for the life of her tell which.

"Meg? So nice to see you. I'm Edith."

Edith shook all their hands, and another woman trailed behind her, offering them water or a glass of wine. Everyone declined except for Rose, who asked if they had vodka.

"It's a bit early for that, isn't it, Mother?"

"Oh, it's not a problem," said Edith. "When brides come here, it's like the celebration is starting! Would you like that on the rocks or with soda?" she asked.

"Rocks, thank you, dear," said Rose.

"Do you have anything caffeinated?" asked Jo. Edith told an assistant to make her a latte.

The room was spare, with putty-colored walls and matching plush carpet. Edith led them into an interior room lined with two racks of white wedding gowns.

"I would have worn my mother's wedding dress if it had been available to me," said Rose. The dress had been left behind in Poland, when they moved away, thinking they would have time to return one day for their belongings. Meryl had heard this story when she herself got engaged.

"Oh, I know, Gran. Mom doesn't have her dress anymore, either. Isn't that right, Mom?"

"That's right," Meryl said.

The truth was, she hadn't worn a dress. She hadn't had the heart to tell this to her daughters when they first asked to see it as young girls, dressed up for their favorite game: playing wedding.

"I don't have it anymore—it must have gotten lost in the move," Meryl told them.

"But what did it look like?" Meg had pressed, her intelligent eyes relentless for the truth and for answers, a budding journalist even as a third grader.

"Like a princess dress!" Amy had surmised.

"Yes," said Meryl, "like a princess dress."

She had not bought anything special for her marriage to Hugh, and even if she had gone dress shopping, she wouldn't have had the sort of entourage that Meg had with her that afternoon. Her mother, while not yet officially boycotting the wedding, had been barely speaking to her. Her best friend at the time was backpacking across Europe and unreachable. And she didn't have sisters.

Meryl had worn jeans and a white lace top that she found in a thrift shop on Greenwich Avenue. The most she could say about the outfit was that it hadn't involved shoulder pads, which was a small miracle in 1984.

Meg approached the first rack of dresses, gingerly touching a sheath dress in ivory duchess satin. Her face was as flushed and happy as Meryl had ever seen it.

"I just can't even believe I'm here, doing this," she said.

The room was bright and airy, filled with the natural light of the three large windows overlooking the street and the town house across from them. Meryl and Rose sat in matching putty-colored chairs, between them a glass table with a vase of white tea roses. Jo slumped into a nearby chair, fiddling with her phone.

Meg followed Edith to the first rack of dresses.

"Do you have a specific silhouette in mind?" the woman asked her.

"Yes, I'm thinking A-line."

Edith nodded in approval.

"Meg, don't be too minimal," said Meryl. "You have every other occasion to dress understated. This is your wedding dress."

"Mom, please. I know what I'm looking for."

The assistant appeared with Jo's latte and a crystal tumbler filled with vodka for Rose. She handed Meryl a glass of champagne. "Just in case," she said.

Meryl gulped it.

Meg and Edith disappeared into another room, with promises to return as soon as she had her "top candidates."

"Cheers," said Rose.

"Mother, really. I wish you wouldn't."

"How about this: When we come for Amy's dress, I won't need a drink."

"We won't be shopping for Amy's dress. Andy's father is designing one for her."

"See! You marry a nice Jewish boy, and you get a tailor in the family."

"Ha! Good one, Gran," laughed Jo. "I need to go find someplace to charge my phone."

"Don't wander off too far," Meryl said. "I want you to see Meg in the dress when she comes out." She turned back to her mother. "He's not a tailor, Mother. He's one of the biggest fashion designers in the world."

"And yet he's still got time to make his future daughter-in-law's dress. A mensch!"

"Okay, Mother. Please don't talk like that around the girls. It's divisive."

"You're being sensitive. Probably because of your fighting with that husband of yours. Woke me up out of a sound sleep."

Meryl looked at her, surprised. "We weren't fighting. It was just a . . . discussion."

Rose nodded knowingly. "Wouldn't be the first marriage to end just as a child is getting married."

"No one's marriage is ending, Mother. Sorry to disappoint you."

• • •

Jeffrey Bruce called Amy into his office.

What did he want? Had Stella said something about Marcus and her? God, Stella would probably love the opportunity to knock her down a few pegs. Or knock her out entirely. And Amy had handed it to her! What had she been thinking?

She felt like she was walking down a gangplank.

But really, what could Stella have said? That they were flirting? Had they been flirting at the bar? She couldn't remember now—anything that had happened before the roof at Rupert's town house was a blur. But everything that happened after was etched like a deep, raw, but delicious scratch down her back.

The way Marcus had looked at her afterwards. His eyes, a smoldering—yes, a smoldering and stormy blue, locked on to hers. He kissed her mouth. "I really wanted you," he said. "I wish I could have tasted you."

Amy's stomach had flipped. Who talked like that? In all their years together, Andy had never said anything like that to her. And never would.

She hadn't slept more than a few hours a night since. She was a walking zombie, fueled only by her guilt and her fear of somehow getting busted.

The worst part—the worst part by far—was that she couldn't stop thinking about Marcus. She wanted to have sex with Andy to press reboot on her body, but she was also afraid that he would somehow sense that another man had been inside her. It seemed impossible that a physical encounter of that intensity had failed to leave a trace.

Her biggest fear, though, was that she would think of Marcus when she was making love with Andy. It was one thing to occasionally find her thoughts drifting to the guy from Spain. That was so long ago, it felt like a dream. And it hadn't been cheating. But this—this was wrong in so many ways. She was engaged. She was in love.

She was standing in front of her future father-in-law.

"Amy! Come in, come in—close the door behind you."

Jeffrey Bruce was, if not classically handsome, a distinguished-looking man with salt-and-pepper hair, a perennial tan, and of course, the most impeccable clothes. He wasn't a big suit-and-tie guy, but even in jeans and a button-down, he looked tailored and regal. He was also warm and informal, and Amy wondered if, even now—as he was potentially about to fire her from her job, from her engagement—he couldn't help being congenial.

"Thanks," she said, for what she didn't know. He had summoned her, and she had appeared.

"How are things on the fourth floor?" he asked, and for a moment she felt a rush of relief. He wouldn't be making small talk if she were busted. Would he?

"Great. Everything's great," she said.

He gestured for her to take the seat in front of him. He perched on the edge of his desk, arms folded, just a few feet in front of her. "That's good to hear. But you know, I didn't call you in here to talk shop."

"You didn't? Okay . . ."

She would deny it. There was no proof. Stella could say she saw this or that, but whom was Jeffrey going to believe—his future daughter-in-law or a jealous staffer? It totally burned Stella's ass that she couldn't completely pull rank on Amy. That's all this was about.

"We have some dresses to talk about, don't we?" he said with a smile.

"Dresses?" The relief almost brought tears to her eyes.

"Why do you look so surprised? Ah, a girl after my own heart. It's hard to think about yourself when there's so much going on at work, I know. But yes, my dear, we need to get started on your wedding gown. But the more pressing issue is the dress for your sister's engagement party. Why didn't you tell me about it?"

"I . . . uh . . . I didn't think about it."

"Andy thought you were being shy. Didn't want to ask too much. But, Amy, I meant what I said about you being our brand ambassador. If it's not too presumptuous of me, I'd like to dress you for any public appearance. There's no better ad for our clothes than you, the woman who is living the lifestyle. Don't you agree?"

Amy felt herself shaking. She held her arms in front of her chest, squeezing tight. *Keep it together.*

"Yes. Of course! I'm honored, Jeffrey."

"Dad."

"Dad."

I'm such an idiot! What is wrong with me? How could I do something so stupid and risk everything?

"I'm not going to have time to design you something custom for the engagement party. But I want you to head down to the showroom today and pick something out. I'm going to need at least two weeks to have it altered properly. Fit is everything, right?"

"Right."

"Excellent." He slapped his palms on his thighs and smiled as if something complicated had just been solved. "And Eileen is going to call your parents this week to have them to Stonehill one weekend soon. I want them to get the lay of the land, feel at home with us having the wedding there."

"Sounds great. Thanks so much. For everything." She found herself tearing up. The guilt was throbbing, unbearable.

Mistaking her tears for a rush of happiness, Jeffrey embraced her. "It's going to be a great year," he said. "All good things."

She stifled a sob, a loud one that would surely have given away the fact that her crying was anguish and not joy. Embraced by her fiancé's father, in the majestic office of his world-famous design company, she felt like a ten-year-old; all she wanted in that moment was her mother.

Meryl, Jo, and Rose moved to a low couch in front of a mirrored wall. At the end of the hall, Meg was busy in the dressing room.

"Shouldn't you be in there with her?" Rose asked.

"I don't know, Mother. I haven't done this before. As you recall, I did my dress shopping alone."

"Yes, well, you were quite good at making decisions for yourself, by yourself, everyone else's opinion be damned."

Meryl felt Jo's curious eyes on her, and could only imagine the questions that would come later. That was fine. It was time to let go of the tall tale of her nuptials. Now the girls could create their own fantasy weddings. Maybe theirs would actually come true.

"Excuse me, Mrs. Becker? Your daughter is here."

The three of them turned—and sure enough, there was Amy, wearing oversized black sunglasses, a navy blue Jeffrey Bruce trench coat, with her brown hair loose and windblown. She looked self-conscious, as if she were stepping into a play already mid-scene.

"Amy! You came after all."

"Yeah. I wasn't so busy at the office as I thought I'd be."

"Come sit next to your grandma," Rose said. There was no space for Amy on the couch, so Meryl moved to a side chair. Rose, flanked by Amy and Jo, had a rare smile on her face. "Now, wouldn't this make a nice picture?"

"Totally. Let's do it, Gran. Selfie time." Jo whipped out her phone and held it out arm's length in front of them, snapping the shot.

Rose bent forward and examined the phone. "What good is it on that device? You can't frame it; you can't put it in an album. You lose your phone and that's it. Gone."

"I can download it and print it," said Jo.

"But no one ever does."

And just like that, her mother went from sounding clueless to speaking the truth. It was the thing about her that was so infuriating.

The dressing room door clicked open.

Meryl gasped.

Meg walked toward them, so slowly and with such poise and grace, it was as if she were walking down the aisle. The ivory dress had a bateau neck and long sleeves, and was head-to-toe duchesse lace with a magnificent A-line skirt.

"The skirt is all hand-appliqué," said Edith.

"What do you think?" Meg asked quietly, turning to face herself in the floor-to-ceiling mirror.

"Oh, honey. It's perfection." Meryl felt her eyes tearing.

"Well, you can't beat that," Rose said to Amy.

Meryl turned to shoot her a warning look, but her mother was oblivious.

"Yeah, well, I'm not Kate Middleton. And neither is she, hate to break it to everyone," said Amy.

"I would normally show this with a waterfall veil, but she could definitely pull off a cathedral if she wants to commit to it," said Edith.

Meg, eyes shining, turned to Meryl. "I think this is it," she said, almost a whisper.

"But it's only the first one," Meryl said, though she couldn't imagine anything more beautiful.

"I know. But this is it."

"God, Meg—it makes *me* want to get married," said Jo.

"You must have some budget," Rose said, looking at the price tag.

Meg looked momentarily stricken. "You don't have to pay for this," she said to Meryl.

"I want to! Mother, please," said Meryl. She would figure it out. She would buy her daughter her wedding dress.

"It's truly stunning on you," said Edith. "Ordinarily, I encourage brides to try on a few gowns, at least for a point of comparison. But honestly . . . you shouldn't even bother."

"Yeah," said Amy. "Why bother?"

Outside, the bright, wide-open street felt jarring to Meryl after the cocoon of the bridal salon. The shopping had taken another hour after the wedding dress selection. Meg had been much less decisive when it came to the cocktail dress for the engagement dinner in Philadelphia. Apparently, Tippy had told her that there would be photographers from the *Main Line Times* and *Philadelphia* magazine, and so she had to be sure to wear something "appropriate and on the conservative side."

"Don't I always dress that way?" Meg asked, and Meryl had agreed that, yes, of course she did. Still, Tippy's comment somehow made Meg second-guess her own judgment as she perused the Monique Lhuillier cocktail dresses.

"Maybe we should have invited Leigh Beauford," she had said. Meryl chose to ignore that, while Jo, getting restless at that point, had perked up suddenly with, "Really? Are you guys using her?"

After much debate, Meg had finally chosen a rose-colored lace dress with a boat neckline, elbow sleeves, and a fitted bodice. The hem hit above her knee, but the overall effect was demure and absolutely lovely.

When the momentous shopping expedition was finished, Meryl wasn't yet ready to separate from the girls. "Let's all get scones at Alice's Tea Cup," she said.

"I have to catch a train," Meg said.

"And I need to get back to the office," said Amy.

"I'll go with you, Mom," said Jo. "Nothing better to do."

But before Meryl could respond, she was silenced by a sudden flash of light. And then, another one.

"Meg, over here!" someone called.

"Oh my God—paparazzi," said Meg.

"What?" Meryl asked. The word didn't sink in, it was so outrageous.

"Hey—other wedding sister. Over here."

Amy stepped forward, smiling, and Meg pulled her by the arm back to Monique Lhuillier.

Meryl looked up the street, hoping for a cab. No luck.

"Mother, back inside," Meg said, ringing the bell to the salon.

Edith opened the door and ushered them in, locking it behind them and closing the shade.

"How did they even know I was here?" Meg asked, looking stricken.

"Did you hear what they called us?" Amy said. "The wedding sisters. Isn't that great! We're like Kimye. Or Brangelina."

"This is not funny, Amy," Meg said. "This is not okay."

"Sweetheart, calm down. You're marrying into a very prominent family. It comes with the territory." Meryl tried to seem casual, to act like it was no big deal. But deep down, it was thrilling. It was one thing to be excited about her daughter getting married. But to think that the larger world of New York—maybe the entire country—was interested?

Scott was right. There was something there—something big. Maybe the idea of a reality show wasn't so crazy after all. Maybe the answer to their money problems was right there, staring her in the face.

"You lie down with dogs, you wake up with fleas," said Rose.

The four of them stood silent, peering out the window.

Jo had to admit, a part of her had been wondering if the Chanel boots woman, aka the Wedding Planner, would be at the bridal salon. Not just wondering, but on some level, hoping. This was the sort of weakness she just couldn't tolerate in herself. How could her heart, virtually in pieces over Caroline, still have the strength to want, to yearn, for the same thing that had gotten her into this horrible misery in the first place?

Maybe the bridal salon itself had inspired such whimsy. There was something about being surrounded by tulle and silk organza and chilled champagne that could make even the most practical woman lose her senses. It wasn't just that she was happy for her sister; there was a palpable giddiness in the air. Even her grandma, who notoriously didn't have a nice thing to say about much of anything, couldn't help but smile at the sight of Meg in head-to-toe lace, so beautiful and luminous, it confirmed what Jo had always thought for as long as she could remember: Meg was the special one.

All of it should have made her miss Caroline more, but instead the dress shopping helped her feel removed from her own misery. Maybe this bridesmaid gig wouldn't be so bad after all.

She was so caught up in the spirit of the afternoon—a spirit that wasn't even diminished by the crazy onslaught of photographers trying to get pictures of Meg and Amy—she asked Toby to meet her at Ocean Grill for a drink.

The seafood restaurant Ocean Grill, on Columbus and Seventy-eighth Street, was the place her parents had always taken them to celebrate excellent report cards and birthdays. Jo loved the towers of seafood on shaved ice, the perfectly chilled shrimp, the "lobster cocktail." It was the first place she'd tried sushi, and when she graduated high school, the first place her parents let her drink a glass of champagne. It wasn't the trendiest place in town, but to Jo it was synonymous with happy times. And she wanted to feel happy, to continue the good vibes of the afternoon.

"This is old-school," Toby said, bending down to kiss her on the mouth. She had a table near the front windows in the barroom. He sat next to her, sweeping his hair away from his eyes in that way he had. She felt a fondness for him, a rush of gratitude that she had such a best friend.

"I know. I love it."

"You look gorgeous. And happy! I take it the dress shopping wasn't such a nightmare after all?"

"No," she said. "It was actually kind of great. The craziest thing was that when we came out, there were all these photographers trying to get pictures of my sisters."

"Why?"

Jo shrugged. "I don't know. Their fiancés have shitloads of money. You know how things are."

"I have shitloads of money. No one's taking pictures of you."

"I'm not your fiancée."

"That can be fixed," he said.

"Okay, stop. You're weirding me out, and I'm not going to be able to ask you what I want to ask you."

"I'm intrigued! Don't let my witty banter stop you."

"That was witty banter?"

"Don't stall. Spill it."

She took a deep breath. "Okay. Do you want to come with me to Meg's engagement dinner?"

"You mean, as your date?"

"Toby."

"What? I need clarification here."

"As my friend."

"Jo, as your friend—who is currently living with you and occasionally having earth-shattering sex with you—I would be delighted to accompany you to your sister's engagement dinner."

"Okay, now I regret asking you."

He smiled and cocked his head—looking adorable, she had to admit. "You won't regret it for a minute. I promise."

Six
Months
Until the
Wedding

Six

Months

Until the

Wedding

fourteen

The engagement party weekend was tightly scheduled with an hour-to-hour agenda that was planned down to the toasts at the Friday night dinner and the Saturday brunch. The toasts brought the first speed bump: Tippy had a special something in mind for the two grandmothers: Reed's mother, Henriette, and Rose.

"My mother won't be able to make it," Meryl told her. "She really feels bad about it, but she needs her rest right now."

What Rose had actually said? "Step foot in that club? Not if you rolled me in my casket."

"Is she unwell?" Tippy asked.

"She's fine." Meryl knew she should have lied—said her mother was sick. But she felt superstitious saying something like that when it wasn't true—as if karma would make it come true somehow. (This illogical thinking was, ironically, courtesy of her mother, who wouldn't speak of Poland yet never met a European superstition she didn't like.)

"I don't understand," Tippy said.

Welcome to the family, Meryl thought.

It was a two-hour drive to the suburb of Philadelphia where the

Campions lived and where the party would take place at their country club. Meryl figured she and Hugh would have a few hours to relax at the Marriott before they were due at the club at six thirty. Jo and Amy were driving separately, and Meg was staying at the Campion house.

"I see you're part of the Campion party room block," noted the woman at the check-in desk.

"Yes, that's right."

Hugh's phone rang. He took the call, walking away.

The receptionist handed her a shiny, black paper gift bag. Looking behind the front desk, Meryl noted a half dozen others lined up, the silver tissue paper peeking out of each one in exactly the same way.

The bag, a thoughtful touch, made her anxious. It was the type of detail she would have to keep in mind for the wedding.

"Enjoy your stay," said the receptionist.

Meryl looked around for Hugh and found him standing off to the side in the hotel's small gift shop. He was on his phone, deep in conversation. She gestured to him but he turned his back to her.

She sighed and sat down to wait on a couch, next to a tray of Philadelphia soft pretzels. Meg had told her many times about the "ridiculously good" Philly pretzels.

Meryl took a bite. Softy, doughy, with just the right amount of rock salt. It was worth the calories, she told herself. And all the more incentive to get Hugh on the dance floor that night—burn off some calories. Finally, she felt relaxed.

Hugh, finished with his call, cut through the lobby toward her.

She stood, brushing the salt off her jeans.

He gestured toward the elevators.

"Mrs. Becker?"

Meryl turned at the sound of her name.

"Hi, Mrs. Becker. It's Leigh. Leigh Beauford—the wedding planner?"

Meryl felt her smile falter. "Hi, Leigh. I guess you're . . . here for the party?"

A very beautiful woman, Meryl noticed for the first time fully. How had she not seen that before?

Leigh reached into a large canvas bag slung over her shoulder and brought out a bottle of wine. She handed it to her. Meryl looked at her quizzically.

"I'm running a little late. They should be in everyone's rooms."

Meryl looked at the bottle in her hands, as if it held the answer to something.

"Have a great time tonight. The menu is fantastic." Leigh smiled and headed for the front desk.

"Who was that?" Hugh said.

"The wedding planner."

"I thought you said no to the wedding planner."

"I did."

"Well, she seems pleasant enough."

"That's not the point," said Meryl. "Who were you on the phone with?"

"Long story. Let's get settled in."

Their room was on the fourth floor. Meryl pulled back the heavy, gold brocade curtains. The view wasn't much: the hotel's circular drive and, across the street, the WaWa convenience store. Still, there was always something romantic about being in a hotel room, and she felt a surge of optimism. Maybe just being out of New York would be the shift she and Hugh needed to reconnect. After all, they were the parents of the bride. This was special. One of the rewards of making it through three decades of marriage was being together on a weekend like this.

She sat on the edge of the bed, watching Hugh unpack. He was still so handsome—barely changed since she first saw him at the front of the lecture hall all those years ago. His hair, sandy blond, now gray. Still thick, still cut in that shaggy way that was slightly bohemian and suggested someone who would never wear a suit to work. His six-foot-three frame still lean, his clothes always classic and so virtually indistinguishable from the khakis and button downs and V-neck sweaters he'd worn in grad school. Meryl imagined standing up behind him, pressing her body against his. It had been months since they'd had sex, and if she remembered correctly, that had been a perfunctory, "eleven o'clock news, mostly dressed in pajamas" event.

Sex was always better in a hotel room. She felt like a different person—or a least a better version of herself. In a hotel room, she was twenty-five again.

Meryl glanced at her own still-packed suitcase. She wished she'd thought to bring nice underwear. Maybe she should have bought something special for the weekend away. There was that store on Columbus, Only Hearts, full of pretty things without being off-putting like the windows of La Perla or Kiki de Montparnasse. Lately all the windows looked like the mannequins were acting out a scene from *Fifty Shades of Grey*.

Or maybe she could just take off her clothes and forget about the underwear altogether.

Hugh turned around and smiled at her. Was he thinking the same thing she was thinking?

He sat next to her on the bed. She'd probably have to make the first move—that's how it had been lately. For years, really. But today, that was fine with her. She stroked his arm, and he leaned forward and kissed her.

"We're going to have a good weekend," he said.

"I know."

"So I don't want what I'm about to tell you to spoil it."

She pulled back. "What?"

"Harrison called," Hugh said. "They're letting me go."

"Letting you go back to work?"

"I'm fired, Meryl. I'm done at Yardley."

She shook her head. "They can't do that."

"It's a private institution. They can do whatever they want."

She stood up and paced, pressing her fingertips into her temples as if exerting hard pressure would make the information feel different as it entered her brain.

"If they fire you, how are you going to find another teaching job? You won't have a recommendation. You won't even have unemployment!"

"Well, I've given this some thought. I don't know if I'm going to try to find another teaching job."

"What? Why not? What are you going to do?"

Hugh looked sheepish. And then she knew.

"I'm thinking now's the time to finally finish the book."

The book. The book that had been languishing for twenty-five years and could take another ten years to finish for all she knew. And what were they going to do for income in the meantime?

"Is that really practical?" she asked, trying to keep calm.

"In the long term, I think it's important. For me—for both of us. And in the short term, we just have to cut back and maybe you pick up a little more work."

As if she wasn't trying.

"Cut back? We have two weddings to plan."

"Well, the girls are going to have to manage their expectations a bit."

"What does that mean?"

"If you don't want to give in and concede that maybe the Campions and Bruces should contribute to the weddings—"

"It's not about them contributing, it's about them taking over. I want to plan our daughters' weddings. I want to plan and throw them—with you. Can you please try to understand that?"

"I do understand," Hugh said. "But you have to meet me halfway, Meryl. Even then, we can only do what we can do. And I think the best way to stretch our budget is to throw a double wedding."

"A double . . . What? No. Hugh, that's out of the question. Amy has felt overshadowed by Meg her entire life. And Meg has always resented how competitive Amy gets. The last thing they will want is a joint wedding. They each need their own special days. And what would our in-laws think?"

"They'll think the truth: that we don't have two hundred grand to throw away."

"Goddamn it, Hugh! Why couldn't you have waited until after the party tonight to tell me this?"

"You're my wife. I needed to tell you the truth."

"Do me a favor—don't go telling anyone else the 'truth.' We don't need the entire engagement party to know you've been fired."

"Meryl, I need you to be supportive. This isn't the worst thing in the world. It's a change I'm ready for. I didn't expect it; I didn't necessarily want it. But it's here, and I'm not going to act like this is a punishment. I'm going to see it as an opportunity."

"An opportunity," she said dully.

"Yes."

Meryl looked at her husband, and in that moment, hated him.

Philadelphia Racquet and Hunt was the oldest private club in the country. Dating back to 1854, it was founded by a group of English men, students at the University of Pennsylvania, who wanted a place to play cricket.

Meryl learned this during Tippy's guided tour.

"The original nine-hole course was built in 1895 by Willie Tucker—he also did St. Andrew's Golf Club and Sand Point Country Club."

With a half hour to go before the guests were due to arrive for dinner, Meryl had asked Tippy to show her the room that would hold the wedding reception. This had launched a twenty-minute tour of the club that culminated in the grand ballroom.

Meryl made no attempt to hide her awe.

"This is absolutely stunning," she said. The room could easily accommodate five hundred people. The floor was marble, with a distinct dance space in the center of the room. The ceilings held half a dozen chandeliers, and the massive windows overlooked a lake and the lush green golf course. How they kept the grass that color in the fall was beyond her, but she could only imagine the vista in the heart of springtime.

"That entire section of the grounds will be flowers," Tippy said, taking Meryl's arm and steering her to another corner of the room. "I'm hoping you can coordinate the floral arrangement with the exterior garden."

"Oh, okay. That might work."

"Visual cohesion is so important. We can discuss it with Leigh," Tippy said.

After the debacle the day of the gift registry, when Meryl had left Leigh Beauford with Meg to get some things done, she'd hoped that would be enough involvement to mollify Tippy. She hadn't heard from her since, and she thought maybe that was that.

Apparently not.

But now wasn't the time to get into it, she knew. Although, now wasn't really time for Tippy to be dictating the floral scheme either, but maybe this entire weekend was going to be one long pitch for how she wanted things done.

"Is your husband here yet?" Meryl asked, deflecting. "I would love to meet him before everyone else gets here." Unbelievably, they still had yet to meet—or even speak to—Reed Campion. He was flying in from Harrisburg, but she thought for sure he'd be at the venue by now.

"No, not yet! I'm sorry. It's been so hectic lately, and unfortunately, it's only going to get worse from here. That's why the timing of this engagement was so important. If anything, I wish Stowe had gotten it out of the way sooner—or waited a few years."

Meryl tried to hide her irritation. "Yes, well, you can't control these things."

"Oh, heavens no. But at least having the wedding here, we can keep a close eye on things. Do it the right way."

Suddenly, the massive ballroom felt like it was closing in on her. "I think we should get back to the dining room," Meryl said.

Cutter Campion, Stowe's younger brother, called out to them from the hall. "Father's arrived. Are you almost done in there?"

"Oh yes," Tippy said, her face lighting up. "Reed is here!"

Meg pulled her dress out of the closet. Tippy had vetoed the one she'd bought at Monique Lhuillier. It was too short. "The photographs are going to run in a lot of places, dear. We have to make sure you look right. It reflects on Reed, you know. It's not personal."

Meg, of course, thought there was nothing more personal than her choice of what dress to wear at her engagement dinner. But Stowe had backed his mother on that one. "She's not getting involved in the wedding planning or any of that. Just humor her for one night, okay? For me?"

Tippy had shown up at their town house two weeks ago with a Carolina Herrera dress in hand. It had put Meg in a terribly awkward position. She didn't dislike the dress. It was beautiful, a floor-length sheath of lilac silk—that wasn't the issue. But she couldn't separate the dress from the politics surrounding it.

Focus on what's important, she told herself. She looked at Stowe, and as always, if she let herself give in to it, if she pushed out all the other noise, her love for him overwhelmed her. She knew what she needed, what would get her in the right frame of mind for the night.

She crossed the room and locked the door. Stowe, sitting on the bed, typing on his phone, didn't notice what she was doing until she was beside him, topless. He looked up and after a moment of confusion, smiled the wide, dimpled smile that had leveled her that first night in Los Angeles.

"God, you're beautiful," he said, tossing aside the phone. He took her face in his hands, kissing her deeply. She heard herself give a tiny moan. The way he made her feel had not ebbed one bit since the beginning. She wanted him more, loved him more, every day. That's why she could say yes to marrying him—her faith that it would continue that way.

He pressed her back, moving on top of her. She fumbled with his belt buckle and the button on his jeans until she found her way to him.

"I love you," he breathed when he was inside her. She couldn't speak, and instead clutched him harder, kissing his neck and letting her body do all the talking.

Afterwards, in his arms, she said, "I wish we could spend the whole night just like this."

"That would disappoint a few people."

"I know," she said wistfully. "I wish it was our wedding night. Then we'd be on our honeymoon tomorrow."

"Soon enough," he said, kissing her and heading for the shower.

Not soon enough for me.

fifteen

When Jo had read "dinner and dancing" on the invitation, she'd thought it meant music people could actually, you know, dance to. But the band—and really, it was more like an orchestra—was not producing anything a person under the age of fifty could move to. If she had known she'd be stuck in her seat all night, she wouldn't have even bothered dragging Toby along. But he didn't seem to mind.

There were eight other people at their table, including Amy and Andy and some of Stowe's friends from Harvard. They were all interesting in their own way, and entirely delighted by Toby's stories of his royal family and itinerant education in boarding schools and summers on the Greek islands. They even found some friends in common, people in London whom Jo had never met nor even heard Toby mention before. They all assumed Toby and Jo were a couple, and she didn't bother to correct them. It was so much easier to play along on nights like this. Besides, with nothing to do but drink—she could barely eat, because of course, there was no vegetarian option on the menu—her buzz was getting epic and she would probably fuck Toby in the coatroom if he suggested it. Right now, she kind of hoped he did.

She looked at Amy, who seemed even more plastered than she was. Jo ducked behind Toby's back and tapped Amy's arm. "Want to get some air?"

Amy nodded.

Outside, it was utterly silent in a way they never experienced in New York City. The grounds seemed to unfold endlessly in front of them.

"I feel like we're in the middle of nowhere," said Jo.

"We are," said Amy, sitting down on the grass. "God, I'm wasted."

"Me too."

"So what's with you and Toby? Are you with him?"

"No. I mean, I'm crashing at his place for a while. And he's been great—a total lifesaver. But we're just friends."

"Is he aware of that?"

Jo sighed, looking up at the sky. Every star was visible; at least it seemed that way.

"Well . . . I kind of slept with him . . . a bunch."

"You should probably watch that." Amy lay down, flat on her back.

"I know. The thing is, I wish I could just be with him. It would make my life so much easier. Like, it could be perfect. I have this great, gorgeous friend who's in love with me—"

"He said that?"

Jo nodded. "And he's got all the money in the world and we could travel and collect art and just . . . well, anything. And idiot that I am, I'm hung up on my college girlfriend, who's planning her own wedding as we speak."

"Caroline's getting married?"

Jo nodded miserably. "Every time I think about it, I feel sick. I seriously never want to be in love again."

"Well, we can't help falling in love. Or lust," Amy said.

"Yeah, but at least you did it in a way that makes you happy."

"It's not that simple."

Jo grabbed Amy's hand, touching the enormous diamond ring. "It looks pretty fucking simple from where I'm sitting."

Then, to Jo's dismay, Amy started to cry.

"Oh my God, what's wrong? Did you guys have a fight?"

Amy shook her head. "No." Her voice broke.

"What, then?"

"You don't want to know."

"Fuck yeah, I do. Spill it."

Amy glanced behind her, back at the building where their families and friends were eating and drinking and dancing, a prelude to the year of celebrations ahead of them.

"I cheated on Andy."

Jo wished she were more surprised. Andy was a nice guy, but he didn't exactly seem like a dynamo in the sack. "What? When?"

"Two weeks ago. And this is the gross cliché part—it was a model from one of the commercial shoots."

"Didn't anyone ever tell you not to shit where you eat?"

"That's all you have to say to me?"

Jo put her arm around her. "I'm the youngest sister. I'm not supposed to have words of wisdom."

"Great."

"But I do."

Amy nodded. She was waiting.

"Figure out why you did it. Either it was just a one-time, mindless fuck—in which case, forget about it—these things happen. But if you've been restless, if on some level, you've been looking for it—you have to deal with it. Before you walk down the aisle."

"That's the thing—I don't know why I did it. I don't think I've been looking for it. But then, how could I cross a line like that? Now—of all times? We've been together for years and I never cheated, and a week after he puts a ring on my finger, I'm banging some stranger on a roof deck. In broad daylight!"

"This story just keeps getting better and better."

Amy put her head in her arms.

Jo rubbed her back. "It will be okay." But what she was really thinking was that this just proved it—love sucked. If even tunnel-vision Amy couldn't make it work with Andy, her perfect-on-paper guy, then who could? Was Meg really going to fit into that Republican, camera-ready family of Stowe's? Was Jo ever going to find another Caroline, and have that Caroline love her back just as much? The answer, on all counts, was probably no. So what was the point?

"We should get back," Amy said, standing up and brushing off her dress.

Jo stood up, and when she turned back toward the clubhouse, she saw Toby headed toward them.

"We've got company," Jo said. "You go on ahead—he probably needs some air too, poor guy. I dragged him into this circus."

"Jo, you have to swear—not a word."

Jo made a zipping motion over her mouth. Amy, apparently satisfied after a moment's hard stare, walked away. She heard her saying something to Toby in the distance, but couldn't make out what it was.

The alcohol in her system must have ebbed, because she suddenly realized how cold it was. She wrapped her arms around herself.

"It's cold out here!" Toby said.

"I know. Sorry I left you to the wolves. Let's head back inside."

He handed her his jacket. "Can we hang out here for just a few minutes?"

"Sure."

"I heard there's a lake somewhere around here. Want to try to find it?"

They walked slowly through the dark.

"I feel like I'm at summer camp," she giggled.

"You went to summer camp?"

"One summer. Between sixth and seventh grades. Totally a disaster. I was the weird New York City girl who couldn't canoe, toast a s'more, or braid lanyards."

"At least you got to go away. I spent every summer, three whole months, with my parents and sister, usually marooned on some remote island. By August, I felt like a character in *Lord of the Flies*."

They walked down a hill, and in the bright, nearly full moon, Toby spotted water in the distance.

"These shoes were not meant for this terrain," she said.

"Get on my back."

"What?"

"Piggyback. Come on—didn't you learn anything at that camp of yours?"

She laughed, took off her shoes, and jumped on his back. He hitched his hands under her legs and carried her the rest of the way to the lake.

"Voilà—your destination, madam," he said, easing her to the ground.

"The only problem is you're going to have to get me back up that hill," she laughed.

"You should know that I'm willing to carry you uphill, Jo," he said.

She couldn't take the intensity of his gaze, and turned to look out at the black water, a reflection of the moon cutting across it like a patch of ice.

"It's so quiet here," she whispered.

"I know. The perfect place to talk."

"Yeah."

She rubbed her hands together, and then put her them in the pockets of his jacket to warm up. She felt something hard and square. Frowning, she pulled it out.

"What's this?" she asked.

He shrugged. "Why don't you open it?"

Suddenly, Jo's heart began pounding, knowing what was going on before her head did. She pulled open the box to find a princess-cut diamond ring set in platinum. It was giant—stunning. It caught the moonlight, dazzling her.

Before she could process what was happening, Toby got down on one knee and took her hand. "Jo, I know you think I'm crazy. But you have to trust me on this: We belong together. I've known it since the first minute I saw you. I held on to that belief even when you were in love with someone else, and even when you told me you couldn't love a guy. But I think you do love me."

He was right. She did love him. She just wasn't in love with him. But since she wasn't ever planning on being in love again, wasn't just plain old love enough?

"Jo," he said. "Will you marry me?"

She hesitated only for a second, pushing thoughts of Caroline far from her mind. Caroline, who was marrying Drew Finley. "Yes. Yes, I will."

He slipped the ring on her finger.

• • •

The head table was closest to the dance floor. Tippy and Reed barely spent a moment in their seats. They danced song after song like it was their senior prom. The salad course (poached shrimp and watercress) had just been cleared, and Meryl and Hugh sat making small talk with the six other couples at the table.

"I absolutely adore the names of your daughters! Just like the characters in *Little Women*," said the woman to Meryl's right. Her name was Sailor Burke, and she and her husband had been friends with Reed since Harvard. She'd never been to Manhattan and found it fascinating that Meryl could raise children there.

"Yes," said Meryl. "Except there were four *Little Women*. We only have three." She looked pointedly at Hugh. "Isn't that right? No fourth child for us."

Hugh took the glass from her hand. "I think you should slow down on the wine, hon."

Meryl had never forgotten about that accidental pregnancy, but her remorse was kicked into overdrive when she was doubting herself. When one of her choices came into question, all the choices over the years fell on top of one another, a cascade of dominoes. But tonight, it was Hugh's choice that was her undoing—his choice to choose this time in his career to take a stand against the culture at Yardley, his choosing the needs of Janell South over the needs of his daughters, and his choosing to dismiss Meryl's intense need and desire to have the weddings.

And really, hadn't that first impossible choice been his all those years ago?

She didn't like to think of it that way. In the rosy glow of retrospect, she had always framed the decision to have an abortion as the choice "they" made. She had only been a sophomore in college. They'd been only dating two months.

She'd thought about it endlessly. It had most likely happened the night of the book party. That first moment of passion, the glorious but unprotected sex in his agent's house. They had not only started a relationship; they'd created a life too. As students of literature, as lovers of art and the life of the mind, they could not help but receive the news in a romantic frame of mind. Hugh had been the first one to speak practically about the matter.

"It's just bad timing," he'd said, as if this were an unfortunate scheduling glitch, a class that had to be dropped.

Meryl hadn't considered an abortion. She had envisioned herself going to class with a baby in one of those slings across her chest; she'd thought about how midnight feedings would barely throw her off her late-night cram sessions. She was in love with Hugh Becker; she knew that. And he loved her—even if they hadn't said it to each other yet.

But Hugh's words, said so calmly, so kindly, and with such gentle certainty, had the effect of waking her from a dream.

She never could have predicted how devastated she felt afterwards. The pregnancy was gone, and there was a gaping hole inside her that she feared would never be fixed. The bleeding felt like a punishment, like it would go on forever, though she knew it wasn't true.

Meryl needed time apart from Hugh, and for once, she really needed her mother. And that's when she made the second mistake, the one that would haunt her as doggedly as the abortion: her decision to confide in Rose.

Had Meryl expected her mother to take the news lightly? Of course not. But nothing could have prepared her for the tears, the howling, and the words Rose uttered as if Meryl had just shot her: "What have you done? Every life is precious. *Every life is precious.*"

Her mother stopped speaking to her. Meryl didn't have the strength to both shut out Hugh and lose her mother. She took baby steps back into her relationship with Rose. They healed. And eventually, her mother called her out of the blue as if nothing had happened. The abortion was never spoken of again. Her mother had forgiven her.

But she never forgave Hugh.

Meryl looked around for a waiter to get another glass of champagne.

Instead she found Polly, the attendant who had greeted her when she first arrived, making a beeline for her. "Mrs. Becker? Your mother is here. Waiting in the lobby."

"On the phone?" Meryl asked. She looked around for her evening bag, realizing she hadn't looked at her phone in hours and probably should have checked it at least once since sitting down to dinner.

"No, ma'am. Here in person."

"Your mother?" asked Hugh, frowning. She ignored him.

Meryl pushed back from the table, realizing only when she stood how very drunk she was. She followed Polly, weaving between tables, certain there was some sort of misunderstanding.

The lobby was several degrees cooler than the dining room, and Meryl shivered in her sleeveless dress. She looked around the room, still not truly expecting to see Rose.

"Mother?"

Rose stood across the way, peering at the ballroom where just hours earlier Tippy had given her a tour. Meryl was acutely aware of the old and the new colliding in a way she didn't find particularly comfortable.

"What are you doing here?"

"I'm here for Meg's little party."

"I mean how did you get here?"

"I dialed 555-7777."

The car service advertised during the late night television her mother watched to combat her insomnia.

"A car service? Mother, that must have cost a fortune."

"Not really. And I'm not paying rent this month, so I don't see how that's an issue."

"I told you, we still have to pay rent on that place until the lease expires."

"I'm not paying rent on a place that kicked me out. This is America."

"Okay, that's a whole different conversation. Why didn't you just come with us this morning?"

"I planned to boycott. I don't condone this, you know."

"Yes, I know. We all know."

"But I also am not going to let these people marginalize me from my granddaughter."

"Mother, no one is trying to marginalize you. You're the one creating the drama. You're so cynical about everything, and this should be a happy time—a celebration! Why do you have to ruin everything?" Meryl heard herself getting louder and louder, but couldn't control herself. It was like locking her keys in a car and then watching it slide down a hill.

"You've had too much to drink." Rose crossed her arms in front of her chest.

"That's all you have to say?"

"For now? Yes."

With little choice in the matter, Meryl led her mother into the dining room. Polly, the consummate professional, had already arranged a place setting next to Meryl. Hugh shot Meryl a look, and she shrugged. Sailor leaned over to introduce herself.

"That's quite a name," Rose said. "Why don't you switch seats with me?" she said to Meryl. "As long as I'm here, I might as well meet new people."

Fine, Meryl thought. Better to keep her occupied. She swapped seats so that she was positioned between her mother and Hugh. The slight change in angle gave her a view of Jo and Toby walking back into the dining room. Jo, catching Meryl's eye, gave an odd little wave. And she headed for the table with her date in tow.

Leave it to Jo to turn a man most women would fall in love with—just based on his looks and title alone—into a pal. A buddy. Her roommate. She'd thought, meeting him Jo's sophomore year at school, that surely they were a couple and Jo just wasn't ready to share it yet. It's not that she thought Jo's attraction to women was a phase—she'd suspected Jo was a lesbian years before she "came out." And just like everything Jo did, her announcement was full of passion and drama: instead of taking Meryl aside, or sitting Meryl and Hugh down together to share the fact that she had a girlfriend or to simply tell them that she was gay, Jo e-mailed them a YouTube video of her speaking from a megaphone from atop the NYU Gay/Lesbian/Trans float at the annual New York City LGBT Pride March. Meryl could barely remember what Jo had said in the video. But she remembered how beautiful she looked, tanned to a golden brown, her long hair waving behind her like a flag, her legs barely covered in tiny denim cut-offs, and a diaphanous peasant blouse. She was like a vision from the 1960s, a child of Woodstock. What really came across in the video had nothing to do with her sexuality, but with her free spirit—the very thing Meryl loved most about her, aside from her sweet and good heart.

"Hey, Gran," Jo said, leaning down and kissing Rose. "I thought you were blowing this off."

"Change of plans," said Rose.

"Well, I'm glad you're here," said Jo, turning to look behind her at Toby. "We have something to tell you guys."

"Something good, I hope," Meryl said.

"We're getting married, Mrs. Becker," said Toby.

"Ha. Very funny. Go on, you two—back to your table. It looks like Reed is about to make a toast. Hugh—do you have something prepared?" She should have thought of this before!

"As a matter of fact, I do. Something short."

Jo leaned down closer to her. "Mom, Toby's serious. He just asked me to marry him." She held out her left hand. And there it was—yet another engagement ring. The third to be bestowed on her daughters in six months.

Meryl's mouth dropped open, and she looked at Hugh. He shook his head ever so slightly, a denial, a rejection.

"May I have everyone's attention for a moment?"

Reed Campion stood in the center of the dance floor with the microphone. Slowly, unwillingly, Meryl took her eyes away from her husband's panicked face.

Meg leaned into Stowe, letting him guide her around the dance floor. She knew some friends who had taken ballroom dancing before their wedding, and clearly she could use some instruction, judging by the way she kept tripping over both feet. But Stowe, Sutton, and Cutter had already taken years of it as children. Who in that day and age sent three boys to ballroom dance lessons? Tippy Campion, apparently.

"I feel bad—I'm a weak partner," Meg said to him.

He pressed his cheek against hers. "You're the best partner. For life. Besides, I can lead. That's what marriage is, right? Sometimes you lead, sometimes you follow. We can't both lead all the time."

Except lately it felt like she was always the one doing the following. She hoped things would be a little more balanced after the wedding. Wedding planning was supposed to be stressful, right? That's why they made all those romantic comedies set around weddings. Drama!

But she didn't want drama. She just wanted to start their life together. She knew what her mother would say: Relax. Enjoy it. It's supposed to be fun. And tonight *was* fun. It was wonderful to have their friends and families meeting for the first time. Everyone seemed happy. And there, on the dance floor, with Stowe's arms around her, the music swelling around them, buoyant like waves, she could imagine how it would be the night of her wedding, when the vows had been taken, the cake eaten, most of the guests had gone. . . . It was almost like the first day of the rest of her life.

"Looks like Dad's going to say something," Stowe said, turning her so she could see Reed taking the mic from the band leader. And sure enough, when the song ended, Reed headed toward the center of the dance floor.

"I don't want to be standing here while he makes a toast—totally awkward," she said.

Stowe nodded and, taking her by the hand, led her to the side, where they grabbed two empty seats at a table filled with Tippy and Reed's friends from the club, including a couple who had seen Stowe grow up and still called him by the nickname "Camp" from his days on the Haverford prep soccer team.

"Friends, family—everyone who has been so wonderful as to join us here tonight. I'd like to take a moment to thank you for being with us to celebrate the engagement of our son, Stowe, to the lovely and talented Meg Becker. We couldn't be more delighted to have Meg joining our family. Where are they?" Reed cupped his hands over his eyes and looked around the room.

"Here, Dad!" Stowe called out.

"Stand up, you two."

Meg and Stowe dutifully got to their feet. She felt herself start to perspire.

"So first, a toast to Stowe and Meg: May your lives together be as blessed as Tippy's and my own have been."

He raised his champagne flute, and the room followed in a wave of raised glasses and murmurs. Someone handed Meg a glass and smiled. Stowe touched his glass to hers and kissed her. She vaguely heard the sound of applause, but mostly she was aware of the heat in the room, the tiny bit of champagne she spilled on Stowe's jacket, and as she looked across the room to where her parents were seated . . . her grandmother?

"My grandmother's here," she whispered to Stowe.

He looked in the direction of her gaze and tightened his arm around her shoulders. "See? Everything worked out just fine."

"We should go say hi."

But Reed apparently was not finished. When Stowe realized his father was still speaking, he squeezed Meg's hand to stay put.

"And while I have you all here, our closest friends and family members, I wanted to share some news so you hear it from me first—before the announcement hits *The New York Times*. I am officially throwing my hat into the ring as a candidate for the next President of the United States of America."

Meg felt her stomach drop—as if she were on a ride at an amusement park hurtling too fast toward some uncertain end.

She looked at Stowe, and he winked at her, his face full of an excitement she had never seen before.

Excitement, not surprise.

She realized she was the only one in the room not applauding. The entire room was on its feet. Tippy joined her husband in the middle of the dance floor and beckoned for Stowe, Meg, Sutton, and Cutter to join them.

And she knew, in no uncertain terms, making her way back on the dance floor to thunderous applause and the sound of the band playing "My Way," that her husband-to-be was a liar.

sixteen

On the surface, it was a normal Monday morning. Hugh with his tattered brown leather briefcase in hand—Meryl could almost pretend he was on his way to Yardley. But she knew that inside the briefcase, instead of student papers to grade and laptop filled with lesson plans, his computer was loaded up with his manuscript in progress.

"Meryl, don't make any commitments with wedding vendors until we finish this conversation," Hugh said, closing the door behind him. By "this conversation," he meant the two-hour argument they had driving home from Philly about Jo's engagement—the third wedding.

"I'd always known suicides were contagious," Hugh had said, "but not engagements."

"That's a terrible thing to say. These are our children."

"Meryl, it doesn't matter. We're throwing one party—*one*—and the girls can share it, or you can hand all this off to their rich future mothers-in-law and let them take care of it. Or we can find some way to space this out over time. But I'm not going to go bankrupt throwing three weddings this year."

It was difficult to argue with him. Two was challenging enough, but now three? She was fighting a losing battle, and her moral high ground had turned into a wet, slushy marsh.

The phone rang, jolting her from her thoughts.

"Hello?" she answered, opening up her DayMinder calendar on the kitchen counter. She still couldn't convert to a digital planner. If she couldn't see the day's tasks written in front of her in her own handwriting, she felt unmoored.

"I'm calling for Meryl Becker," a woman said.

"Speaking."

"Hi, Meryl—this is Jennifer Jedell from *New York* magazine. I'm working on a piece about your daughters' engagements."

"My daughters?"

"Yes. It's quite a story and apparently keeps getting better. A political powerhouse, fashion royalty, and actual royalty. I mean, bravo, if I do say so myself. We haven't seen a trio of New York women marry this well since the Miller sisters in the late '90s."

Meryl had no idea how to respond to that.

"Can you tell me anything about the wedding plans?" the woman asked.

"It's still early."

"Will all three weddings take place within this calendar year? Because frankly, that makes it an even more interesting story."

A little too interesting, Meryl thought.

"We really don't know yet."

"Okay, well, let me give you my contact info. It would be a huge help if you could keep me posted."

After the initial surprise wore off, the publicist in Meryl snapped to attention. "Whom are you speaking to for this article?"

"I can't share my sources. But if your daughters would like to cooperate, I would of course welcome their input."

"What did you say your name was again?" Meryl wrote her name and phone number down, and as soon as the call ended, Googled her. The search produced a dozen articles about socialites and celebrities, with snarky headlines like, PRETTY IN THE AGE OF SUCK CITY. The content of the articles had no less bite. She immediately called the girls and left them voice mail messages.

"It's Mom. If a reporter from *New York* magazine calls, don't speak to her. And call me later."

Will all three weddings take place within this calendar year? That makes it an even more interesting story.

How interesting was the story if the weddings all took place within the same *evening*?

Very interesting, Meryl would imagine. The publicist in her, dormant, underemployed, kicked into high gear. She felt a simmering sense of purpose. If she couldn't manage the weddings the way she wanted, she could at the very least manage the press.

Next she left a message for her friend Shelley Kale, the books editor at *People* magazine. Same with her contact at *Vanity Fair.*

Her phone rang. Scott.

"Hello?"

"Meryl—tell me that it's true."

"What's true?"

"Your youngest daughter just got engaged to a Danish lord?"

Meryl had to think for a minute. Toby *was* technically a lord, though she never thought of him that way. Another set of imposing in-laws-to-be. But the countess couldn't possibly be worse than Tippy.

"Yes, Jo got engaged this weekend."

"This is big. Huge. Meryl, I know you're hesitant about exploring a TV deal, but as your friend, I have to tell you: You're sitting on a gold mine here."

"There's just a lot going on—"

"I have to go to London for a week. Then I'll be in New York. We should really sit down and put together a game plan."

A game plan?

"I don't know—"

"I'll touch base soon. And, Meryl—have fun with it!"

Fun with the wedding planning. That was a novel idea.

The photos from the Milk Studios shoot came back phenomenal. At least, that's what Andy said.

Amy could barely look at them.

"You did a great job," he said to her. "I'm glad you went along."

"I really didn't have much to do with it."

"Why don't you ever want to take credit for anything?"

The *New York Post* was open on her desk, Page Six. "Is that your sister?" Andy said, peering over at it. Another article about the "wedding sisters," and another photo of Meg. This time, she was walking out of Monique Lhuillier, caught in motion, her sunglasses in one hand on her way to her face, but the shot happened first. It reminded her of that famous Ron Galella photo of Jackie Kennedy on the city street.

"Yeah. It's from the day she was dress shopping. They were waiting outside like wolves."

Andy leaned forward to read the short piece:

Here Come the Brides

Wedding sisters **Meg**, **Amy**, and **Jo Becker** will all be walking down the aisle in **Monique Lhuillier**. Youngest sister Jo just this weekend announced her engagement to Danish **Lord Tobias Hedegaard-Kruse**. Oldest Meg is marrying the son of Republican Senator (and presidential hopeful) **Reed Campion**, while middle sister Amy is hitching her wagon to the **Jeffrey Bruce** fashion empire. The wedding dates have not been set.

"You're not all wearing Monique Lhuillier," Andy said.

"Can your dad call someone? This is just obnoxious." Of course the paper used Meg's photo yet again. And what was with them saying she was "hitching her wagon"? What was that supposed to mean?

The bottom line was that no matter what they wrote or didn't write about her, she didn't want her engagement in the limelight—not today. It wasn't just the guilt that was eating at her. It was also the fact that she couldn't help but wonder if "the incident," as she'd come to think of cheating—signified something she couldn't ignore. Jo was right. Amy had to figure it out. But how?

"Gotta run to a meeting with Stella." He kissed her on the forehead and left her with a screen filled with images of Marcus. Her eyes gravitated to the shots in which he wore the white T-shirt and chocolate brown leather jacket. Moments before those were taken, he had been talking to her. And it was that brief conversation that pressed pause on her life as Andy Bruce's fiancée. For two minutes, she was just a girl talking to a gorgeous guy. And while she hadn't admitted it to herself in that moment, she had been flooded with hot, agonizing desire.

Amy closed the window of images and put her head in her hands. This was a mess and she was going to fix it. She was going to throw herself into wedding planning. That would keep her focused on the right thing, the important thing: Andy.

She texted her mother. *Come with me to look at invitations this week?* She needed coffee.

Amy headed to the elevator bank. There was a department assistant she could send to the Starbucks across the street, but she needed fresh air. Maybe she would stay away from any shoots until after the wedding. Just to be safe. She didn't know how she'd explain that to Jeffrey, but she was sure Stella wouldn't complain.

The first elevator made a ding and the doors slid open. She walked inside, looking at her phone. Her mother had responded to her text, *Later this week. And did you get my message about the New York magazine reporter?*

What *New York* magazine reporter?

"Amy!"

She looked up and the phone fell from her hand. Marcus bent down to retrieve it for her, and she bent down at the same time and they nearly collided.

"What are you doing here?" she said, taking the phone from him, trying not to look at his face. She was like Perseus trying to avoid Medusa. Or was that Athena trying to avoid Medusa?

"I have a meeting with Stella and Mr. Bruce. This is my agent, Karen."

Amy shook hands with the young woman, barely able to register her. It was all she could do to maintain some semblance of a normal, professional demeanor.

"This is Amy," Marcus said. "She was at the spring shoot."

"I guess the shots came out pretty damn well," Karen said.

"They did! We just got them in late Friday. I was away, so I just saw them this morning."

"They want to talk to me about expanding my relationship with the brand," Marcus said.

"What?"

He smiled and shrugged. "That's what they said."

The doors opened into the lobby.

"Who said?"

"Mr. Bruce and Stella. Your boss who was at the shoot?"

His agent's phone rang. She answered quickly and gave Marcus the "one sec" finger.

"Hey," Marcus said when Karen was out of earshot. "So great to run into you. Really."

Amy couldn't speak. All she could do was soak in his eyes, his lips, the perfect contours of his face. She felt herself leaning toward him, a plant in photosynthesis.

"I have to go," she said. He touched her arm. Her heart fluttered.

"You ran off before I could get your number last time." His phone was out, and he handed it to her. "Type it in for me, okay?"

She took it wordlessly, the screen swimming before her eyes, blurry and unreadable. She couldn't type—she couldn't think. "I don't know. . . ."

He took it back from her. "It's just ten digits, Amy." He smiled to show he was joking.

How was she going to know what this was all about? There was only one way.

She recited her phone number and then rushed out the revolving door.

Meg and Stowe did an awkward dance around each other that morning. Stowe made a point of bringing her coffee while she dressed and offering to stop by Whole Foods for groceries for dinner on his way home. But Meg kept her eyes glued to her phone, silently scrolling through news sites as she stood at the kitchen counter, eating a toasted bagel. The news of Reed's candidacy was everywhere, including Poliglot. Kevin had cobbled together an article based on secondhand sources.

He hadn't responded to her calls or e-mails all weekend.

Meg dropped her plate in the sink, dreading the office but unable to stand being around Stowe. She had every intention of maintaining the wall of silence that had stood between them since Reed's announcement Friday night—not an easy task, considering the entire weekend was a celebration of their engagement, culminating in brunch at his parents' for fifty people.

But then she got the Google Alert.

"You've got to be kidding me," she muttered, clicking the link to the headline reading HERE COME THE BRIDES. A photo of herself outside Monique Lhuillier filled her screen.

"What?" asked Stowe, jumping at any chance for a dialogue. The last words she'd spoken to him were "You lied to me," to which he'd replied, "I didn't know." To which she'd replied, "Bullshit."

Meg didn't answer, simply sliding her phone across the kitchen counter. He looked at it and said, "I guess we'd better get used to it. Soon, it won't just be the *Post*."

"Yeah, thanks for the news flash. I *do* work in the media, you know. If I still have my job, that is."

"Meg, please stop with this anger. I know you're frustrated. But I didn't lie to you. I didn't know he was declaring a run for the ticket. I mean, in politics nothing is out of the question. But I absolutely did not know."

It was nothing she hadn't heard all weekend. And what she hadn't been able to articulate through her hurt and fury was the one thing that he couldn't explain away:

"But you wouldn't have told me anyway."

He paused, then took her hands and pulled her in front of him. He forced her to look at him before he said, "Honestly? I don't know. It would have been tough for me, and maybe that's why my dad didn't put me in that position. He really likes you, Meg. He really likes *us*. I think he was protecting our relationship by not telling me."

"I wouldn't have leaked the news. Does he think I would do that? Does he think I couldn't handle being put in that position?"

"Babe, again, I don't think he wanted you to have to make that choice."

"Why couldn't he have just told me and let me work with the story? It would have been huge for me."

"It just would have looked like nepotism. It wouldn't have made you look like a great reporter. Just the opposite."

Meg froze. She hadn't thought of it that way. She was so twisted up inside over the idea that Stowe had lied to her, and that Reed had gone out of his way to keep a tremendous scoop from her, that she didn't think of it from the rational angles.

"Look, I know this is difficult for you. But there are going to be some conflicts of interest that come up over the next year, and we're going to have to learn to trust each other and deal with them. I love you. I will not lie to you. But at the same time, I want to protect you and I think my dad does, too. Please don't see this as you versus us. You're one of us, now. You're going to be my wife."

He kissed her, and she felt a flood of relief. She hated fighting with him. Not talking to him all weekend had left her feeling hollowed out inside. A part of her had wondered if she should call off the engagement, how messy it would be if she did. But she had told herself that once she ripped the Band-Aid off, she could focus more on work. Let Amy and Jo be the wedding sisters. One day, the wound would heal and this would all just be a painful memory.

She had woken up in the middle of the night sobbing. Stowe held her, but she only indulged in a moment's embrace and then pulled away. He lied to me, she told herself. He chose his parents over me, and he always will.

But hearing his words of reason, looking into his eyes, smelling his morning scent and the freshly laundered smell of his shirt and feeling the strength and warmth of his arms around her, she had to wonder if she'd overreacted.

"I'm sorry," she said. "I just need to know that it's you and me—not you and your parents with me as an afterthought."

"Why do you feel that way?"

She shrugged. "I don't know."

He kissed her, and she held him tight.

"It's going to be okay, Meg. You just have to trust me a little more."

She nodded. She had the urge to tell him how she was anxious about going into the office, that she felt like she'd failed. But she didn't want to make it seem like she was picking the fight again.

"I have to get to work," she said.

Stowe seemed slightly disappointed, as if he'd thought maybe they had time for makeup sex. And maybe they did. But she wasn't ready. It would have to wait for tonight, when she'd cleared the air with Kevin and figured out this new reality of being the future daughter-in-law of a maybe future president of the United States.

By the time Meg reached the Poliglot office, she was feeling better.

She slid her ID card through the metal reader, and the arm opened for her. She fell into a tide of people headed toward the elevator bank. Maybe she could even call Reed later to get a few words from him. Yes! Why hadn't she thought of that sooner? She didn't break the story—but she could supplement what they already had. It was more than any other reporter on the desk would get on their own.

Kevin was hovering near her office. Not technically waiting for her, but close enough. He followed her inside and closed the door.

"I was blindsided," she said.

"Becker. This isn't good."

"I hate being put in this position," she said.

"I don't blame you. I don't like it either. And unfortunately, Meg, this probably isn't the last time it's going to happen."

"What's that supposed to mean?"

"I mean, you're on staff here, your future father-in-law is running for president of the United States. Conflict of interest? I'd say yes."

"Kevin, please. I'll handle it, okay."

Silence.

"Meg, I think we need to talk about you stepping down."

Meg looked at him, mouth agape. "Down from what?"

"Your position here."

"What? Two weeks ago you were talking about a promotion."

"I guess I was being overly optimistic."

"You aren't serious."

"Let's be honest: You're no longer a neutral, outside observer."

"You didn't seem to mind that possibility when you asked me to break the news on Poliglot."

"But you didn't, did you?"

"So that's what this is? You're punishing me?"

He shook his head. "No, Meg. I'm not. I'm just stating the obvious. You're no longer a neutral third party to the ground you cover here. So it's best if you resign."

"That's not how it works, Kevin."

"Isn't it, though? What happened when Maria Shriver found herself married to the governor of California? She resigned from NBC, citing a conflict of interest."

"She was the first lady."

"He was just a governor. We're talking the White House, Meg. I'm sorry, but I have to do what's best for the site. I'd like you to be out of here by noon. And we'll tell everyone you're moving on for other opportunities. Sound good?"

Meg couldn't speak. She watched him walk out of her office.

Her first thought was to call Stowe, but his phone went straight to voice mail. She dialed his office line, and his secretary told her he was in meetings all day.

She felt completely ganged up on: by the Campions with their closed circle, their family secrets. By Stowe for keeping her out of that loop. By Kevin, who had turned on her.

Meg called the one person who was always on her side, and always would be. "Mom, I'm coming home for the night."

seventeen

It was a day Meryl had dreaded: packing up her mother's apartment. But at least, unexpectedly, she had reinforcements: both Hugh and Meg came along to help her.

Hugh began folding the unconstructed moving boxes into shape, while Meg unspooled the roll of Bubble Wrap.

Rose sat on the couch, resting back and closing her eyes.

"Mother, you really didn't have to be here. You could have just stayed at my apartment," Meryl said.

She wished her mother had just let her and Hugh—and, thanks to her surprise visit, Meg—do the packing on their own, but instead she had insisted on coming along.

"It's some extra time with Meg," Rose said. Meg's appearance yesterday had been a bonus for all of them. Though she suspected the visit was not so simple as Meg had made it out to be when she said breezily, "Things are quiet at work and it was just a spur-of-the-moment decision."

Meryl didn't push. She figured she'd talk to her during the packing up. And then her mother insisted on coming along. Always a private person, Rose no doubt hated the thought of Meryl and Hugh—especially Hugh—going through her things unsupervised.

"Let's get organized," said Rose.

Meryl and Hugh glanced at one another.

"We *are* organized, Mother," said Meryl.

"You two pack up the living room and kitchen, I'll do the bedroom," said Rose. "But first I'm just going to take a quick rest."

She closed her eyes again, pressing back into the cushions.

"Fine," said Meryl.

Meryl and Meg started in the kitchen. When Meryl had moved Rose into the apartment a decade earlier, she put the fine china and silver into storage. All they had to deal with were basic dishes, glasses, and mugs from Pottery Barn, serving trays and a few vases from Simon Pearce, and the Nespresso machine Meryl had bought her for her birthday five years ago.

"So what's really going on with Gran?" Meg asked quietly. "Is she sick? She seems competent enough to live here if she wants to stay independent."

Meryl glanced up from rolling a vase in Bubble Wrap. "You don't find some of the things she says slightly out of touch with reality?"

"Maybe. But that's just Gran. Hasn't she always been that way?"

"Oh, honey. I don't know. And I'd rather talk about what's really going on with you."

Meg, busy with a row of mugs, didn't look at her when she replied, "Mostly just work stuff." But then, haltingly at first and then tumbling in a rush of words and tears, Meg explained that she had lost her job and she feared that in a marriage to Stowe, she would lose *herself*. "I just couldn't go back to his house last night."

"*Your* house. It's your house too now, Meg."

Her daughter's shrug was exaggerated, like a child's.

"The few months leading up to a wedding are stressful for a lot of couples," Meryl said. "Sweetie, don't lose perspective. You love him. And he's a good man. And you'll find another job. It's probably time to make a move anyway. You've only worked at one company since college. Of course they take you for granted."

If Meg heard her, she gave no indication.

"Rose is asleep—out cold," Hugh commented, walking into the kitchen. "I'm going to start on the bedroom. We don't need to be here all day."

Meryl sighed. "Fine. She's not going to like it, but you're right—we should just keep things moving."

"Dad, it's great you were able to take off from work," Meg said.

Meryl and Hugh glanced at one another.

Before he could speak, Meryl said, "Your father has decided to take a leave of absence from Yardley."

"Really?" said Meg, her brow furrowing. "Is everything okay? Is it—are you taking sabbatical to finally finish the book?"

Again, Hugh looked at Meryl. She nodded ever so slightly.

"That's part of it," Hugh said, shifting uncomfortably. "Let's focus on the task at hand here and we can talk about all that later."

Meg's phone rang. She pressed it to voice mail. Meryl resisted the urge to ask who it was; the call left Meg so distracted, she drifted back to the living room.

"Let's get this over with," said Hugh.

Rose's bedroom was pristine, the austere, Shaker-style quilt pulled tight, the curtains closed, the nightstand empty. It was so neat and lifeless; it gave Meryl a pang, as if her mother had died. She shook the thought away and surveyed the room. There were two small closets, one on either side of the heavy wooden bureau holding the television set.

"So what's the game plan with this stuff?" said Hugh.

"I want to bring the bedding to our apartment so she feels at home, pack the clothes into garment boxes, and move anything else in the closet into storage." She paused. "She's going to kill us for going through her things."

"Please—she should be thanking us."

"Well, don't hold your breath."

Meryl stood in front of the open closet, her hands on her hips. Her mother's clothes hung neatly on the metal rack. Rose was not a fan of color, so the blouses were all white, cream, or black, and the skirts were black or gray or muted shades of moss green or slate. The dresses were all solid colors—no prints. Despite their limited palette, the clothes were all chic, timeless, and surprisingly expensive—silks, wools—labels from

Saks Fifth Avenue and Bergdorf and cashmere sweaters from Manrico on Madison.

"How bad does it look in there?" Hugh asked.

"Luckily, it's mostly clothes. But there are a few boxes in the back." There had been a time when her mother had slight hoarding tendencies, and Meryl suspected the boxes harbored the last of her "tchotchkes," as her mother called them.

In the very back of the closet was a stack of oil paintings, a few Meryl recognized as having hung in the old apartment.

"Hugh, look at these. Do you remember them from my parents' old place?"

"Meg loved that one—the Russian ballerinas. Maybe your mother will let her take one to her place in D.C. Help her make it more of her own place."

Meryl smiled. "Oh, Hugh, that's a wonderful idea."

"I'm going to get those garment bags. Left them in the living room."

At the bottom of the stack was a painting she'd never seen before. It was a blue and white water pitcher on a wooden table, a still life that seemed it might have been a copy of a classic work. She looked at the signature. *Roza Olszewski*. She didn't recognize the name.

Meryl turned it over, looking at the back of the canvas. A manila envelope was taped there, sealed with wide clear packing tape. She looked around for Hugh, but he was still in the other room.

She carefully peeled the tape away from the envelope, trying not to tear it but failing. Her heart pounded. She told herself she wasn't doing anything wrong, but the fact that she was about to break open the envelope to see what was inside made it impossible to pretend this was just a casual glance.

The envelope was packed thick with papers. She carefully withdrew the entire stack and set it on the floor beside her. She fanned it out and discovered photos among pencil sketches that were yellowed and curled with age. The subjects of the drawings—flowers, birds, trees—were so simple, they were clearly the work of a child. At the bottom, in the large awkward scrawl of a child, the name Roza Klasczko.

Other drawings, more sophisticated, were signed the same way. And then the photos: a girl of about eleven, with blond curls and a narrow face—much like Meg as a child—standing next to a dark-haired young boy. Her hand was on his shoulder. The children, sandwiched between a man and a brunette woman, stood outside a café in some European city. Poland?

More photos: the same girl with the woman and the boy, at a breakfast table, smiling and laughing. And then, a photo of the girl, now thirteen or fourteen, with another couple, blond and handsome but serious-faced, outside a farmhouse. And another of the teenaged girl with three smaller children, all blond and smiling. Behind them, a handmade sign on the wall, and on the table, a birthday cake.

Meryl, perspiring, quickly flipped through the photos until she saw a still older version of the girl, now with the woman Meryl recognized as her grandmother—her mother's mother, Rachel Weiss. Finally, a setting she recognized: her grandparents' old house in New Jersey.

Meryl's mind tensed like a muscle, the pieces of the puzzle forming before she fully computed that she was looking at a puzzle in the first place. Clearly, these were the first, the only, photos of her mother as a child she had ever seen. But who were the adults? Aunts and uncles? And the boy? Were these people a few of the many family members who did not leave Poland in time, never to be seen again? Of course, Meryl understood why Rose never talked about the country of her birth. Her parents left when she was seven, just before the Nazi invasion. But most of her family had not been so lucky.

But if her mother had left at seven, settling in New Jersey, shedding her Polish identity like a diseased skin, how could there be photos of her in Poland as a teenager?

"Meryl?"

She jumped, shoving what she could underneath the canvas. Hugh loomed above her, holding a stack of garment bags.

Those drawings. That unfamiliar name.

"Do you need help with the closet?" Hugh said.

It was just too much—all of it. Her mother, the weddings, Hugh and his job, the money, Meg fighting with Stowe . . .

"I can't finish this today," Meryl said, overwhelmed and near tears. She wanted to crawl into the nearest bed and throw the covers over her head.

"Okay, okay," said Hugh, leading her to the edge of the now unmade bed and pulling her close. "Don't get upset. It will get done. It will all get done."

The apartment would get packed, but what about everything else? Hugh had been right all along. There was no way to throw three weddings. Even if he'd had a job, it was way beyond their means. She should just forget about her stupid pride and let Tippy Campion take over. She was sure Eileen Bruce would be happy to help with Amy's wedding. And Jo—well, maybe she could wait awhile since her engagement seemed impulsive, to say the least.

She looked at the pile of paintings on the floor. In her hand, she still clutched some of the photos. "Hugh, look at these. I think this girl is my mother."

He flipped through the photos. "She looks like Meg."

"I have no idea who any of those other people are. And this is clearly not the U.S., even though she said she was here by that age."

He shuffled through the pictures again. "You're right. But why would she lie about that?"

Meryl took the photos and slipped them into her handbag. "I don't know."

Jo had never experienced someone sucking up to her so completely. And this wasn't some obsequious kid at school, or Amy trying to manipulate her into a favor, or even someone at work trying to get her to switch shifts. This was a real person, a professional, treating her like she was royalty.

Which, she almost was. Sort of.

The real estate agent steered her through the lobby of 56 Leonard Street. She was an attractive woman, probably around her mother's age—but so Botoxed, it was tough to say. She wore a lot of jewelry and carried a Chanel bag. Her name was Katherine Green, but she told them to call her Kat.

"As you can see, this building is as much a work of art as it is a home." She said this to both of them, but she looked at Jo. Toby had made it clear that when it came to apartment hunting, it was "whatever his fiancée wanted."

Toby's parents, the Lord and Lady Hedegaard-Kruse, had decided that since their son was engaged to be married, it was about time he had his own apartment. It was their engagement gift. The count and countess, traveling through Hong Kong, made no mention of when they might have time to meet their future daughter-in-law.

"We'll be lucky if they even make it to the wedding," Toby had informed her. She could see that he tried to make light of it, but there was an obvious undercurrent of hurt.

"Who did that sculpture outside?" asked Toby.

"The Indian artist Anish Kapoor," she said. "The tower itself was designed by Herzog and de Meuron."

Toby looked at Jo and they both shrugged.

"Sounds good to me," said Toby.

The building was sixty stories tall and designed with staggered units so the tenants' panoramic views were not obstructed by so much as an inch. The effect was that of a giant mah-jongg tower made of glass and steel.

She took them up a private elevator to the thirtieth floor. The elevator opened directly into the apartment, a massive space as light and open and airy as if she were standing suspended in the middle of the sky.

"As you can see, we have fourteen-foot windows, a custom-sculpted fireplace, and these kitchen islands are available in this trademarked piano shape."

She took them outside onto the wraparound deck.

Jo looked at Toby. This place was beyond. She thought of the tiny little dark space she'd shared with Caroline in Greenpoint. Who needed passion when you had these views?

"You absolutely *must* see the bathrooms. They are my favorite feature of these homes."

They followed Kat, the sound of her high heels echoing through the place.

She slid open a door, and Jo laughed in delight. Even the bathroom had floor-to-ceiling windows! The tub was a freestanding chalk white oval, deep as a small pool.

"These vanities are one of a kind, and while these marble tiles are designed to go with the space, you can also talk to them about retrofitting with tiles of your choice."

Toby turned a faucet on and off. Jo wanted to jump into the tub.

Could she really call this place home someday?

Kat led them back into the living room. "When you're ready, I'll take you to the roof. You would have a sky estuary with a seventy-five-foot infinity-edge lap pool."

"A lap pool," Jo repeated, stunned.

"Ms. Becker, Lord Hedegaard-Kruse, the amenities are truly the best you will find in the city—any city: fitness center and yoga studio, a library, private dining salon, a catering kitchen . . ."

Jo smiled and bit her lip. It sounded crazy to hear someone address Toby as "Lord."

"What do you think, Jo?" he asked, leaning against the piano-shaped island in the center of the sparkling, ultramodern, off-the-charts kitchen.

"I say when can we move in?"

eighteen

Meryl surveyed the dismantled living room. "We can finish tomorrow," she said.

"Tomorrow? Why not just get this over with?" asked Rose.

"Hugh has to get to the library, I'm hungry, and Meg has to get back to D.C. before rush hour."

"Everyone's abandoning the sinking ship," said Rose.

Ignoring her, Meryl suggested they at least grab lunch. Hugh passed on the idea, but Meg suggested Isabella's on Columbus.

Sitting in the signature wicker chairs by a table overlooking the street, Meryl tried to forget about the troubling photographs in her handbag.

"I'll have a Diet Coke," Meg told the waitress, a beautiful young woman, no doubt an aspiring actress. Meryl remembered reading recently that Jennifer Aniston had waited tables there just before she was cast on *Friends*.

"Vodka on the rocks," said Rose.

"Mother, it's the middle of the day," said Meryl. But then she gave in and ordered a glass of prosecco. She deserved a drink.

Hell, it would be easier if they were all a little tipsy.

Rose pushed her glasses higher on the bridge of her nose and turned to Meg. "So why aren't you at work? And don't give me any of that 'oh, it was just a spontaneous day off' crap."

Meg reached for her water glass, then sat back against her seat and tucked a lock of her gold hair behind her ear. She sighed. "I lost my job, Gran."

"You got fired! Meryl, did you know about this? She got fired! What for?"

"I wasn't fired. They just feel that . . . with Reed running for president, that I might have a conflict of interest down the line. That it might get in the way of my reporting."

Rose shook her head and made a *tsk-tsk* sound.

The waitress, mercifully, appeared with their drinks. No one spoke until Rose, after a few sips of her vodka, said, "You see? A woman is better off alone than with the wrong man."

"Mother!" said Meryl.

Rose shrugged. "If you don't teach them anything, Meryl, then you leave it to me. So, stop your crying."

"Oh, for God's sake."

"Gran, it's not Stowe's fault."

"Then why are you sitting here with us instead of in Washington with him?"

Good Lord, her mother had a way of cutting like a knife.

Meryl, realizing the lunch conversation was already off the rails, decided there was no sense delaying the inevitable.

"Mother, stop it. Meg, I'm actually glad you're here today so we can discuss something. But before I get into that, let me just say you'll find a new job—no doubt a better job. And then you'll look back and say it all happened for a reason and you're thankful it did. That's how life works. Isn't that right, Mother?"

"That's how life works in movies, certainly."

I give up.

"Thanks, Mom," said Meg. "I appreciate it. I know it will work out. And honestly, part of this is just me freaking out a little because I guess I didn't fully realize how much the Campions' high profile would affect my life. That's why I needed to come home—to kind of . . . regain my equilibrium." She reached across the table and squeezed Meryl's hand, as if reassuring her. "So what do you want to talk about?"

This was it. The point of no return.

"Meg, you know I'm so excited about planning this wedding. And the reason I was irritated by Tippy's insistence that I use the wedding planner is that I don't want someone else taking over."

"Yeah, I know. Believe me, I don't want that either. I was just trying to be diplomatic."

Meryl nodded. "The thing is, what I'm learning about wedding planning is that it's about choices. You can't get everything you want, so you prioritize. From my perspective, and tell me if I'm wrong here, having autonomy over this thing is a big priority."

"Definitely," agreed Meg.

Meryl took deep breath. "Okay. The challenge I'm having is that your father and I now have *three* weddings to plan. It's just not feasible financially—not without outside help."

She could see Meg struggling to maintain a neutral expression. "You want Tippy and Reed to pay for the wedding? I mean, they will. That's . . . it's not a problem."

"But what do *you* want, Meg?" Meryl asked, thinking of Hugh's admonishment—this isn't about you. As much as he'd failed to be a partner in this whole thing, on that point at least, he'd been right.

"I don't want this to be a burden on you and Dad."

"It's not a burden—you're our daughter! I've thought about this day since you were all little girls. Remember how you used to dress up as brides with your tissue paper veils?"

Meg laughed. "Yeah. Jo always refused to wear a dress."

"And Amy always complained you took the better dress."

"I sense a 'but' coming in all of this," said Rose.

Meryl could throttle her. Really.

She turned to Meg. "Your father and I can pay for a wedding. One wedding. For the three of you."

"Okay. What does that mean?"

"A triple wedding! I like this idea!" said Rose.

"You do?" said Meryl.

"Wait—hold up: You mean Amy, Jo, and I all get married together?"

"Essentially. Yes."

"You realize Amy will *never* agree to that. She'd rather have the Bruces do her wedding."

"Let me worry about Amy. I'm asking you."

Meg nodded, thinking. "If it's a choice between you throwing my wedding along with my sisters, or having Tippy do a Campion extravaganza that will probably turn into a campaign PR piece—I choose you and my sisters."

Meryl felt weak with relief. Meg was the one she didn't want to disappoint. If Meg was okay with it, she felt right in her heart. And as for Amy and Jo—they'd get on board. Somehow.

"When are you going to tell Amy and Jo?"

"If you can stay in the city for a few more hours, I'll ask them to come to the apartment tonight."

"You know what would be lovely?" said Rose. "A wedding at one of the old estates they have in Westchester or Long Island . . . one of those famous old mansions that they rent out."

"That's a great idea, Gran. Maybe that will help convince you to actually come to the wedding," Meg teased.

"Well, it's Amy's wedding too. And Andy is a nice boy."

"It's also Jo's wedding. And I can't see you approving of that match."

"Meryl, I might not know much," Rose began, "but I know that pair will never make it down the aisle."

Meryl's phone rang.

She didn't recognize the incoming number, and an unfamiliar woman's voice asked for her by name.

"This is Meryl Becker," she said.

"Joan Glass from *People* magazine returning your call."

Meryl glanced across the table at her mother and Meg. She held up a finger to say *one second* and walked to the front of the restaurant, where she began pacing in front of the bar.

"Yes, thanks for getting back to me. The reason I'm calling—"

"Your daughters. The Wedding Sisters."

"Umm, yes. How did you know?"

"I read the papers, Mrs. Becker. Let's talk about this in person, shall we? My office, four o'clock today? I don't mean to rush you, but that's the nature of the beast these days, ticktock."

Across the restaurant, she saw Meg take her mother's hand. She knew with a sinking feeling that neither one of them would approve of this meeting. Then she thought of how Meg had lost her job and the manila envelope stuffed into her handbag. With everything going haywire, it was up to her to take control.

"I'll see you at four," said Meryl.

The *People* magazine office on Sixth Avenue took Meryl back to the days when she belonged in Midtown. There had been a time when Meryl had lunch or coffee with magazine editors a few times every week. In the beginning, she was just trailing her boss, a silent guest at glamorous restaurants like La Grenouille, present only to listen and not speak. And then, she got her own corporate card and started taking out a few editors on her own. Younger editors who were on the rise, just as she was. She had been certain at that time that rise, she would.

Those had been the glory days of publishing: expense accounts, lavish book parties. Jackie Kennedy as celebrity book editor. Meryl, in her early twenties, felt important. She felt a part of something. When she became pregnant with Meg, there was no question she would go right back to work after the baby was born.

But when she first held that tiny bundle, Meg with her ocean blue eyes, those tiny hands—someone so vulnerable and pure, she felt like she should be taking every breath for her—she wavered. She told herself that in six weeks she would be ready, and not to think about it again until that day was closer.

That day never came.

At Meg's one-week checkup, the pediatrician, holding the stethoscope to her tiny chest, looked up at Meryl and said, "I hear something."

Meryl didn't know what he meant. She was still half euphoric and completely sleep deprived. Her brain processed conversation like mush.

It wasn't until the doctor suggested they take Meg back to the hospital for an ultrasound that she snapped out of it and realized something might be wrong. She left Hugh a message, but he was teaching. Still, she didn't panic. Later, she would realize she was half in denial, even when the doctor told her that Meg had a ventricular septal defect—a hole between the left and right ventricles.

"These sometimes self-correct. But with the size we're dealing with, I think we're looking at surgical intervention," he said.

Meryl thought she would dissolve into a puddle right then and there. She realized she could no longer indulge in her own needs, worries, or fears. She needed to talk to Hugh, but this, in the days before cell phones, would require a stop at a pay phone, and she couldn't imagine taking that sort of time. She needed to get Meg home. Meg, who was crying and hungry. Meg, who had a gaping hole in her heart.

The following weeks were a blur of trips back and forth to New York–Presbyterian's Cornell Medical Center. Even thirty years later, walking south on York, she could remember pushing the baby carriage fueled by what was a constant sense of panic. Meg was in congestive heart failure much of the time. She was "failing to thrive." At the six-week mark, Meryl gave notice at her job.

The cardiologist couldn't seem to give her a direct answer when she asked about the timing of the surgery.

"Hugh, you have to come with me to the next appointment. I don't think the doctor is being straight with me," she said.

Meg's heart defect scared Hugh. It scared Meryl too. But Hugh handled it in a different way. A detached way. It was the first time she saw that dichotomy she had come to resent so very much: his endless emotional investment in his students, and his maddening, cool practicality when it came to Meryl and the girls. She had caught a glimpse of it when he suggested the abortion, but that might be unfair. And now, again, he was more concerned with Janell South—a student who really, in the end, betrayed him—than with the girls. He was more excited about the prospect of finishing the Alcott project than the weddings. This was Hugh—she'd known it for years. Lived with it for years.

The question now was did she want to continue living with it?

She hated to admit that her mother had been right with her quip in the bridal shop. Somehow, these engagements had turned an unwelcome spotlight on the musty old problems with Hugh she'd thought she left stuffed in the back of her mental closet. But here they were, out in the daylight, unpleasant and undeniable.

"Mrs. Becker, thanks for making it in on short notice," said Joan Glass, who greeted her with a warm smile and a businesslike handshake.

"Please, call me Meryl." Joan appeared to be close to Meryl's age. She had thick blond hair threaded with gray that she wore in a sensible cut just skimming her shoulders. She wore a crisp white blouse and chunky gold necklace. Her pants were well tailored. She was shorter than Meryl and she didn't wear heels.

Meryl liked her immediately.

Joan led her down a corridor lined with framed covers of the magazine, a walk down memory lane of Meryl's life in pop culture: John Travolta from his *Saturday Night Fever* days. Princess Diana with a baby Prince William, JFK Jr. as Sexiest Man Alive.

Joan's office was also filled with photos: Joan with Emma Stone, Joan with Steven Spielberg, Joan with Kim Kardashian.

Meryl sat in a plush chair opposite the large glass desk. Joan sat behind the desk, and by way of opening the conversation, referenced the books editor whom Meryl had first contacted.

"You work in publishing?" said Joan.

"I used to work in publishing. The industry has changed a lot."

"Haven't they all! Believe me, magazines are racing to adapt to this bold new digital world as well. But in some ways, books have it easy—just the format is changing. For us, the substance of what our readers are interested in has undergone a sea change."

Meryl nodded.

Joan pointed to something behind Meryl—a photo of Joan and Julia Roberts. "No one cares about movie stars anymore," said Joan. "Did you ever think we'd live to see that day?"

"No," said Meryl truthfully, although she suspected the question was rhetorical.

"It's all about reality stars, and real-life fairy tales. People want to believe it can happen to them. That's why we're so interested in your family."

"You are?"

"Absolutely. As I mentioned on the phone, your girls were on my radar before you even called. And I hear through the grapevine there's a *New York* magazine cover story in the works."

Meryl nodded. "The writer called me for a comment, but I didn't speak with her."

"A hatchet job. That's all that writer does. We can get something up fast and scoop whatever it is they think they're going to say that's newsworthy in that piece."

"Get something up? You mean, online?"

Joan nodded. "A quick online story to establish ourselves as the source for all things Becker sisters. Followed by a print piece next month that expands on it. Sound good?"

"You want to run a story about my daughters in the magazine?" Meryl had to bite her lip to maintain a poker face. She hadn't known what to expect from the meeting—maybe drum up some interest in covering the wedding in the spring—vague interest that she could parlay into something concrete from a smaller publication. All she'd known was that the latent publicist in her had felt the need to take control of the press surrounding the girls. She hadn't expected this.

"Yes. But as I said—first, online to get ahead of this thing. And we want exclusive rights to the wedding photos."

"Exclusive rights?"

"Which we'll pay for, obviously."

Meryl's pulse began to race. "What are you offering?"

"Look, it's an interesting story. Your girls are beautiful and on their way to something. The fiancés are all media magnets. But they aren't Kardashians. You know what I mean?"

Meryl knew she was suddenly in the middle of a negotiation. No, they weren't Kardashians. They were so much more than that. What was it that *New York* magazine writer had said?

"There hasn't been anything like this since the Miller sisters in the '90s," said Meryl. "And with my daughter's future father-in-law potentially the next president of the United States, I'd argue you could be asking for a scoop on the next Jackie Kennedy."

Joan leaned forward, clasping her hands in front of her. "What's the date of Meg's wedding?"

Meryl was taken aback by the familiar way Joan used Meg's name.

"Actually," Meryl said slowly. "The date we choose might be for all three girls. We're considering a triple wedding."

Joan's face flooded with color. She clapped her hands together, not bothering to conceal her delight. "Meryl, tell me the date is in May."

"We're looking at May or June."

"We need May to make the summer wedding issue. So here's my offer: If you schedule the wedding in May, and if we get exclusive rights to photos, *and* all three girls make it down the aisle—this publication is prepared to pay in the high six figures."

Meryl gasped. "I don't know what to say."

"Say you'll consider it. Let me talk to my people about the dollar amount, have the paperwork drawn up. You can talk to the girls. And we can take it from there."

Joan stood and Meryl followed her lead. Her legs felt shaky.

"But in the meantime, at the very least, let's get that online piece in the works. I'm going to take you over to my assistant to take all your information and your daughters', and we'll start setting up the interviews. Sound good?"

"Yes," said Meryl.

They shook hands outside her office. An assistant appeared to show her to the lobby.

"Looking forward to speaking soon, Meryl," called Joan. "Get ready to be a household name!"

Before Meryl reached the subway, she texted Hugh to leave the library early and meet her at home. He responded that he was already working from home. Perfect.

What would Hugh make of all this? On the one hand, this was a practical solution to the money problem. On the other hand, Hugh hated anything that smacked of ostentation or appeared to be attention seeking. A *People* magazine spread would certainly qualify on both counts.

It shouldn't even matter. She should just tell him this is what's happening. He said he didn't want to spend too much money on the weddings, and now he wouldn't have to. Might even make some money on the weddings. How's that for problem solving?

The one thing it didn't solve, however, was losing the apartment. That was unsolvable. And every time she thought about it, she wanted to punch Hugh.

And when Meryl walked into the apartment, the impulse to punch Hugh intensified. Dramatically.

Hugh was not alone. There, at the dining room table, behind a mountain of accordion files, index cards, and books, was a teenaged girl.

"Hon! Great timing," said Hugh, standing up with a smile. "I've been wanting to introduce you two. This is Janell South. Janell, my wife, Meryl."

"Nice to meet you, Mrs. Becker," said the girl politely. She was short and slight, a tiny slip of a thing, with dark skin and green eyes. Her hair was a cascade of dreadlocks to her waist. Meryl felt a ping of alarm; what was he doing with the student who essentially cost him his job? *In their apartment?*

"Hugh, can I . . . can we talk in the other room for a minute?"

She closed the bedroom door with a louder slam than she'd intended.

"What the hell is she doing here?"

"She's my new research assistant."

"Are you out of your mind? The press is following our daughters around—how long before they take an interest in you and your 'research assistant'?"

"I'm not even going to dignify that with a response. I couldn't care less about all that media nonsense. This is a stroke of genius! One of the things holding me back on this project has been time management. Without a day job, and with a little help, I know I can get this thing to the finish line. Remember when I tried to get Meg involved? I wanted her to be my research assistant that summer between junior and senior year of Yardley? I thought it would be a great thing to include on her college applications. But she wasn't interested."

"No, Hugh. She wasn't."

"Most seniors at Yardley already have internships. I feel so bad that Janell lost her scholarship. I think the least I can do is give her a chance to bolster her high school transcript with a research internship."

"So which is it, Hugh? Is she helping you, or are you helping her?"

"Both! That's why it's so perfect!"

"Are her parents okay with this?"

"She lives with her aunt."

"Okay—her aunt. Her guardian—whomever. You have to be careful, Hugh. She's a minor."

"Her aunt doesn't care and her social worker thinks it's very constructive for her. It seems the only one who has a problem with it is you." He put his hands on his hips, and Meryl sighed. She didn't have the energy to argue. Not when there was so much other, very real stuff to get straightened out.

"Fine, Hugh. Whatever. But she has to leave now. We've got family business to take care of."

"It's going to have to wait an hour or so. We're in the middle of something that I need for—"

"*People* magazine is offering us over half a million dollars for the rights to photograph the wedding."

"They can't be serious."

"They are. The triple wedding. Hugh, it's a big deal. I know I was resistant at first, but you might be on to something here. We just have to get the girls on board."

nineteen

Amy wanted to confess.

It was the only way for her to (a) make sure she didn't cheat on Andy again and (b) walk down the aisle in a white dress without feeling like the world's biggest fake.

Andy would be hurt, angry. But she knew him well enough to believe he would forgive her. They could, they *would*, work through it. Maybe they could postpone the wedding. They didn't have to rush to make a May wedding date. That had been her stupid idea just to one-up Meg. And now it was coming back to bite her in the ass. Well, she deserved it. As Jo would say, karma's a bitch.

She had been all set to just get it over with—to go home from the office with Andy and tell him over dinner. And then she'd gotten the call—no, the summons—from her mother. Amy had told her mother it wasn't a good night, but Meryl insisted.

"I have news," she said. "And all you girls need to be here."

Her mother could be so dramatic sometimes. But apparently Meg was in town, so maybe it was important.

Amy was the last one to arrive at the apartment. Her parents and sisters were sitting in the living room already. And her grandmother.

"Finally," said Jo. "I'm starving."

"I didn't bring food," snapped Amy.

"No shit—but the sooner we get this show on the road, the sooner we can order Chinese."

"Girls, please," said Meryl. "Amy, sit down, hon."

"Okay, you're freaking me out," said Amy. "Is something wrong? Are you sick?" Her eyes grew wide. That's it. Her mother was dying. Her cosmic punishment.

"No, sweetie, nothing is wrong."

Amy squeezed onto the couch between Meg and Jo. Her grandmother sat on the love seat, and her father in his Eames chair.

Meryl remained standing. "So, as you know from the Page Six articles and the photographers outside Monique Lhuillier and the call I got from *New York* magazine, your engagements have inspired a lot of media interest."

Had her mother really called them there just to lecture them about avoiding the media? Amy had already gotten the memo from her mom's nearly hysterical call about not talking to that reporter. Just because her mother worked in book publicity, she thought she was a PR guru. Amy had told Jeffrey about it, and he told her that all publicity was good publicity. And really, he should know.

"Photographers wait outside Toby's apartment building every morning now," said Jo.

"Really?" Amy resisted a surge of jealousy. Why her?

"Girls, the attention is just going to increase. That's why we need to start taking control of the publicity. I met with *People* magazine today. They want to do a story on all of you that will run online, ahead of anything *New York* magazine publishes, and then an expanded piece in the magazine next month or so."

"We should really run this by Jeffrey's PR team," said Amy. It wasn't surprising that *People* wanted photos of the wedding. The Bruces were the biggest fashion family in America. But Jeffrey was so into maximizing publicity, it was possible he was already talking to someone about the wedding.

"No," said Meryl, so sharply, it startled her. "We are not running this by anyone except the people in this room. Girls, we have three weddings to plan—and frankly, your father and I simply can't afford it."

"Mom, the Bruces will take care of anything we need—"

"What I need is for you to be quiet and listen! Your father and I have been trying to figure out what to do. Look, girls, I'm sorry we didn't tell you sooner, but your father is no longer with Yardley."

"I thought you said it was a sabbatical," said Meg.

"When did you go on sabbatical?" said Amy.

"He's leaving Yardley," Meryl repeated. "And so, financially, things are challenging. But talking to the editor at *People* today offered a solution for this. They will pay us—a lot of money—for the exclusive rights to the wedding photos."

"Cool," said Jo.

"But there are two conditions: one, the wedding takes place in early May so they can run this in their June wedding issue."

"What do you mean, 'the wedding'? Whose wedding?" Amy asked, confused. Was this all about Meg again?

"That's the second part. We discussed the idea of a triple wedding."

Amy's mouth dropped open. This had to be a joke. She turned to Meg, but she only nodded calmly.

"That's so crazy, it's kind of genius!" said Jo.

"Mom, please tell me you're joking," said Amy slowly.

"She's not joking," said Hugh. "And I'm asking you girls to seriously consider this. It's unconventional, but we've always done things our own way, haven't we?"

"That's one way of putting it," said Rose.

Amy looked at her grandmother, who was now a fixture in their midst after a lifetime of being largely absent; at her father, who she could only guess quit his job to write that book; and at her mother, who was . . . Was she wearing red lipstick?

"I'm all for it," said Meg.

"You are?" Amy couldn't believe it.

"It will be fun!" said Jo. "Like when we were kids."

"Shut up, Jo. Of course you don't care. This engagement is just another one of your random impulses. Does it even mean anything to you?"

"I find it really hard to believe you're judging *my* engagement," Jo said pointedly. And Amy regretted, oh how she regretted, confiding in her.

"I think we all just need to calm down," said Meg.

Meryl, her arms crossed in front of her chest, glared at Amy. "I would like for you, just once, to think of someone other than yourself," she said.

Amy felt like she'd been slapped. Of course, *she* was the selfish one. Meg was handling this elegantly and perfectly, Jo was down for anything, and Amy was the bitch for stating the obvious: This was crazy.

Meryl closed the door behind the girls, wishing she could go with them. The apartment felt claustrophobic, the tension of the conversation still sucking all the air out of the room.

"That went well," said Hugh. If Meryl didn't know better, she would think he was being sarcastic. But Hugh didn't do sarcasm. As usual, he'd just misread the room.

"In what sense? That it didn't devolve into physical violence?" said Meryl.

Rose barked a laugh.

"Oh, come on, Meryl. The girls squabble. But Jo and Meg are fine with it, and Amy will come around. You did a good job."

She had to admit, his praise felt good. But what would have felt better was him being a partner to her—at least once—when it really counted.

"Amy will do whatever Meg does. She always has. It's money in the bank," said Rose.

"Okay, Mother, I don't know if this is your idea of being support-ive, but please just stop."

For the second time in her life, her daughters had drawn her mother out of her closed-off shell and awakened an odd hybrid beast—part wisdom, part irritation.

Twenty-eight years ago, it had been Meg's heart condition that pulled her mother out of her silence and resentment. Rose couldn't keep quiet when something needed to be said, and when Meg called her crying, insistent that the doctor wasn't giving her clear answers, Rose had stepped in.

"Your father's old friend, Sol Klein, is on the board at CHOP," she'd said. The Children's Hospital of Philadelphia. It was the place to go, her mother insisted. Meryl couldn't make any more decisions at that point. She was confused. Now the cardiologist was throwing around terms like "tetralogy of Fallot." Meryl sat on the floor of the Yorkville Library, Meg in her lap, paging through a cardiology book, trying to make sense of it all because the damn doctor wasn't telling her anything useful. Every three days was the same agonizing routine of chest X-rays; a visit with Dr. McFlynn, where he asked how much she seemed to be eating; and then an assessment of how much weight she was failing to gain.

"Do you think she needs the surgery soon?" Meryl asked. She dreaded both a yes and a no. A yes would get it over with, but a yes meant surgery. A no meant more uncertainty, but it sustained her perhaps irrational hope that surgery could be avoided.

She couldn't sleep. She watched over Meg with a compulsion, as if only her vigilance would solve the problem. As if the answer could be found in the uneven rise and fall of her tiny chest. Her mother said to her, "There are two types of problems in life: fixable and not fixable. This is fixable. So let's fix it."

The doctor at CHOP was different. He was decisive. There was no reason to wait. Meg, her heart the size of a walnut, would have surgery in a matter of days.

There had been an unreal quality to handing tiny Meg off to the anesthesiologist. The woman was already wearing a surgical mask to cover her mouth. All Meryl could see—and would always remember—was the woman's bright blue eyes, and the way she said with such confidence and certainty, "We're going to get this fixed."

And then there was nothing for Meryl and Hugh to do but wait. There was a certain closeness in that, a solidarity. And Meryl had known that while she had traversed the past few months feeling alone, she wasn't. She had Hugh.

Meryl's phone rang. Her first thought was that it was one of the girls—together, walking to their dinner, they'd decided on a mutiny. No wedding.

"Hello?" she said.

Hugh was already retreating to his office. And her mother had moved to the couch and picked up a copy of *New York* magazine.

"Meryl, it's Scott."

"Oh!"

"Is this a bad time?"

"No—I just, I wasn't expecting you. I thought it was . . . Never mind. How are you?"

"I'm good—back in New York. A project is getting some traction, so I'll be here for a few days. Any chance you're free for a drink one night this week?"

Meryl glanced at her mother. "Sure. Thursday night?"

"Sounds good. I can come to you this time. Want to do that place you originally mentioned on Eighty-fifth?"

"Perfect."

"See you Thursday."

She felt a surge of energy, an almost giddy excitement.

"Who was that?" asked Rose.

Meryl jumped—she'd forgotten she was in the room. "Oh—just a friend."

"What friend?"

Meryl hesitated. "An old friend from Nana and Grandpa's place at the shore," she said. Really, she had nothing to hide.

Rose squinted at her with suspicion. "What friend from the shore? You didn't have any friends."

"First of all, Mother, that's not true. And his name is Scott."

"Erma and Lew's kid—with the limp?"

"No! That was Sammy Goldberg. Scott was the lifeguard at the beach."

Rose shook her head. "Don't be ridiculous, Meryl. You're too young to be running around with that lifeguard. And don't tell your grandmother."

Meryl looked at her, her heart thumping with alarm. "Mother, what are you talking about? I'm a grown woman. And Nana is gone."

"Well," said Rose, "as a grown woman, you should certainly know better."

Andy, easygoing (or was it passive?) as always, took the news of the triple wedding calmly. "Really, babe—whatever you want. It's not a big deal."

She had texted him to meet her for dinner. Andy, thinking she was going to eat with her parents, had made plans to have a beer with a friend in the Village. But he met her at the Mexican place Toloache when she said it was important.

"What about your parents?" she asked, pouring herself another margarita from the pitcher.

He shrugged. "They'll be cool with whatever. They did their whole big wedding thing, like, ten years ago. They don't need this for themselves."

"What whole big wedding thing?"

"They renewed their vows. When they got married the first time, they were basically broke, so it wasn't exactly a dream wedding for my mom. So I guess it was a do-over."

Amy swallowed hard. Would she end up wanting her own do-over if she agreed to this crazy idea?

"But what do *you* want?"

"I want whatever you want. Really. Your big family is kind of fun for me. It's so different than what I had growing up. I like Meg and Jo. And Stowe's cool. I don't know this other dude, but we had a few drinks at the engagement dinner. I think it could be cool. Kind of different."

Amy nodded. "But what about the *People* magazine thing?"

"Oh please, you know Dad will *love* that. You in a custom Jeffrey Bruce wedding gown on the cover of *People* magazine? All good."

"You think we'll get the cover?"

"I mean, if they're paying money, yeah. Unless some celebrity runs off and does something crazy, I think you'll be on the cover. They're not spending money to bury you in the back."

"Oh my God! You're right!" Amy laughed, feeling genuinely excited about things again. She smiled at the image of the three of them smiling out from every newsstand in the city. Of course, the photographer would probably put Meg in the center.

It was counter-logical, but while a triple wedding did steal the spotlight from her—it actually cast a more intense glow. And maybe Andy was right—it would be fun. With everything that was going on—like the temporary insanity with Marcus—it might be advisable to embrace a wedding scenario that was about more than just her. There was no second-guessing, no postponing—this thing was happening. It was a freight train.

All she had to do was go along for the ride.

Meg knew that running off to New York had not been the most mature thing to do. But it had worked out for the best. If she hadn't been there to support her mom in the wedding decision, Jo and Amy might not have gone along with it.

She just had to get Stowe to accept it.

The way she saw it, she'd lost her job over Reed's presidential run. She'd taken one for the team. Now it was Stowe's turn.

"Hello? Babe, I'm back." She tossed her keys into the bowl on the entrance table and shrugged off her coat.

"In here," Stowe called out from the kitchen. Meg walked through the house, and he intercepted her in the living room.

He hugged her. "I missed you," he said. "I wish you hadn't run off like that."

"I needed some time. To process everything," she said.

"I know. And I know I said this on the phone, but I just want to reiterate: It will work out. Probably for the best."

Meg was surprised by how good it felt to be in his arms, to hear his reassurance despite her lingering doubts about how much he knew and when. But really, she had two choices: move on from it or end it. And she didn't want to end it. She loved him. She wanted to be his wife—as complicated as that might be. She now knew their challenge—and every relationship had them—was to help him find the balance between his life as a Campion and his life as her partner.

"I love you," she said.

"I love you too."

Why was he whispering?

Meg pulled back, a sudden unease chilling the warm glow of her homecoming. "Is someone here?"

As if on cue, Hunter Cross strolled into the room. Meg gasped, feeling as if she'd walked in on Stowe in bed with someone.

"What are you doing here?" she asked bluntly, realizing her response lacked a certain grace. Why did Hunter Cross rankle her so much? Maybe it was because from the first moment Meg saw her in Reed's office, things had been going haywire.

Hunter smiled, pulling a pen from the knot in her high ponytail. "We're working," she said. Hunter was dressed in a cream-colored blouse and matching pencil skirt. The blouse had a black, gauzy loose bow that tied at the neck in an oversized way that was dramatically chic. Meg felt sloppy and wrinkled after the three-hour drive, but she stood up straight and tucked her hair behind her ear and said with all the regal authority she could muster, "Well, you'll have to excuse us. The workday is over and I need to talk to my fiancé."

Hunter looked to Stowe, and he nodded. "We can finish this tomorrow," he said.

Hunter nodded. "I'll get my things."

When she retreated back to the kitchen, Meg glared at Stowe. "What's this all about?"

"Campaign stuff."

She looked pointedly at her phone. "At . . . nine at night?"

"I just got back from the office an hour ago."

Meg walked to the kitchen, to see exactly what they were "working" on. The marble island in the center of the kitchen was filled with files, two laptops, and two legal pads. And an open bottle of wine.

Hunter was packing up her papers and computer into her Louis Vuitton briefcase. She glanced up at Meg. "You'll have to get used to unconventional business hours," she said. "A campaign is twenty-four–seven."

"Stowe isn't running for office," said Meg.

Hunter smiled tightly. "When one member of the family runs, you all run. Really, Meg—if you're going to marry into the Campions, you need to get with the program." She brushed past her on her way to the door.

Meg, her hand shaking, poured herself a glass from the open bottle of cabernet. She heard Stowe walk into the room, but didn't look at him.

"What's the problem?"

"Do you want to tell me what that was all about?"

"I do—if you can stop looking at me like I did something wrong."

"I don't like her."

Stowe laughed. "Really? You hide it so well. Come on, Meg—you don't like being told what to do. Ever. But that's Hunter's job—to tell people what to do, say—sometimes even what to think. It's not personal."

"When she's sitting in my house at nine at night, drinking wine with my fiancé when I'm out of town, it feels very fucking personal."

"Meg, come on. You don't really think I have something going on with my dad's press secretary?"

"No," she said. "I don't."

"So then what's this about?"

"You tell me? What business do you have to discuss that was so important?"

"Well, there are decisions to be made."

"Like what?"

"My dad wants me to take a leave of absence from the firm to help with the campaign full-time."

"Well, that's not going to happen." But she could see by the look on his face that she was probably the only one of that opinion. "Is it?"

"I don't know, Meg. This is a really big deal—a once-in-a-lifetime thing. I'm really proud of him, and frankly, I'm honored that he wants me on board."

Meg leaned over the counter, her head in her arms. "Isn't this something we should be discussing before you talk about it with Hunter Cross?"

"I wanted to get all the information before I talked to you—what it would really entail, when it would start—"

"Goddamn it, Stowe!"

"What? Why is this such a problem for you?"

"Because I'm completely shut out! All of this affects me too, you know. I just lost my job—in case you forgot. And yet every single decision is made behind closed doors—even the doors of our home."

"I know it might feel that way, but it's just because this is all new and everyone is figuring things out."

He hugged her, but this time, she found no solace in his arms.

"Are you going to do it?" she said. "Quit your job?"

"Not quit. Just take leave."

"You'll never go back."

"Meg, no one knows what's going to happen down the line. We need to just take it one step at a time."

"I have some news too, you know." She pulled away from him, finished her glass of wine in one gulp. And she poured another before saying, "We're having a triple wedding. Me, Amy, Jo—same day. One party. And it won't be at your parents' country club. You can do the honors of telling your mother."

twenty

At the top of Meryl's list of a million and one things to do: find a wedding venue.

Tippy had suggested, if they insisted on throwing the wedding in New York, that they consider the Vesper Club.

"They have rooms for at least some of the out-of-town guests to stay in, and then of course, the Carlisle is nearby for the rest."

Leigh, learning of this plan, called Meryl and told her that while she "didn't hear this from her" the Vesper Club was "not a good idea." When Meryl asked why not, Leigh said the sister club to the organization, the Women's National Republican Club, had recently been very vocal about not wanting lesbian members, and the Vesper Club was not far behind.

"I don't think Jo would feel comfortable getting married in a place like that, even if she *is* marrying a man. Do you?"

Meryl, surprised that Leigh knew enough about Jo to make such an observation, admitted that, no, the place didn't sound like the right fit.

So there was that.

And just as pressing, the interview dates needed to be set with *People*.

She waited until 9 A.M., and then called the number for Joan Glass's assistant to schedule the interviews for Meg, Amy, and Jo. Getting voice mail, she left a message, checking against the note she'd made last night about what days worked for which of the girls.

That's when the screaming started.

The sound coming from her mother's room, shrill and primal, froze Meryl for a second. The startled reaction of her body debating fight or flight, before it put the alarm in context.

She rushed into the bedroom to find her mother exactly how she had found her back in her own apartment: perched at the edge of the bed, staring straight ahead.

Meryl sat next to her and put her arm around her. "Mother, it's okay," she said, trying to sound calm even as she felt herself panicking. What was this about? And for the first time since packing her mother's apartment, she thought about the drawings and the photos. She'd been so distracted by getting the girls on board with the triple wedding and *People* magazine, she'd completely forgotten about the envelope she'd stuffed in the bottom of her bag.

Now, obviously, was not the time for it.

After Meryl spent a few minutes talking calmly to her mother, Rose snapped out of it.

"You were doing it again," Meryl said.

Rose looked at her. This time, Meryl understood that her mother was aware of it. Was, in fact, as alarmed as she was.

"You're going to have to see someone," Meryl said.

"What good will that do?"

Meryl was encouraged by the response; it wasn't a no.

The wedding calls would have to wait. People would have to wait. Meryl needed to find a psychiatrist. And she wanted someone today.

Her phone rang. She let it go to voice mail while she rifled through one of the mini legal pads she kept in her desk, looking for the numbers Dr. Friedman had given her a few weeks ago. After an hour of phone calls to the insurance company and leaving messages for half a dozen psychiatrists, she could do nothing but finally get dressed and wait.

Meryl looked at herself in the mirror. Yesterday, on the way to meeting with Joan, she had stopped into Sephora. She just wanted to kill a few minutes—she had been early—but ended up buying a new lipstick. One of the saleswomen, in her all-black uniform and headset—looking more like a backup dancer at a concert tour than the type of makeup ladies who used to help her mother back when they shopped together at Saks—picked one out for her. It was deep red and matte, the brand Nars. It had been a long time since Meryl bought—let alone wore—makeup aside from mascara. But she had to admit, gazing into the handheld mirror amidst the blaring hip-hop music, that it looked good. And it felt good.

Maybe it was time to do a little more in the sprucing-up department. She knew—as if Hugh didn't remind her enough—that none of this was about her. But she was a part of it. She was the mother of the brides. She should look presentable. More than that, even. She should look good. She should feel good. It was time to start enjoying this moment a little more.

"The house phone rang," Rose said, appearing in the bedroom doorway. Her glasses seemed more enormous than usual, and Meryl remembered Amy calling her Grandma Owl, though not to her face.

"Oh, it's probably a package at the front desk. I'll get it later. Thanks."

"No, actually your *machatunim* is on the way up."

"What?"

Meryl knew what she meant—*machatunim* was Yiddish for "in-laws"—she just couldn't make sense of it. Was her mother still having an episode?

The doorbell rang.

Meryl, with one more glance in the mirror, hastily pulled a cardigan over her T-shirt and hurried through the apartment to the door and looked out the peephole. Sure enough, Tippy Campion, in all her Tory Burch–wearing, bleach-blond-haired glory, waited on her doorstep.

Oh my God.

"Tippy. What a surprise. Come in."

"It wouldn't be a surprise if you answered my calls," she said.

"What calls?"

"I called you late last night—later than I should, admittedly—and just an hour ago. I finally reached your husband, who told me you were home."

Meryl turned and looked at her mother, who shrugged. A small smile played on her lips. Great. At least someone was amused.

"I didn't know you were in New York," said Meryl.

"Well, here I am. So would you care to tell me what this triple-wedding nonsense is all about?"

"Come in. Let's sit in the living room. Would you like coffee?"

Meryl had known this conversation would have to take place. She just imagined it happening over the phone—where she could present her justification matter-of-factly and then pretend to have another call and get out of the conversation quick and easy. Of course, Tippy would not like the change in wedding plan. For reasons Meryl could imagine, and probably for reasons Meryl didn't even yet know about. But none of that was Meryl's concern. Meryl's job was to keep things on track.

"I don't want coffee," Tippy snapped. "I want to know what this is all about. Stowe communicated very little to me over the phone except that this was Meg's wish and he was willing to go along with it. But I can't imagine he's very happy about it, either. So I would appreciate it if you would tell me what's going on."

"It's my fault," said Rose.

Both women looked at her, and Meryl didn't know who was more surprised—she or Tippy.

"Hello, Rose. I didn't see you standing there," said Tippy, fighting through her irritation to find her manners. "How are you?"

Impeccable manners. Meryl had to respect that. She did just barge in there, but at least she called first. Note to self: check voice mails more often.

"I couldn't help but overhear the conversation," Rose said. "And I have to admit the change in wedding plans are my doing."

Was it Meryl's imagination, or was her mother's Polish accent suddenly twice as heavy?

"You?" said Tippy, echoing Meryl's own thoughts.

"Yes. It's a Polish tradition."

"Triple weddings are a Polish tradition?" said Tippy.

"If three daughters get engaged the same year, it's bad luck not to get married on the same day."

Meryl had to bite her lower lip not to laugh. She couldn't tell if her mother was messing with Tippy for sport, or if she was actually trying to somehow come to Meryl's aid.

"Well, with all due respect, Rose, we can't be ruled by superstition."

"I had a double wedding," Rose said, as if Tippy hadn't spoken. Meryl covered her mouth with her hand. There was no other way to stifle the smile. Her mother most certainly had *not* had a double wedding. Now she knew that the answer to her question was both: her mother was messing with Tippy *and* she was coming to Meryl's aid. "I dreamed of the same for my daughter, but I wasn't blessed with another daughter. And then my daughter has three daughters! God works in funny ways."

"Yes," Tippy said, glancing at Meryl. "But I don't think . . ."

"I don't know how much time I have left," said Rose. "But now, whenever God comes for me, I go happy."

"Okay, thank you, Mother. I think you should rest now," said Meryl.

"I should go rest now." She retreated back into her bedroom.

"Meryl . . . ," Tippy said.

"I understand your concern," said Meryl. And then, the olive branch she had been planning. "But if it makes you feel any better, I will definitely need Leigh Beauford's help. In fact, she can come with us when we go dress shopping for Meg's sister."

"I thought Jeffrey Bruce was doing her dress?"

"My youngest. We have three, remember? Triple wedding?"

Tippy paled. "I'll talk to Leigh."

Meryl told herself that the decision to stop by the hair salon had nothing to do with drinks that night with Scott.

She had a wedding coming up. And before that, bridal showers and all the photos that entailed, and anyway, it was time. So she stopped in at the Aveda salon on Eighty-sixth Street, where she told Jo-Ellen, the woman who had cut her hair for years and years, that she was ready to cover up the gray.

Jo-Ellen was delighted and didn't question the sudden decision, though Meryl still had found it necessary to justify the change with, "For the wedding . . ."

Meryl had never colored her hair before. So she didn't know what to expect when it came to turning back the clock on her hair, which had been gradually graying since her midforties. Maybe I'll color it, she had thought once. When it gets really "bad." And then one day a woman at the checkout counter at Eli's had commented that she really liked when women let their hair stay natural. That's when Meryl realized she was nearly completely gray. The thing was, she hadn't noticed. And then when she did notice, she didn't care.

But now she did.

"Oh my God," she said, looking in the mirror. She looked, if not ten years younger, at least more like herself of ten years ago. And it was a welcome sight.

She had an hour before meeting Scott. The bar—or, as the place billed itself, gastropub—was just two blocks from Aveda. She didn't want to go home first, didn't want to go through the trouble of explaining her hair to Hugh. He would notice—of course he'd notice. He might have his head up his ass half the time, but he wasn't blind. Maybe he'd even like it.

Did she want for him to like it? Did she even care anymore?

As for her evening plans, she'd told Hugh she was having drinks with an old work friend.

"You think it could lead to something?" he asked.

She'd bitten her lip. "No. It's just drinks."

Bondurants had very few tables, but she'd called ahead to reserve one. She was the first to arrive, and sat reading the menu over and over again. She was so nervous, and she knew that alone was a sort of betrayal of Hugh. To combat her guilt, she reminded herself that she was meeting him for a reason. Wasn't she?

Without watching the door, she somehow sensed when Scott walked in.

She stood to greet him and he kissed her on the cheek.

"Is it my imagination or do you look different?" he said, looking her up and down in a way that made her blush.

"I'm not sure," she said, resisting the urge to touch her hair.

He sat across from her, looking around the small room. The bar was already packed.

"Interesting place," he said.

She couldn't tell if he meant that as a compliment.

"There's a Ranger game on tonight," she said. "This is the only bar in walking distance without a screen."

"No, this is great."

They ordered drinks. Another thing about Bondurants—which she hadn't known ahead of time—was that there was no table service, so Scott had to walk up to the horseshoe-shaped bar and order for them. Another minute to collect herself.

Scott returned with their drinks—a club soda for him, and prosecco for her.

"You don't drink?" she asked. She knew that wasn't something you were allowed to ask. But she felt a compulsion to hear everything about his life.

To her relief, he didn't seem to mind the question. "I don't anymore. Got a little out of hand when I was younger. You know how it is in your twenties."

She didn't say anything. Then, "I had three kids in my twenties."

He whistled. "I can't imagine. How old were you when you got married?"

"Twenty-three."

"What's it like? Being with the same person for . . . how long has it been again?"

"Thirty years," she said.

"Impressive."

"It's not easy."

"No kidding. I've never had a relationship last longer than a year."

"I'm sorry."

"Don't be. It's fine. I have no complaints. The truth is, I prefer being single. I really enjoy never knowing what life is going to bring my way—who I'm going to meet. Running into you, for example."

Meryl gulped her drink, coughing on the bubbles. "Running into me."

"Crazy, after all this time. I still remember that night on the board-walk. God, we were so young."

Meryl couldn't look at him. She was afraid of what her eyes would give away. She was still that girl on the boardwalk. And that kiss suddenly felt like very unfinished business.

"So—a lot's happened in the last few weeks," he said.

"What?" She looked up, conversationally disoriented.

"Hasn't it? Your third daughter got engaged, and I feel like I'm reading another article about the wedding every day."

"Oh—yes. A few things here or there, but—"

"You know what I mean. Really, it has all the makings of a phenomenon, Meryl. We need to talk about the show."

The show. As if it were already a thing.

"I know there's an interest in my girls—"

"A rabid interest."

"Okay, well. Yes. But the thing is, they don't want that kind of exposure."

"Have you actually talked to them about it?"

Meryl shook her head. "No. There's been too much going on. But the truth is, I could barely get them to agree to the triple wedding," she said.

"So that's true? I thought that was just gossip."

"No. It's true."

"You sure you don't want a publicist?"

"I'm already in talks with *People* magazine. I have it covered," she said.

"Good for you! Maybe when all this wedding stuff quiets down, we can talk about bringing you into my production company's marketing department. I mean, if you'd be interested in something like that." His dark eyes flashed at her.

She felt a surge of energy, a sense of possibility. She touched her hair. "That could be interesting," she said evenly.

"But in the meantime, talk to your daughters about the show. And I'll write up a pitch."

"Just like that?"

"Sure. I can see the show, Meryl. I already have a sense of your daughters' different personalities. And of course, I know you. The missing puzzle piece is your husband. How does he fit into all of this?"

Meryl's stomach tightened. She sipped her drink. "Oh, I don't think Hugh will go for this."

"Look, Meryl, not everyone is going to understand our vision," Scott said. "People take a little convincing sometimes. If this stuff were easy, everyone would have a show, right?"

"I suppose," she said. "But please—don't do anything yet. I have a lot to think about. And it's really up to my family."

"Understood. But, Meryl—don't take too much time thinking. Hot today, gone tomorrow. You know the life cycle of these things."

She nodded.

He raised his glass. "To old friends," he said. "And new beginnings."

They touched their glasses together, but she knew no matter how intrigued she was, the show would never happen. No one would agree. So why did she keep talking to Scott about it?

She just wanted an excuse to keep seeing him.

The apartment was dark by the time Meryl walked in at ten thirty.

It was possible Hugh was still awake, watching TV in bed. But she hoped not. She wasn't drunk, but she wasn't exactly sober. She realized now, in the quiet stillness of her home, the excitement of the evening behind her, that she shouldn't have lied about whom she was meeting. The next time she saw Scott—and she was sure there would be a next time—she would tell Hugh the truth. She had nothing to hide.

"Well, well—look what the cat dragged in." Her mother switched on the living room light.

"Jesus! You scared me. What are you doing sitting there in the dark?"

"Don't try to change the subject."

Meryl shrugged off her coat. "Mother, I'm not in the mood for this. I'm going to sleep and you should too. Good night."

Rose followed her through the hallway. "You are a married woman," she said.

Meryl turned and walked back into the living room. "Mother, since when do you care about my marriage?"

"I care about marriage as an institution!" she said.

"Shhh! Hugh is sleeping."

"How *convenient* for you. Were you out with that lifeguard?"

Meryl sighed. "Don't say it like that. I wasn't out with him in that sense. And he's not a lifeguard anymore, Mother. He happens to be a very successful TV producer."

"You shouldn't lie to your husband."

"Oh! That's rich coming from you. You know what, Mother? You shouldn't lie to your daughter."

"I don't lie to you. I tell it to you straight—even when you don't want to hear it. Like right now."

"Really? You know what I want to hear? I want to hear why you were in Poland as a teenager when you told me you moved here before the war."

It came out before she could stop it. It came from a place of pure hurt and frustration—all the years of being judged by her mother, all the years of being held at a distance yet smothered at the same time. And it came too from a place of worry that something was deeply wrong—had long been deeply wrong—with her mother.

Her mother sat down, her lips pressed together in a thin, white line. Clearly, no response was forthcoming.

"Mother, I'm not angry. I want to help you. I just want to know the truth."

Still, nothing. Meryl, trying to stay calm, walked back to her bedroom. It was almost dark, but the TV was still on and the room was lit by the glow of *Last Week Tonight* on HBO. Hugh was still propped up on his pillows, his reading glasses on, a library book folded open on his chest. Moving slowly and quietly, Meryl opened her closet and retrieved the manila envelope from its hiding spot under a pile of shoe boxes. She tiptoed across the room and closed the door behind her.

A part of her wanted Hugh to wake up, to be by her side. But would it be any comfort, any support? She didn't know anymore. She'd forgotten what to expect from her own marriage.

Her mother had left the living room. Heart pounding, Meryl slowly walked to her bedroom. She couldn't put this off any longer.

She didn't bother knocking, and opened the door to find her mother sitting on the edge of the bed, in the same position as she'd found her in the times she was screaming. But she wasn't making a sound, just staring straight ahead, her hands folded in her lap.

Meryl swallowed hard. She wasn't ready for this.

And then Hugh appeared in the doorway. She was flooded with relief.

She looked at him gratefully, and his gaze fell to the envelope in her hands. He nodded, squeezing her arm.

Meryl opened the envelope and spread the drawings and photographs on the bed.

"You went snooping through my things," said Rose.

"I was helping you pack the apartment."

"Some help."

Meryl picked up the photo of the eleven-year-old girl, the young boy, and the dark-haired couple. "Who are these people?"

Rose barely glanced at the picture. "That's me."

Meryl nodded. "You look just like Meg. Or, rather, she looks just like you. Who are the adults?"

"Relatives."

"You said you came here when you were eight."

"What is this, an interrogation? So I was off by a few years."

Meryl tried to show her the photo of the teenager, but Rose refused to look at it. "This is more than a few years. You have to be at least fourteen here."

"You know I don't like to think about the family that didn't make it out of Poland. Why bring up the past when we have so much to look forward to now. Our family is the future—the girls and their marriages. If you can manage the wedding," she said with a contemptuous glance at Hugh.

"I'll let you two talk in private," he said.

"No, you two go talk in private," said Rose. "Meryl, clear your conscience instead of pestering me."

Meryl turned to glance uneasily at Hugh, but he was already gone. "Fine," she said, standing up. "Have it your way—as usual, Mother."

twenty-one

Jo stared at the image of herself on the cover of *New York* magazine. THE WEDDING SISTERS. It had been taken outside Monique Lhuillier, Meg in the center, flanked by Amy and Jo. Amy, the only one looking directly at the camera, was also the only one who looked happy.

The tagline of the article: THE NEW FACES OF MARRYING WELL.

"Don't make any plans for next Thursday night," Toby said, bringing a cup of coffee into the bedroom and handing it to Jo.

"This article makes us sound like gold diggers," Jo said.

"American media is a funny thing. I kind of love it. Did you hear what I said about next Thursday?"

"Yeah," she said, reaching for the mug. "What's next Thursday?"

"My parents are coming to town."

She'd known she would eventually have to meet the count and countess. But the introduction had been abstract. Even Toby hadn't seen them in close to a year, so she figured she had some time.

"Apparently, they are quite eager to meet their future daughter-in-law."

"In a bad way?"

"No—of course not. My parents are way too self-absorbed to give you too much thought. Trust me, this is just another thing to check off their to-do list before the next trip to Ibiza. Or Belize. Or wherever. Don't worry—we just have to suffer through one dinner, and then we won't hear from them again until they show up at the wedding. If they show up at the wedding."

"Oh, Toby. Of course they'll be at the wedding."

But they had flaked on Toby's college graduation, so who knew what these people were capable of? Jo felt bad that his parents were so detached. It had to be lonely for him. She had the impulse to invite him dress shopping with her and her mother, but it was bad luck for him to see the dress, so what was the point?

"You're right—they will be. I'm sure they'll want to see with their own eyes that I've gone through with it."

"What's that supposed to mean?"

"Well, because of the trust fund."

"What trust fund?"

"I come into my inheritance when I marry. We all do."

Jo dropped the magazine. "Is that what this engagement is all about?" she asked.

"What? No! Jo, don't be ridiculous. You know how I feel about you—how I've always felt about you. I'm not doing this for the money any more than you are."

Wow. Okay, that was fair. Why should she accuse him of ulterior motives when she was the one who'd done the complete 180?

"I'm sorry. I just . . . This never came up before."

He shrugged. "It's not a big deal. A technicality. Oh—almost forgot." He pulled out his black American Express card and slid it across the table. "For the dress."

"Toby—you don't have to do that. Really."

"I want to. Maybe you'll even let me see you in it before May. I'm not sure I can wait." He smiled.

"It's bad luck," she said.

He kissed her. "I don't believe in luck."

• • •

Meryl rushed into Jane restaurant. Scott gave her a wave from his table in the center of the room.

"I have maybe twenty minutes," Meryl said, out of breath.

"I know, I know—you're in demand. But this is worth your time, trust me. You cannot imagine the number of calls I got this morning," he said, hugging Meryl in greeting. He smelled painfully good.

"I have a dress-shopping appointment at Marchesa in an hour. Or rather, a pants fitting. My youngest wants to wear white silk Marchesa skinny pants down the aisle."

"I love it! Now, here's the deal: I got three calls from networks this morning asking me about a potential show with you and your daughters."

"Scott, I told you not to pitch it yet. I haven't even spoken to my family."

He held up his hand. "I didn't pitch it. The networks I've worked with came to me."

"Came to you? Why?"

"Because this is what I do, Meryl. They thought I might be able to approach you. And yes, I'll admit, when they called, I told them I happened to know you personally. But that's as far as the conversation went. That's why I needed to see you immediately. This is hot, Meryl. This isn't just shooting the shit between two old friends. There's real money here."

Was it indecent to order alcohol at eleven in the morning on a weekday? Probably.

"I'll have a mimosa," said Meryl.

"Just coffee for me," said Scott.

"Now you're making me feel bad."

"If I had three daughters getting married in a matter of months, I'd be drinking too."

She laughed. "Yes, well—when you put it that way. So this is all because of the *New York* magazine article?"

"That was quite a piece. Calling your daughters the modern-day Paley sisters?"

Meryl beamed. "It's very exciting. But the show just isn't a good idea.

Between you and me, sometimes I feel getting these three girls down the aisle will be the death of me."

"That's not the way this article makes it sound."

"Yes, well—don't believe everything you read."

"What's going on? I mean, aside from the stuff with your husband. I can imagine it's stressful for him to be unemployed when there is a wedding to plan. That's why this show is such an opportunity, Meryl."

"He's not . . . unemployed. He's writing a book." Suddenly Meryl felt prickly and defensive for Hugh. "We're all just doing the best we can," she said.

"I get that. And this show can make your best all that much better."

It was tempting. But everything with her mother was making her anxious. She felt vulnerable. Uncertain.

"It's not a good time."

"Meryl, I didn't get where I am by taking no for an answer." He put his hand on hers, and she felt the familiar pull toward him, an attraction that had first set root in her when she was just a girl. But there was no place for that now, as much as she'd liked, for a fleeting moment, to believe there was.

"I appreciate that. But this isn't just about business. It's personal."

"Yes—it's personal, and it's business. The two aren't mutually exclusive." He smiled.

"Scott, between you and me, I have a lot to deal with now aside from the wedding. You know my mother—you must remember her from, God, when she was my age."

"Of course. Your mother always wore those enormous round sunglasses."

"She wears enormous round glasses, period. All the time. My girls used to call her Grandma Owl."

He laughed. "I can't wait to meet them. So what are you saying? She needs to be on the show? We can make that happen."

"No—no. Absolutely not. Things have been difficult with her lately. At first I thought maybe she had dementia. Now I don't know. Depression, maybe. And I have this feeling . . . a really distressing feeling that she's lying to me about something."

"Lying about what?"

Meryl found herself tearing up. "The past. Her past. I don't know. There's just so much going on at once. The last thing any of us needs or wants is a bunch of cameras following us around."

"I know you feel that way now. But in a few months, this stress will be behind you and you'll change your mind. And if we don't start getting footage now, it will be too late. This time leading up to the wedding is crucial. Meryl, I don't want you to miss this opportunity."

She pulled back. "You don't want *me* to miss it? Or yourself?"

"That's not fair."

She nodded. "Maybe. Maybe not. But I don't need another thing on my plate right now. I'm sorry, but I'm going to have to pass on this."

"Meryl, as your friend, I think you're making a big mistake."

Was he right? When all the excitement died down, would she be kicking herself for not exploring this?

"Scott," she said. "It wouldn't be the first time."

Jo wanted to wear Marchesa because of an outfit she'd seen on Pinterest. It was a white satin minidress with scalloped layers in front paired with white satin skinny pants. She'd seen it over a year ago, long before weddings were even a thought. Still, she'd had the fleeting but unforgettable notion that she would someday get married in something exactly like it.

Only three places in the city carried Marchesa bridal, and one of them was on Wooster Street in SoHo. She was due to meet her mother at ten, but she thought she'd get there a little early just to get the lay of the land before her mother swooped in and started micromanaging. She didn't want to try on a dozen dresses. Jo knew how she wanted to look on her wedding day, and it was just a matter of whether or not this particular bridal boutique had what she needed to pull it off.

"Jo!"

She looked up automatically at the sound of her name, and then noticed a swarm of photographers advancing toward her. Flashes went off like mini explosions, leaving her momentarily paralyzed. She might have stood like that, a deer caught in the headlights—or in this case, flashing lights—but someone grabbed her by the arm and said, "Follow me."

It was the wedding planner, aka Chanel Boots. Aka Leigh Beauford. Aka the recent guest star in a few unwelcome but extremely hot dreams.

Leigh was somehow equipped with an umbrella despite the clear weather, and she used it as a shield and buttress as they pushed through the throng of photographers to the front door of the bridal boutique. All the while, they were shouting Jo's name, asking about Toby—she thought she even heard Caroline's name.

Once inside the shop, the sales rep locked the door and pulled down blackout shades.

"Okay, that was insane," Jo said. "We have to warn my mother."

"I'm calling her now," said Leigh.

"Tell her to ring the shop when she's outside. We'll open up for her," said one of the saleswomen.

Jo glanced at Leigh, who was talking intently into her phone. She wore a robin's egg blue trench coat; a red, blue, and gray Burberry scarf; charcoal gray pants that flared at the bottom; and gray Louboutins. Her chocolate brown hair framed her face in perfect layers, cascading down her back. Her fair skin was flawless, her almond-shaped dark eyes intense. Jo looked at her hands, the long tapered fingers, the short nails polished the color of the inside of a conch shell. Jo imagined those hands on her body, and immediately shook the thought away.

"I've called security to clear the perimeter of the store," said the first saleswoman, Jacqueline. "Your mother should be fine. Do you want to start looking at a few things, or wait for her?"

Jo looked at Leigh.

"We should probably wait for her mother," Leigh said.

Jacqueline drifted away. Jo and Leigh were left on the sales floor with a tray of champagne.

"I didn't know you were coming today," Jo said.

"Your mother asked me to help out. I think with the triple wedding, she's more comfortable with the idea of outside support."

Jo nodded, fighting the urge to check her appearance in the mirror. Jo never felt self-conscious. She was nothing if not comfortable in her own skin. And damn this chick for throwing her off her game. What was her deal?

Their first encounter in the shoe department of Bloomingdale's had felt like a flirtation. But that was before Leigh had known there was any professional connection between them. Really, what were the odds? So whatever that had been—it didn't matter.

"It just kind of feels like a waste of your time," Jo said. "I mean, I know what I want here, so—"

"Think of me as being in a support role," Leigh said coolly. "And I need to coordinate the entire event, so having a sense of all the moving parts is important."

"Okay. Whatever."

Jacqueline rushed back across the room. "I'm opening the doors for your mother and the photographer now."

"What photographer?" Jo and Leigh asked in unison.

Meryl breezed in through the newly unlocked entrance to the salon, followed by two men lugging equipment.

"Thanks, Jacqueline," said Meryl. "You're a lifesaver. And thanks for being flexible about the cameras."

"Mom? What's going on?"

"Hi, sweetheart. Hi, Leigh! It turns out *People* wants a few shots of dress shopping for the piece, and since Meg is already finished with that and Jeffrey doesn't want his design revealed until the wedding, that only leaves today. Just pretend they're not here."

Jo looked at Leigh, and they shared a spontaneous and unnervingly intimate glance.

"Uh, don't you think you should have asked me if I'm cool with it? It seems a little invasive," said Jo. Somehow, everything that came out of her mouth right now was making her sound like a raging bitch.

"Honey, you know what we're working on here. Please just roll with it. Like I said, pretend they're not here."

Jo sighed, pulled her phone out of her bag, and showed Jacqueline a photo of the satin rose dress.

"Ah. That was many collections ago. And not bridal. But let's see if we can replicate the aesthetic. Of course, we don't have those pants. But we can always have something made."

Jacqueline pulled a few dresses and put them in the fitting room. Jo glanced behind to find Meryl, but her mother was busy talking to the photographer.

"I can help you," Leigh said, following her into the room.

"Just come out when you're ready," Jacqueline said. "I'm going to pull a few more looks for you. And I'm calling over to Marchesa to see if they have anything from their other collections that might be more what you're looking for."

Leigh closed the door.

Jo looked at her, swallowing hard. "Like I said earlier—I don't really need help."

"We need to talk."

"We do?" Was she missing something?

"Yes. Obviously, there's an attraction between us."

Oh.

"I don't know what to say." Jo shifted uneasily.

"I think we need to defuse the situation so we can get on with working together."

"Defuse it . . . how?"

She walked to Jo, took her face in her hands, and kissed her.

The room fell away.

She smelled like vanilla and honey and just a hint of something floral. Jo's body responded even as her mind buzzed like it had just been plugged into a socket. Her mouth moved with Leigh's like they'd kissed a hundred times before, yet with the spark and wonder of the completely new.

Leigh pulled away first.

"What was *that*?" Jo said, catching her breath.

Leigh reached out and stroked Jo's hair.

Jo's heart pounded. She thought of her mother on the other side of the door. The *People* photographer. Jacqueline.

"We're doing this here?"

"Lord, you are young. No, not here. I'm staying at the Soho Grand. Meet me for a drink tonight?"

Jo's mind raced, already calculating where she could tell Toby she was going. "Yes."

"Perfect. So, now that that's settled—let's find you a wedding dress."

• • •

Meryl had begun measuring days in terms of progress versus setbacks. Today had been mostly progress: Jo was set with Marchesa, Meryl had successfully made an appointment for her mother to see a psychiatrist, and she had closed the door on that whole reality show thing. And now she had no reason to see Scott, and really, nothing good would have come from that.

She looked at Hugh next to her in bed, his reading glasses slipping down the bridge of his nose. When was the last time they'd made love? Did he even think about her that way anymore?

Meryl slipped out of bed to the bathroom. She looked at herself in the mirror, still not used to her "new" brunette hair. Hugh's only comment about it had been, "Interesting." She'd asked him, "Interesting good or interesting bad?" He said, "Whatever makes you happy." She'd found that comment maddening.

Her phone rang.

"Want me to get that?" Hugh called.

"Yes—if it's one of the girls, I'll be right there."

She began removing her mascara.

"Meryl?" Hugh called out.

She wiped her eyes and walked back into the bedroom. He handed the phone to her wordlessly.

"Hello?"

"Meryl—it's Scott."

Meryl froze, then reminded herself that she hadn't done anything wrong. She glanced uneasily at Hugh. "Scott, this isn't a good time—"

"I've got great news. E! wants to take a meeting."

"What? Scott, I told you I don't want to do this."

"You'll feel differently when you're in the room with them. Trust me."

"No—I won't. Now, please, stop talking to people about this. Just tell them it's not happening."

Hugh mouthed to her, "Who is that?"

"I have to go," she said, and hung up. She sat down on the bed, not looking at Hugh.

"Meryl, what's going on?"

"Nothing," she said, thankful—so thankful—that it was the truth.

"It didn't sound like nothing."

And so she told him—about running into Scott the night Tippy Campion came to dinner. About meeting him at City Bakery, and Bondurants, and Jane. About the reality show.

"Are you having an affair?" he asked.

"No!" she said. "Absolutely not."

"I can't believe I even have to ask you that."

"I'm telling you the truth—there's nothing going on."

"Nothing except you running around with some strange man behind my back."

"I don't have to tell you every move I make. You certainly don't tell me! At least I'm not making major decisions that threaten us financially, make us lose our home, without talking to you. I'm trying to fix the hole you put us in!"

"So it's back to that again. You're still mad about Yardley."

"Damn right, I am. You decided to risk your job right when we needed money for the girls."

"That problem's solved, Meryl—you have *People* magazine footing the bill."

"Eventually! When it's all over. In the meantime, all the money we've laid out—the credit cards maxed. I won't feel okay until they get their photos and hand us the check."

"It will be fine, Meryl."

"And that's just the wedding. Where are we going to live come August? Do you know what our options are for what we pay to live here? We'll be lucky to find a studio. In Greenpoint."

"And you think your ex-boyfriend is going to solve that with a TV show about our daughters? Are you out of your mind?"

"He's not my ex-boyfriend. And I told him I'm not interested in a show."

"So why is he calling you at ten at night?"

She didn't have an answer for him.

Hugh gathered up his pillows and a blanket and moved to the couch.

Certain places in New York City seemed designed for cinematic drama. The lobby of the Soho Grand was one of them.

To Jo, it felt like the set of an urban fairy tale with its turquoise chairs, its looming wall clock framing the reception desk, the floor-to-ceiling steel birdcages, and the potted plants with their large, drooping fronds, and in the center of it all, an incredible bottle glass staircase.

Leigh had texted Jo, reminding her to be discreet. *Photographers are everywhere.*

In the elevator, Jo's hands were slick with nervous perspiration. She'd be anxious meeting up with Leigh under normal circumstances, but the subterfuge added a level of intensity that made it almost unbearable. She was so stressed, she was nauseated.

She stood outside the hotel room for a few seconds, taking a moment to collect herself. She even gave herself a minute to think about Toby, and mentally shelved her guilt—to be dealt with later.

Leigh opened the door quickly and ushered her inside like she was ferrying state secrets across the border.

"I feel like I should be wearing a trench coat and dark glasses," she said.

"Maybe next time."

Leigh was more casually dressed than she'd ever seen her, in faded jeans and a simple white short-sleeved V-neck T-shirt. She held a glass of red wine in one hand and she was barefoot. Her toenails were painted dark red.

The room was low lit, all muted, neutral shades with big windows and a view of the Empire State Building, which glowed purple in the distance.

"Can I get you a glass of wine?" Leigh asked, kissing her on the cheek.

"Um, sure."

Jo sat on the couch and Leigh joined her with a bottle of cabernet and a glass.

"This place is amazing," Jo said.

"Yeah. I like it. I planned an event here once that went off really well, and I've been staying here ever since."

"How long have you been doing the party-planning thing?"

"Since college. I started working at this party-planning company when I was at Penn undergrad, and then a few years ago, I met Tippy at an event and she started requesting me for all her events."

Jo nodded. "Impressive."

"What do you do? I haven't really gotten any sense of that."

"Nothing right now. I was working at a coffee shop, but I got fired."

Leigh laughed. "Okay, that's not *impressive*."

"I'm not like my sisters. Amy was always obsessed with clothes. Meg studied journalism at Georgetown. It's just taking me a little longer. I'll figure it out."

"I'm sure you will," said Leigh. She moved closer to her. "You okay with this?"

"With what?"

"Being here tonight. With me."

"Yeah. Of course. I want . . ."

"What?"

"I want you. I've been thinking about you since that day at Blooming-dale's."

Leigh smiled. "I couldn't resist talking to you in the shoe department. And then to walk into the registry and find you were part of the family I was working with? I've learned to be prepared for anything when I'm working with clients, but I had a hard time keeping a straight face."

"Yeah. I guess 'straight' face is the right way to put it."

They laughed.

"So . . . where do we go from here?" Jo said.

"Look—we just need to get this out of our systems. We have to work together for the next few months. You're getting married, I don't date. So let's just defuse the tension, and we can both move on."

"Really? It's as simple as that?"

"Yeah," said Leigh. "Pretty much."

"Why don't you date?"

She smiled. "My biggest client is gunning for the Republican nomination for president of the United States. And most of my other clients are friends of his, political beasts."

"You mean—you're not . . . out?"

"No."

"Oh my God, that's so '90s."

"You're young," said Leigh.

"You're condescending," said Jo, smiling.

Leigh took the glass from her hand and set it on the coffee table. Then she kissed her, deep and full, her arms slipping easily around Jo's body. Jo felt herself flood with heat and lust and a yearning she'd never felt, not even with Caroline. When Leigh slid her hands under her shirt, she gasped.

"Oh my God," Jo said. "Don't stop. . . ."

Leigh stood, took her by the hand, and led her to the bedroom.

By midnight, Jo knew she had to leave or she'd have a hard time explaining herself to Toby.

"So what's the deal?" Leigh asked. "What made you decide to marry that guy?"

Jo propped herself up on her elbow, staring at Leigh's beautiful profile, the slope of her nose, the curve of her cheek. Leigh turned to look at her, and Jo kissed her full lips.

"I don't know," said Jo, almost whispering. "It seemed like a good idea at the time. I was really heartbroken—my ex . . . she just decimated me. Marrying my best friend was a really comforting idea. But I'm going to call it off."

"What? Why?" Leigh sat up.

"I thought . . . when I said yes, I thought it was better just to be safe than to risk feeling what I feel right now—with you. I thought I never wanted that again. But now that I feel it, I do want it. I want you."

"Jo, that's not what tonight was about. I told you—I don't date. I don't get involved. We had a good time, I'm glad we did it. But that's it—it's done. We can't do this again. I thought you understood that."

"I did—in theory. But it's different now."

"No," Leigh said, shaking her head. "It's not. Jo, you don't have to marry that guy. But I assure you, if you don't, you still won't be seeing me like this again. The next time I see you will be shopping for your wedding invitations. Or I won't be seeing you at all."

Three Months Until the Wedding

twenty-two

"Are you sure you can't come? I mean, it *is* the place we're getting married. Probably." Meg poked her head out of the bathroom. "And can you throw me my robe?"

"It's probably the place, or we're *probably* getting married?" Stowe said, rolling over in bed.

"Very funny."

"I still don't understand why you won't even consider the Vesper Club. It's a great space, and my parents have belonged there forever."

"My mom said there's logistical issues. Whatever that means. Besides, if we're doing this in the spring, we might as well look at outdoor options."

"Come back to bed and we can discuss it." He gave her a wink.

"I have to get going, Stowe. I barely have time to shower. I have an early train."

Meg had a million errands to do in Manhattan before their afternoon appointment to drive out to Long Island and see the historic estate that was their number one candidate for the wedding. Stowe had not been terribly impressed by the photos online.

"Come on—it's beautiful," Meg had said.

"Yes, but it doesn't have the same *meaning* the club has for my family."

"Well, this day is about more than your family," she said. It had become such a sore subject; they both left it at that.

Stowe pulled himself out of bed, wearing only a pair of navy and green plaid Polo boxers. His dark hair was tousled, his blue eyes bright with energy, and she was so in love with him, she wished they could rewind to the night of their engagement and plan to elope.

"I want to go with you," he said, handing her the robe. "But it wouldn't look right if I didn't show up for one of my last days at the office."

"I know. I get it. At least one of us has a career to look after."

"Babe, you'll find a job."

"Easy for you to say." She closed the bathroom door and pulled off her tank top.

After a few seconds, he knocked. She opened it an inch. "I'm serious—I have to get in the shower."

"It's easy for me to be optimistic about your job prospects because I happen to have one for you." He grinned.

"Oh yeah? What's that?"

He pushed the door open and slipped his arms around her naked body. "God, you are beautiful."

"Stowe . . ."

"Oh yeah—the job thing. Mrs. Campion, you are all work and no play."

"I'm not Mrs. Campion yet." Still, the sound of it thrilled her.

"How'd you like to come work for my father's campaign? In the press office."

"What? Where is this coming from?"

"My dad. His idea entirely. He likes you a lot, you know."

"Stowe, I'm flattered. But I don't know if that is a good idea."

"It certainly helped George Stephanopoulos's career."

That cut her protests short. George Stephanopoulos, of ABC News, at age thirty had served as then Governor Bill Clinton's press communications director during his 1992 presidential campaign.

"I'll think about it. It just feels like . . ."

Stowe pulled her close. "You worry too much."

She breathed against him, kissing his chest. He kissed the top of her head. "Now, go find us a place to get married."

Meryl waited in the lobby of the psychiatrist's office while her mother had her session. She checked the time. In two hours, they had to head out to Long Island to see Longview, the Georgian Revival mansion her mother had once visited with Meryl's father on a sightseeing day trip. A place she had never before mentioned to Meryl, but had apparently never forgotten.

The historic home had 160 acres of formal gardens, lakes, grand allées that were something out of another time and place. It had taken a few calls from Tippy to make sure the venue was available on the date of the wedding, May 7.

It was now looking like it would be an outdoor wedding. Kristin Miller, the *People* photography editor going along with them to scout the location, confirmed that it was an incredibly scenic place. "From a photography standpoint, you couldn't ask for much more on the East Coast."

Hugh was bringing Janell. Apparently, she was into photography and wanted to take some nature shots. Meryl didn't want Janell there—a walking reminder of the inevitable loss of their apartment. Meryl was still angry.

"Don't you think it's inappropriate to bring a former student to a family event?" she had asked.

"Hon, with the *People* magazine editor and wedding planner tagging along, it's not exactly an intimate event," Hugh had responded. "Besides, she's doing a lot of good work for me. Hard work—for free. Why not let her have some fun if we're taking a trip out to the country for the day."

Meryl let it go. Hugh hadn't been too hard on her about the whole Scott thing, so she really needed to deal with her anger about his job already. And it wasn't Janell's fault. She was just a kid.

"You're still here?" Her mother loomed over her, her handbag casting a shadow across Meryl's lap.

"Mother! You startled me. Of course I'm still here. I'm taking you back home." She stood up. "How did it go?"

"I think it's a waste of time."

"Of course you do."

"Did you tell her about the . . . episodes?"

"My sessions are private," she said.

"Okay, fine. Whatever works for you. Do you still want to come with us to Longview?"

"Of course! It was my idea. I should at least get a trip out of it."

Meryl noticed the papers in her hand. "What's that?" Meryl said.

Rose looked down, as if having forgotten about whatever it was she was holding. She tore the paper in half and handed it to Meryl.

Meryl stopped walking, piecing together the two halves of the prescription, squinting to read the doctor's scrawl. Prozac and Ativan.

"Mother! Why did you do that? We'll get these filled on the way."

"I'm not taking that garbage."

"The whole point of coming here is to help prevent those episodes, Mother. You know that. You don't have to take this stuff forever. What did she say about it?"

"This is a waste of time, Meryl. At my age, you are who you are." She paused, looking at her. "You, however, still have room for improvement."

Amy closed the door to her office, turned on her computer, and tried to muster some excitement. She had to leave work early today to meet everyone for the drive out to Long Island to see their wedding venue.

She was exhausted. She'd barely slept last night after the text at eleven, just before she had been about to turn off her phone. Marcus, asking if she was "around." And if she wanted to "hang out"? At eleven at night! Andy, fortunately, had been in the bathroom—hadn't heard the jarring little ping. She had deleted it. But she couldn't delete it from her mind. No more than she could delete the memory of the joy of fucking him.

And more unpleasantness: typing an e-mail informing Stella she would miss yet another meeting. She didn't know why she cared so much—it's not like Jeffrey Bruce was going to fire her for taking the time to find a wedding venue for her marriage to his son. She just hated the way Stella looked at her—like she was a mouse the cat dragged in and she now had to deal with. If Stella could make her wear a Post-it on her forehead that read DEAD WEIGHT, she would do it. Amy wanted to prove her wrong.

At least Andy would be at the marketing meeting. "I trust you to check the place out. If you like it, I'll like it," he had said.

Andy was so easygoing. Maybe too easygoing. Meg had admitted that Stowe balked at the triple-wedding idea—which Amy thought was totally normal.

A knock sounded at her door.

"How's my brand ambassador doing this morning?" Jeffrey walked in, dressed in his uniform of faded jeans and a button-down shirt and blazer. A garment bag was slung over his shoulder.

"Hi, Jeffrey! I'm just finishing up a few things. I'm going to see the venue today. For the wedding."

"I know—exciting stuff. I brought you something to wear."

He unzipped the bag with a flourish to reveal a chocolate brown, knee-length pony-print skirt.

"Oh—thanks. But I feel okay in what I'm wearing. Thanks for thinking of me, though."

"You might feel okay in what you're wearing, love, but it's not from this season. Andy told me that *People* photographers are going along." Jeffrey tapped his temple to indicate, I'm always thinking about these things.

"Oh. Got it. Okay. Thanks."

"The blouse is in here, too. I'm sending up the boots. Just wanted to hand-deliver these to tell you to enjoy. And we'll see you kids at dinner tomorrow night." He held her by the shoulders and gave her a kiss on the cheek.

"Thanks, Jeffrey."

"Dad!" he said with a wink on his way out the door.

Amy sighed. It was a pretty skirt.

Her office door opened again. Stella.

"I just got your e-mail. If you're not making the meeting—again—I need that Excel sheet with all the SKUs for the upcoming shoot."

Amy nodded. "Sorry about missing the meeting, but I'll—"

The door slammed shut.

Her phone vibrated with a text.

I'm cool with you blowing me off last night, but now I'm literally a block away. Shooting today in Chelsea Market. Meet up after?

Marcus. Amy was flooded with guilt. She had to put an end to this—whatever this was.

She could just text him to leave her alone. But she couldn't help but want to see him one last time. It was weak, she knew. But she was going to end it—or stop it before it became something to end. Was that so wrong?

Meet me in the Starbucks in the Google building.

Now?

Y.

She found Marcus sitting at the counter, at the window facing Ninth Avenue. He handed her a cup.

God, he was beautiful.

"I got you a latte," he said.

"Oh—that was . . . Thanks." She slid next to him. "I can't stay long. I just wanted to tell you that I can't see you again."

He smiled. "You could have just texted me that. It's not like—you know, we're not a couple breaking up or anything. But I'm still glad you showed up."

"Yeah. I felt like I should explain."

"You have a boyfriend. A fiancé."

"You know?"

"I mean, your ring is kind of hard to miss." He shrugged. "But sometimes that doesn't mean . . . Well, people have all kinds of deals. But it's cool. It was fun while it lasted. And maybe since I'm doing so much work for the company now, it's better not to mix it all up, you know?"

"I think you're right." *Especially since my fiancé is Jeffrey Bruce's son.*

He leaned over and kissed her on the cheek. "Don't look so freaked out. It's all good." The closeness of him, the smell of him, made her blood rush fast and hot. She wanted to say, I take it back—never mind. Let's do this. Whatever this is.

Was she ready to walk down the aisle, never to feel this way again? As if reading her mind, he touched her face in a gesture so intimate, she felt as much his lover as she was Andy's. More so. How could she feel this way? He was a stranger. He was nothing to her.

He kissed her, and for a heart-stopping moment, she gave in to it. But then she pulled back, breaking the spell.

"I have to go." She pulled her bag off the back of the chair abruptly, and in that moment, caught a glimpse of someone outside the window. Someone looking right at them.

Stella.

Longview was the type of house Meg had dreamed of living in as a little girl. In middle school, she had been friends with a girl who was heiress to a beef fortune. They lived on Park Avenue during the week, and during the weekends drove out to Long Island to their estate. It also had a name, though Meg could no longer remember it. But she had fallen in love with the house, and all her romantic fantasies—she was still too young to care that much about boys—centered around a glamorous life in a historic, stately home on the Long Island Sound.

Longview was not on the water, but the 160 acres of grounds included ponds and lakes and picturesque little streams running alongside beds of flowers imported from all over the world. It was one of the nicer days in late February, and nothing was in bloom, but she had seen the photos on the Web site.

Now that she was seeing the estate in person, she felt confident Stowe would love it as much as she did.

"The house was completed in 1906," said their guide, Cliff, a handsome, slightly effeminate guy in his late twenties with dark hair combed in a 1950s style, wearing a sweater vest and a bow tie. "John Longchester built it for his bride, Amelia, since she agreed to move here from England."

"Now, that's what I call a compromise," said Meg, laughing.

No one so much as cracked a smile. What was everyone so grumpy about? The guide was probably annoyed with the size of the group. And they were an odd bunch: Meryl and Hugh, her father's research assistant—why she was along, Meg couldn't begin to imagine—the wedding planner, an editor from *People* magazine, and their six-foot-five, tattooed African American photographer named Paz.

When they showed up at the front door of the estate, Cliff had said, "Well! Today you have enough people for the wedding party right here."

Clearly, he had very little grasp of the scope of the event being planned.

The tour started indoors.

"These chandeliers were originally candeliers. This entire interior underwent a renovation in the 1920s. The mirrors are Chinese Chippendale. The carpets are from 1760, made in England. That Wedgwood bust is of Cicero, and the other is, of course, John Milton."

They traipsed through the house, Leigh taking notes. Jo seemed to be trailing her like a puppy, Meg noticed. What was that all about? Amy was moping like she'd rather be getting a root canal. Her mother was so busy talking to the *People* editor, Cliff had to shoot her a warning look like an irritated elementary school teacher. And her father had his usual dreamy, distracted expression, which told her he was thinking about his book. The house no doubt reminded him of some Alcott family trivia.

"You'll notice the laurel leaf moldings in the ceiling are mirrored in the rug. And all these portraits on the walls are of the original family members. Most are by John Singer Sargent. As a painter, he was known for depicting his subjects exactly as they were to him—not sugar-coating it."

Jo leaned in, examining a painting of a woman with stringy pale hair and a bulbous nose. The only attractive part of the portrait was the emerald-cut ruby around her neck.

"Not a looker, was she?" Jo said.

"Well, courtship was not based nearly so much on today's notion of romantic love," said Cliff. "It was a man's job to make money, and a woman's job to marry it and care for the home and family. People were very sensible."

Meg, impatient, checked her e-mail. The wedding was in May, and at this rate, they would still be in the middle of this tour.

"You mentioned on the phone that there is a glass-enclosed atrium leading to the gardens?" said Leigh.

"Yes, but I thought you'd like to see the upstairs first? The third floor has fourteen working fireplaces. The master bedroom has a Chippendale mahogany bed dating back to 1750."

"It sounds fabulous. But I think we can get right to the areas of the house that are relevant to the event we're planning."

Finally, Tippy's event planner was proving herself useful. Meg knew her mother would never risk being rude simply in the name of hustling things along.

"Very well."

Cliff clearly hated them, but at least Meg had a fighting chance of making it back to D.C. in time for a late dinner with Stowe.

"This south terrace provides the primary transition between the house and gardens. When we do outdoor affairs, this is usually the reception area for the place cards and possibly a small bar. The grounds have many distinct areas, including the lotus pool, the walled garden, the allée of linden trees, the rose garden, the pond, and the south lawn. Most of our weddings take place in the walled garden. So, in the interest of brevity, I'm assuming that's where you'd like to go first?" he said pointedly to Leigh.

"Sounds good to me."

The group followed Cliff down a stone path. Even in the winter, the grounds were beautiful. Meg could imagine the place in full bloom. She sighed happily, genuine excitement about the wedding coursing through her.

"Longview is the preeminent example of an English naturalistic garden. You won't find a better experience of this on the East Coast. All of this will be in full bloom in May."

High brick walls surrounded the garden; they entered through ornate iron gates.

"The flowers are organized in formal plantings. The bridal path—" He gestured along the stone walk. "—is lined with wild bluebells.

Ladies—" He turned to Meg and Amy and Jo. "—you will walk right up to here, the garden's edge, culminating near the lotus pool."

"Where do we put the chuppah?" said Rose.

Meryl looked at her sharply. "Nowhere, Mother. We're not having a religious ceremony."

"You don't even need a formal altar, because it's framed by the pillars there. The statue spouts water in the warm-weather months, but we can turn that off if you prefer," said Cliff.

"I prefer a chuppah, is what I prefer," grumbled Rose.

"Since when do you care about a chuppah? We never even belonged to a synagogue."

Meg looked at her father.

He smiled and held out his arm, bent at the elbow. "Let's test out the aisle."

Meg looped her arm through his, laughing as they walked down the bare walkway. She had to admit that despite a bumpy month or so, things were looking up. Paz took a few shots of the lotus pool. Meryl and the editor conferred in low, delighted voices.

"It's so desolate!" complained Rose.

Everyone turned to look at her.

"Oh, it's just this time of year," said Cliff quickly. "I assure you, in three months, it'll be an entirely different tableau. Didn't you see the Web site?"

"Web site? I thought we drove all the way out here to see it in person. I could have stayed in the apartment to look at a Web site."

"Gran, you were here yourself in the summer," said Meg gently. "You're the one who suggested this place."

"Well, not every idea is a winner," said Rose. The group settled into silence.

"I have a question about the flow of the guests," said Leigh. "Can we walk back up to the south terrace? I want to run through the transition from cocktails to getting everyone seated."

"Certainly," said Cliff, clearly relieved to hear a voice of reason. "And again, there is more than one way to do this. But I will show you our preference and we can adjust accordingly."

They all began walking back up to the house. Meg pulled her phone out of her bag and texted Stowe, *It's going to be beautiful.*

"Where's Amy?" said Meryl.

Everyone looked around. She wasn't there.

Jo tried to catch Leigh's eye, but she was studiously avoiding her.

Back at the south porch, Jo waited for her mother and Cliff to become absorbed in some detail or another, before pulling Leigh's arm. "I need to talk to you."

"This isn't the time or the place, Jo. Come on."

Leigh was so measured, so distant. It was like the night at the Soho Grand never happened.

"Well, you haven't answered any of my texts or calls, so . . . when?" She knew she sounded like a child, like she was twelve instead of twenty-three. And she knew that she was the one getting married, but she couldn't help it. She wanted Leigh, had to have her. Wanted her more than she had even wanted Caroline. And now she was looking for a sign. Could she really walk down the aisle with someone she wasn't in love with? It had seemed reasonable that night in Philadelphia, outside, running around like silly college kids again. It felt reasonable walking around that gorgeous Leonard Street apartment building, the home they would make together. But it felt decidedly, completely wrong when she had been in Leigh's bed. And just as wrong now, standing next to her, in the place where she was supposed to get married.

"Jo, I told you how this was going to go. Don't make it difficult. I'd really like it if we could be friends."

Jo's phone rang. She sighed. Toby. There had been a time when Toby was her friend.

Now, he was going to be her husband.

Meg found Amy back in the garden, sitting on a stone bench.

Meg waved her along. "Everyone's back up at the house."

"I'm just going to hang out here for a bit."

"Why?"

"It's so peaceful. Even if it is desolate like Gran said."

"Are you okay?"

"Yeah. I'm fine." Amy sat with rounded shoulders, her hair falling into her face, her hands knitting together as she picked off her nail polish.

As much as Amy drove her crazy, with her petty competitiveness and insecurity, she was her sister, and Meg loved her and didn't want to see her upset. And clearly, she was not happy.

"So what do you think of this place?" Meg asked, sitting next to her. The stone bench was cold through her wool pants. "I really like it. I can see it working. The scale is so big that honestly, it would be too much for just one of us. But the three of us—it will be pretty amazing. Perfect."

Amy started to cry.

"Hey. What's going on? You don't like this place?"

Amy shook her head. "It's fine."

"Did you have fight with Andy?"

"I'm sorry. This is all my fault," she sobbed. "I never should have planned to get married so quickly. This was your time, and I stepped on it—and now look."

"It's fine—really. I don't mind this triple-wedding idea. Besides, it burns my future mother-in-law's ass, and that makes it *totally* worth it for me."

Amy didn't even crack a smile. "I should have waited a year."

"Amy, honestly, the logistics of the wedding are the least of my problems."

This seemed to momentarily snap her out of her funk. "Don't tell me you're fighting with Stowe?"

"Not fighting. Just . . . not connecting. I don't know. It's probably me. It's like, the closer I get to becoming part of his family, the more I wonder if I should. I'm really afraid it's going to take over my life. It's already cost me my job."

"Marrying the man you love is more important than a job."

"Easy for you to say. You have both in one package."

Amy suddenly started sobbing, her head in her hands. "I don't know if I do."

Meg put her arm around her, drawing her close. "What does that mean?"

"I don't know if I love him. Not the way I'm supposed to."

"Oh, Amy. This is probably just stress about the wedding."

"Yeah. And maybe you're just stressing about the wedding."

"Maybe I am. That's what I've been telling myself."

They sat in silence, looking out at the acres of grounds.

"Can I ask you something?"

"Sure."

It was strange—Amy had never confided in her. She always preferred talking to Jo, never wanting to admit weakness to Meg, even though Meg probably could have given her some experienced advice. That she was turning to her now—well, she must really be desperate.

"Are you ever attracted to other men?"

Meg wished she could tell Amy that yes, she was—because clearly that was what she needed to hear. But the truth was that she had not been, not since the first day she met Stowe.

"I haven't been with Stowe as long as you've been with Andy," she said carefully. "So no, I haven't been attracted to someone else yet. But I'm sure, over the course of a lifetime together, it will happen. It's normal to be attracted to other people, Amy. We're human."

"What if I acted on it?"

"Did you?"

Amy nodded. Fresh tears.

"Does he know?"

Amy shook her head. "No. But this woman at work saw me with him—I was just trying to say good-bye. End it—and it wasn't even anything to end. Just one time. And now I'm afraid she's going to tell Andy!"

"That would be really stupid on her part."

"Why?"

"Haven't you heard the expression 'don't shoot the messenger'? The person who delivers unwanted news always gets burnt by it. If she tells him, it could really backfire on her."

"Not as bad as it will on me."

"Who was the other guy?"

"Ugh, I don't want to talk about it. And he's really—It doesn't matter." She paused, peering into the distance. "Is that Gran?"

Sure enough, their grandmother was slowly making her way down the stone path. "What are you girls doing hiding out here?" Rose called out.

When she was closer, within comfortable earshot, Meg said, "We're just talking. Where's everyone else? Are they finished?"

"Finished? We're going to be here for hours!"

"Oh."

"What's the problem?" Rose said, pushing up her glasses. Meg slid over to make room at the end of the bench. Rose sat, leaning forward to get a closer look at Amy.

"Nothing, Gran. Everything's fine."

"Um-hmm," she said. "Which one of you is having second thoughts?"

Meg and Amy looked at each other. Amy shook her head, ever so slightly.

"No one's having second thoughts, Gran," said Meg. "We're just taking a little breather from the tour."

"Well, have it your way. You can lie to me if you want. I see nothing wrong with a good solid lie every once and a while. The world couldn't exist without them. Just as long as you don't lie to yourselves."

twenty-three

Jo looked across the breakfast table at Toby and thought, *I have to tell him.*

She had exactly one hour before her *People* magazine interview, where she would be expected to say whatever it was that excited brides-to-be said. She would talk about her engagement, the dress, the honeymoon. She would talk about how she and Toby met.

How they fell in love.

Except, they hadn't. Or rather, she hadn't. He knew that she wasn't madly in love with him. She'd been clear about that. And he didn't care. But he also didn't know she was now infatuated with someone else. This thing with Leigh—and it could only be called a "thing" because it barely existed—it wasn't a relationship, it wasn't a friends-with-benefits situation. It had been a one-night stand, but Jo couldn't accept that it would never be anything more. That it would never happen again. And even if Leigh stuck by her insistence that they just be friends—at least Jo knew she could feel passion again. That she wasn't dead inside after Caroline, and that she shouldn't want to be.

The entire thing was making her sick. She was exhausted. Her nerves were so bad, she'd thrown up twice.

"Toby," she said quietly.

He looked up from his iPad, shaking a lock of blond hair from his face. With the light coming in off the park, he was lit from behind, like a photo from an Instagram "Hot Guys with Coffee" series. He deserved to be with a woman who was in love with him. There were probably legions of them out there.

"What time's your interview?" he asked. "Should I roll with you?"

"No, I'm just going to go myself. It shouldn't take too long." Truthfully, she had no idea how long the interview would take. Her mother had simply told her to show up at the apartment at ten wearing the Jeffrey Bruce outfit Amy had messengered over, black pants and a black blouse with a mandarin collar. I'm not wearing this, she'd muttered to herself, and paired the pants with a faded gray Lucky brand Union Jack T-shirt.

"Cool," said Toby.

"Listen," she said, unbuttoning the top button of the pants, which were too small for her. "I'm thinking maybe this is a little crazy."

"It's totally crazy. So just rock it. You look gorgeous." He jumped up from his seat and walked around the table to hug her.

She slipped her arms around him and tried to muster something resembling the yearning she felt for Leigh whenever she was anywhere near her. Nothing.

"I mean us. What we're doing," Jo murmured against his chest.

"It's not crazy. It's perfect," he said, stroking her hair.

She pulled back. "Aren't you even upset that I'm saying that? That I'm thinking it?"

"No. Look, your mother and your sisters are in fairy-tale-wedding la-la land, and we're different. We're getting married because it works for us. We don't expect it to be something it's not."

Jo crossed her arms. "What do you expect it to be?"

"I expect to spend my life with my favorite person in the world, a beautiful woman I want more than I want anyone else."

"What about what I want?"

"You want security. A safe landing. And sometimes you like it when we fuck. That's more than a lot of people have going into a marriage."

"What if I'm attracted to other people?" Jo bit her lip.

"Then be with them. Like I said, this isn't your parents' marriage."

"Do *you* plan to be with other people?"

He shrugged. "Probably. I mean, life is long. Why not?"

"Toby, what the hell? What's the point in even doing this?" She paused, remembering their last conversation about marriage. "Is this about your trust fund?"

"No. I mean, yes, I'm happy to get it. And I have to marry someone eventually. But I'm picking you because of the way I feel about you and because I think we have as much of a chance of being happy together as anyone else who maybe goes about things more . . . conventionally. I'm in love with you; you're not in love with me. I can live with that, Jo."

But I don't know if I can.

"Jo, go do the interview. Get some pictures taken—we'll hang them in the entrance foyer to the place on Leonard Street. And then we're going to have an epic life together."

It was useless. There was nothing to say that would provoke Toby into being the one to break off the engagement. If it was going to happen, it was on her. Jo didn't know what to do. She wished she had a sign from the universe, but she suspected she was on her own with this one.

There was just one other person she needed to talk to. And that person wouldn't be happy about it.

Meryl sighed.

The apartment had never looked more beautiful. It was magazine ready. And it should be for the weeks of work that Meryl had put into it: fresh paint, a new coffee table, photos that had been sitting in piles for months if not years finally framed.

Preparing the apartment for the *People* magazine shoot had been bittersweet. After decades in the same place, she was seeing it through fresh eyes. She looked at the pencil marks near her bedroom closet, where she had measured the girls' growth through high school and middle school, the initials *M, A,* and *J* etched into the eggshell-colored paint. She had never covered the marks, but in August when they were forced to move, she would leave them behind forever. In the girls' bathroom, she noticed for the first time in years the place where the tiles were crooked, where she and Hugh had an ill-fated turn at home renovation. One of the tiles was handmade by Meg, a Mother's Day craft from school. It was a blue tile with a red heart. Meryl traced it with her finger, wondering if she could somehow take it with them.

"I don't know why they want to photograph us here and not at our own apartments," Amy had said.

"They'll do that too," Meryl told her.

Meryl suspected part of the reason they wanted photographs in the childhood home was because she'd told them the anecdote about them dressing up as brides as little girls, walking down the aisle together.

"That's priceless!" said Joan.

"I have photos of it somewhere."

Now, in the apartment, the writer Kristin and the photographer wanted them to re-create that scene. Amy and Jo visibly balked at the idea, while Meg simply hung back silently.

"Girls, come on," said Meryl. No one moved, and if she'd had a cattle prod handy, she would have gladly used it. What was with the three of them?

Hugh was working at the dining room table—the academic at home. The fireplace was lit. Kristin had commented that she rarely saw a working fireplace in Manhattan. Meryl hoped that made it into the article.

It was hard for her to believe that, after twenty years, they would have to move out this summer. She shook the thought away.

"They walked down this hall," Meryl said to Kristin, turning to shoot the girls a death glare. "And I'll never forget what they were wearing, because they squabbled about it every time. Hugh walked Meg first, then Amy, then Jo." Meryl looped her arm through Amy's and dragged her down the hall toward the kitchen like a recalcitrant dog on a leash.

"Well, we can get that shot later," Kristin said, glancing at the photographer. "Let's get a shot of Mr. Becker working on his book."

Hugh, suddenly more animated than he had ever been during the entire wedding-planning process, smiled and then bent over his laptop as if mid-sentence.

"The book is nonfiction, correct?" asked Kristin.

"That's right. It's a definitive look at the Alcott sisters. I published a book about Abigail Alcott—the model for the mother in Louisa May Alcott's *Little Women*—in the 1980s. I've been working on this off and on since then. The challenge was making it less academic and something the commercial audience would like."

Meryl looked up. She didn't know that. Why had he never mentioned it? Or had he shared this with her, and she simply never registered it?

"And how is it coming along?"

"Extremely well. I think I've finally cracked it. I have a new research assistant—a high school student helping me in her spare time. Her input has been invaluable. She brings a less rigid approach. It's changed the entire tenor of the project."

"How did you find a high school student who was interested in researching the Alcott family in her spare time?"

Hugh launched into Janell's background and her arrival at Yardley as a scholarship student. One of his students. Until . . .

Meryl shot him a warning look. Hugh was not going to get into all that. Not with *People* magazine.

"Hugh . . ."

"So they fired you? For standing up against an unfair policy? In defense of your student?"

This, from the photographer.

"It wasn't, in theory, an unfair policy," said Hugh. "In fact, I'd helped enact it a few years ago. But it had been established during a certain climate of cheating—of a sense among students that they could do no wrong, that they were privileged, they were owed good grades somehow. But that didn't apply here. And maybe doesn't apply most of the time. Like laws or policies or anything else, I felt the 'one strike you're out' rule should be reexamined. But I was alone on that. It's worked out for the best, however. Janell and I are, as my mother used to say, making lemonade out of lemons."

Kristin was typing furiously into her laptop. Meryl looked around the room frantically, wondering how to intervene.

"Kristin, maybe you want to get started with Amy? I know she might have to get back to the office," Meryl said. "Hugh, can I speak to you for a minute?"

She dragged him into his office and closed the door.

"What the hell? Why would you get into all that? You want the whole world to know you were fired from your job?"

"I'm not ashamed of what happened at Yardley, Meryl. I'm sorry you are—but that's really your issue. Kristin wants to write about the girls because they're real people—not celebrities. So we're real people with real problems. And it's not even a problem—it's all worked out for the best. Why do you feel the need to control everything? We're a family, and that's what they want to see."

"Sure! Why don't I just tell them how my mother hates you because you told me to have an abortion and we didn't raise our kids Jewish. Since we're being real!"

A knock on the door. "Um, Meryl?"

Kristin. Oh God. Had she heard them?

Meryl slowly opened the door.

"Sorry to interrupt," Kristin said. "I'm just looking for Jo? Our photographer wants a group shot."

"Of course. Let me find her."

With no luck in the bedrooms or kitchen, Meryl finally found the bathroom in the hallway outside the bedrooms locked.

"Jo? Are you in there?"

"Yeah."

"Are you okay?"

A pause, and the sound of the door unlocking.

Jo opened it a few inches, looking pale—almost green.

"What's wrong?"

"I don't know." Jo sat on the floor.

"Are you sick?"

"I think I'm just stressed."

"About what?"

"I don't know if I should go through with this whole thing."

Meryl felt herself go pale too. "What 'whole thing'? The wedding?"

"Yeah."

"Jo, it's normal to be stressed in the months leading up to the wedding. I think Meg is feeling the same way. Even Amy doesn't seem herself. But you have to stay focused on the love that brought you to make the commitment in the first place."

"Mom, I'm sorry, but I have to break the engagement. I can't—"
Jo leaned over suddenly and retched into the toilet.

"You *are* sick, poor thing."

"I keep waiting for it to pass, but it doesn't. I've been nauseated off and on for weeks. And I'm so tired, Mom. All I want to do is sleep."

"For weeks?"

Jo nodded.

Meryl reached for the towel rack to steady herself. She could feel herself back in her dorm room, saying those exact words to Hugh.

"Jo," she said slowly. "You're not stressed. You're not sick. You're pregnant."

One
Month
Until the
Wedding

twenty-four

Hunter Cross read from her laptop, glancing up every few seconds to glare at Meg after particularly offensive passages. It was as if she had the *People* magazine piece memorized.

"'While the three sisters have had a picture-perfect road to the altar, the father of the bride, sixty-year-old Hugh Becker, has had a bumpier time of late. He recently was fired from his twenty-year teaching position at the prestigious Yardley School when he stood up against what he believes to be an unfairly dogmatic policy toward academic cheating.'"

Hunter closed her laptop with an aggressive slam. "Do you understand," she said to Meg, "that we cannot afford a whiff of scandal right now?"

Meg looked at Stowe, crossing her arms. To say she felt ambushed was a gross understatement. She thought he'd called her to the Campion campaign headquarters for a strategy session—not a crucifixion over the *People* online article—which in her opinion was completely positive.

"That comment would make sense, Hunter, if there were any 'whiff of scandal' in this piece."

"Your father was fired from his job—essentially for defending academic dishonesty. Don't you think that's something you should have mentioned to us ahead of time so we could do damage control? If you're going to be a member of this team—"

Meg cut her off. "Correction, Hunter—I *am* a member of this team. More importantly, I'm a member of this family. Which is more than you can say. So why don't you adjust your attitude."

"This is extremely unprofessional," Hunter said to Stowe, packing her laptop into her oversized Hermès bag. "And I think Reed would agree with me." She stalked out of the office.

"Thanks for the ambush!" Meg said to Stowe.

"I could say the same to you."

"What's that supposed to mean?"

"Why didn't you tell me your father was fired? You said he was on sabbatical to finish his book."

"That's what my parents told me! And frankly, it's none of my business and none of yours."

Stowe inhaled deeply. "I'm sorry, babe, come here. Please calm down." He reached for her hand, and she begrudgingly gave it to him. She leaned on the edge of his desk, avoiding eye contact. Surprisingly, she felt tears in her eyes.

"Every time I think things are back on track, that they're finally clicking, something happens to ruin it," she said, her voice wavering.

"Nothing's ruined," he said. "This is just politics. It's a game, and you're learning to play it. And part of that game is knowing that in this stage of things, everything matters. Everything is our business, because the whole world is watching my father. I know it's an adjustment. But know that I love you and we're on the same team."

"It doesn't feel that way. It feels like you and Hunter are the team. And I keep walking in from the outside."

"That's not true."

"I don't like her."

"Okay, I get that. Loud and clear. But did you like everyone you worked with at Poliglot? It's just a job, Meg. And it's going to be great for you. For us."

He kissed her and she felt her body relax, the tension ebbing.

"I'm sorry I didn't tell you about my dad's job situation. But I really didn't know until the day of the interview. And even then it didn't seem like a big deal—at least, not the way Hunter is making it out to be. My father is a good man. He cares so much about his students. He stood up for something he thinks is right. I don't see how that can hurt Reed."

"Well, it will get spun. The way Hunter spoke about it—she was just relaying the way the other side will talk about it. That's her job. None of this is personal." He stroked the lock of her hair that came loose from her ponytail.

"I guess a lot of the stress will be off after the wedding," she said.

"Yes. Oh! Before I forget, there's a scheduling conflict with the honeymoon."

"What kind of conflict?"

"My father has his first major campaign event in the South. We have to be there."

"When's the event?"

"May tenth. Three days after the wedding."

"Are you sure?"

"We can't miss it. I'm sorry."

Meg nodded. She had to be professional—adult. She could look on the bright side; it would be her first appearance as a member of the Campion campaign team. A short time ago, she would have been traveling to the event just attempting to get an interview with Senator Campion and members of his team. Now, she'd be the one granting or denying access to the press, giving a few sound bites herself.

"We'll reschedule the honeymoon. And maybe we can find something romantic to do in . . . Where are we going, exactly?"

"Texas."

"Honeymoon in Texas," she said, smiling.

He hugged her. "I love you."

"I know," she said.

Jo was embarrassed to tell the Marchesa team that after custom-ordering the white satin pants, they now had to be completely retailored to accommodate her pregnancy.

"Thanks for coming with me," she said to Leigh. Her mother had bailed last minute, saying something "came up." She was too busy now with wedding preparations and the press to deal with minutiae like a bridal outfit that would no longer fit on the wedding day. "I need a second opinion."

"Not a problem," said Leigh, holding open the door to the Marchesa showroom. "That's what I get paid for."

As if Jo needed a reminder that their relationship was purely professional. But she was thankful that the Campions were putting Leigh up in New York for the final weeks leading up to the wedding, for last-minute emergencies and finalizing details. And of course, it stoked Jo's fantasy that there would be a repeat of the Soho Grand night. But just a fantasy, that's all it ever would be from now on.

Leigh shrugged off her coat, revealing a black floral print Ted Baker dress, cinched at the waist, very 1950s. Jo wanted to tear it off her.

Instead, she dutifully changed into the pants and stood on a pedestal in front of a massive mirror so the tailors could adjust the waist, while Leigh perused the racks of dresses.

"How far along are you?" asked a woman bending at Jo's waist with a fistful of pins.

"Almost three months," said Jo.

She couldn't believe it. In fact, saying the words aloud felt like a joke—a lie. Glancing in the mirror, she caught sight of Leigh looking at her. Their eyes met, and Jo's heart beat faster.

"How exciting!" said the woman.

"What? Oh. Yeah."

Exciting was one word for it. Terrifying was another.

She was going to be a mother. Her own life was a confusing tangle, a mess. She hadn't even had time since college to find a real job. And now she was going to have a baby before the end of the summer? A baby?!

Jo wanted to see it as a gift—as the "blessing" that her gran and her mother had insisted it was. But she just couldn't see it as anything other than the colossal mistake it was.

Toby wasn't helping matters. When she told him the news, he'd been calm and supportive at first, telling her he'd go with her to have the abortion. And then she told him there wasn't going to be an abortion.

"Why the fuck not?" he'd said. Just like that: Why the fuck not?

"For one thing, I'm pretty far along. And another, it's just not something I want to do. It doesn't seem right in this situation. I mean, we can afford it. We're getting married."

"But I don't want a kid," he said. "Jo, the whole point is that it's you and me—to travel, to party, to *live*. Where does a baby fit into that?"

"I don't know where it fits in! But it's in my goddamn body, for one thing. So it's got to fit in. Or we can just call this whole thing off."

No, he said. He didn't want to do that. He didn't want to "lose her."

Yet they'd barely spoken in the week since she broke the news. Toby was suddenly very busy.

"You're all finished, love. You can change out of these now," said the seamstress.

Jo stepped down and headed back to the dressing rooms. She closed the curtain on her dressing area, stepping out of the pants carefully. She looked at her body. The new curve of her lower abdomen was subtle but unmistakable. It was already difficult to fit into her tightest jeans. She felt betrayed by her body. Her body, which had responded to Toby's touch, had allowed her to get pregnant. The same body that wanted Leigh so very badly.

Damn it.

She pulled on her cargo pants and sweater, sitting on the floor to get her high tops laced.

Leigh pulled back the curtain. "You ready to go?"

"I could have been naked in here."

"I could see you underneath the curtain, sitting. Come on—I have to meet Tippy at the Vesper Club to go over plans for the rehearsal dinner."

"I thought the rehearsal dinner was at Landmarc?"

"It is. But I'm staying at the Vesper Club this week."

Jo smiled. "No more Soho Grand?"

"Jo." She shook her head.

"Leigh, what the hell am I doing?"

"You're doing the right thing," Leigh said, glancing behind her. She walked into the dressing room and closed the curtain. Sitting on a leather bench, she sighed. "What do you want to happen, Jo? Do you want to be a single mother? You don't even have a job."

"I want to have a job. I always planned on having a career. I just haven't figured it out yet."

"Well, figuring it out with a rich husband and a beautiful home for your baby is better than the alternative. Trust me. I'm older than you, and I've seen a lot more of the way the world works."

"I don't know how you can be so practical about things. So detached."

Jo pulled herself off the ground and faced the mirror. If she looked at Leigh, she wouldn't be able to hold it together.

But then Leigh appeared behind her, meeting her gaze in the reflection. "I work hard at it."

"Why?" Jo said, turning around. "Haven't you ever been in love? Don't you want that?"

"I can't afford it."

Jo pulled her against her body, pressed her mouth to Leigh's lips, holding her so hard, she was sure she was hurting her. Leigh's entire body stiffened, pulling away slightly before she gave in, kissing her back with a ferocity that told Jo once and for all that she wasn't alone in this.

"Goddamn it," Leigh said, pulling away.

"I want to be with you," Jo said. "For real. I want—"

"Just get married, Jo. Just get married, and get on with it."

"What's so important?" Meryl asked Hugh. "I just canceled on Jo. We were supposed to go to Marchesa."

"Janell has something to show you."

The girl approached her nervously. "My friend has an, um, internship at a cable network. They do documentaries and stuff. Anyway, um, she knows I'm working with Mr. Becker, so when she saw this, she e-mailed it to me."

She handed Meryl a document. The letterhead read, SCOTT SOBEL PRODUCTIONS. She skimmed it, and her heart started to pound. Then she started over from the top, reading more slowly.

It was a pitch for a "docu-soap" called *The Wedding Sisters,* from "Executive producer Scott Sobel." It cited his litany of hits, and announced the *The Wedding Sisters* as his first documentary venture. It named everyone in the family, with descriptions that made them sound like something out of a cheap romantic comedy. "Meryl Becker, the midlife striver, a more relatable Kris Jenner; Hugh Becker, the befuddled father, a quiet academic unwillingly swept along the tide of his daughters' sensational marriage matches and media appeal; Meg Becker, a Grace Kelly–look-alike ice queen whose perfection snagged her a modern-day JFK Jr.; Amy Becker, the classic middle child always struggling to keep up, marrying her college sweetheart who just happens to be the heir to an all-American fashion empire; Jo Becker, a gorgeous bisexual who snagged a Danish royal. Rose Kleinman, an enigmatic octogenarian hiding a family secret. *The Wedding Sisters* is an examination of our culture's obsession with perfection, the billion-dollar wedding industry, and one family's determination to have it all."

Meryl dropped the papers and covered her mouth. "Oh my God. Can he do this?"

"I don't know, Meryl—can he? Did you sign anything?"

"No! Absolutely not. I told him the girls would never agree to a show. And he can't do anything without us. I just . . . Why would he shop this around?"

"Excuse me," Janell piped up, "but—he doesn't need your permission, 'cause this isn't a reality show. It's, you know, him just putting together a story."

"What does that mean?" said Hugh.

"We're the subjects. Not the participants," said Meryl weakly.

"Happy now?" said Hugh.

For Amy, it was the dress that made the wedding feel real.

Everything else—the invitations, the menu tasting, the cake, the visits to Longview—all had an abstract quality. It could be happening to someone else. Maybe it was because she was doing everything with her sisters, and they had to agree on everything unless Leigh stepped in as a tiebreaker. But the fittings for the Jeffrey Bruce gown were all her. They made her feel like a bride.

She knocked on Jeffrey's office door, and he called out for her to come in.

"Am I too early?" she said.

"No, no—come in. I'm ready."

He was wearing his tortoiseshell reading glasses, and he removed them and left them on his desk, walking to the closet.

She smiled as he pulled out the dress. "I can't believe this is the final fitting."

"We are getting close! Come on, sweetheart—to the fitting room."

They walked down the hall to one of the fitting rooms where they auditioned models for the runway shows. It had huge windows, lots of natural light, dressing rooms, and wall-to-wall mirrors.

Amy changed into the gown with the help of one of Jeffrey's seamstresses. The organza and tulle ivory dress had a boned bodice and full skirt. It was a fairy-tale dress, fit for a princess. Amy didn't understand how Jo and Meg could be so understated with their dresses. It was their wedding day!

She stepped onto the elevated platform so Jeffrey could assess and make any adjustments.

"Oh my God, it looks amazing," Amy said, gingerly touching the skirt.

"The bustle needs a little work. Nancy, be a doll and excuse us for a few."

"Can I see the back?" Amy said, turning to look over her shoulder. "Wow. The bustle. It's so . . . bridal."

"Is that a bad thing?" said Jeffrey.

"What? No! It's my favorite part of the dress."

"Just checking. It's normal to get cold feet, you know."

"I don't have cold feet," she said. "And if anything, this gown makes me even more excited."

"That's good to hear," he said, his eyes meeting hers in the mirror. Something about his expression made her stomach tense.

"Yes, well, it's true."

He nodded, as if contemplating something. He knelt down, working with the lower portion of the dress. When he spoke, she couldn't see his face. "I heard about your little tryst. With the model."

Amy gasped. It was all she could do not to topple off the pedestal. "Oh my God. I can explain. . . ."

Fuck you, Stella. Meg had been wrong. Stella had told on her, and no one shot the messenger—though at that moment, Amy would have gladly pulled the trigger.

"Amy, listen, these things happen," Jeffrey said. "I just need to know you're going to be discreet."

Discreet? What was he talking about? Did he think—?

"What? No—Jeffrey, it will never happen again. I'm really appalled and ashamed of myself. Andy deserves better. It will never, *never* happen again." She started to cry, which only mortified her further.

He put his arm around her. "Then there's no problem! Don't get so upset. That wasn't the purpose of this conversation. No one should cry in their wedding dress, right?"

She tried to crack a smile, but couldn't manage it. "Okay," she whimpered. "But honestly, I feel sick about it."

"Amy, doll, just forget we ever had this conversation. I only wanted to talk to you because I don't want anything to jeopardize the wedding. You know how the press can be."

Suddenly Amy's remorse was eclipsed by something worse: the slow realization that Jeffrey was more concerned about the wedding and all the publicity he was getting from his new "brand ambassador" than he was about his son's feelings.

It was clear now who had been leaking everything to the press, tipping the paparazzi off as to where she and her sisters would be and when.

"I should tell Andy the truth," she said quietly, more to herself than to Jeffrey.

But he heard her loud and clear. "Absolutely not!" he said. She looked at him, startled. His expression softened. "Trust me on this: Some things are best kept to ourselves, even if the impulse is to be honest. Honesty is not always the best policy, despite all conventional wisdom to the contrary."

"I just think we should enter into this marriage without any secrets between us."

"Amy, relationships are fragile. They are tenuous under the best of circumstances. We wouldn't want Andy to think he'd made a mistake proposing."

What?

"Andy wouldn't think that. We love each other. He'll be upset. He'll be angry. But it won't change anything. I really believe that."

"Amy, let's not put that to the test."

"What's that supposed to mean? Are you saying he doesn't love me?"

"No. I'm saying he wasn't sure about getting engaged."

Amy felt the room tilt. She stepped down from the pedestal, nearly tripping over her dress. Jeffrey reached for her arm, steadying her.

"He seemed sure when he asked me," she said, her voice faltering.

"Of course he was. But he needed a little convincing about the timing."

"What? Did you tell him to propose to me?"

"I wouldn't put it that way."

"I need to . . . Can we finish the dress some other time?"

"Amy, you're taking all of this the wrong way—"

"I'm sorry, Jeffrey. I just need to get back to work." She pulled up her dress so it didn't drag on the ground, and made her way to the door.

"Amy—one more thing. I'm promoting you. To associate director of marketing."

She turned around. "Huh? I mean . . . really?" She hadn't even recovered from the last five minutes. She certainly wasn't read to process this.

Jeffrey nodded with a smile. "How does that feel, Brand Ambassador?"

"Does Stella know?" Translation: Stella is going to kill someone. Most likely me.

"Stella's been fired."

Twenty-four Hours Until the Wedding

twenty-five

"Please don't tell me this entire crowd is here because of the rehearsal dinner," said Hugh.

The Time Warner Center was surrounded by television crews and paparazzi. Meryl, Hugh, and Rose lingered in the cab while she dialed Leigh for help finding a back entrance to the building. "What a circus!"

"A circus is more dignified," Rose huffed.

"Yes, well—it's a circus that is paying for itself. So please let's just find a way inside."

The press had been calling her for days for details about the rehearsal dinner. The truth was, Meryl didn't have very much information to give.

Maybe out of spite over the triple wedding, or maybe because she simply didn't give Meryl much of a thought, Tippy had been uncommunicative about the evening's event. The only things Meryl knew were that (a) it was taking place in the Landmarc restaurant at the Time Warner Center, and (b) Tippy lent the venue some sterling silver from her personal collection for use during the party. Meryl had asked Leigh for more details, and she said her mandate had been "light and springy."

Whatever that meant.

"Just be thankful you only have to go along for the ride on this one. You'll have plenty to manage tomorrow," Hugh said.

Leigh directed them via cell phone to a side street entrance.

"I'll check you into your room—just meet me on the fourteenth floor. The lobby is filled with press too."

All the out-of-town guests were staying at the Mandarin Oriental hotel, including Meg and Stowe. Dinner that night was at Landmarc restaurant, and the following afternoon, four buses would transport guests to Longview.

It had been Hugh's idea—at the last minute—to get a room at the Mandarin. He was in a celebratory mood: after the *People* magazine article ran, a major publishing house called him about his manuscript. For the first time in thirty years, he had a book deal.

She was proud of him.

Standing in the room, looking out at the view of Central Park South, Meryl hugged herself. Having just showered, she wore one of the hotel's white terry cloth robes. She had only about twenty minutes to do her hair and makeup and change into her Jeffrey Bruce dress. It was a pale rose silk with beaded side panels. He'd also made her a dress for the wedding, a stunning empire neck, floor-length gown with a beaded bodice and a cinched waist. A panel of cascading ruffles draped along one side. It was midnight blue, Meg's favorite color.

It was odd how she had looked forward to this weekend for months— for years, really—and now that it had finally arrived, she couldn't enjoy it.

The apartment. Scott. The documentary.

She'd called Scott half a dozen times since Janell showed them the pitch. He never returned any of her messages.

A knock on the door. Hugh answered it.

"The photographer needs to talk to you for a minute," Hugh said.

It was Paz, from *People*.

"Can I get into the dining space for a few shots before the guests arrive?"

"I don't think that will be a problem. Let me just call the manager." Meryl made the arrangements for Paz, and then pulled her dress from the closet.

"I need to talk to you for a minute," said Hugh.

"I have to get dressed—"

"Meryl, relax."

But she couldn't—not until she was at the restaurant with a glass of wine in her hand. Or maybe not until the girls were walking down the aisle. Or until they'd said their vows, *People* got all its contractually promised photos, and all that was left was the seated dinner for 350 people under the tent on the lush grounds of Longview. Until then, there was nothing anyone could say that was of interest to her.

"I can't, Hugh. I'm sorry. I just can't."

"Meryl, I got this room so we could relax a little. And celebrate."

She nodded. "I'm proud of you for the book deal, Hugh. I am."

"I don't mean celebrate the book deal."

She looked at him blankly. "What, you mean, the wedding?"

"The book deal, the wedding—yes, of course. But also . . . the parents at Yardley are petitioning for my reinstatement."

"You mean you might get your job back?"

"I *will* get my job back."

"I don't understand. Why now?"

"Because of the *People* magazine article. Parents saw a different side of my dismissal. The administration hadn't been forthright about exactly why I was fired. Now the parents are coming to my defense. They want more transparency when it comes to dealing with cheating accusations, and they want a review board they can participate in. And they want me reinstated to act as their liaison to make these changes."

"I can't believe it was that simple."

"It's not simple. It's actually complicated. *People*'s angle on how and why I was fired helped tremendously. And the publicity about my book deal gives Yardley a way to rehire me while saving face—bringing me back on scholarly merits, that sort of thing."

Meryl barely dared to ask the next question. "Do you think . . . we can keep the apartment?"

He nodded, smiling.

She threw herself into his arms. "Oh, Hugh—I can't even tell you what this means to me."

"I know. And I'm sorry it's been stressful. But things are looking up."

"Do you really think so?"

He nodded. "Yes. So let's try to enjoy this weekend, okay? The worst is behind us."

Meg and Stowe walked into the Landmarc dining room, hand in hand.

The space was a spring wonderland filled with flowers and Japanese paper lanterns and sterling silver buckets packed with Cristal. The bar was decorated with tall sterling silver vases from Tippy's personal collection and filled with white gerbera daisies.

"Green goddess?" offered a passing waiter holding a tray of the party's signature cocktail, a cucumber martini flavored with elderflower essence. Leigh had specially ordered pale green martini glasses.

A single long table, set for one hundred, was decorated with glass vases and Lucite troughs encasing the green stems of shaved horsetail surrounded by chartreuse cymbidiums, hydrangeas, mini lavender calla lilies, and tall square lavender votive candles.

"Oh, Stowe, it's perfect," she breathed, leaning against him. He squeezed her hand.

Across the room, Amy and Jo waved at her. Her sisters looked beautiful—Jo, her long hair loose, wearing a black silk romper with ropes of delicate gold chains around her neck and thin gold bangles on her tan wrists. At seven months pregnant, she was barely showing. "I was the same way," Meryl had told them.

And Amy wore a pale yellow A-line silk dress, her hair up in a French twist.

Toby slipped his arm around Jo and gestured for Meg to come join them.

"Let's go say hi to my sisters," she said.

"There you two are!" Tippy walked over to them, brisk and focused. "Stowe, Hunter is looking for you."

Meg looked pleadingly at Stowe—*Don't do it, not tonight.*

"Mother, we just got here. Let me say hi to a few people, and then I'll find Hunter."

"She said it's important."

"Tippy, I think we should put a time-out on work talk tonight,"

Meg said. It was the first time she had ever contradicted her mother-in-law-to-be, and it felt good. Damn good. Like something she should do more often.

"My dear, you do look lovely. And I know you don't want to take any of the attention away from yourself and your sisters. But you must know by now that there is no such thing as a time-out in this business. This is what you've signed up for, so please don't make a fuss."

It took all Meg's restraint not to throw her green goddess in the face of the Queen Bitch.

"Hon, I'll be right back. Let me just get this out of the way."

And all she could do was watch as Stowe retreated, Tippy's hand on his arm, out the door of the restaurant and back into the Time Warner Center atrium.

It was never going to change. If Meg couldn't even have his focus at the rehearsal dinner for their wedding, when would she ever? And if she was now a member of the campaign team, why was Hunter still calling Stowe aside separately? Anything that concerned him now concerned her too.

She had just turned to follow after them when her mother intercepted her.

"Oh, Meg! You have never looked more beautiful," her mother said, brushing her cheek against hers. Meg thought the same of her mother. She looked absolutely radiant, happier and brighter than she'd seen her in months. Maybe years.

"Come this way. Gran wants to get a picture of you three girls all together. Now, where did Jo run off to? She was just here a minute ago."

"Mom, I have to check on something. I'll be back in a few minutes. Sorry." She left her drink on a table and hurried out of the restaurant.

Where would Stowe and his mother have gone? She turned right and pushed through the double doors leading to a long corridor with signs directing her to the restroom. She walked the length of the hall, but they were nowhere in sight.

She opened the door to the ladies' room just in case Tippy and Hunter had ducked inside for a tête-à-tête. Meg had a few words for both of them—primarily consisting of four letters.

Instead, she found her sister at the sink, dabbing away tears with a paper towel. Leigh was by her side.

"Jo—are you okay? What's wrong?"

"Nothing," she said, trying to hide the paper towel in her handbag and bending over the sink, washing her hands.

"She's fine," said Leigh.

"Um, clearly not."

"Meg, it's okay. I just needed a few minutes."

"Leigh, can you excuse us for a minute?"

Leigh nodded and exited the bathroom with what seemed like huge relief.

"Did you have a fight with Toby?" she asked Jo.

"No."

"Is it—? Everything's okay with the baby, right?"

Jo's hand moved instinctively to her belly. "Yes—yes. The baby's fine."

"Then what?" Meg put her beaded clutch on the sink and reached for her sister's arm. "Tell me."

"I'm in love with Leigh," Jo said before dissolving into a fresh round of sobs.

"Leigh? The wedding planner?"

Jo nodded.

"Um, okay, but considering you're seven months pregnant and standing outside your wedding rehearsal dinner, I'm not sure what to make of that."

"Neither am I."

"Are you two . . . involved?"

"We hooked up once. But that's all it will ever be. Leigh's not out; she's worried about her job. She doesn't want me."

"Do you love Toby? At all?" Meg asked, hugging her tightly.

"Not like that, I don't."

"Jo, and I say this from a place of caring—why the hell did you agree to marry him?"

"It seemed like a good idea at the time. And in some ways, it still does. In a lot of ways, actually. Did you see my mother-in-law out there?

You can't miss her. Bright red hair. Already drunk. She gave me this."

Jo pulled up her shirtsleeve to reveal a canary diamond bracelet.

"Oh my God. That's magnificent."

"I can't accept it. But it was easier than to argue—you know what I mean?"

"Jo, you don't have to do this. If you're having doubts——"

Jo pulled back, looked at herself in the mirror, and said, "Please don't lecture me, Meg."

"Okay, I won't. But come back to the party soon. Promise?"

Jo didn't respond.

All one hundred guests were finally seated at the single table running the length of the restaurant. Meg didn't breathe easily until she saw Jo seated next to Toby. Across from them, the aforementioned countess, with flaming red hair and a bawdy laugh, was busy moving name cards around.

Meg tried not to stare, looking instead at the printed menu in front of her—the one that was at each place setting: for an appetizer, a choice of endive salad or warm goat cheese profiteroles. For the main course, either hand-cut filet mignon, pan-seared scallops, or grilled salmon with a sorrel vinaigrette. For dessert, blueberry crumble, crème brûlée, or a chocolate cake with green tea buttercream and semisweet chocolate truffles by Silk Cakes, the same bakery that created their three (three!) wedding cakes for the reception the following night.

A waiter filled everyone's glass with champagne. After the encounter in the bathroom, and Stowe's tight-lipped response when she asked what was so damn important that Hunter had to pull him aside during a wedding rehearsal dinner, she gulped it. And then asked for a second.

"Excuse me. Can I have everyone's attention?"

Meg, startled, turned to look at her grandmother, who was now standing.

Rose clanged her knife against her wineglass until the table fell silent. "Thank you! Now, I don't know the rules for this sort of thing. Maybe the toast comes later. In my day, we did things much simpler. And my own daughter didn't even have a wedding—she ran off and eloped. But my granddaughters certainly made up for it with this—well, let's call it what it is: theater of the absurd."

"Mother," Meryl whispered loudly.

"But if I've learned anything in my years, it's that the how and the why of the marriage doesn't matter. Not as much as I thought it did, at least. All that matters is the commitment to family. My husband and I had forty-five years together. And not all of them good. But we had the years—that's the point. And my daughter stuck it out. Thirty years under her belt, right, Meryl? And for the life of me, I couldn't tell you what those two have in common."

Meg glanced at her parents. Her mother was bright red. And she could have sworn her father was stifling laughter.

"And so, to my beautiful, intelligent granddaughters, I say this: I might not agree with this circus. I might not even agree with your choices in husbands. Well—yours I do, Amy. Regardless, to all of you, I'm proud of your willingness to make the ultimate promise any person can make to another: to be true to them, always. And part of being true is being truthful. That's the hard part. Meg, Amy, Jo—I see you struggling with your truths. And I feel responsible. I set a bad example. And so my wedding gift to you is something I was unable to give even my own husband: my truth."

The room had fallen absolutely silent.

"My real name is Roza Klasczko. That's the name I was born with. During the war, when my parents and brother were deported to the death camps, I hid with a Catholic family and took their name to survive."

Meryl gasped. Meg looked at her in alarm, reaching over Stowe to touch her shoulder. Her mother didn't respond, her eyes locked on Rose.

"When the war ended, I waited and hoped for my parents and my brother to return. They never did. Relatives I never met came for me, to bring me to America. My name changed again, and I never spoke of the other names—or the other people—I left behind. But I speak of them today, in honor of the future—in honor of the greatest blessing, my first great-grandchild." With that, she looked pointedly at Jo. "So, to you and Toby, to Meg and Stowe, Amy and Andy—I wish you true love and a long life together." She raised her glass. "To family."

Meryl was statue still, her face pale underneath her makeup. One of the guests, a woman Meg didn't recognize, was crying. Slowly, everyone stood and raised their glasses.

"To family," said Hugh.

Meg turned to Stowe—and that's when she noticed he was texting under the table.

She glanced across the table, and sure enough, Hunter was looking at her phone.

"Can I talk to you for a minute?" Meg whispered in his ear, her hand squeezing his arm. Hard.

"Now?"

She stood up and walked away from the table, not sure where she was going, just knowing she needed to get far out of the earshot of the guests before she exploded. Stowe followed her. She kept walking until she was back outside the restaurant, in the hallway where she'd originally gone looking for him and Hunter.

Meg pulled her engagement ring off her finger. "Did you hear a word my grandmother said? If you can't give me an insanely good fucking reason why you were texting Hunter Cross while my grandmother was giving a toast to our marriage—and, in case you missed it, dropping a major fucking bombshell—you can take this ring back right now. We can just call the whole thing off. Because I am not doing this for the rest of my life."

"Meg, please—there's something you need to know about."

She pressed the ring into his hand and walked to the bathroom.

He ran after her. "Meg—wait. Okay. I didn't want to tell you about this now—I wanted you to enjoy the night. But Hunter got an alert about an article that went live this afternoon."

"So? This is exactly what I'm talking about—"

"It's about your family. And it's not good."

Meg froze. "What do you mean?"

He tapped into his phone and handed it to her. The headline filled the screen: LIES OF MATRIMONY: THE SECRETS BEHIND THE YEAR'S MOST SCANDALOUS WEDDING.

Meg's hand shook so hard, Stowe had to hold the phone for her. He put his arm around his shoulder as she skimmed the words, barely processing them—not wanting to process them.

She didn't know what was the most offensive, inflammatory, unbearable part. The photo of her mother having dinner with a strange man, a man identified in the article as "reality TV mega-producer Scott Sobel." The piece implied that not only was a "docu-soap" about the Meg and her sisters in the works, but that Meryl was "in bed" with Scott in more ways than one. Or the part about her father being fired from Yardley for having an affair with one of his students, whom he continued to see on a regular basis. And that secrets and lies are just "par for the course" in this "family that makes the Kardashians look like the Brady Bunch."

"Oh my God," Meg said, reaching for the wall to steady herself.

Stowe looped his arm around her waist. "It's going to be okay," he said.

"We have to tell my mother."

"We can manage this, Meg," said Hunter, coming up behind them.

"Fuck off, Hunter. You're the one who brought this into my engagement dinner. But I'm not going to have you ruin my wedding. So please don't be there tomorrow."

"Meg . . . ," said Stowe.

"I mean it," said Meg. And she walked off to find her mother.

The
Wedding
Day

twenty-six

The show must go on. Or, in this case, the half-million-dollar wedding.

But for Meryl, the joy was gone. She woke up with her mother's revelation hanging over her like a lingering, unshakable nightmare.

Her mother, a "hidden child." She'd read about these children, stashed away in convents and the homes of Catholics to spare them as their parents were carted off to their deaths. She'd read a few books, even saw the Polish film *Ida*. But she never imagined—her own *mother*.

She wanted to know more—to know everything. If her grandparents had died in concentration camps, who were the people Meryl had grown up *thinking* were her grandparents? And why had her mother chosen to keep all of it inside for her entire life?

But last night had brought no more answers. Her mother left the dinner early, exhausted. And this morning, there was no time. So the hidden truths of her family would have to stay hidden a few hours longer.

At least now the photographs made sense.

Before going to bed, Meryl looked at them, crying so hard, she knew her eyes would be swollen in the wedding pictures.

"Meryl, the car's here," Hugh said. It was the most he'd spoken to her all morning.

She felt he could give her a little more empathy, considering the stunning revelation her mother had just dropped, but she also knew that he was furious about the article—the article that Scott Sobel had so clearly planted.

"This could undermine everything positive with Yardley that came out of the *People* article," he had said.

"No, no—it won't!" Meryl had insisted. "It's just a tawdry gossip site."

But the worry set in, gut deep.

It was all her fault. She had let the wolf into the henhouse. In her frustration with Hugh, in her fear of losing control of the wedding, in her impatience with her own life, she had welcomed the distraction of Scott Sobel. It had been, in its own way, as selfish as Hugh throwing away his job. More so, probably, because Hugh at least lost his job taking a stand for something. Both of them had turned away from their marriage. And now she wasn't quite sure how to lean toward it again.

But today was not about her or about Hugh or even about her mother. She had to focus on the girls. She would at least get *that* right.

The weather, thankfully, was picture perfect: bright blue clear skies, shining sun, a gentle breeze. And as the car pulled up to Longview, she could see that it was in glorious full bloom, as Cliff had promised.

She headed toward the house, Hugh following close behind with their garment bags. In the distance, she heard the hammering of last-minute construction.

Leigh was halfway down the lush green front lawn before Meryl noticed her.

"How's everything going?" Meryl said.

"Under control. There just seems to be some confusion about the bouquets. I know it's my job to smooth over this sort of thing, but sometimes there's just no substitute for Mom."

"Of course, Leigh. And you've done a fantastic job. I know I was resistant at first—"

"That's one way of putting it." She smiled.

"Yes, well, I'm the first to admit now that I don't know what I would have done without you. I know my daughters feel the same."

An odd look crossed Leigh's face. "Well, just doing my job. But thank you."

Cliff greeted them at the front door. He was dressed in a seersucker suit with a deep purple calla lily in his lapel.

"Don't you look nice!" said Meryl. And she started to feel the first tingle of optimism.

"I got a sneak peek at the brides, and they are *perfection*."

"I can't wait to see them myself! Heading up there right now."

"Actually, first—can you just take a look at the bouquets?" asked Leigh.

Meryl bit down her impatience and followed her to the kitchen, where the source of the problem was being refrigerated.

"I brought them out for some photos, and Jo insists this is not what she asked for. She said she wanted the ranunculus."

Jo's lily of the valley bouquet, wrapped in fern, was exactly what Meryl remembered her ordering.

"The other two are fine?"

"Yes." Leigh showed her Meg's bouquet, mini calla lilies, the stems wrapped in chartreuse silk ribbon, and Amy's ranunculus wrapped in a green leaf secured with pearl pins.

Meryl sighed. "I'll talk to Jo. Where is she? Upstairs?"

Leigh nodded, and Cliff escorted Meryl up the central staircase. He consulted his phone. "The band is here. I'm going to show them where to set up. You should get dressed. The family photographer and the *People* photographer are battling it out for time, and you're not camera ready, my dear."

Meryl hurried down the hall and knocked on the closed door.

"What?" barked Jo.

"It's Mom."

No reply. Meryl tried the knob and the door opened. Jo stood by the window. From behind, in her skinny satin pants and short cocktail dress, her hair nearly to her waist, she looked like a teenager. But when she turned, Meryl's eyes went straight to the unmistakable curve of her belly.

"I never should have worn this," she said, tugging at the dress. "If I had known I was pregnant—"

"Nonsense! You look beautiful!" Meryl picked up the white floral wreath from the bed and handed it to her. She had said all along she wanted to wear flowers instead of a veil. "I want to see this on you."

"Not now. I can't deal. Did you see the bouquet? I didn't ask for those flowers! The bouquet was supposed to match these flowers."

"What are these flowers?"

"How the hell should I know? This is not my thing!"

"Hon, I was there at the florist. You did agree to the lily of the valley."

Jo turned and looked out the window. "I can see the garden from here. Are they . . . Is that a chuppah they're setting up?"

"Yes," she said.

"Because Gran—"

"Yes. Now, hon, I have to get dressed. Do you want me to try to get a last-minute replacement bouquet?"

"No. I don't want to carry a bouquet."

Meryl, about to protest, thought better of it. The time for fighting over things, fighting *for* things, was over. All that mattered was that Meg, Amy, and Jo were walking down that aisle in two hours.

"Mom, who are those people filming down there?"

Meryl moved toward the window. The distance was a blur without her glasses.

"I don't know."

"It's not the *People* photographers."

"I'll go check it out." She kissed her cheek. "Go meet your sisters downstairs. Paz is waiting."

Meryl let herself out of the room, and nearly colliding with Meg, let out a yelp.

She was a vision in head-to-toe lace, her gold hair loose to brush her shoulders, the ends curved ever so slightly inward toward her collarbone.

Her cheeks blushed pink with excitement—or maybe it was the work of the makeup artist. But somehow she looked incredibly young and radiant and elegant and sophisticated all at once. Meryl's eyes brimmed with tears—her daughter was the most perfect bride she'd ever seen.

"Oh, my baby—look at you!"

"Mom—don't! It's too early to cry. And I just got false eyelashes put on."

"False eyelashes?"

"Yes—just a few single ones on the top. See?" She leaned toward Meryl, her pinky finger hovering near her eyelid.

"The photographer is ready," Meryl said.

"Listen—I need to talk to you."

"Oh God. Don't tell me there's another problem. Jo just informed me she's not carrying a bouquet. The photographer really wants symmetry when you girls walk down the aisle—"

"She's not upset about the bouquet."

"Yes, she is. I just spoke to her."

Meg put her finger to her lips and gestured for Meryl to follow her into one of the bedrooms. Once inside, Meg kept her back against the door.

"Don't press your gown—"

"Mom, listen to me. Last night, before dinner—before the whole article fiasco—I found Jo crying in the bathroom."

"It's just pregnancy hormones, honey. I mean, planning a wedding is stressful enough—"

"It's not pregnancy hormones. She's in love with someone else."

Meryl felt her stomach knot. "She's still upset about Caroline?"

Meg shook her head. "She's in love with Leigh."

"Leigh? Leigh who?"

"Leigh—the wedding planner!"

Meryl sat down heavily on the antique four-poster bed. It creaked and groaned under her weight. "In love with her? How? They barely know each other."

"Oh, they *know* each other. A lot better than any of us realized."

"Okay—just wait a second. So Jo and Leigh have been having an affair?"

"Apparently."

"Is Leigh asking her not to get married?"

"No. From what I can tell, Leigh is telling Jo to forget about her and do the practical thing. I told Jo she doesn't have to do this—she can call it off. But she wouldn't listen to me."

"Oh my God."

"She can't marry him, Mom. I mean, things aren't perfect with Stowe. But I love him—I'm in love with him. There's no one else for me. How can she walk down that aisle and say those vows if she doesn't feel the same about Toby?"

"I'll talk to her," Meryl said, but it was an automatic response. Was she really going to walk out there and tell her daughter to be a runaway bride? It was unthinkable.

"She won't listen to you," said Meg.

"Meryl, I hate to interrupt, but I need you for a second."

Leigh.

Meryl tried to assume a normal facial expression. She tried not to blurt out, *Are you in love with my daughter?* She just had to hold everything together. Keep the wedding on the tracks.

It wasn't her place to second-guess her daughter's complicated emotions, or to tell her to turn her back on her fiancé. Jo was an adult now—she would have to make adult decisions, and live with them. Everyone did.

"Meryl, we have a situation in the garden. Could you please go check on what's going on? We sent a staff member to talk to them but—"

"Them? Them *who*?"

"The documentary filmmakers."

Amy looked at herself in the full-length mirror. The dress, with its tiny seed pearls and princess skirt, was a fantasy come to life. Her hair, in a chignon, was exactly how she'd imagined it on her wedding day, ever since she was a little girl. The reflection even caught the window behind her, out of which she could see the beautiful walled garden, where in less than an hour, guests would take their seats.

Amy couldn't sit in her dress, and so with time to kill before the photographs, she had been left to pace the bedroom. There was no TV, no computer. Just a stack of magazines and a coffee table book on English gardens.

Left alone with her thoughts, she couldn't ignore the nagging, gnawing feeling. Just wedding-day jitters, she told herself. Still, she wanted a distraction. So she reached for one of the magazines, *Vanity Fair,* and flipped through it.

Marcus smiled up at her, shirtless, wearing only a pair of Jeffrey Bruce distressed jeans.

That's when she knew what she needed to do to put an end to the nagging feeling.

She opened the door and called for Leigh. "Can you please get Andy for me? I need to talk to him for a sec."

And then Amy waited, telling herself she was doing the right thing. The minutes ticked by like hours until finally, a sharp knock.

Andy.

"Hey," she said, opening the door.

"Wow. You look . . . You look incredible, Ame. But I thought I wasn't supposed to see you in the dress. My dad wouldn't even show me his sketches. Holy shit, that thing is amazing. That skirt is big. Was that your idea, or his?"

"I said I wanted a ball gown," she said, swallowing hard. Now that he was there, in his wedding tux, smiling at her, the impulse to talk to him seemed like a bad one.

He kissed her on the cheek. "You okay? I have to get back down there—that *People* photographer has us jumping through hoops. Not literally, obviously."

"Yeah. Okay. The thing is—I need to talk to you."

Andy glanced at the door, then back at her. "Right now?"

"Yeah. I'd say let's sit, but . . . I can't sit." She hesitated, but knew there was no time for stalling. "I have to tell you something. It's been weighing on me, and I can't walk down that aisle without—"

"You hooked up with that model," he said bluntly.

She gasped. Even though she'd planned on confessing, even though those very words had been on the tip of her tongue, hearing them come out of his mouth was like a slap in the face.

"You knew?"

"I heard rumors. Fashion is a small world," he said. "I tried to, um, ignore them."

"Why? Why didn't you confront me?"

"I guess I didn't want to hear it from you. I wanted to keep it as rumors."

Amy sat on the bed, not caring that the crinoline crunched underneath her. "Oh, Andy. I'm so sorry. It was nothing—really. I don't even know why I did it." She couldn't stand to look at him. She felt tears threatening to undo her eye makeup.

"You're going to mess up your dress," he said.

"That's it? That's all you're going to say?"

"What do you want me to say, Amy?"

A quick knock at the door, and Meg called from the hallway. "Amy— the photographer is ready for us."

"Go," Andy said. "Everyone's waiting."

Scott Sobel, crashing her daughters' wedding. With a camera crew.

"What the hell are you doing here?" she yelled, marching up to Scott.

"We're just getting some B roll and then we'll be out of your way," he said, barely looking at her, snapping his fingers at one of his crew and pointing to the chuppah.

"This is a private event—you can't be here."

"This property is open to the public until one P.M. today."

Another guy advanced to the front row of seating, getting a shot of the view from where the officiant would be standing.

"I've got this, Meryl," said Hugh.

In her outrage, she hadn't seen him cutting through a row of chairs, knocking a few over in his haste. He took her arm, moving her aside before ripping the expensive-looking Sony camcorder from Scott's hands and smashing it to the ground.

"Are you out of your fucking mind?" Scott yelled. "That's destruction of property."

"This is my daughters' wedding day. Get the hell out of here."

Scott turned to another cameraman. "Keep shooting."

Meryl thought she knew her husband. She thought, after thirty years, there were no surprises left. But Hugh, seeing the second cameraman panning his camcorder up and down the aisle, took a few steps toward Scott and punched him in the face.

"Hugh!" Meryl instinctively grabbed him, holding him back. It was what women did when their men got primal in movies. She just never thought she'd ever play that role with her cerebral, amiable husband.

Scott, on the ground, his hand covering the spot where Hugh landed the blow, looked up in disbelief. Then anger. Then fury. "I'll see you in court," Scott said.

"Back at you," said Hugh. "I hear libel can be *very* costly."

By then, Cliff and Leigh had rushed down the lawn, followed by Reed's security.

Meryl took Hugh's hand. "Let's go," she said.

Hugh didn't move, didn't seem to hear her. He was breathing hard. She moved in front of him, her back to Scott, and looked into his eyes.

"Hugh . . ." She squeezed his hand. And then everything caught up with her, the good and the bad, the past and the present and the future all colliding in a crushing wave of emotion. She started to cry.

Hugh put his arm around her, steering her away from the commotion as the security team hustled Scott and his crew off the property.

Together, they walked up the aisle, hand in hand, back to the house.

"Three generations of beauty. How fabulous!" Paz said.

It was warmer than Meg had anticipated, and after forty minutes of Paz photographing her with her sisters, and then the three of them with their mother, and then with their mother and grandmother, she was dripping with sweat and ready for a complete makeup and hair redo.

"Stop your sweet-talking and just take the photo. I'm roasting out here," said Rose.

Meg noted that her gran's face was pale and shiny with perspiration.

"We need to take a break," Meg said.

"Okay, ladies—that's a wrap."

Finally dismissed, Meg walked Gran back to the house. Then, in the cool privacy of the second-floor bedroom, she took off her dress and changed into a robe so she could cool down.

"I don't see why we couldn't do the photography after the ceremony," she grumbled to the makeup artist.

"You're going to do plenty after—with your new husband," said the makeup artist.

New husband. Meg smiled.

Someone knocked on the door.

"It's me," said Amy. "Open up."

The makeup artist pulled open the door. "I'm almost ready for you."

"Okay, great. Meg, listen—Reed's being a pain in the ass."

"What?" she said, trying not to move her face.

"He won't pose in any photographs with Dad."

Meg turned to her, and the makeup artist groaned in protest. "Why the hell not?"

"I don't know! Stowe's talking to him now."

Meg jumped out of her seat and slipped her feet into the nearest pair of mules she had lying round.

"Where are you going?"

"To see what the hell is going on!"

"It's bad luck to see your husband before the wedding."

"That's only if you're in your dress. And the only bad luck is if his father doesn't get in the damn photos."

Meg took the stairs two at a time, rushing out the south terrace to the lawn, where Paz had the cameras and lights set up. Sure enough, her father, Jeffrey, and the count were sitting on a bench. Reed was nowhere in sight.

She found Stowe on the sidelines, with Hunter hovering nearby, of course.

"Stowe! A word, please." She beckoned him over, and he followed her back onto the patio. Hunter followed until Meg yelled, "Stay out of this, Hunter! I told you not to come, and I *will* call security and have you escorted off the property."

"Jesus, Meg. Calm down. What's wrong?"

"Why won't your father pose for the *People* photos? You know we have a deal with them."

Stowe sighed, running his hand through his hair. He looked so handsome in his Jeffrey Bruce tux, a single mini calla lily pinned to his lapel to match her bouquet. As usual, things with him were almost perfect. But today, "almost" wasn't good enough.

"Just let it go, Meg."

"Just let what go?"

"Look—my dad can't be in any photographs that can be used against him—twisted around by tabloids. That article that posted last night about your father and the high school student—"

"Are you kidding me? You know that's all bullshit."

"Of course I know! But it's exactly the type of salacious thing my dad has to stay very far away from. It's a sensitive juncture in this campaign, Meg. He doesn't even have the Republican nomination yet. After Texas, things will be a little more secure—"

"No! It's not right. This is our wedding day. This has nothing to do with politics. This is a family day—a family event."

"Babe, I know. And for me—for us—it's about becoming real family. And part of being in my family is rolling with some of the inconvenient aspects of living in the public eye. I told you before—it's just a game. It has nothing to do with what's real—with us. I love you. My dad loves you. And he likes your dad—he does. This is just a minor inconvenience in the big picture of things. In the big picture of what I hope is a very long, amazing life together. I can't wait to walk down that aisle, say our vows in front of all these people, and wake up tomorrow as husband and wife. Please, please focus on what's important. Okay?"

"Okay," she whispered.

He kissed her, and it felt like a finger pressed to her lips to silence her.

When she turned back to the house, she had tears in her eyes. But like her dress, they were not something she would reveal to him before the ceremony.

twenty-seven

With nearly all the guests seated in front of the hastily constructed chuppah (adorned with white roses transferred from the arbor), Meryl urged her mother to sit down. Rose looked pale and sweaty.

"Are you all right?" she asked her.

"Of course I'm all right. This is what happens when you have a wedding in the dead of summer."

"It's spring, Mother." She looked around for Leigh, but couldn't find her. "Just wait here. I'll go get you a bottle of water."

Meryl hurried up the garden path, trying not to break out in a sweat herself. Where was Leigh when she needed her?

Meryl couldn't help but admit to herself that Leigh had been a lifesaver. She had made the most of a near-perfect setting, a garden abundant with roses, ivy, and purple hydrangeas. Leigh had demarcated the beginning of the aisle with white garden boxes planted with tall pomanders of sterling roses surrounded by lavender and violet hydrangeas at the base. The purple flowers had been Amy's request. And the aisle itself, adorned with a crisp white linen runner, culminating in the arbor covered with dozens of white roses.

There had been so many details along the way, so many people to please and to answer to, so many fires to put out. All handled—a boulder pushed up a hill—with the help of the wedding planner. The wedding planner with whom, apparently, one of the brides was in love.

Meryl didn't want to think about that. It was time for Jo, her impetuous flower child, to grow up.

"Meryl—there you are. Listen, I just want to make sure your guests know not to post any photos of the girls coming down the aisle until after we've got it up on the magazine's site," said Joan.

"It's in the program—I feel confident we'll be fine with that," said Meryl.

"Paz said he already got some fabulous shots staged in front of the grand allée and near that large fountain—"

"Joan, please grab a seat. I have to take care of one thing and I'll see you after the ceremony."

The house was bustling with movement and energy, the hallway outside the kitchen was filled with catering staff prepping for the tented cocktail reception following the ceremony.

"I'm sorry to bother you," she said to a passing woman, "Can you please get me a bottle of water? I need to take it down to the ceremony."

The woman looked at her blankly.

"Ella necessita una botella de agua, por favor," said Leigh.

Meryl turned around. "I was looking all over for you."

"Everything okay down there?" Leigh said. "I think we're all set."

The woman returned with a bottle of Poland Spring. Leigh handed it to Meryl. "Enjoy the ceremony."

"You should probably walk down with me now. We're getting close," said Meryl.

"I'm going to stay up here—keep things on track."

"Oh, no. Don't worry about that. Everything's fine and Cliff is here."

"Really, Meryl. Go on. Like you said—it's getting close."

Meryl knew she was right, but she found herself rooted in place. "You don't want to watch Jo get married," she said.

"Excuse me?"

"I know. I know that Jo is in love with you. I just didn't realize it was mutual."

"Meryl, I don't know what you've heard, but I assure you I'm a professional—"

Meryl reached for her arm. "Do you love my daughter?"

Leigh looked like a deer caught in the headlights. After a startled pause, she recovered enough to say, "I don't have room for love in my business."

"What do you mean? What business is that?"

Leigh squared her shoulders. "The Campion business."

Meryl looked at her, not comprehending at first. "Oh. You can't be serious."

"I'm very serious. And so are they when it comes to appearances and the people with whom they surround themselves. So I would appreciate it if you never mentioned this. To anyone."

"Leigh, I've grown quite fond of you. And I'm not saying this for my daughter, though maybe, God help me, I should have said it to her: There is no job, no career, no appearance, no amount of money—that is more important than love. Jo is going to marry Toby today, and she might not love him, but that's a situation she is going to have to figure out for herself. But you should not intentionally set out to live a life without love. And you should realize that now, while you're young—before it's too late."

Leigh's dark eyes met hers, unblinking. "Your daughters are waiting for you. I'm sure it will be a beautiful ceremony."

Meg was the first down the aisle on her father's arm.

Calm, cool Meg walked slowly but with sure steps, her arm loosely linked through Hugh's. Meg, in her lace gown, the cathedral veil covering her face, seemed to float down the aisle's white runner.

In that moment, Meryl felt herself standing in the doorway of the girls' childhood bedroom, watching a mirror image of this procession amidst piles of princess dresses and tissue paper, small hands clapping and tiny voices rising with excitement for their chance to walk down the aisle.

She bit her lip to hold back tears.

Stowe met them halfway so Hugh could then turn around and

retrieve Amy, while Meg and Stowe took their places before the officiant—a nondenominational minister named Olympia whom Jo had found on TheKnot.com and, after exchanging e-mails with her, insisted be the one to marry them. It had been Jo's sole request for the entire event.

All eyes turned to Amy, walking a bit faster than Meg but also pulling off her statement gown, looking every bit the budding fashion icon the media—and Jeffrey's PR team—was making her out to be. When the handoff happened between Hugh and Andy, Meryl had a flashback to the first time Andy showed up at their apartment, an eighteen-year-old kid who had called Amy "dude."

But it was Jo who really set her off. Jo, her baby—the tomboy who would never wear a dress and, God love her, stuck to that even on her wedding day. Even as a pregnant bride. Jo, who was getting married while she still didn't know the meaning of love, or perhaps was getting married because she didn't want to go through the trouble of figuring it out. Either way, it wasn't Meryl's choice to make or her mistake to fix. If there was one thing she'd learned in all of this, it was that sometimes she had to just let go.

"Don't they look beautiful?" she whispered to Rose.

"This is the craziest thing I've ever seen."

When all three couples were assembled before the officiant, the music quieted. The only sound was the much-needed breeze rustling through the trees.

"Welcome, friends and family. We are so grateful that you could be here with us for this special—truly remarkable—wedding celebration. Today, we have not one, but three sets of love to celebrate, not two but six lives to join in matrimony. It is always a blessing to find love, but for three sisters to find love at the same time—well, that is truly miraculous."

"That's one way of putting it," deadpanned Rose.

"Mother! Please."

"But though we celebrate their unions on the same day, the unions are not the same. All loves are unique, and in the spirit of that, Jo and Toby, Amy and Andy, and Meg and Stowe have each written a personal introduction to the traditional vows to best convey their feelings for one another, and their deepest commitments as they enter into the bonds of matrimony. Today, the last becomes the first, as we begin with Jo and her betrothed, Tobias."

That had been quite the argument—who should say their vows first. Meg had thought she should go first since she was engaged first. Amy thought she should go first since she had been with Andy the longest. And Jo, as was typical throughout the process, didn't have much to say. In the end, the officiant had suggested reverse birth order. "In all things, a progression," she had said. And that had settled that.

Toby turned to Jo, taking both her hands in his. "Jo, I fell in love with you the first time I saw you. And I wish I could say that was the beginning, but it wasn't half that easy." The crowd laughed. "Finally now, after all these years, our feelings have met at a place where we are able to start a life together. And today, standing before all our friends and family, I give myself to you."

Meryl dabbed at her eyes.

Olympia nodded. "Tobias, please repeat after me, 'I, Tobias Hedegaard-Kruse, take thee, Josephine Becker, to be my wife. To have and to hold, in sickness and in health, for richer or for poorer, I promise my love to thee for as long as we both shall live.'"

He slipped the ring on her finger, and Meryl reached for Hugh's hand.

Olympia turned to Jo. Meryl saw her mouth, "Are you ready?"

Jo nodded. "Toby, I always knew you were someone I could count on—through bad and good. We've had so many years of friendship. And now . . . and now . . ."

As she faltered, Meryl saw her glance down at a crumpled piece of paper in her hand. But she didn't continue. After an awkward pause, Olympia asked gently. "Shall we move on to the 'I do' part?"

"No!"

Three hundred and fifty heads turned in unison to find Leigh walking down the aisle, gasps and whispers in her wake.

"Oh, my good Lord," Meryl said.

"Is something wrong?" Hugh whispered.

"That will depend on how you look at it."

Leigh stopped a few feet behind the row of couples.

"Leigh! What do you think you're doing? Sit!" Tippy hissed, standing up from her aisle seat and marching over to her, "Sit down right this minute."

Leigh, to her credit, didn't miss a beat. She seemed so focused on Jo, it was as if there were no one else in that garden. And maybe that's exactly the way it felt to her.

"Leigh?" Jo said, as if she didn't quite trust what she was seeing and hearing.

"I was wrong," Leigh said.

"You were?"

"Yes. I don't think you should go through with this."

"Are you out of your mind?" said Toby. "Someone get her the hell out of here."

Tippy was by that point physically trying to remove Leigh from the aisle.

"Leave her alone," Meryl said, jumping up to pull Tippy away.

"This is the best wedding I've ever been to," said Rose.

Jo stepped away from the chuppah, rushing to Leigh's side.

"I love you," she said to Leigh.

"I love you too. I'm an idiot."

"No. You're amazing." They kissed.

Reed stood from his seat and turned to face all the guests seated in the rows behind him. "I apologize for this inexcusable display and interruption." Then, to Leigh and Jo. "Leigh, needless to say, you are fired. Jo, you should at least have the decency to step aside, stop shaming your sisters, and let them continue with their wedding."

Jo turned to Meg and Amy. "I'm so sorry," she said, tears of happiness streaming down her cheeks.

The countess rushed to Toby's side and ushered him away. "I want that bracelet back!" she yelled at Jo.

"Jo, you two should maybe head back to the house," Meryl said.

Jo and Leigh looked at each other before marching back up the aisle together.

"Everyone, this is unexpected," said Olympia. "But the path to true love, as they say, never runs smooth. So now, please let us turn our attention back to the two couples standing before you who are ready to take their vows—"

"I'm not ready to take my vows," said Meg suddenly.

"What?" Stowe took her hand. "Babe, just calm down."

"No," she said, lifting her veil. "Your vows will be a lie. You might love me, but you don't honor me—or my family. You don't know how to put me first—put us first. And you never will."

Sobbing, she ran to Meryl's side. Meryl, heart pounding, realizing she had utterly lost control of the situation, that it was completely off the rails, looked frantically at Hugh. He took Meg by the arm and walked her back up the aisle, presumably to the house.

"This is not what we signed on for," said Joan, stepping over people to reach Meryl's seat.

"I can't worry about your stupid magazine right now!" snapped Meryl.

"Fine. You can worry about it tomorrow, when you don't have your check."

"Perhaps we should take a ten-minute break and then continue," said Olympia, trying to remain serene under pressure and almost succeeding.

"There's no point in continuing," said Andy. "If anyone should be walking away from this thing, it's Amy and me." He turned to Amy. "And you know it's true."

Jeffrey stood. "Everyone, let's just calm down."

"I didn't mean to hurt you. You're one of my best friends," said Amy, her voice breaking. "I'm so sorry."

"Ame, don't. It's not totally on you," he said, pulling her into a hug. "I was never that into it. All this, I mean. And we were never really . . ."

"I know." Amy whispered back.

Olympia looked helplessly at Meryl.

Meryl knew what she had to do. After nine months of putting the wedding together, of pushing so hard to make it happen in a big, glorious way, it had now come down to her being to one to say, "Everyone, I apologize. We appreciate all of you being here on this day. But it seems clear that no wedding will be taking place after all."

Cliff, appearing from out of nowhere, took the microphone.

"Please, everyone—if you would all follow me to our tented reception,

I'm hoping you will at the very least enjoy the cocktails and hors d'oeuvres being served."

Meryl watched in disbelief as the rows of guests emptied, the buzz of conversation filling the air like a swarm of bees.

"Your daughters are a piece of work," said Reed.

"It's not our fault your son couldn't close the deal," said Hugh.

"Close the deal? My son dodged a bullet today!" And with that, Reed stormed off, Tippy trailing behind.

Olympia walked to them. "Mrs. Becker, I don't know what to say. . . ."

"Oh, believe me—you're not alone in that."

"I wish there were something I could do to salvage this day."

"There is," said Rose.

Everyone turned to her. "Mother, please—not now."

"I never did get to see you and Hugh exchange vows."

"What?" said Meryl.

"Is that true?" said Olympia.

"Yes—she ran off and eloped!"

"Mother, you wouldn't even speak to Hugh. You said you wouldn't come to the wedding."

"Well, I'm here today. I came for a ceremony, and I want a ceremony. So let's have it."

Olympia smiled. "We could renew your vows."

"What? No—that's crazy," said Meryl. "We have to go up to the house—the girls need us."

"We need this," said Hugh.

"We do?"

He held her hand. "Okay, Olympia—we're ready when you are. Oh—just one thing." Hugh reached for the chuppah and pulled out a handful of roses, handing them to Meryl.

"Hugh, we'll start with you. Repeat after me. . . ."

Hugh held both Meryl's hands, looking her in the eyes. "I, Hugh Becker, take thee, Meryl Becker, to be my wife. To have and to hold, in sickness and in health, for richer or for poorer, I promise my love to thee for as long as we both shall live."

"And Meryl—."

"Wait, I know what I want to say." Meryl, looking into the eyes of her husband, realized she had wanted to say these things for a long time. "Hugh, I'm so sorry I doubted you. And there have been many times. But you've proved me wrong. And as much as this day is a disaster—I'm thankful for the chance to say once again that I take you to be my husband, in sickness and in health, in employment and unemployment, in the home we share now or whatever new home we make in the future—I will love you always."

"You may now kiss the bride," said Olympia.

twenty-eight

"I don't see what you're so upset about," said Rose, pouring herself a vodka and settling on the couch. "Better now than later."

"Really, Mother? That's what you have to say?" Meryl, having kissed Meg and Amy good night as they retreated to bed, was ready to put the disastrous day to rest. But she couldn't—not yet. "That certainly wasn't your philosophy when it came to telling me the truth about yourself."

She glanced at Hugh, and he nodded, kissing her on the cheek before withdrawing to their bedroom. After a long pause, Rose finally said, "It was my truth to tell. Or not."

"Well, I'm glad you finally did. But I still need to know: Who were the people I always believed were your parents?"

"Nana was my mother's first cousin. When she came to Poland to find her family, I was the only one left. They spent months tracking me down. No easy feat, since we were placed with families under such secrecy, there was no record of who was where."

"Why didn't you ever tell me?"

"I wanted to leave it behind. And I thought all these decades that I had. But seeing the girls about to get married, a new generation about to be born—I couldn't hide it anymore. I realized it would be lost forever. My parents—my brother—would be lost forever."

For the first time in her life, Meryl saw her mother's eyes fill with tears.

She took her mother's hand, her skin so soft and thin, it was like touching mercury, like her hands could just slip away from her.

"You kept this bottled up for too long," she said. "You need to talk to someone."

Rose looked at her, her blue eyes direct and unwavering. "I am. I'm talking to you. My daughter."

In the morning Jo awoke with an instant sense of well-being. She couldn't, at first, recall exactly why. And then it all came rushing back to her.

She turned over to look at Leigh, sleeping inches away from her in the big bed at the Soho Grand. The place where it all began, where she finally realized how she really felt.

Jo spooned against her, and Leigh responded by reaching for her arms and pulling them tighter. "What time is it?"

"I don't know," Jo said. "Late, probably."

They had not gone to sleep until three in the morning. It was as if they wanted to cram a year's worth of relationship into one night. "I just want to be at that place where we're together—and that's it," said Jo.

"We are together. But there's still a lot to get to know—to figure out."

"I've already figured out a lot," said Jo. "I won't be in a relationship where I have to hide it."

"I don't want that either. I think that's part of what last night was all about. I had to really blow things up in a big way so I couldn't chicken out!"

"Well, that was big, for sure."

Leigh had told her about Meryl's impromptu little speech just before the ceremony. "It was weird," Leigh said. "It was as if someone were telling me something I was hearing for the first time, yet knew all along. I was barely thinking when I walked down that aisle. I just knew that you and I still had so much to talk about—and I didn't want that conversation to be over."

Jo reached for her phone. "I'm almost afraid to turn it on," she said. She hadn't spoken to Toby since he stormed away from the ceremony. The count and countess had whisked him off in a car by the time she went looking. And Jo had been so caught up in the moment—a moment she didn't want to end—she hadn't let herself think about the fallout.

She regretted hurting Toby. But she had told him she didn't love him in that way. She had told him that from the beginning, and he had insisted it didn't matter. Well, he had been wrong.

But she was still carrying his baby. There was no grand gesture on Leigh's part that could change that.

"Don't turn on the phone. I'm not ready for reality," Leigh said.

"I know, but my mother is probably having a heart attack today. She was cool about it last night, but now that she's had some quiet and time to think about it, she must be losing it. Not to mention the whole *People* magazine deal fell apart. The deal was we all had to walk down the aisle."

"Oh, please—like this isn't an even juicer story for them?"

As soon as Jo's phone was on, it vibrated. Eight messages. The most recent was from Meg.

Her sisters. She'd barely even had time to think about what they must be going through. Why had Meg bailed on Stowe? And had Andy found out about Amy's cheating on him? Meg and Amy had both spent the night at their parents' apartment, since clearly they couldn't very well go back to the homes they'd shared with the men they left at the altar.

"I have to stop by my parents' later," she said. "You know we're the only ones who are happy this morning."

"And I am happy," Leigh said, propping herself up on her pillows and taking Jo's hand. "Even though I'm unemployed."

"Maybe it's time to start your own wedding-planning business," Jo said.

"Maybe," she said. "I did plan the most talked-about wedding of the year."

296 • jamie brenner

"I wouldn't say most talked about—"

"Jo, I hate to break it to you, love—this wedding will live on in New York gossip-column infamy."

"Ugh. You're right. I should call my sisters." Jo dialed Meg.

She answered immediately, sobbing.

"Meg—I can't understand you. Just calm down. It's going to be okay. You guys can work it out. Stowe loves you. It's not like—"

"No! Stop," Meg said. "Didn't you get my message?"

"I didn't listen to it." Her stomach tightened. "What is it?"

"Gran's dead."

It was Hugh who'd found Rose unresponsive in her bed.

Meryl slept late, completely wrung out—emotionally and physically.

But Hugh was incapable of sleeping in, so when he awoke, he decided to talk to Rose—to thank her for making the disastrous wedding worthwhile in at least one respect. He had felt, as he told Meryl the night before, that he finally had her mother's blessing.

He called 911 before he woke Meryl.

When the paramedics arrived, they ushered Meryl and Hugh out of the room, firing a litany of questions at them: "What medications was she taking? Did she have a heart condition? High blood pressure?"

While she sat on the couch, trying to stay calm and answer the questions as accurately as possible, with Hugh beside her and holding her hand, the other paramedics emerged from the bedroom, grim faced.

"I'm sorry—there's nothing we can do."

Meryl screamed, a bloodcurdling cry that finally roused Meg and Amy from their sleep.

Hugh stood up. "Can you give us some idea of what happened?"

"We're not sure," the young man said. To Meryl, he looked like a kid. "At that age, these things happen. Sometimes they're just ready to go."

Meryl held on to Hugh. Sometimes they're just ready to go.

twenty-nine

By Jewish custom, the mourning period would last seven days and nights, a period called "sitting shiva."

Since Meg and her sisters had been raised pretty much agnostic, to see her mother embrace such a traditional ritual of mourning was surprising.

They would stay at their parents' apartment all week, day and night, while friends and family stopped by to pay their respects, bringing them food and company. It was nice in theory—the family would not be left to mourn alone. But three hours into the first day, she wondered how she would last a week.

Of course she was mourning Gran—she was bereft. It was the first death of anyone close to her, and Meg knew that at age twenty-eight, she was lucky in that regard. But she felt claustrophobic in her parents' apartment, an odd sense that on the *Monopoly* board of life, she had been sent back to the starting point.

It was not lost on her that the day of the funeral was the day she and Stowe would have set off on their honeymoon—if the honeymoon hadn't been usurped by the Texas campaign trip, that is.

Had she done the right thing? She felt she had done the only thing she could. She didn't want to wake up five years from now, with children, alone in a marriage. At least now, she could start over. And she was starting over: with her career. Someday, with her love life—although that seemed impossible to imagine right now. And, in some ways, even her family life. Somehow, over the past nine months, the long-standing dynamics of her family had shifted in a way she couldn't fully pinpoint. Her parents seemed closer. She and Amy had a better understanding of one another. And Jo—well, Jo was Jo. But Meg also felt she had somehow lost her identity in the mix. She was no longer the one who had it all together—who could do no wrong. Now she was just as much of a mess—if not more of one—than the rest of them.

The front door opened. Her mother had left it unlocked so guests could easily arrive and depart. Surprisingly, it was Cliff from Longview.

"I hope I'm not intruding," he said, handing her a tray of cookies from Bouchon Bakery.

"No! Not at all. Come on in."

"I read about your grandmother in the paper this morning, and I just had to pay my respects. Your poor mother—what a week."

"This is so lovely of you, Cliff." It was hard to believe that her life was such that her grandmother's death made the front page of the *New York Post*. And the news had brought out the oddest assortment of well-wishers: Janell South and her older sister, her father's new literary agent, the chancellor of Yardley. Baskets of baked goods and trays of cold cuts had arrived from *People* magazine, Marchesa, and E! television. It seemed the wedding might have been a failure, but people were still banking on the Wedding Sisters.

"Hugh, I don't want people with their phones out. No photos, no texting. All I need is for someone to live-tweet our shiva," Meryl had said that morning, covering the mirrors. Apparently, that was also part of the shiva tradition—no vanity. A dramatic turn from the past nine months, which had been all about how they looked, what they were wearing, whom they were dating.

They had been brought down to earth, and Meg wasn't sorry for it. She'd just wished it had happened some other way.

"Hon, relax. It's just family and friends," said Hugh.

Four days. Was that all it had been since she'd seen Stowe? Four days ago, she was minutes away from becoming his wife. And now she was likely never to speak to him again.

Not a call, not a text, not a word since her outburst at the altar. Their only contact with the Campion family had been an e-mail from one of Tippy's assistants about the logistics of returning the wedding gifts.

He hated her, she was certain. From his point of view, she had just bailed out. She had wanted something he couldn't give, and when he told her his limitations—or shown them, really—she had blown the whole thing up in spectacular fashion. And most unforgivable—at least in the Campion world—she had done so publicly.

It had all been too good to be true. He had been too good to be true: too handsome, too intelligent, too successful. Everyone said they were the perfect couple, and she had believed the hype. Maybe this was what happened to you when things went pretty damn smoothly for twenty-eight years; you didn't know to look over your shoulder, waiting for the other shoe to drop.

But she loved him—had fallen in love with him that first night under the California stars at the Standard Hotel. Maybe that one magical night was all it should have been, and everything since had been her fault—her hubris for thinking she could have a lifetime of that magic.

The apartment was stifling.

Meg slipped out the front door, closing it behind her and leaning against it. The hallway felt ten degrees cooler and was mercifully quiet. She closed her eyes until the ping of the elevator arriving down the hall forced her back to attention.

She turned to go back inside.

"Meg!" Stowe walked toward her, wheeling a travel bag behind him.

"Oh my God. What are you doing here? I thought you were in Texas."

"I was." He stopped, awkwardly, a few feet away from her.

Meg didn't know whether she should hug him or keep her distance. There was too much to process—her overwhelming joy at seeing him, her utter shock at seeing him, and her fear that he showed up out of propriety yet hated her for leaving him.

"I came as soon as I heard the news about your grandmother. I'm so sorry."

"Stowe, I don't know what to say. You didn't have to do that. I mean, considering . . ."

"I know I didn't have to. I wanted to."

Meg gave a bitter laugh. "You know, the irony is that when we were together, you never would have left a campaign event to be with me."

"That's not true. I know you felt that way, and yes, there were times when I put my parents' wishes first, but I was wrong. I realize that now."

"Stowe . . ." She glanced back at the apartment.

"Don't run away from me, Meg. Not today. I'm standing before you, telling you that I heard you. I heard you three days ago, standing at the altar. I wish I'd heard you sooner. I wish it hadn't happened like that. But it doesn't have to end like that."

"It doesn't?" she whispered.

"No. Not if we don't let it." He pulled her to him, and she held on to him as if her life depended on it, choking back sobs.

"But your mother hates me," she said, pulling away and wiping her eyes with the tissue she had folded in her sleeve. She hadn't been without a tissue handy for three days straight.

"She doesn't hate you."

"She does."

"Well, she'll just have to get over it. And didn't you tell me your grandmother didn't talk to your father for years? That worked out okay in the end, didn't it?"

She burst into tears again. "Yeah."

He took both her hands in his and got down on one knee. "Let's give this a go, Meg. I'm not ready to give up on us. Are you?"

"No," she said.

"You were right. So let's see what we can be when we put each other and our relationship first. Do you want to give it a go?"

"I do," she whispered.

thirty

It was a day that made Meryl miss her mother.

Standing on the terrace, looking at the autumn trees framing the East River with their leaves turning pale gold, she could almost feel her. On this momentous occasion, there was the sense that Rose was with them. Or maybe that was just wishful thinking. But so what? Meryl would just have to wish.

"Mom, we've been looking all over for you. Come on—it's time."

Meg appeared, cradling Jo's two-month-old daughter in her arms.

"Meg! You're in your dress. You shouldn't be holding Rose. You know she's been spitting up all day. Where's Jo?"

"Jo and Leigh are dealing with the caterers. Something came late or is missing . . . I don't know. But Olympia wants us all in our places."

"Give me the baby," Meryl said, reaching for her granddaughter, pressing her lips to her tiny head covered in feathery pale hair.

She followed Meg inside, where the bridal party—consisting of Jo, Leigh, and Amy—waited in the living room. The groom's party consisted only of Stowe's youngest brother, Sutton. His father and Cutter, at a campaign event, declined to attend. Tippy, at the last minute, was a surprise appearance. Meryl supposed if there was anything that could rise above politics and ambition, it was motherhood.

The rest of the twenty guests—including Janell, now a freshman at Penn, Hugh's book publisher and publicist, and Toby, Jo's friendly coparent—gathered around the small chuppah made of birch branches. Leigh and Jo, working together now in their new company Leigh & Jo Weddings, designed it themselves.

Amy, the only one dressed extravagantly, in a dress designed by her new boss, Diane von Furstenberg, marched over to Meryl in a huff. "We can't start yet—Dean isn't here!" she said. Dean, the latest in a seemingly endless string of outrageously attractive but completely casual boyfriends.

"Amy, your sister has waited long enough for this moment. She's not going to wait a minute longer for Dean. And I suggest you text him and tell him to wait twenty minutes so he doesn't interrupt the ceremony."

"So annoying," Amy muttered.

Some things never changed, and there was comfort in that.

"Mom, I can take her," Jo said, reaching for her daughter.

Before handing her off, Meryl breathed in that special baby scent, thinking for the umpteenth time that she'd never known love like this. It was different than with her own daughters. Not stronger, but somehow richer. More poignant. There was the overwhelming sense, holding the incredible bundle of new life, of time marching on. Of the continuum of family. Of being part of something greater than herself—something she helped build that would, like the seasons, change but always renew.

"Everyone, if you could please gather around," said Olympia.

There was no aisle to walk down. Hugh stood by Meryl's side.

"You look more beautiful today than you did on our wedding day," he whispered. Stowe and Meg walked hand in hand, taking their places in front of Olympia.

"Friends and family, we are so thankful you could join us here today to celebrate the union of Meg and Stowe. As you all know, it was a *little* bit bumpy getting to this afternoon." When the laughter settled, Olympia said, "But I have rarely seen true love without a bit of drama. It keeps life interesting, does it not?"

Meryl noticed Jo and Leigh exchange an intimate, satisfied glance, while Amy checked her phone—no doubt texting her date.

Stowe and Meg beamed at one another. "I'm ready," she said with a smile, glancing at Meryl. In that moment, Meg was her little girl playing dress-up again. She blinked back tears.

"Well, one down. Two to go," Meryl whispered to Hugh, squeezing his arm.

"Please—let's not think about that right this minute. Let's just enjoy the fact that for now, we did good, didn't we?"

"Yes," she said, reaching for his hand. "We did."

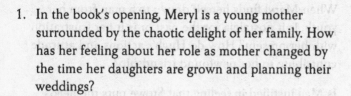

1. In the book's opening, Meryl is a young mother surrounded by the chaotic delight of her family. How has her feeling about her role as mother changed by the time her daughters are grown and planning their weddings?

2. As Meryl anxiously gets ready to meet her future in-laws, her husband says, "Remember, it's not about you." Is Meryl making the wedding about herself, or is she really doing everything in the best interest of her daughter?

3. Out of the three sisters, the oldest, Meg, is the first to get engaged. Would the engagements that follow for Amy and Jo have happened if not for Meg's wedding plans? Why or why not?

4. How are the stresses of the Becker family's wedding plans universal, and how are they unique to this particular family?

5. How do the traditional expectations and etiquette of wedding planning affect the families? Should such rules still apply in modern times?

6. Meryl has always had a strained relationship with her own mother, Rose. Is Meryl at all responsible for their rift? Why or why not? In what ways does the wedding planning further push them apart, and in what ways does it bring them closer together?

7. Meryl is upset not only with the timing of Hugh's work crisis, but also with the position he takes on the controversy. Is she right to be annoyed with him, or should she be more supportive? Do you empathize with Hugh's stance at his school, or is he being reckless?

Discussion Questions

8. When Meryl finds herself drawn to a man from her youth, is it nostalgia for the past or is it her frustration with her present? How do Hugh's actions and attitude contribute to her newfound friendship?

9. Is Meg justified in feeling that Stowe puts the needs of his family before their relationship? At what point in a relationship should a person's priority shift from their nuclear family to their significant other?

10. Youngest sister, Jo, has always been a free spirit and impetuous. In what ways does this serve her well and in what ways does it hurt her?

11. How does Amy's feeling of being in constant competition with Meg affect her choices throughout the book? Is there a sense that this competition has diminished by the end of the book, or is it more likely this will always be the dynamic between the two sisters?

12. Has Hugh changed as a husband by the end, or has only Meryl's perception of him changed?

13. On a wedding day full of surprises, whose actions were the most unexpected? Did the sisters end up where they belonged?

14. How do you imagine the lives of each of the three sisters ten years after the book ends?